Shakespearean Drama, Disability, and the Filmic Stare

I0585820

Shakespearean Drama, Disability, and the Filmic Stare synthesizes Laura Mulvey's male gaze and Rosemarie Garland-Thomson's stare into a new critical lens, the filmic stare, in order to understand and analyze the visual construction of disability in adaptations of Shakespearean drama. The book explores the intersections of adaptation studies, film studies, Shakespeare studies, and disability studies to analyze twentieth and twenty-first century representations of both physical disability and "madness" in global cinematic film, television film, and digital broadcast cinema adaptations of Shakespeare's works. *Shakespearean Drama, Disability, and the Filmic Stare* argues that the filmic stare does not differentiate between male and female characters with disabilities, or between powerful and powerless figures in disability representation. This multi-disciplinary volume is ideal for disability studies scholars, Shakespeare scholars, and those interested in adaptations of Shakespeare's famous works.

Grace McCarthy earned her PhD in English and Film Studies from Wilfrid Laurier University in 2020. Her research focuses on disability studies and Shakespeare studies. She has previously published in *Early Modern Literary Studies* on adaptation and Shakespeare. Grace was the recipient of a SSHRC and an OGS award in addition to the Award for Outstanding Work at the Graduate Level.

Routledge Studies in Literature and Health Humanities

Shakespearean Drama, Disability, and the Filmic Stare
Grace McCarthy

To learn more about this series, please visit: https://www.routledge.com/ Routledge-Studies-in-Literature-and-Health-Humanities/book-series/RSHH

Shakespearean Drama, Disability, and the Filmic Stare

Grace McCarthy

Routledge
Taylor & Francis Group

NEW YORK AND LONDON

First published 2021
by Routledge
605 Third Avenue, New York, NY 10158

and by Routledge
2 Park Square, Milton Park, Abingdon, Oxon OX14 4RN

Routledge is an imprint of the Taylor & Francis Group, an informa business

© 2021 Taylor & Francis

Library of Congress Cataloging-in-Publication Data
A catalog record for this title has been requested

ISBN: 978-0-367-75647-5 (hbk)
ISBN: 978-0-367-75649-9 (pbk)
ISBN: 978-1-003-16337-4 (ebk)

DOI: 10.4324/9781003163374

Typeset in Sabon
by Taylor & Francis Books

Contents

Figures

Acknowledgements

Shakespearean Drama, Disability, and the Filmic Stare is the culmination of seven years of academic study, and almost nine years of research on rheumatoid arthritis, with which I was diagnosed as an undergraduate student while still hunting for my niche in Shakespeare studies. I realized (far too late in my studies) that the questions I really wanted answers to were "Do I still fit in Shakespeare? Where are the characters who reflect my new reality, and the reality of so many others?" This book speaks to, but perhaps does not fully answer, those questions. What I hope this book does successfully do is create a new framework and new space for discussing representations of disability in film adaptations of Shakespeare and highlight the intersectionality of disability studies more generally. I had help and support from more people than I can possibly acknowledge while researching and writing this book. To everyone whose lives intersected with mine while I wrote, thank you.

I owe thanks to the Social Sciences and Humanities Research Council of Canada and the Government of Ontario. The research and revision process for my book was aided by an Ontario Graduate Scholarship and a SSHRC Doctoral Fellowship.

As I explored Shakespeare and disability in my graduate studies—which ultimately led to this book's existence—I was blessed with phenomenal supervisors. Russ Kilbourn, Anne Russell, and Terry Reilly were all at the helm with me at different times during my studies, and this book quite simply would not exist without their support and enthusiasm. Additional inspiration, support, and constructive comments on this project from its earliest stages to its current form came from Jing Jing Chang, Sandra Annett, James Overboe, Sarah Hatchuel, Eileen Harney, Melissa Brennan, Julia Empey, Heather Olaveson, Rebekah Ludolph, Sanchari Sur, and the members of the GSEFSA Reading Group. I am deeply grateful to everyone at the University of Alaska Fairbanks and Wilfrid Laurier University who was involved in the process of conceiving, researching, and writing this book.

Staying healthy (or at least functional) while writing a book is important, and I extend warmest thanks to all the doctors and nurses in Fairbanks, Anchorage, Kitchener, and Waterloo who listened, responded, and worked closely with me to keep me human and as healthy as possible. Special thanks to the nurses in my infusion clinics in Fairbanks and Kitchener—you made those spaces wonderful to write in and cheerfully worked around my laptop and frankly unreasonably sized stacks of books.

I am immensely grateful to Simon Smith, Sam Misra, Brooke Southgate and Claire Meldrum for their friendship and support during the writing of this book. Everything from walks to midnight chats to professional questions and courtesies helped bring this project to its final form.

Many thanks also go to my family, for their love, support, and willingness to read, comment, or cheerlead as I was writing, revising, and preparing my manuscript. I could not have done this without them.

Finally, thanks to Chris, my best friend and phenomenal partner. I love you and thank you for everything.

A Note on the Text

Unless otherwise noted, all Shakespeare quotations come from the second edition of the *Riverside Shakespeare*.

Introduction

One of the most pervasive myths with which the current critical reclamation of disability in early modern literature struggles is the idea that disability is a "modern" phenomenon, or one whose birth took place in the nineteenth century. Rosemarie Garland-Thomson points to North American Freak Shows and so-called "Ugly Laws" to contextualize disability in western society,[1] and Martin Norden points to texts such as *The Hunchback of Notre Dame* and *A Christmas Carol* to contextualize both literary representations of disability and their film adaptation counterparts.[2] Based purely on these examples, it is all too easy to assume that disability was not theorized and not present in texts prior to the consumptive protagonists in Victorian novels. However, early modern scholars, including Sujata Iyengar,[3] Allison Hobgood, David Houston Wood,[4] Genevieve Love,[5] and Elizabeth Bearden[6] have worked to highlight and analyze bodies in the works of early modern authors from Aphra Behn to John Webster, connecting early modern ways of understanding the body and mind—including humoral theory and Robert Burton's *Anatomy of Melancholy* (1621)[7]—to twentieth- and twenty-first-century understandings of disability, physical difference, and mental health. In addition, Tobin Siebers takes a broad look at art history, embodiment, and aesthetics to argue that disability has always existed in art.[8] The exemplary work being done by these scholars is largely confined to the fields of literature and disability studies, however, and is not necessarily applicable to film adaptations or Digital Broadcast Cinema (DBC) productions of the early modern dramatic texts. Extant critical work tends to follow one of two trends: critics either use the early modern play texts as a jumping off point to speak broadly about disability in the late sixteenth to early seventeenth centuries, as Iyengar, Houston Wood, and Hobgood do, or they focus on a single play text and key stage performances, as in the special Shakespeare edition of *Disability Studies Quarterly*.[9] Film scholars who engage with disability, including Norden and Sally Chivers,[10] tend to take a long view, looking at changes in the representation of disability across film history largely without engaging with Shakespeare film adaptations.

This book both dovetails with the reclamation of early modern disabilities and expands into film and adaptation studies with a focus on Shakespeare film adaptation. As one of the most adapted authors in the western canon, the corpus of Shakespeare film adaptations is quite large, and therefore any exploration of

DOI: 10.4324/9781003163374-1

disability in that corpus requires some delineation to create a workable sample size of film texts. It is easy to say that Shakespeare studies, even Shakespeare film studies, has been approached from the perspective of every conceivable critical-theoretical discourse. Yet there is a lack of critical attention in English and film on disability, giving lie to the saturation argument. Additionally, studios are wary of green-lighting film projects of plays that aren't fairly mainstream; my choice of plays is therefore limited to those that have been adapted into film or were conceived and shot as DBC productions. Unfortunately, plays like *The Spanish Tragedy* (Thomas Kyd, 1582–1592) and *Gorboduc* (Norton and Sackville, 1561) have not made their way to the silver screen.

Within Shakespeare film studies are a number of useful taxonomies and methodologies for categorizing Shakespeare film adaptations. These include Jack Jorgens' division between the theatrical, realistic, and filmic modes of adaptation,[11] as well as delineations between anglophone and non-anglophone films,[12] and Sarah Hatchuel's taxonomy based on the distance a film adaptation is from the original Shakespearean text.[13] Samuel Crowl and Hatchuel also distinguish between Shakespearean adaptations and Shakespearean "spin-offs."[14] In order to create a manageable pool of texts for my discussion, I have taken a bricolage[15] approach to extant Shakespeare film scholarship, and have borrowed elements from a number of different scholars to delineate the bounds of this project. Broadly speaking, my discussion will focus on a cross-section of global Shakespeare film adaptations that feature disabled characters in order to explicate the filmic stare.

Chapter 1 explicitly lays out my critical-theoretical framework, what I call the filmic stare, which is used to analyze primary film texts throughout the rest of the book. The filmic stare is analogous in structure to Laura Mulvey's male gaze, albeit with ideological underpinnings borrowed from Rosemarie Garland-Thomson's sociologically determined stare. Chapter 1 both explicates the theory and demonstrates the breadth of applicability of the filmic stare by using primarily (though not exclusively) non-Shakespearean film examples. The filmic stare as a new critical-theoretical framework is significant because it creates a critical lens with which to analyze disability in film without sacrificing a film studies approach predicated upon formal analysis. Much of the extant criticism on disability in film comes from a cultural or advocacy point of view, which elides many of the cinematic aspects of adapting characters with disabilities. To take a brief example, when film reviewers or disability advocates explore a film representation of disability, they often assess that representation on the basis of medical accuracy. Assessing medical accuracy falls back into the trap of fidelity, as medical accuracy is a form of fidelity to a constructed ideal of the 'real.' Therefore, in much popular criticism, the notion of what is medically accurate is synonymous with a 'positive' review. I take a significantly different approach to defining positive and negative in film representations of disability. Insofar as the filmic stare is concerned, medical diagnoses of fictional characters are impossible, and therefore a positive representation of a disability is one in which the character is humanized and given agency. A 'negative' representation would be one that dehumanizes a character with a disability, suggests that a disabled life is not worth living, or perpetuates overcoming narratives (a narrative in which the focus is on a character with a disability succeeding in spite of the disability). My definitions and my methodology as laid out here both support the scaffolding of the filmic stare and constitute something of a 'political' dimension to my argument, as it is in reaction to the narrative trends that Hollywood has been reproducing and reiterating since the days of the Nickelodeon theatres.[16]

Chapters 2 and 3 focus on physical disability in *The Tempest*, *Richard III*, *Titus Andronicus*, and Akira Kurosawa's adaptation of *Hamlet*, *The Bad Sleep Well*. Rather than divide this section by gender or genre, I have focused on class and disability. Figures like Titus Andronicus, Lavinia, and Richard III are all privileged, high class characters, with a combination of acquired and congenital physical impairments. Conversely, Caliban is a subaltern—and often racialized—product of a colonialist mindset with subtle, yet textually unstable congenital physical impairments.

Unlike Richard III and Caliban's congenital disability (referred to as "monstrousness" by Trinculo and Stephano), Titus and Lavinia experience 'imposed' disability; i.e., disabilities resulting from injuries inflicted on them intentionally by another character. This type of disability functions differently from congenital disability, at least partly in the sense that it functions to punctuate a sudden shift in identity as well as metaphor. Gender remains a part of the discussion in this chapter, as the difference in the suppression—but not the construction—of disability between male and female characters is present when considering physical disabilities.

In Chapter 3, the focus will be on Caliban, and his many and varied representations. As a subaltern subject whose textual descriptions all come from questionable sources, Caliban is a unique case study in terms of disability. The methodology for this chapter will incorporate my critical framework, but in the context of an enhanced post-colonial approach, taking into account the difference in class between Caliban and other characters (many of whom are socially and/or financially powerful). Class will be seen as important an element to the construction of Caliban as a disabled figure as gender is to characters like Ophelia.

Chapters 4, 5, and 6 focus on films that represent mental disability, for which I use the early modern term 'madness.' I address madness in such depth primarily because, in the wider context of disability studies and film, physical disability is often discussed in more detail than mental disability. The focus on physical disability can be at least partly attributed to the fact that such disability is visual; it is easy enough to see when someone is missing a limb, but it is far more difficult to see (and therefore theorize) when someone is experiencing clinical depression. The 'invisibility' of mental disability has led to less overall critical attention being paid to characters with these types of impairments. Although the Shakespearean text renders both physical and mental disability verbally and in a linguistic sign system, the shift to an audiovisual medium introduces a shift in the relative representation of physical and mental disability because of the shift to a visual and aesthetic sign system. By focusing on mental disability, I am able to privilege a critical aspect of disability studies that often is denied top billing in research.

Chapter 4 will explore madness as it relates specifically to Hamlet, the titular prince of Denmark. I will briefly explore early modern under-standings of madness, before introducing the filmic stare and questions of how a largely invisible disability is represented for a visual medium. Mad characters deviate verbally and physically from what Ronald Berger calls "social scripts."[17] These deviations also frequently veer wide of the kind of realistic portrayal many sociologists call for and end up being valued nega-tively without deeper analysis. My main texts for this chapter will include film adaptations of *Hamlet* directed by Laurence Olivier, Kenneth Branagh, Michael Almereyda, Franco Zeffirelli, Grigori Kozintsev, and Vishal Bhard-waj. My main focus will be on the tools with which directors represent madness, and ultimately, I will argue that, while male and female madness alike have been critically discussed as separate phenomena, in the context of film representations of madness, because the tools used in film to represent male and female madness are the same, the representations are far more egalitarian than critics have previously acknowledged.

In Chapter 5, I take up representations of madness in Ophelia. My discus-sion explores tensions in critical trends between feminist and disability studies focused readings of this iconic character, including tensions between madness as a form of specifically female communication and the stigma that still sur-rounds mental disability. I also read patterns in constructing Ophelia's visual synecdoche as part of representing her madness through the use of the filmic stare.

Chapter 6 addresses madness in both Macbeth and Lady Macbeth. In addi-tion to adaptations of *Macbeth* directed by Orson Welles, Robert Goold, and Justin Kurzel, I also include adaptations directed by Jayaraj, Vishal Bhardwaj, and Akira Kurosawa. My discussion highlights the visual trend of creating Lady Macbeth's visual synecdoche around her hands, and the near-ubiquitous use of subjective realities to showcase madness in both Macbeth and Lady Macbeth. Including both Macbeth and Lady Macbeth in this chapter highlights that, while the specific synecdoches and subjective realities may be different in their details, the building blocks of visual representations of madness are the same regardless of gender.

The final chapter of this book combines analyses of both physical and mental disability in male and female characters in DBC. The process of filming and editing live stage productions is significantly different from typical Hollywood or BBC filming processes, and so this chapter will examine the technological differences, the resulting representations, and how my critical framework applies to DBC. I will also explore the expansion of the filmic stare into what I call the DBC-specific meta-stare. The meta-stare refers to the multilayered mediation of stares unique to DBC productions, in which the broadcast audience has the opportunity to not only stare at characters onstage, but also the theatre audience. This chapter will primarily address DBC productions of *Titus Andronicus*, as this text explores both physical and mental disability in male and female characters. I will also briefly explore a DBC production of *The Duchess of Malfi* in Chapter 7.

In engaging with the reclamation of disability in early modern scholarship and in the field of Shakespeare film adaptation, this book develops and explicates the filmic stare, its expansion into the meta-stare, and lays out a framework for analyzing the representations of mental and physical disability in film adaptations of early modern drama that acknowledges the complexities of interdisciplinary scholarship.

Notes

1 Garland-Thomson, Rosemarie. *Staring: How We Look*. New York: Oxford UP. 2009. 72–3; Garland-Thomson, Rosemarie. *Extraordinary Bodies: Figuring Physical Disability in American Culture and Literature*. New York: Columbia UP. 1997. 55.
2 Norden, Martin. *The Cinema of Isolation: A History of Physical Disability in the Movies*. New Brunswick: Rutgers University Press. 1994. 91, 33.
3 Iyengar, Sujata. *Disability, Health and Happiness in the Shakespearean Body*. New York: Routledge. 2015.
4 Hobgood, Allison P. and David Houston Wood, eds. *Recovering Disability in Early Modern England*. Columbus: Ohio State UP. 2013.
5 Love, Genevieve. *Early Modern Theatre and the Figure of Disability*. London: The Arden Shakespeare. 2019.
6 Bearden, Elizabeth. *Monstrous Kinds: Body, Space, and Narrative in Renaissance Representations of Disability*. Ann Arbor: University of Michigan Press. 2019.
7 Burton, Robert. *The Anatomy of Melancholy*. Ed. Floyd Dell and Paul Jordan-Smith. New York: Tudor Publishing Co. 1927.
8 Siebers, Tobin. *Disability Aesthetics*. Ann Arbor: University of Michigan Press. 2010. 4.
9 *Disability Studies Quarterly*, 29.4 (2009). MLA International Bibliography. Web. May 12, 2015.
10 Chivers, Sally. *The Silvering Screen*. Toronto: University of Toronto UP. 2011.
11 Jorgens, Jack. *Shakespeare on Film*. Bloomington: Indiana UP. 1977. 7–12.
12 Hatchuel, Sarah. *Shakespeare from Stage to Screen*. New York: Cambridge UP. 2004. 16.
13 Hatchuel, 16–17.
14 Hatchuel, 16–17; Crowl, Samuel. *Shakespeare and Film*. New York: WW Norton and Co. 2008. xiii–xiv.
15 Sanders, Julie. *Adaptation and Appropriation*. London: Routledge. 2006. 6.
16 See Martin Norden's *Cinema of Isolation* for an in-depth historical look at Hollywood's use of the overcoming narrative.
17 Berger, Ronald J. *Introducing Disability Studies*. New York: Lynne Rienner. 2013.

Bibliography

Aebisher, Pascale. *Screening Early Modern Drama*. New York: Cambridge UP. 2013.
Bearden, Elizabeth. *Monstrous Kinds: Body, Space, and Narrative in Renaissance Representations of Disability*. Ann Arbor: University of Michigan Press. 2019.

Berger, Ronald J. *Introducing Disability Studies*. New York: Lynne Rienner. 2013.

Burton, Robert. "Part One, Member 1, Subsections 1–5; Part One, Member 3, Subsections 1–3; Part One, Member 2, Subsection 1; Part One, Section 2, Member 3, subsections 1–10." *The Anatomy of Melancholy*. Ed. Floyd Dell and Paul Jordan-Smith. New York: Tudor Publishing Co. 1927.

Chivers, Sally. *The Silvering Screen*. Toronto: University of Toronto UP. 2011.

Crowl, Samuel. *Shakespeare and Film*. New York: WW Norton and Co. 2008.

Disability Studies Quarterly, 29. 4 (2009). MLA International Bibliography. Web. May 12, 2015.

Garland-Thomson, Rosemarie. *Extraordinary Bodies: Figuring Physical Disability in American Culture and Literature*. New York: Columbia UP. 1997.

Garland-Thomson, Rosemarie. *Staring: How We Look*. New York: Oxford UP. 2009.

Hatchuel, Sarah. *Shakespeare from Stage to Screen*. New York: Cambridge UP. 2004.

Heyer, Paul. "Live from the Met: Digital Broadcast Cinema, Medium Theory, and Opera for the Masses." *Canadian Journal of Communication*, 33 (2008): 591–604.

Hile, Rachel E. "Disability and the Characterization of Katherine in *The Taming of the Shrew*." *Disability Studies Quarterly*, 29. 4 (2009). MLA International Bibliography. Web. May 12, 2015.

Hobgood, Allison P. and David Housten Wood, Eds. *Recovering Disability in Early Modern England*. Columbus: Ohio State UP. 2013.

Iyengar, Sujata. *Disability, Health and Happiness in the Shakespearean Body*. New York: Routledge. 2015.

Jorgens, Jack. *Shakespeare on Film*. Bloomington: Indiana UP. 1977.

Love, Genevieve. *Early Modern Theatre and the Figure of Disability*. London: The Arden Shakespeare. 2019.

Norden, Martin. *The Cinema of Isolation: A History of Physical Disability in the Movies*. New Brunswick: Rutgers University Press, 1994.

Sanders, Julie. *Adaptation and Appropriation*. London: Routledge. 2006.

Siebers, Tobin. *Disability Aesthetics*. Ann Arbor: University of Michigan Press. 2010.

1 Staring, the Filmic Stare, and Theorizing Disability

Linda Hutcheon argues that Shakespearean film adaptations are highly palimp-cestuous,[1] haunted not only by the play texts—themselves highly unstable—but by the theatrical performance histories of the plays. As Samuel Crowl says of Richard Loncraine and Ian McKellen's 1995 film adaptation of *Richard III*, "even repeated viewings of the film, often experienced with classes of appreciative students, have failed to erase from my memory the thrill of the stage performance—an experience that I compare unfavorably with the tepid amusement provided by the film."[2] Add filmic influences, new technologies, and, especially as we move to late twentieth- and twenty-first-century film adaptations, the film histories of each play to this already complex set of palimpsests, and it is easy to see where aesthetic nervousness, as Ato Quayson terms the discomfort of engaging with disability, might tempt scholars to skim over the representations of disability as sites of analysis in favor of other concerns. Given this complex web of histories, influences, and hypotexts, it is unsurprising that representations of disabilities in film adaptations of early modern drama are both diverse and frequently lack a disability-studies grounded analysis. To thoroughly analyze and categorize the many and varied representations of disability in film adaptations of early modern drama, I will construct a critical and theoretical framework using influences from disability studies itself as well as film, sociology and literary studies scholars who address texts and characters that feature representations of disability. I will, as Tobin Siebers does,[3] privilege disability as an identity category, with the nuance and weight of identity categories such as race, gender, or class. As a result, my critical-theoretical framework will explore the construction of representations of disability on film in a manner similar to constructing gender, race, or class on screen.

Film, as an audiovisual medium, requires as much thought and multi-layered understanding in both the crafting and consumption of representations of disability as does a sociological, literary, or medical paradigm. The characters in these film adaptations are not real people, they are representations, and what these representations tell us is valuable, even if they are not medically accurate representations of a given physical or mental impairment. To discover meaning in these representations then, I will explore three main areas. (1) The points of tension between fields under the umbrella of disability studies—specifically the

DOI: 10.4324/9781003163374-2

differences between a film-centered approach to disability studies (the aesthetic approach) and a social sciences approach (the sociological approach)—in how disability is theorized, defined, and constructed. (2) The interconnected web of shots, angles, and cinematographic techniques that comprise the filmic stare, and (3) choices made by the director, editor, and actors that highlight or suppress impairments and disabilities. My approach is neither proscriptive nor prescriptive, but rather descriptive and analytical. By exploring these three areas, I have developed the filmic stare, a critical theory describing the cinematographic construction of visual representations of disabled bodies based on the unconscious social, cultural, and physiological reactions to disabilities, and valuing those representations as sites where those unconscious assumptions and/or reactions can be explored and challenged in nuanced and complex discourses. The filmic stare is strongly influenced by Laura Mulvey's concept of the male gaze, Rosemarie Garland-Thomson's concept of the stare, and disability aesthetics, all of which I will explore in more depth later in this chapter. To demonstrate the breadth of applicability of the filmic stare, I include a few non-Shakespearean films in my discussion. I will begin with a brief overview of disability studies as a field before focusing on disability studies as it relates to film studies. Finally, I will lay out Garland-Thomson's stare before defining and applying the filmic stare.

Disability studies is an umbrella field encompassing many sub-fields; however, Ronald Berger and Catherine Kudlick offer excellent starting point definitions for a humanities-based exploration of disability. Berger defines the field of disability studies as "an interdisciplinary field of inquiry that includes representation from the social sciences, the humanities and the medical and rehabilitation and education professions."[4] Kudlick adds that disability studies "invites scholars to think about disability not as an isolated, individual medical pathology but instead as a key defining social category on par with race, class, and gender."[5] Within disability studies, however, are disagreements about defining disability, representing disability, and the ways in which disability and society interact. Sociology has developed disability theory in three waves, beginning with the medical model which gave way to the social model, which in turn gave way to the cultural model.[6]

The medical model is an essentialist theory which holds that disability is located in the physical body and requires medical intervention to 'normalize' a non-normative body—or mind, in the case of mental disability. In the 1970s, however, the social model of disability rose to popularity. Rather than locating disability in the body, the social model locates disability as a relationship between an individual with an impairment and a society whose architecture, customs, and assumptions are ableist—that is, assumptions which prejudice against or disregard the needs of disabled people[7]—and need to change to accommodate more variations of the human body and mind. Finally, the cultural model, which arose in the wake of the passage of the Americans with Disabilities Act in 1990, argues that disability is a point of group identity and personal and cultural pride. These models demonstrate an evolution in the theorizing of disability from an essentialist approach that understands disability as a property of an inherently deficient (and therefore inferior) individual to models which posit that disability can be celebrated as a matter of group identity, a part of the broader fabric of human diversity, and as a site of cultural resistance to socially constructed conceptions of normality.[8] The medical model has largely fallen out of favor in both the academic theorization of disability and in practical applications of theory in social, legal, and governmental settings and policies.

I do not wish to give the impression here that the progression from the medical to the cultural model is somehow inevitable, or that the progression represents linear progress. While the US focuses on the cultural model of disability,[9] that emphasis is challenged by UK disability theorists, including Tom Shakespeare,[10] who argue that the social model of disability is most relevant and politically effective.[11] Tom Shakespeare specifically argues that "US-style cultural disabilities studies" focuses on "rhetoric" to the extent that embodiment, and even action (social, legal, political, etc.) are neglected.[12] A common thread I highlight here is that both cultural and social models of disability have been criticized for omitting the body. Whether that omission is through a focus on the relationship of the individual to society at large,[13] or the "linguistic turn,"[14] setting embodiment to the side ignores the material reality of a body with impairments. The focus on rhetoric and the linguistic turn seems to inherently invite what Ato Quayson terms "aesthetic nervousness."[15] Quayson specifically locates aesthetic nervousness in the literary text, arguing that "aesthetic nervousness is seen when the dominant protocols of representation within the literary text are shortcircuited [sic] in relation to disability."[16] Because Quayson locates the "final dimension of aesthetic nervousness [...] between the reader and the text,"[17] however, the linguistic turn in disability studies and its resulting tendency to omit the body may itself be a form of aesthetic nervousness that reflects the discomfort with a body that is aesthetically different from what a non-disabled individual might expect in the real world. Quayson nods to this idea in his book when he notes that "for the reader, aesthetic nervousness overlaps social attitudes to disability that themselves often remain unexamined in their prejudices and biases."[18] Situating aesthetic nervousness between the reader and the text mirrors Garland-Thomson's stare, which takes place between real people in the real world, and invites an expansion of that relationship, to a viewer and a film text. By situating aesthetic nervousness in literary texts, however, Quayson notes issues in disability representation and begins to articulate the aesthetic turn in disability studies more widely.

Barker and Murray argue that Quayson and Siebers—and I add Michael Davidson—"point to disability's pivotal role in complicating and enriching notions of the aesthetic because of the difference disabled bodies and minds bring to the process of representation."[19] Rather than focusing on language or linguistic representations, Siebers and Davidson focus on visual representations of disability and the aesthetic therein created. Siebers argues, "What I am call-ing 'disability aesthetics' names a critical concept that seeks to emphasize the presence of disability in the tradition of aesthetic representation,"[20] to place the visual aesthetic at the forefront of analysis and discussion. The significance of prioritizing a disability aesthetic is twofold. First, this approach grounds dis-ability aesthetics in embodiment by focusing on the body as "both the subject and object of aesthetic production."[21] Grounding analysis in the body and in embodiment in general directly addresses the criticism that metaphorical and linguistic treatments of disability fail to confront the "material conditions" or lived experiences of persons with disabilities.[22] Second, as Barker and Murray argue, prioritizing disability aesthetics has pushed disability studies as a field "beyond making distinctions between 'positive' and 'negative' representations," and "toward a better understanding of the complex nature of many disability narratives."[23]

Moving beyond positive and negative classifications of representations of disability is aptly demonstrated by Siebers in his modern art examples[24] and by Davidson in his analysis of Maurice Ravel's *Concerto for the Left Hand*.[25] In the context of film studies, however, there seems to be a lag in understanding and analyzing complex representations of disability and a resurgence of aesthetic nervousness. Reviewers tend to seek out medically accurate representations and lambast films that deviate from "inspiration porn," a term that denotes an overwhelmingly positive narrative that represents disability as something that is overcome by the protagonist.[26] *Forrest Gump* (1994) is worth a mention here, as the film, while widely beloved, is also an ableist combination of overcoming narrative and inspiration porn. Davidson points out a corollary to the desire for inspiration porn in self-help literature, noting that "[a] good deal of self-help literature has been written to explain how to 'endure' or 'triumph over' such adversity, and figures who do—Helen Keller, Christopher Reeve, Stephen Hawking—are celebrated as exemplars."[27] Keller and Hawking have both been the focus of feature film adaptations that explore their lives, and the ableist, overcoming narratives that Davidson identifies are reflected in the films. How-ever, in a film studies paradigm, a more nuanced and complex representation— or a representation designed to elicit shock and/or body horror—in concert with disability aesthetics is a critically valuable example to discuss.

Often, discussions of disability as identity in film studies are limited to broad categories that define character types. Martin Norden explores this phenom-enon,[28] arguing that the first filmic representation of the disabled villain was Richard III.[29] We can also recognize what Norden calls the "charity cripple," with Dickens's Tiny Tim being the most well-known example.[30] Tiny Tim is also the epitome of the disability-as-shorthand style that sociologists decry. We know exactly two things about Tiny Tim: he is Bob Cratchit's son, and he has an unspecified physical disability, therefore he is worthy of a viewer's (or reader's) pity. Tiny Tim's entire identity as a pathetic figure is couched in his physical disability to the exclusion of any other identity. Tiny Tim is also a relatively   minor   character   in   Dickens;   we   see   similar   shorthand characterizations—defining a character through assumptions based on their disabilities—throughout literature and film for minor characters.

When scholars like Garland-Thomson and Norden argue that the same kind of shorthand is used for main characters (again, *Richard III* is a common example), however, the argument falls apart. The sheer volume of critical scholarship on Shakespeare's protagonists suggests a depth and breadth to these characters that belies the easy argument that a disability eclipses and erases all other traits and abilities of a character.[31] I will privilege the representation, not the diagnosis. My methodology breaks with the sociological methods and models insofar as I also use the term madness as a broad signifier of mental disability instead of attempting to diagnose characters with specific mental illnesses and/or disabilities. Disability as an identity category, underpinned by disability aesthetics, will be the overarching idea behind the filmic stare and will sandwich filmic representations of disability between identity and a foundation of genre and medium.

When dealing with representations of disability in film adaptations, genre plays a critical role. I argue that disability as an identity category in film and Digital Broadcast Cinema (DBC) adaptations of early modern drama is visually constructed by a combination of genre and generic conventions and medium to produce a representation of disability. Films which are explicit in their genre tend to use a specific set of techniques to create a sense of verisimilitude about their visual representations of disability, whereas art films tend to suppress or omit representations due to their requirement for compulsory able-bodiedness (specifically in Greenaway's *Prospero's Books*) to highlight a specific storytelling and/or visual style. Because Shakespeare film adaptations span so many different genres, I will address the issue of genre more specifically in later chapters, leaving my discussion of genre and the suppression or highlighting of disability more general here.

In addition to genre dictating whether disability is highlighted or suppressed, medium is also critical in the representation of disabilities because Hollywood tends to only green-light film adaptations of well-known plays. As a result, there are many, many *Hamlet* film adaptations, depending on how the films are categorized.[32] DBC, however, is not constrained by Hollywood's methodologies for play selection. As a result, a wider variety of early modern plays have been simulcast for audiences in cinemas worldwide. Many were also filmed and later repackaged as DVDs or downloadable content for consumers. The significant production and technological differences between cinematic film and DBC productions are such that I will categorize the two as related, but distinctly different media. Chapter 7 will address DBC productions in detail. In terms of my film selections, I will discuss Anglophone films from the United States and the United Kingdom, which use the Shakespearean text. This eliminates some phenomenal Anglophone genre films (including the 1956 sci-fi film *Forbidden Planet*, an adaptation of *The Tempest*), but that limitation creates space to also include non-Anglophone films from Bollywood, Soviet Cinema, and Chinese cinema that hew closely to the original Shakespearean plotlines and include representations of disability. These parameters create a pool of films that still vary in their genre, medium, and use of technology to help construct a representation of disability.

In categorizing my chosen film adaptations by genre and medium, I also address the changes in genre and film technologies across time. The shift from celluloid to digital changed the way that physical disabilities are represented. This change is particularly evident when the Olivier and Cumberbatch *Richard III* film adaptations are compared. Olivier's hunchback was a practical effect that is often visually minimized by Olivier's framing and composition choices, as well as the costume design.[33] Thanks to digital and CGI technologies, viewers of more recent *Richard III* films have a more intimate relationship with Richard's impairment than before. The iconic shot of Cumberbatch's bare back, with its digitally composited S-shaped spine and textured hunch, disallows the audience any plausible deniability in terms of confronting a non-normative body.[34] The camera insists on looking not at a costume that has been padded, but a visually non-normative body without the illusory comfort provided by a costume. This example highlights how advances in film technology and film grammar alike change representations of disability onscreen.

Film theorists who engage in disability studies focus more on representation than reality. The point of the most significant slippage between disability studies as addressed by film versus sociology (or really any liberal arts field versus any social science or hard science field) is the difference between reality and representation. In film representations, even those films which present images of historical figures, real people, and real disabilities are not at stake in the same way they are in a sociological or medical study of disability. If Benedict Cumberbatch's Richard recalls Mel Brooks' Igor (*Young Frankenstein*, 1974), then the sociological instinct to immediately dismiss the representation as negative—that is, a medically inaccurate representation, or not adhering to an overcoming narrative—ultimately fails to even value the representation as a site for analysis, let alone to explore the representation. Metaphor, irony, and representations that interrogate assumptions and/or stereotypes through images that might be considered negative are worthwhile grounds for a more in-depth analysis, particularly in the context of disability aesthetics. The use of rhetorical and formal filmic techniques that create a representation that might seem negative can create space for more nuanced representations than representations that are tied to medical accuracy.

Additionally, visual representations of disability can and often do inspire aesthetic nervousness in viewers who are unused to seeing disability in any capacity. Many disabilities, both physical and mental, can be invisible. An invisible disability may affect an individual without creating a visibly non-normative body. Most mental disabilities manifest in terms of behavior that breaks unspoken social scripts rather than visually non-normative bodies. People may go through their day-to-day lives never realizing that they are seeing disabilities, so to be suddenly confronted with a disability—which, insofar as film is an audiovisual medium, *can never be wholly invisible*—can be unsettling and lead to a knee-jerk dismissal of the representation out of sheer discomfort and surprise. A theatrical example of this can be found in Richard Ouzounian's *Toronto Star* review of the 2008 Stratford Festival Production of *Taming of the Shrew*. Ouzounian writes, "Hinton has decided that Katherine has an actual physical deformity and has her hobbling across the festival stage as though she were Richard III instead of Katherine."[35] Ouzounian is the most openly dismissive, but by no means the only reviewer to critique Katherine's disability without analyzing the effect of the representation on the narrative. Rachel Hile's thoughtful analysis of Katherine's limp and its inclusion in stage performances—despite a theatrical history of omitting the limp—begins to explore disability not only as another visual facet that affects the meaning of the text, but also as a component of Katherine's identity. These examples serve to underscore the idea that representations function as more than simply education for those who do not experience disability, or as an overdetermined representation that "functions only as a visual difference that signals meaning."[36]

Theorizing Disability

Depending on the specific field and assumed audience, theorizing disability takes on many different forms. One point of tension that transcends divisions between academic disciplines, however, is the distance between theory and the body. Contemporary scholars point out the difference between embodiment and representation of disability, but that difference is hardly unique to the twentieth and twenty-first centuries.

Burton's *Anatomy of Melancholy* (1621)[37] is one of the earliest texts to theorize and categorize (primarily) mental impairments. Interestingly, Burton acknowledges what would come to be one of the persistent slippages in theorizing disability: the inherent connection of the mental and physical. Burton describes the connection vividly:

> For as the body works upon the mind, by his bad humours, troubling the spirits, sending gross fumes into the brain, and so disturbing the soul and all the faculties of it [...] with fear and sorrow &c. [sic] which are ordinary symptoms of this disease: so, on the other side, the mind most effectually works upon the body.[38]

Of course, Burton is working with humoral theory, the dominant medical model of his day, but even modern theorizing of mental disability—particularly mental impairments considered invisible, such as depression, dyslexia, or autism—tends to forget that these invisible disabilities are a result of physical processes in the brain and body. The division between the mind/brain and the body is a point of criticism against the social model, which theorized disability to the point of entirely excluding the physical body from the conversation.[39]

Elizabeth Bearden both reiterates and complicates Burton's assertion that the mind and body are interconnected in her conception of "the interdependence of body, space, and narrative in the moral and aesthetic production of early modern disability."[40] Reiterating the "tight body–mind connection"[41] that Burton and humoral theory nod to, Bearden also highlights the inherent capacity for change and fluidity that the mind–body connection implies based on classical understandings of disability from Aristotle and Pliny the Elder, among others.[42] Bearden also references the geographic, map-oriented space in which disabilities were often understood, specifically citing Gleeson's theory of geographies in which "bodies are enabled and disabled by particular geographies."[43] In terms of understanding narrative representations of early modern literary and theatrical representations of disability, Bearden reminds us that "most formal assessments of fictional technique and content emphasize mimetic representation,"[44] so it is reasonable to assume that playwrights were drawing, at least in part, on the evidence of disability in the world they knew. As far as specific dramatic narratives are concerned, Bearden notes that "people with impairments were of great interest to Renaissance authors," and argues that narratives with disabled protagonists—such as perennial token disability example Richard III—tend to follow Mitchell and Snyder's narrative prosthesis. However, she also argues that genres that "focus on the multiplicity of monster" tend to behave more like memes, pointing to the fluidity of representation as well as of disability itself.[45] Bearden and Burton focus on embodiment and medical representations of disability, but how are these concepts represented when it comes to early modern stage representations?

Genevieve Love, in her book *Early Modern Theatre and the Figure of Disability*, argues that when the "physically disabled character, with missing limb and prosthesis" enters the stage, he "enters from war, he enters to show, he enters to fight, he enters to the rescue [...] he enters to *work*." Love elaborates that work as twofold embodiment: of the theatrical slippage between imitation and identity, and the textual slippage between various editions of play texts and theatrical performance.[46] These "likeness problems," as Love names them, draw a clear, straight line from theatrical issues of embodiment and representation to similar issues in film adaptations of these dramatic texts. Likeness problems also reflect the tensions in the differences between the aesthetic and linguistic turns in disability studies. It is one thing to read on a page, "Enter the Cripple,"[47] and another entirely to watch a—likely physically able—actor embody that character on a stage. That kind of embodiment on stage runs the risk Davidson identifies as allowing "dominant social norms to be written on the body of a person who is asked to step offstage once their metaphoric exchange is made,"[48] particularly as the imitation of disability Love identifies in stage representations ultimately lacks both the mind–body connection Burton explores[49] and the passability[50] that Bearden theorizes. And yet, film adaptations take just as much of their 'likeness' from stage productions as from the play text. For Love, then, the figure of disability on the early modern stage is a representation of disability that highlights the stylization of early modern dramatic practices and functions as a metaphor that makes immediately visual some of the ethical and material issues surrounding making a disabled figure 'work' onstage. How these issues are handled in film adaptation will be addressed throughout the book, but this section highlights how theorizing disability in the early modern period is melted into the hypotexts that form the foundations of adapting disability.

The various classical and early modern theorizations of disability explored by Bearden, Burton, and Love, particularly in contrast with the terminology used colloquially today, reminds scholars and disability theorists that while the many and varied ways of describing mental and physical disability may be useful constructs, they can also lead to challenges in defining disability. Many individuals and organizations have spent time attempting to define disability in various contexts, including the medical, governmental, educational, and social.[51] For the purposes of my discussion, the only divisions I will make between disabilities is to separate mental and physical disabilities. I address mental and physical disabilities separately because while the mind and body do influence each other, on-screen representations rarely show the interplay between the mental and physical in the same character. In addition, mental and physical disabilities are represented using different cinematographic techniques. Separating mental and physical representations of disability will help to focus later discussions of the filmic stare. I will not make a distinction between chronic illness (e.g., cancer, autoimmune diseases, asthma, diabetes, etc.), congenital physical or mental difference (e.g., mental illnesses, learning disabilities, polydactylism, etc.) and acquired physical or mental difference (e.g., violent or accidental loss of limbs, traumatic brain injury due to violence, accidents, or substance abuse, etc.). Distinguishing between these types of disability is outside the scope of this discussion, and a significant aspect of the filmic stare requires refraining from medically diagnosing fictional characters. My rationale for this elision, which will undoubtedly prove controversial, is twofold. First, disability studies as a field and the language and categories used to classify and describe disability have been evolving since at least the mid-1500s, and so to restrict myself to any temporally specific taxonomy or terminology contextualizes Shakespearean characters in a time and place that may or may not be relevant to my case studies. I will, however, use the terms 'disability' and 'impairment' throughout the book, maintaining their separate, specific definitions. That is, I will use impairment in speaking specifically about a character's body or mind, and disability when broadly discussing a character's relationship with society. My specific use of these terms firmly positions my arguments equally within disability studies and within a film studies paradigm.

Second, in avoiding a strict diagnosis and in using a broad understanding of disability, I can explore the film representations of these characters through the lenses of cinematic realism and disability aesthetics without the complexities required for a medical diagnosis or sociological analysis. While disability scholars often argue that "people who have disabilities do not want to be treated as ill, and people who are ill do not want to be treated as disabled,"[52] drawing a hard line between disability and chronic and/or long-term illness is something that physicians, advocates, and patients (myself included) struggle with. Where precisely that line might be drawn is a topic deserving a book-length treatment, and I have not the space to do it justice here. Working with a broad definition of disability and counterposing that definition with an early modern understanding of the health of the body and mind provides the broadest possible spectrum of disability. That breadth allows for an in-depth and nuanced understanding of broad categories of disabilities that apply to Shakespeare's characters and allows me to sidestep the trap of attempting to diagnose 400-year-old literary characters according to anachronistic categories.

My goal is neither to refute nor support any one of these diagnoses but rather to explore the often-nebulous representation of mental disability on film. Mental impairments—a term I use to reference a wide spectrum of mental disabilities, including but not limited to traumatic/acquired brain injuries, congenital brain deformities, mental illnesses, and learning disabilities—are often invisible in the sense that the individual's body does not visibly reflect the mental impairment. However, stigma and rumor can affect the power dynamics in a relationship if the other party is aware of an individual's mental impairment. In using the terms mental disabilities, mental impairments, and—for the early modern-specific examples in later chapters—madness,[53] I intend to use the broadest terms possible. The medical, advocacy, rehabilitation, and sociological fields require the specificity of language to demarcate differences between neurological, physiological, and/or morphological deviations from the accepted norms to recognize, manage, treat, and otherwise address what is an immensely complex system of impairments. One of the main criticisms of mental disability in film is the elision of (or incorrect representation of) symptoms and the lack of documentary-style realism in the portrayal of mental illness.[54] This criticism, however, is frequently laid at the feet of the actors and directors who are perceived as having failed to do the research, or who are perceived as playing to stereotypes about mental impairments. To reiterate, my intention is not to diagnose. As a result, the distinctions between specific diagnoses, and even specific terms like 'madness' and 'distraction,' can be allowed to blur to a certain extent in the context of the filmic stare. The web of cinematic techniques that allows us to see the on-screen representation of mental disability is my focus, not the accuracy of the performances themselves. A brief example from *Hamlet* speaks to two key challenges involved in addressing mental disability on film: terminology and legitimacy.

The many, many film adaptations of *Hamlet* have led to libraries full of critical studies and diagnoses. Hamlet the character has been scrutinized through a variety of different lenses; from the mad Hamlets of the 1700–1800s, to the Freudian Hamlets—on stage as well as screen—in the 1930s, 40s, and 50s,[55] to the depressed Hamlets,[56] to the intellectually disabled Hamlets,[57] to the twenty-first century autistic Hamlets.[58] In that list alone is a series of diagnostic terms, and it does not even address Carol Thomas Neely's chosen term "distracted," or Neely's—and other critics'—choice *not* to use the term disability. Neely argues that "madness in [*Hamlet*] is dramatized through a peculiar language more often that through physiological symptoms, stereotyped behaviors, or iconographic conventions, although these are present."[59] She goes on to note that the text leads to an "unfolding of different types of distraction," and reveals that "distinctions between female distraction and feigned madness and melancholy are represented in *Hamlet*."[60]Chapters 4 and 5 will deeply engage with Neely on gendered representations of disability, but for my discussion here about terminology, I want to highlight the multitude of terms that have been applied to madness in early modern texts and clearly state my commitment to the term disability to cement the continued relevance of early modern texts and their adaptations to the field of disability studies.

Additionally, *Hamlet* scholars must deal with the four-hundred-year-old question: is Hamlet's madness real or feigned? This question will be addressed in more depth in Chapter 4, but for the purposes of theorizing mental disability in the context of the filmic stare, the diagnosis, and the question of whether the mental impairment is real or not matters less than the fact that mental disability is being represented visually on film. Lindsay Row-Heyveld's *Dissembling Disability in Early Modern English Drama* thoroughly explores the anxieties behind early modern representations of feigned disabilities and their representations on stage, although her chapter on madness focuses primarily on *Antonio's Revenge* (John Marston 1600–01) rather than *Hamlet*.[61] Even if Hamlet is feigning madness, he is still figuring a representation of madness. Whether or not Hamlet is a reliable narrator of his own madness is not the focus of this book, however. Real or feigned, madness is represented in the play and it is the representation itself that is important, not Hamlet's trustworthiness as a narrator. Hamlet's representation (as well as the actor playing Hamlet's representation) is informed by socio-cultural assumptions about disability. The locus of my interest is how the representation is constructed cinematographically, not whether the representation is accurate in a given historical-cultural context.

My avenue into theorizing disability in film and DBC adaptations of early modern drama runs through Garland-Thomson's concept of the stare. At its most basic, Garland-Thomson's theory of the stare describes an interpersonal interaction in the real world. A normate—defined by Garland-Thomson as a white, heterosexual male in his mid-twenties who is fit, successful, physically abled, and conventionally attractive—stares at a person with a disability, feels and acknowledges a discomfort with and lack of knowledge of persons with disabilities, and the discomfort and lack of knowledge leads to an unconscious, negative othering of the person with a disability.[62] Garland-Thomson is describing an interaction in the real world, with real people and physical eyeballs. She argues that these real-world interpersonal interactions are always dynamic, whereas "literary representation sets up static encounters between disabled figures and normate readers."[63] Sociology as a field is concerned with reality and real life, and sociologists who focus on the multi-disciplinary field of sociology tend to be writing from a semi-activist perspective; that is, they are focused on identifying social circumstances that create barriers for persons with disabilities and suggesting ways to circumnavigate and/or remove those barriers.

Garland-Thomson's stare acknowledges the tensions between expectations of polite behaviour and the gut-level instinct to stare at that which we do not understand. However, her theory rests on a point of tension and turns on an assumption of othering.[64] The point of tension is knowing that staring is somehow taboo and in conflict with the desire to see and understand that which is foreign to us. However, the acknowledgment that a physical impairment is foreign also acknowledges the othering of the bearer of the impairment. Being othered by an impairment does not necessarily have to be negative; in fact, when two individuals with different impairments meet for the first time, that stare can be an acknowledgment of a shared reality that is other. That said, however, Garland-Thomson also sets up a power dynamic in her stare: the normate starer and the impaired staree.

Social and cultural relationships regarding race and gender still apply in this situation, and, as a result, the dynamic of staring always involves an imbalance of power. Interestingly, the list of normate attributes inevitably follows the same order: sex, race, sexual orientation, level of ability. Arguably, this hierarchy and its ubiquity underpins part of the ideology at work in the stare. It lists in descending order the importance of the traits individuals and societies consider when assessing a new individual. Depending on the rhetorical desires of the speaker, the order may change slightly; particularly in contemporary American politics, race will often come before gender. These traits automatically paint a picture of where an individual fits into the larger social order. Abled is so much the assumed default state that it rarely, if ever, is added to the list. Like all these terms, however, abled/disabled makes a very neat binary and like the binaries white/not white, male/female, heterosexual/homosexual, binary understandings are inherently oversimplified.

For example, a large percentage of the population wears glasses or contact lenses. Each of those individuals has a visual impairment; however, stigmatizing language is not applied to individuals who use corrective lenses, and those of us who wear glasses do not consider ourselves disabled. With the proliferation of prescriptions for corrective lenses, the wearing of glasses was folded into the paradigm of able-bodiedness. Even those who wear contact lenses are never said to "pass" as visually abled; they simply wear contacts. Glasses and contacts are also referred to by their names rather than being labeled as "assistive devices," as canes, walkers, or braces often are. By normalizing the use of glasses and contacts, power dynamics between individuals are largely unaffected by these ubiquitous assistive devices. Spectacularly visual impairments affect power dynamics, e.g. a missing limb, the use of a wheelchair, or even something as simple as needing a large-print version of a document on a legal-sized sheet of paper rather than the typical letter-sized sheet. Assistive devices and large print are most common in terms of physical impairments, but mental impairments affect power dynamics as well. Garland-Thomson's stare focuses primarily on visible, physical impairments because that is what is visible in real life. In terms of developing a filmic stare, however, I will include mental impairments/disabilities.

Film is an inherently visual storytelling medium, and one of the challenges of filmmaking is to create a visual representation of what is invisible. For mental impairments, generally that means a visual and aural break from the unacknowledged but binding social scripts that govern behavior. Breaks with social scripts are often a property of the mise-en-scène, however, they can also be a property of the cinematographic construction of the filmic stare.

Filmic representation of disability, the overall focus of this discussion, has received many of the same criticisms as the plays: there is a fundamental difference between disability as a character attribute and the experiences of real people;[65] the representations oversimplify disability;[66] disability onscreen has become shorthand for either villains or the helpless.[67] In short, the underpinning issue returns once again to language, metaphor, and visual shorthands. Inherent in these criticisms is also the assumption that literary and filmic representations must be true-to-life. However, my discussion will privilege realism—the verisimilitude of a film to the believability of its characters and events—rather than reality—the real world that you and I live in. To theorize disability for film studies, I will set aside criticisms based on a desire for medical fidelity. To theorize disability based in filmic realism opens up the possibility of an argument that I, like the social model of disability, have so completely divorced disability and body that there is no body left, only theory.[68] However, representation in popular culture is critical for viewers too.

Images of disabled bodies onscreen allow those who identify as disabled to feel their own embodiment. That line of discussion leads us to the question of assumed audiences and the audiences who physically go to the theatre to watch the film. In the context of this discussion, I will base my arguments on an assumed audience, e.g., the audience the director imagines when they construct their film. The composition of the real audience, while a subject worthy of scrutiny, requires an ethnographic study, which unfortunately lies outside the bounds of this project. Because the majority of directors and actors in these films are white, male, and able-bodied themselves, arguably they assume an able-bodied audience. The question of audience is another place we see differences between the aesthetic and sociological approaches to disability in film. Some scholars want empowering, uncomplicated, and positive representations of disability in film to dispel stereotypes and educate a normate audience on the realities of living with a disability. Directors, who are often addressing thematic concerns unrelated to the representations of disability, draw on the existing theatrical and filmic traditions.[69] Many of these traditions are exactly what sociologic scholars point to when they talk about derogatory and/or negative representations of disability. As we can see, the disparity between the goals of the directors, actors, scholars, and audience members is at least partially the result of different discourses and paradigms. Current debates in Hollywood about the casting (or not) of disabled actors and the lack of disabled filmmakers address the real-world bodies at stake in creating film representations. Unfortunately, the real-world side of Hollywood casting and the diversity of its filmmakers falls largely outside the bounds of this discussion.

In terms of a formal theoretical structure for analyzing disability in film, Norden's *Cinema of Isolation* is one of the few texts that lays out a formal structure beyond the common metaphoric understandings of disability (e.g., the dichotomy between disability denoting a pure vs. a villainous character). Norden argues that, between the birth of cinema in the late 1890s and the passage of the Americans with Disabilities Act (ADA) in 1990, representations of disability in film overwhelmingly isolate the impaired individual both visually and geographically within the narrative.[70] Isolation often narratively precedes exploitation, "kill or cure,"[71] or the impaired—and usually secondary—character becoming a prop for the protagonist's emotional journey.[72] Norden's focus is on early silent film and film from the twentieth century addressing disabled veterans, but the isolation and exploitation frameworks he lays out are useful in wider discussions of film and disability.

Exploitation in this context refers to two different scenarios. Norden defines exploitation in early cinema as the casting of physically disabled individuals in early silent film who resembled the stars of the film. These individuals would be inserted into the shot to demonstrate the "after" of a fight, vehicle crash, or other accident, in which a character lost limbs; most commonly a leg or an arm.[73] However, exploitation also referred to films where the narrative revealed a false disability assumed by a character, either to create a more pitiable beggar persona or to exploit individuals and organizations.[74] False disability, imported to film and television from theatrical and social roots,[75] is included in Disney's *The Hunchback of Notre Dame* (1996)[76] when the gypsy beggars are revealed to be feigning disabilities, and an episode of the BBC's *Dr. Who* in which a suspect in a murder investigation inadvertently reveals that he is not paraplegic.[77] Exploitation narratives may or may not include the death of the impaired imposter; kill or cure however, ends in death far more often than cure.

The OED dates the phrase "Kill or Cure" to the mid-1700s, and the phrase was used to refer to last-ditch attempts to heal patients; these cures were often so extreme that the patient would either be cured, or the cure would prove fatal.[78] Norden uses the term to describe films where the disabled character is either cured of their disability at the end of the film, or they die.[79] Death may be a result of the disability itself, but more commonly death is some kind of sacrifice that buoys and/or spurs the development of the abled protagonist. Norden's kill or cure dovetails nicely with Mitchell and Snyder's theory of narrative prosthesis,[80] in which the development of the narrative and the disability are tied together; at the conclusion of the narrative the disability is resolved either through—an often miraculous—cure or death. Davidson adds that "what John Hockenberry calls a 'crip-ex-machina' provid[es] the able-bodied viewer a measure of compassion for the victim while permitting an identification with the able-bodied hero who survives."[81] Kill or cure is so common in narratives that feature disability that it arguably becomes the basis for some of the criticism regarding the oversimplification of disability. Often, the narrative frames a disabled character's death in terms of a useful death as opposed to a useless (or burdensome, restricted, painful, etc.) life, which elides kill or cure with the death of a secondary character to forward the protagonist's development. This false binary—abled life vs. disability and death—creates emotional moments in narratives as a plucky underdog sacrifices their life or a pitiable character succumbs to a disabling illness, but critics argue that the "better dead than disabled" ideology fails to consider that a disabled life is valuable and worth living.[82] One poignant example is Clint Eastwood's 2004 film, *Million Dollar Baby*, in which Maggie Fitzgerald commits assisted suicide after becoming quadriplegic; the film's sympathetic portrayal of Fitzgerald's choice suggests that there are no alternatives to death in the case of acquired disability.[83] It is worth noting that the majority of films Norden addresses involve acquired, physical impairments, largely because of his interest in disabled veterans on screen. So already we see that film theorists tend to work with a small slice of defined impairment, precisely because physical and mental disability is so individualized. That individuality is also at least partly responsible for normates accusing individuals whose disabilities are more extreme of monstrosity.

In choosing and defining a specific kind of impairment, filmmakers must eventually ask at what point disability and monstrosity converge. "Monster" as a term was used in medical texts, from the 1400s to the 1990s, to describe "a fetus, neonate, or individual with a gross congenital malformation, usually of a degree incompatible with life."[84] Bearden adds that "renaissance writers frequently used monstrosity to imagine what we now call disability," further arguing that "as a precursor to modern concepts of disability, monstrosity portends, shows, and teaches us much about our tendency to ascribe disability with meaning."[85] Monstrosity and the grotesque are themselves a significant aspect of literary and cultural theory, but Garland-Thomson's exploration of freak shows in the early 1900s refuses the abstraction of criticism and insists on the reality of the—arguably disabled, socially relegated to freakishness and monstrosity—body.[86] Monstrosity also seems to presage disability aesthetics and Siebers' insistence that disability aesthetics works to make the historical presence and influence of disability overt.[87] There is a reason disabled subjects persist in artistic representations.

A well-known character of literature and film referred to as monstrous is Quasimodo (Victor Hugo, 1833, novel; *The Hunchback of Notre Dame* 1911, 1939, 1956, 1986, 1996, films). There are many adaptations of Victor Hugo's novel, each with its own changes to the original plot, but the central arc of Quasimodo's narrative is of a physically disabled bell ringer in Notre Dame, who falls in love with a gypsy woman; ultimately his love goes unrequited, and in Hugo's novel, both Esmeralda and Quasimodo die at the end. Quasimodo's impairments are examples of congenital disability—an impairment an individual is born with—and acquired disability—an impairment acquired in life.[88]

Quasimodo, unlike many characters with disabilities, is a subaltern figure, socially isolated from infancy. Many of the characters in later chapters are privileged figures, with impairments that are less visually arresting than

Quasimodo's; as a result, any monstrosity attached to them will often be metaphorical rather than the classical definition of half-human, half-animal monstrosity,[89] or even the medicalized definition of congenital impairments usually incompatible with life.[90] For the purposes of a discussion about disability and cinematic realism, however, I draw a line at the classical definition of monstrosity. Characters who are human with visible physical impairments—for example, Quasimodo—will be considered disabled whereas characters who are not fully human—such as *Forbidden Planet*'s (1956) Id monster version of *The Tempest*'s Caliban—will be considered outside the scope of this discussion because they are monsters outright as opposed to monstrous human figures.

Many of the early modern characters I will discuss have acquired disabilities, and those disabilities are often acquired through punitive acts of violence. Suddenly and violently acquiring a disability raises the question of trauma. For example, the wounds incurred via battle, violent punishment, or accidental maiming certainly result in impairments that can be called 'disabilities', but if the act of violence is the substance of the scene (as in the Taymor and Howell adaptations of *Titus Andronicus*), then shouldn't that be considered first? In these instances, the character incurs a disability, perhaps, but do they not also incur a psycho-emotional and physical trauma?

For the purposes of exploring representations of disability and the filmic stare, we can and arguably should separate acquired disability from trauma. If the focus of a given scene is the sudden, violent acquisition of an impairment, the resulting trauma certainly qualifies under many definitions of disability. Some might argue that films that focus on PTSD also focus on trauma. In those cases, there is a risk of conflating trauma and a specific kind of mental impairment. My discussion is intentionally broad and identifying exactly where the trauma/PTSD line lies is, unfortunately, outside the scope of this project. Additionally, theorists who have been reclaiming an early modern understanding of disability don't necessarily construct disability—mental or physical—based on how the disability was acquired or how traumatic that acquisition may have been.[91] This style of thinking is more common in sociological texts, such as when Martin Norden argues that "[...] the only thing the movie leaves unanswered about Hook is his pre-disablement identity."[92] From a sociological perspective, it makes sense to inquire about Captain Hook's life prior to the loss of his hand. From an aesthetic perspective, it makes less sense because the film offers us nothing *but* the representation of the disabled Captain. The representation is what I focus on.

The Filmic Stare

Like Mulvey's gaze, and to some degree Siebers' disability aesthetics, Garland-Thomson's stare is inherently ideological; the stare is based on largely unconscious ideas about disability that are pervasive in society and reveal themselves in various media. A poignant example of the unconscious ideology behind the stare is that up until the 1970s, many US states had on their books "ugly laws": restrictions placed on individuals with visible physical impairments, preventing them from being seen in public places.[93] Additionally, although freak shows largely fell out of popularity in the early 1900s,[94] their ideological legacy of an other who exists to be stared at persists in tandem with the manners with which many are inculcated as young children: don't stare, it's rude to stare, stop staring.

But what are the ethical implications of staring, particularly in a disability studies context? As with many multivalent and interdisciplinary issues, context is key. Between two passers-by on the street, staring runs the gamut from microaggression to an active, productive desire to *see* and to *learn*, as Garland-Thomson notes.[95] In literary disability studies, Quayson argues that,

> the representation of disability oscillates uneasily between the aesthetic and the ethical domains, in such a way as to force a reading of the aesthetic fields in which the disabled are represented as always having an ethical dimension that cannot be subsumed under the aesthetic structure.[96]

Quayson positions the oscillation between the aesthetic and the ethical in texts as coextensive with a discomfort of disability in the real world. In my discussion of the filmic stare, I will locate the ethical dimension of disability studies that Quayson identifies more generally in the specific context of staring, disability aesthetics, and film studies.

For Davidson, staring is both visual and embodied, as he frames the *Concerto for the Left Hand* not as highlighting Paul Wittgenstein, who commissioned the work, as a musician with a disability, but rather in terms of disabling Ravel, the composer.[97] In focusing on Ravel's process for creating a piece of music for an artist with an impairment, Davidson argues that "by enabling Wittgenstein, Ravel disables Ravel, imposing formal demands upon composition that he might not have imagined had he not had to think through limits imposed by writing for one hand."[98] The assumed embodiment that Davidson attributes to Ravel here is similar to the adage "walk a mile in someone's shoes," and becomes a physical form of staring through embodiment. Literature and aural art, however, while it may encourage empathetic embodiment, does not necessarily invite staring. Visual arts, on the other hand, not only invites but insists upon viewers staring. Passive staring is the fact of Mulvey's male gaze and my filmic stare existing; as Garland-Thomson points out, staring is both an active choice and a physiological imperative—sometimes our bodies and brains engage in staring before our higher cognitive functions kick in to remind us not to passively stare. What separates the gaze, the stare, and the filmic stare from a passive act, however, is the active critical work behind them and the awareness therein of the aesthetics and complexities of representation at play. Staring with purpose—or positioning staring through the lens of the gaze or the filmic stare, in the context of film studies and disability aesthetics—helps to combat the short circuit caused by aesthetic nervousness. Ableism is a difficult bias to confront and address, which means that unethical representations of disability do and will continue to exist. Looking away from representations of disability out of discomfort, or passively staring, ignores the very real fact that a problem or bias cannot be addressed, examined, or—crucially—changed until it is articulated and there is a framework in place for moving through nervousness into a productive conversation. The filmic stare will contribute to the articulation of both problematic and praiseworthy representations of disability, and encourage the already exemplary work of disability studies in addressing and understanding the complexities of aesthetic representations, and providing a framework for the ethical considerations that arise from those conversations. Unlike Garland-Thomson's stare, which is couched in the interpersonal interactions of the real world, the filmic stare is concerned with how a stare is constructed by a given film's cinematography, editing, and mise-en-scène, dovetailing with disability aesthetics to highlight the influence of disability on aesthetic representations of disability in film.

The filmic stare stands in an analogous relation to Mulvey's male gaze, although the gaze has a psychoanalytic ideological foundation not shared by the filmic stare. The filmic stare describes the web of techniques including the stare of a normate subjective camera (cinematography and mise-en-scène), the stare of normate characters within the film's diegesis, and the stare of an assumed normate audience—similar to Quayson's construction of aesthetic nervousness but adapted for film studies. Taken together, these techniques and the ideological underpinnings explored by Garland-Thomson, create a visual representation of a character with a disability as a staree. Mulvey appropriates psychoanalytic theory in "Visual Pleasure and Narrative Cinema" to "demonstrat[e] the way the unconscious of patriarchal society has structured film form."[99] The filmic stare, by contrast, is largely detached from psychoanalytic criticism, and rather than focusing on how the "unconscious of patriarchal society" constructs visual representations of gender, it focuses on how the unconscious of normate society constructs visual representations of disability. In the context of constructing a visual representation of the human form, Mulvey, Garland-Thomson, and Siebers agree that looking at the human form is fascinating. Mulvey explores the scopophilic and voyeuristic aspects of gazing,[100] but Garland-Thomson defines staring as "an interrogative gesture that asks what's going on and demands the story," creating "a circuit of communication and meaning-making."[101] Garland-Thomson also identifies the unconscious responses to staring at non-normative bodies: fear, distaste, a lack of understanding, dehumanization, and asexual objectification.[102] The filmic stare describes the cinematographic construction of visual representations of disabled bodies based on the unconscious social, cultural and physiological reactions to disabilities, and, in the vein of disability aesthetics, values those representations as sites where those unconscious assumptions and/or reactions can be explored and challenged in nuanced and complex discourses.

I will begin a more in-depth exploration of the filmic stare by examining the function of the different shots that help form the cinematographic web of techniques. The choice of shot distance and framing is critical in high-lighting or downplaying the visual impact of an impairment. I argue that there is no such thing as a truly invisible impairment in film; however, if the impairment is out of frame or consistently hidden by shot distance or composition, then what is literally out of sight may be largely out of mind. While some shots are used to highlight an impairment or a break with social and/or behavioral scripts, others ultimately suppress the visibility—and therefore the impact of—those same impairments. My discussion of the use of shots in the filmic stare will examine the following: close-ups, medium shots, wide shots, subjective shots, and empathetic shots. Each type of shot is used differently to help create the filmic stare, and some shots, close-ups in particular, function differently for mental vs physical impairment.

Close-ups and extreme close-ups in Hollywood are affective; that is, they are used to evoke emotion in audiences as well as focusing on critical details. When a film includes a character with a physical impairment, directors often choose to focus close-ups on the impairment—or visible assistive device. Garland-Thomson argues that a function of literature and film's compression of narrative to a medium-specific length is that a disabled character is reduced to the symbolism or stereotype of their impairment.[103] What close-ups do for disabled characters onscreen is twofold: the impairment (and/or assistive device) is highlighted, causing the visual fragmentation and objectification of the disabled character, and the close-up in combination with the fragmentation and focus on a visible impairment creates a visual synecdoche of the character. In the creation of the visual synecdoche, a split between the sociological and aesthetic approaches of looking at disability is highlighted. Looking at just a still image of a close-up, or just the shot in isolation, it is easy to understand where Garland-Thomson and other sociological disability theorists find evidence to support their understanding of filmic representations of disability.

A close-up creates an emotional reaction to a highly visible facet of a character that often becomes the shorthand for characterization. A sociological approach to disability assumes that the part becomes the whole, rather than a representation of a whole that is arguably more complex within the total formal system of the film. Within narrative storytelling, the sociological insistence on avoiding shorthand becomes a major handicap to film as a medium. Visual storytelling is more complex, nuanced, and engaging when visual shorthands (in the form of the close-up shots currently being discussed) are interpreted in a wider filmic context. The rhetorical term synecdoche applies to these shots/stills because the aesthetic understanding of representations of disability in film recognizes that the close-up is part of the whole. That whole may be the film's total formal system or the shot's place in a sequence; in either case, the part, decontextualized from the whole, is not enough to serve as the basis for an evaluation of a representation.

A synecdoche can also exist in contrast with the larger thematic material of a film. For example, in Martin Scorsese's *Hugo* (2011), repeated close-ups of Inspector Gustave's knee brace draw attention to the impairment, and audiences can assume that this impairment is what makes Gustave socially isolated and even cruel to orphans in the Gare Montparnasse railway station. Late in the film, however, Gustave reveals that it is not his impairment that shapes his worldview, but rather his experiences as an orphan and as a soldier. This revelation throws audience assumptions—influenced by the filmic stare—about Gustave into conflict with the revelation that he is, in many ways, a foil for Hugo. While Gustave's visual synecdoche (his knee brace and accompanying limp) informs his character, it is ultimately not neatly resolved with his function in the film.

In addition to creating a visual synecdoche, close-ups function to fragment and objectify disabled characters. Often, discussions of fragmentation and objectification are connected back to Mulvey's theorization of the male gaze.[104] In the context of an aesthetic approach to disability in film, however, the fragmentation of a non-normative body complicates Mulvey's gendered reading. Often, the fragmented and objectified body is male. In contemporary film adaptations of early modern texts, the male disabled body leads to adaptive challenges, particularly when the film adaptation of the Shakespeare play is being treated as a star vehicle. To varying degrees, the play text dictates specific character impairments to the adaptor—for example, Richard III must have physical impairments, but the severity of the impairments is left ambiguous, as I will discuss in detail in a later chapter—and the star wants the prestige of performing Shakespeare. As a result, the director and star are largely locked into the character's disability, but the way the character is shot complicates the heroic aspects of the character with the character's disability.

The filmic stare theorizes that along with the discomfort and fear inherent in the stare comes the asexual objectification of a character with a disability. Asexual objectification is a common aspect of the assumptions made by individuals who do not experience disabilities about individuals with disabilities, highlighting a social and cultural discomfort with the sexualization of an individual with a disability.[105] In order to reframe narratives around the idea of asexualized disability, films either place the disabled character on the periphery, where questions of sex and sexuality are outside the narrative scope of the film, or they change the central relationship of the film so heterosexual, abled sexuality is not challenged. An example of this second strategy is *The Miracle Worker* (1962), where the focus is on Helen Keller and Annie Sullivan's student-teacher relationship. While *The Miracle Worker* provides the audience with a relationship to follow, the relationship is based on the isolation of Keller and Sullivan, and ultimately reflects the isolation around which Norden centers his *Cinema of Isolation*. Additionally, Keller and Sullivan, through their isolation, are placed outside of the typical expectations of abled woman- and girlhood and therefore do not threaten the status quo of abled, heterosexual sexuality. Alternatively, films might provide a disabled character with a potential love interest in an attempt to resist the asexual objectification of a protagonist or central character, but in many cases the disabled character dies or commits suicide to "free" the love interest from what audiences likely assume will ultimately be a sexless, caregiver relationship. Examples of what many theorists[106] describe as an attitude of "better off dead than disabled" include films like Thea Sharrock's *Me Before You* (2016), where the main character commits assisted suicide explicitly to free his caregiver to have a normative heterosexual relationship. There has been some resistance to this idea, largely in the late twentieth and twenty-first centuries.[107] In films which do challenge the idea of asexualized disability (in which a disabled character is given a love interest and lives to the end of the film), we see different types of conflicts and discomfort.

Norden cites Hal Ashby's *Coming Home* (1978) as one of the first films to explicitly address the sex life of a disabled character.[108] Much of Norden's focus with *Coming Home* is on the process of filming, specifically the use of a special camera dolly that placed the camera on the same level as characters in wheelchairs, thereby avoiding high angle shots, which are often interpreted as ascribing powerlessness to the subject in the wheelchair.[109] It is fascinating to observe the filmmaker's cognizance of the typical film apparatus that inherently places characters with assistive devices in shots that suggest a lack of power. However, in terms of the construction of the filmic stare, removing high angle shots does not deconstruct the network of shots which comprises the filmic stare, it just shifts the nuance of the disability aesthetic created by the film. Part of the narrative tension in this film comes from the fact that Sally and Luke's relationship is an affair: Sally's marine husband is in Vietnam at the time of the relationship. Although the high angle shots of individuals in wheelchairs are removed from the film, narrative tensions still ultimately create what Margrit Shildrick refers to as a "dangerous discourse;" that is, a discussion of a sexual relationship that is ideologically problematized by two different but intersectional theoretical paradigms.[110] In the case of *Coming Home*, the two critical paradigms at work are disability studies and feminism. However, not every film that rejects asexual objectification then problematizes the relationship to the point of dangerous discourse.

Josh Boone's film adaptation *The Fault in Our Stars* (2014)[111] is exceptional in that it not only highlights the story of two visibly disabled teenagers, but in adapting the story it resists infantilizing or asexually objectifying the film's protagonists even as it resists ideologically problematizing the romantic sexual relationship. Admittedly, the film is not a perfect fit in the context of resisting a kill or cure narrative; Augustus's death because of a cancer relapse and widespread metastasizing is included in the film, and we are told in the opening scene that Hazel's lung cancer is terminal, so "cure" was never truly an option for either character. However, Hazel does survive the run time of the film, which focuses partly on her sexual desires—an arguably feminist perspective. This film (and the John Green YA novel on which it is based) pulls no punches in exploring teenage sexuality intersected with disability. Hazel relies on additional oxygen, wearing a cannula[112] for much of her screen time. During the foreplay leading to her first sexual experience, Hazel stops, telling Augustus "I can't breathe."[113] The next shot onscreen is a two-shot of Hazel and Augustus, lit beautifully, as he helps her put on her cannula. The tension here stems from three places: first, is the anxiety of Augustus, who will be revealing the site of his amputation to Hazel for the first time. This is almost immediately laid to rest by Hazel herself, telling Augustus to "get over yourself." The second point of tension is when Hazel announces that she cannot breathe. The stakes here are higher than normal teenage sex; more than getting pregnant or falling prey to an STD, sex without her cannula could be dangerous, even deadly for Hazel. The reseating of the cannula is handled smoothly, matter-of-factly. The third point of tension, which exists throughout the film, is highlighted in this scene: the question of the male gaze and its relationship to the filmic stare. For the male disabled bodies in *The Fault in Our Stars* and *Coming Home*, asexual objectification is usually uncomplicated by the gaze. Female disabled bodies have a more complex relationship with asexual objectification and the male gaze.

Both the male gaze and the filmic stare visually fragment the object of the look; the function of that fragmentation is significantly different depending on the film in question. *The Fault in Our Stars* forces the stare and the gaze into elision by focusing on a female protagonist whose assistive device cannot be hidden by fragmentation. Any close-up of Hazel will reveal some part of her breathing apparatus: a close-up on the face, or medium shot of the top half of her body will reveal the cannula and tubing. Any shot of the lower half of her body at any scale will reveal her oxygen tank. No matter how Hazel is fragmented, her visual synecdoche remains in the frame. This is not to say that the inclusion of the breathing apparatus negates the effect of the gaze. Rather, the film goes out of its way to make Hazel attractive despite the physical changes that typically come with cancer treatments. *The Fault in Our Stars* revels in the inherent contradiction of a beauty shot of a female character wearing a cannula. The contradiction also upsets the objectification we see with a character like Gustave (*Hugo*, 2011), where the creation of his visual synecdoche means removing his face from close-ups to focus on his leg. Hazel's synecdoche insists on the inclusion of her face because that is where a nasal cannula goes, therefore humanizing her through the inclusion of her face in both the gaze and the filmic stare.

Hazel is an unusual case in terms of the gaze being complicated by the stare. One of the major issues with finding examples of female characters with disabilities is that Hollywood tends to cast women in caretaker roles, rather than in roles where they are the disabled character. Another significant complication is that Hollywood still holds actors and actresses to unwritten standards which imply a narrow spectrum of physical beauty. Outside of biopics like *Soul Surfer* (2011), where the film is an adaptation of a real-life individual's experience, blindness and deafness are the two most common impairments embodied by female characters in narrative film. These impairments are less visible than a missing limb or assistive device. We may occasionally see a pair of dark sunglasses on a blind character, but films such as *Wait Until Dark* (1967) and *The Miracle Worker* (1962) forego that shorthand in favor of being able to fully see the faces of Audrey Hepburn and Anne Bancroft. Additionally, in the case of a close-up on a blind character or other fragmentary shot, there is no real visible reminder of the disability, potentially creating an "out of sight, out of mind" situation. We might know intellectually that Hepburn is blind in *Wait Until Dark*, but when a close-up of her face is meant to reveal emotion, it is easy to forget that her character is blind. A similar situation is created when a female character is deaf.[114] When we can visually forget that a character has a physical impairment, arguably the gaze can take over. As a result, the filmic stare, and the disability itself are subtly visually suppressed. This kind of visual suppression of disability is unusual, particularly with male characters. For female characters with physical impairments, largely invisible disabilities like blindness and deafness often mean that close-up shots are analyzed through the gaze rather than the filmic stare. More visible disabilities like the loss of a limb or assistive devices tend to be categorized under the filmic stare rather than the gaze.

Asexual objectification, close-up shots as suppression of disability, and the tensions between the gaze and the stare become more significant when we step out of the realm of physical disabilities and discuss mental disabilities. Film is a visual medium and, as a result, no disability on film is ever truly invisible. Bolter and Grusin note that Classical Hollywood gives us a specific strategy for visualizing mental disability: hypermediacy.[115] An excellent example is Scottie's breakdown in *Vertigo*. The sequence begins with a close-up of a sleeping Scottie, and then coloured filters begin to overlay the mise-en-scène in an alternating pattern. Next, the sequence transitions to a series of animations, beginning with a representational bouquet of flowers which morphs into abstract shapes. Then the sequence cuts to a fantastical version of the courtroom scene, featuring a woman who looks like the painting of Carlotta Valdez that Madeleine had spent so much time staring at. Then the camera zooms in on a necklace around Carlotta's neck, before finally cutting to double exposure images of Scottie walking toward an open grave. Upon looking into the grave, the camera cuts to a photographic image of Scottie's face over a background that gives the perception that the image of Scottie's face is falling. These hypermediated images convey Scottie's state of mind as he falls into acute melancholia. The sequence closes with a close-up of Scottie violently waking up. Hypermediacy owes a certain debt to cinematic expressionism in the movement away from objective realism to show the invisible disability that is the acute melancholia to which Scottie succumbs at this point in the film. Hypermediacy becomes a crucial aspect of the filmic stare in *Vertigo* because in rejecting realism, it allows the viewer to see Scottie's mind shift from nonmelancholic to melancholic. Understanding that the shift in Scottie's mind has occurred, and making that shift visible, highlights the change Scottie experiences from a normate mental state to a state of mental disability.

Hitchcock spends a lot of time in *Vertigo* balancing expectations of masculinity—that Scottie should end up with one of the two women with whom he is associated in the film—with the socially emasculating and isolating effects of Scottie's acrophobia and melancholia using the filmic stare. As a part of the western film canon, *Vertigo* has been extensively discussed in the context of the male gaze and masculinity; Scottie lusts after Madeleine for most of the film, but in the end, he is unable to possess her. Rather than explore Scottie's emotional journey through a more psychoanalytic lens, however, I want to look at the filmic stare and Scottie's asexual objectification in the film. It is important here to underline the fact that mental disability and the resulting asexual objectification is not limited by gender in the context of the filmic stare.

As a direct result of his acrophobia, Scottie is asexually objectified by the men around him at the hearing to decide if Madeleine's death from falling out of the bell tower the first time was Scottie's fault. Scottie's asexual objectification is encapsulated by the language used by the judge to describe Scottie's inaction, particularly in phrases like "fear of heights makes him powerless," "it is a pity, knowing her suicidal tendencies, he did not make a greater effort the second time," and "he could not face the tragic results of his own weakness and ran away."[116] Terms like "powerless," "greater effort," and "weakness" all imply that acrophobia—and by extension, mental disability in general—is something that can simply be overcome with willpower, like a hatred of Brussel sprouts. That assumption is inherently ableist, and it positions mental disability in a specific body and then minimizes the effect of the disability on the mind and body. Therefore, Scottie is othered for his perceived inability to "man up" and "overcome" a disability in a society that neither understands nor accommodates mental disability. The dialogue others Scottie, and because his inaction—in the period seen as unmanly[117]—is so intimately linked in the film narrative to a female figure, the scene contains undertones that suggest that Scottie has failed in his masculinity and therefore he is neither masculine nor virile in the eyes of the judge and jury in the scene. The effect of the filmic stare is that Scottie, a male character, is asexually objectified as a result of his acrophobia and the effects that has on the diegetic perceptions of his masculinity, despite the filmic stare being uncomplicated by the gaze.

Close-ups are good for highlighting small impairment details, affecting audience emotions, and serving as the anchor points for the construction of the stare, but some disabilities do not lend themselves to this kind of shot. Medium and wide shots function in the structure of the stare to establish not only larger-scale visual impairments (e.g., a character sitting in a wheelchair, using crutches, or whose overall stature requires a point of reference to be noticeable, as with dwarfism or giantism) but to make visual the breaking of social and behavioral scripts that so often accompanies the representation of mental impairments. I discuss medium and wide shots together here because these types of shots are the most critical in terms of constructing a visual representation of impairment on screen. Close-ups might affect the viewer and draw their attention to a specific impairment or prosthesis but staring insists on the visibility of the impairment in a wider frame. The medium and wide shots are also the places where the interplay between a desire to highlight or suppress disabilities is most visible. In a close-up of a non-normative body or assistive device, it is impossible not to face the visual reality of disability. Wide and medium shots allow for composing the mise-en-scène to either subtly highlight or minimize impairments and disabilities by removing them from the audience's line of sight. The difference between highlighting and suppressing the stare in medium and wide shots is more than simply maintaining or fragmenting the stare across the run time of the film. The difference also serves to help highlight or suppress disability as an identity category in the analysis of the characters. The techniques for highlighting or suppressing a disability and/or impairment are slightly different depending on whether the impairment and/or disability in question is physical or mental.

For physical disabilities, the medium and wide shots serve to contextualize the impairment. For example, a medium or wide-angle shot is required for a character in a wheelchair or with a prosthetic limb for the assistive device to appear in the frame. If the impairment and assistive device affect only the lower half of a character's body, then in medium shots and close-ups of faces, and shot/reverse shots sequences, we will not see the device or impairment. The wheelchair is simultaneously the most and least visible assistive device in film. In wide shots, the readily visible wheels invite audiences to stare. In medium shots, where the wheels are not visible, the back and arms of the wheelchair—particularly the wheelchair designed for Sir Patrick Stewart in his role as Professor X (Marvel's X-Men franchise 2000-present)—merely look like the back and arms of a customized office chair. If the scene is set in a time/location where being seated is expected, the disability and accompanying assistive device are once again visually out of frame and out of mind. Audiences cannot stare at an impairment that is suppressed either by not being in frame or by the mise-en-scène of the film.

Crutches, braces, and canes are even easier to hide within a frame, and these smaller assistive devices can also be discreetly hidden in wide shots by the mise-en-scène. For example, it is incredibly simple to borrow an old theatre trick and put a cane or a crutch in a character's "upstage" hand—the hand furthest away from the camera. This technique goes a long way toward allowing the actor's own body to hide the assistive device, and if the cane is not accompanied by a visible limp, audiences can easily miss the presence of the device in the mise-en-scène. If a leg brace cannot be put on the upstage leg for some reason, strategically placed props or other actors can be used to minimize the visibility of the assistive device. By hiding the visible sign of the disability at every opportunity, the filmic stare is weakened. The fragmentation of the stare subtly suppresses the presence of disability in the film overall, leading to a critical focus on other aspects of the film.

Films can also go in the other direction and highlight a physical impairment or assistive device in wide and medium shots. Inspector Gustave (*Hugo*, 2011) is an excellent example of highlighting a disability in this fashion. Gustave's brace is on his downstage leg—the leg closest to the camera—in most of his wide shots. Even in medium two-shots with Gustave and Maximilian, the dog rarely significantly hides the brace. This subtle but consistent highlighting of the impairment maintains visibility, refusing to allow audiences to forget about or not acknowledge the impairment outside of the close-ups. The filmic stare is therefore maintained throughout the film, not only when close-up shots thrust the impairment into the viewer's face. Scorsese plays many of these moments for comedy; however, comedy generally presupposes an unspoken understanding that requests the viewer's visual attention and permits laughter as a result of the intensified visual engagement. The laughter may be uncomfortable, if viewers are reacting to a "better them than me" instinct.

The foregoing examples involve relatively straightforward shots, which fit neatly into narrative cinema conventions. However, art film, a modality which fundamentally changes the construction of the mise-en-scène, cinematography, and editing, significantly shifts how cinematography is interpreted in the context of the filmic stare. The filmic stare in art film will be addressed in more depth in later chapters; I mention this here only as a reminder that different filmic modes can and do affect the use and interpretation of these strategies for highlighting or suppressing assistive devices and prostheses. Prostheses and assistive devices, however, are only useful as a synecdoche or motif if the film is addressing a character with a physical impairment.

Because characters with mental impairments rarely embody anything as visual as prostheses or missing limbs, directors fall back on the breaking of verbal and behavioural social scripts to demonstrate such disabilities. Often the verbal deviations are in the early modern texts; play scripts are blueprints for another kind of visual medium, making the adaptation of the idea of the text different than a literal transposition of the words from play script to screenplay. Characters deviating from verbal social scripts also creates a meta layer in the representation of mental impairments in both theatre and film. The breaking of a social script draws attention to their existence of such scripts, the screenplays that underpin the visual, and the dialogue. In terms of the specifics of dialogue, verse, and prose, books have been written about early modern wordplay and the challenges of adapting that language to film.[118] Visually, however, the breaking of behavioural scripts is where directors frequently choose to use wide and medium shots to represent mental impairment, regardless of whether the film is an adaptation.

To take an example from the canon of early modern film adaptations, in John Webster's *The Duchess of Malfi* (1612), Ferdinand's lycanthropy exists not in speech, but in behavioural changes. *The Duchess of Malfi* focuses on the titular duchess, her twin brother Ferdinand, and their older brother the Cardinal, as Ferdinand and the Cardinal plot to keep their recently widowed sister from remarrying. However, the duchess secretly marries Antonio, and her brothers hire an old soldier, Bosola, to spy on and eventually murder the Duchess and her children. As a result of this murder, Ferdinand goes mad— he is diagnosed with lycanthropy—and Bosola ultimately avenges the duchess by killing the Cardinal and Ferdinand.

In James MacTaggart's 1972 BBC adaptation of *The Duchess of Malfi*, we often see Ferdinand and Bosola plotting while framed in a relatively tight two-shot.[119] This focus allows the audience to focus on the language and plot elements that are being communicated. Once Ferdinand succumbs to his lycanthropy however, we see him primarily in wide shots, often being restrained by two other men. When he escapes, we need the space of the wide shot to show that Ferdinand is scrabbling about on the floor, attempting to escape further restraint. This framing underscores the fact that the impairment—the lycanthropy and the accompanying distortion of perception—are unique to Ferdinand. We in the audience have (hopefully!) never experienced the change in perception that comes with lycanthropy, so we cannot empathize with Ferdinand. The characters who are charged with keeping Ferdinand restrained cannot share that reality with Ferdinand either. The impairment is entirely Ferdinand's, and it isolates him to a large degree. The disability comes in the sudden shift in Ferdinand's dis-ability to interact with society. Whether this is framed in terms of Ferdinand's inability to interact with society or society's inability to accommodate Ferdinand is a question for disability activists; the representation itself demonstrates an isolation of experience, which reflects the disability. The impairment is individual, which is why physical impairments are shown in close-up. Disability is about the relationships surrounding the individual with the impairment. That is why the medium and wide shots are so critical for mental impairments: since the impairment itself is problematic to show, the disability becomes the anchor point for the stare.

A common criticism of films that feature disabled characters is that these characters are frequently disallowed from looking. That is, characters with disabilities in protagonist roles who visually dominate films have few to no optical POV shots attributed to them. Norden references the many scholars who have noticed this and made the claim throughout *The Cinema of Isolation*. Garland-Thomson, Berger, and Barounis all add that characters with disabilities are rarely the center of their own stories, and the point of view of the story is rarely that of the character with a disability. This is common enough that pop culture websites like TV Tropes have also commented on the lack of disability points of view. Even within the parameters of early modern film adaptations, subjective optical POV shots attributed to characters with disabilities are not common. Some of the subjective shots are necessitated because the character in question is the main character, and do not necessarily add to the framework of the filmic stare. Subjective shots that contribute to the filmic stare come in two varieties: self-reflexive and empathetic.

A particularly interesting example of a self-reflexive subjective shot is in the 2016 *Richard III*.[120] *Richard III* follows Richard of Gloucester as he murders and schemes his way up the line of succession to the English throne despite his physical disabilities. The play then tracks Richard's downfall as Henry Tudor, Earl of Richmond (later King Henry VII) defeats him at the Battle of Bosworth Field. In Dominic Cooke's 2016 film adaptation of *Richard III*, Richard is locked away in a small room, having just been crowned king, when the camera cuts to an optical POV shot of Richard examining his own distorted reflection in the blade of a dagger. The tight framing and the distortion caused by the metal means that it takes the viewer a second or two to comprehend the on-screen image. A combination of the framing and shallow focus means that the viewer's stare must intensify, first to understand what they see, then simply because the image invites staring. Richard's face is as distorted by the metal as his stature is distorted by his impairment, and as his gaze is distorted by the reflecting surface. Richard has heard himself described as an "elvish-mark'd, abortive, rooting hog,"[121] and refers to himself along these same lines many times. Arguably, Richard has internalized his own impairments. How Richard stares at himself is up for debate, but assuming a normate viewer, the viewer's alignment with him at that moment positions them to be both staree and starer. This subjective, self-reflexive shot encapsulates and amplifies for a cinematic paradigm the experience that Garland-Thomson describes in her theory of the stare. That is, by aligning a viewer with a character with whom we are not meant to identify, the sense that we cannot and do not understand or empathize with the character is enhanced by the sense that, momentarily, we are literally behind their eyes. The discomfort of being behind the eyes of a character so emotionally and physiologically different from the assumed audience amplifies the othering that Garland-Thomson refers to. The duration of the shot, as well as Richard's manipulation of the blade during the shot, thereby changing the angle we see without a transition, adds intensity to the interaction. This type of subjective shot de-centers the audience. By aligning the audience with the disabled character, the audience is forced to both stare and, through their alignment with the character, be stared at.

Most subjective shots are not into a reflective surface, however, and it is difficult to insert effective self-reflexive POV shots for characters with mental impairments (although Branagh's "To be, or not to be" speech into the mirror presents an interesting example). In addition, not every character to whom subjective shots are attributed is Richard III. In cases where audience sympathy is desired, often empathetic subjective shots will be used. This style of shot gives the viewer a glimpse into the character's subjective reality, in essence communicating to the audience what a non-normative mind perceives. Scottie's nightmare in *Vertigo* is an example of this. Empathetic subjective shots extend a hand to the audience and bring them closer to what a given character is experiencing. Narratively these shots add detail to a character arc, but in addition to the diegetic function, seeing what a character with a mental impairment sees is the closest the audience can possibly come to experiencing the character's reality and finding empathy.

To explore an example of an empathetic subjective shot, I return again to Hitchcock's *Vertigo*. To visually represent Scottie's acrophobia,[122] Hitchcock originates the dolly zoom—a technique wherein the camera simultaneously zooms in and tracks out. The dolly zoom would go on to represent everything from Brody's realization of the shark's presence (Spielberg, *Jaws*, 1974) to Frodo's perception of the black riders on the wooded road (Jackson, *The Fellowship of the Ring*, 2001). In *Jaws* and *Fellowship*, the shot signifies a realization of an atmospheric shift; in *Vertigo*, however, the dolly zoom is a subjective shot that allows the viewer to see what Scottie sees both at the beginning of the film when he nearly falls off a roof, and when he is chasing Madeleine/Judy up the bell tower. In momentarily sharing Scottie's subjective reality, the viewer may feel either empathy or sympathy. An assumed normate viewer may be unable to share Scottie's reality, but by seeing it on screen, the subjective shot has the potential to bridge the understanding gap assumed by the filmic stare. The dolly zoom has the potential to communicate the enormity of the shift in Scottie's vestibular system and sense of proprioception.[123] Again, depending on the actual rather than assumed viewer, these shots may still lead to the objectification of the character. Scottie is scorned by other men in the film because of his impairment;[124] along with that scorn comes emasculation and arguably asexual objectification. Whether the empathetic subjective shot is successful in bridging the understanding and objectification gap in a given film, these subjective shots open the door to understanding by allowing the audience to momentarily share a character's subjective reality.

Very occasionally, subjective shots will be both self-reflexive and empathetic. The best example of this kind of shot is Julia Stiles' Ophelia,[125] standing on the lip of a pool and looking at her reflection in the water. Audience members familiar with the story recognize this bit of narrative foreshadowing of her drowning. In addition to the foreshadowing, however, this shot speaks to every audience member who has ever stood on the edge of a body of water or precipice and heard the little voice inside them ask "what if I step off the edge?" Here the director is (consciously or otherwise) asking the audience to stare, be stared at, and find empathy in meeting "their own" eyes. That level of self-reflection and understanding is intimate, deeply uncomfortable, and again breaks the comfortable fourth wall assumed in the voyeuristic experience of watching film.

To conclude this chapter, I briefly return to Crowl and his reading of Loncraine and McKellen's 1995 *Richard III*.[126] Specifically, I will address the moment in which Richard makes something of a production of using his mouth to assist in the transfer of his ring to Lady Anne's hand in the wooing scene. The film was inspired by a stage production of the play, and in adapting this moment Crowl notes that,

> the ring business is retained and given an added emphasis, courtesy of a close-up, as the camera allows us to see the ring momentarily disappear into McKellen's mouth before his good hand retrieves it and slips it on her finger. This gesture, as well as neatly paying Anne back for her spitting at him, appropriately reflects the vulgar daring of Richard's wooing and the oral fantasy of his devouring appetite for power: now it is *his* saliva that provides lubricant for the ring.[127]

I agree with Crowl that this emphasized moment smacks of Richard's petty revenge and lust for power. However, his reading of a scene deeply colored by Richard's impairments is buried in metaphor and medicalization, as opposed to engaging with the embodied and cinematographic aspects of the representation. Crowl's reading ultimately suggests that the use of Richard's mouth to remove and transfer his ring to Anne is pathologized separately, and therefore ultimately disconnected from, Richard's physical disability, except perhaps as an overly moralizing metaphor. Perhaps this reading is, as Quayson describes, "shortcircuited"[128] by the presence of disability and the aesthetic nervousness between viewer—in this case Crowl—and the film text. A reading of the ring sequence which more fully explores the embodiment of Richard's disabilities and avoids diagnosing Richard with an oral fixation or positioning his physical impairments as a narrative "crutch"[129]— to use Mitchell and Snyder's term—will use the filmic stare. The filmic stare focuses on the creation of a visual synecdoche for a character with a disability, a resistance to diagnosing fictional characters, and an interconnected web of cinematographic techniques that helps us understand the nuts and bolts of the construction of a cinematic representation of disability.

The ring sequence is filmed in a high angle close-up, specifically to give the viewer a clear look at Richard's face, both insisting on his humanity and reminding the audience that Loncraine and McKellen have visually highlighted Richard's mouth as part of the visual shorthand that grounds Richard's physical embodiment. The angle and distance of the shot, while insisting on Richard's humanity by focusing on his face rather than a close-up of one of his physical impairments, also seems to suppress the visibility of those impairments; his hunch, limp, and unusable arm are not in the frame. However, the "out of sight, out of mind" idea that viewers may, albeit briefly, forget that Richard has physical impairments if the camera fragments the actor's body in such a way that the character figures in the frame without their impairments is not a concern here. Because Richard's mouth has already been set up as part of his visual synecdoche, we are reminded that there is a concrete, embodied reason for Richard to use his mouth to transfer the ring outside of an oral fixation or petty schoolyard tit-for-tat revenge.

The verbal dexterity Richard is so well known for is literalized in the highlighting of McKellen's mouth and is expanded in its interaction with the rest of his body, particularly the impressive dexterity of his right hand. Part of Richard's embodiment of his dexterity, then, is as a direct result of a lack of dexterity in his left hand and arm, and the "situated knowledge adher[ing] in embodiment"[130] demonstrated through the practicality of using his mouth to aid in a task that typically requires two hands. Not having the physical dexterity of a normate—to use Garland-Thomson's term[131]—means that Richard must embody a different kind of dexterity, not that Richard has an oral fixation. Richard's embodiment of his physical impairments is inextricably tied to his physical, mental, and verbal dexterity through the small moment of using his mouth to facilitate the removal and transfer of the ring. That Richard uses his dexterity for murder and power-grabbing is incidental to his impairments, rather than his impairments being the causal agent of Richard's crimes.

As Crowl's reading of the sequence demonstrates, Shakespeare film adaptations and critical engagement with those adaptations typically shy away from close engagement with disability studies. Where engagement does occur, as with the many iterations of *Richard III*, that engagement falls into the traps of aesthetic nervousness, pathologizing, and the limits of the linguistic turn—whether that language uses English grammar or film grammar—to downplay or entirely sidestep embodiment. The use of the filmic stare cracks open *Richard III* and other film adaptations of early modern drama in order to reexamine the representations of disability therein from an aesthetic point of view, valuing disability as a site worthy of critical analysis and highlighting the complexities of representation in the tradition of disability aesthetics. This is especially useful for engaging with embodiment in physical disabilities—as noted with *Richard III*—exploring representations of mental impairments in film, which in general is a somewhat neglected area of disability studies in film, and finally for understanding the multilaminated nature of mediating disability in a hybridized form like DBC. The subsequent chapters in this book will bring the filmic stare to bear intersectionally with gender and class to reveal the ubiquity of impairment and disability, as well as the surprisingly egalitarian nature of film representations of disability. Ultimately, the filmic stare is a critical step in bringing film disability studies into step with current trends and definitions from cultural and literary disability studies.

Notes

1 Hutcheon's term refers to a hypertext that is haunted by its hypotext to such an extreme degree that the two are distinct works, but are so entwined as to be nearly impossible to discuss separately. See Hutcheon Linda. *A Theory of Adaptation*. 2nd ed. New York: Routledge. 2013. 6–8, 20–2.
2 Crowl, Samuel. *Shakespeare at the Cineplex*. Ohio: Ohio UP. 2003. 109–10.
3 Siebers, Tobin. *Disability Theory*. Ann Arbor: University of Michigan Press. 2008. 1–33.
4 Berger, Ronald J. *Introducing Disability Studies*. New York: Lynne Rienner. 2013. 3.
5 Kudlick, Catherine J. "Disability History: Why We Need Another 'Other'." *Rethinking Normalcy: A Disability Studies Reader*. Ed. Tanya Titchkosky and Rod Michalko. Toronto: Canadian Scholar's Press. 2009. 31–7.
6 Berger, 26–30.
7 "ableism, n." *OED Online*. Oxford University Press, September 2019. Web.
8 Berger, 30.
9 Berger, 34.
10 I will refer to Tom Shakespeare by his first and last name throughout this book to avoid confusion with William Shakespeare. Shakespeare, Tom. *Disability Rights and Wrongs Revisited*. 2nd ed. London: Routledge, 2014.
11 Shakespeare, Tom, 268–9.
12 Qtd. in Iyengar, Sujata. *Disability, Health and Happiness in the Shakespearean Body*. New York: Routledge. 2015. 4.
13 Shakespeare, Tom, 269; Berger, 28–9.
14 Siebers, *Disability Theory*, 2–3.
15 Quayson, Ato. *Aesthetic Nervousness: Disability and the Crisis of Representation*. New York: Columbia UP. 2007. 32.
16 Quayson, 32.

17 Quayson, 32.
18 Quayson, 33.
19 *The Cambridge Companion to Literature and Disability*. Ed. Claire Barker and Stuart Murray. Cambridge: Cambridge UP. 2018. Kindle Edition. 20.
20 Siebers, Tobin. *Disability Aesthetics*. Ann Arbor: University of Michigan Press. 2010. 2.
21 Siebers *Disability Aesthetics*, 1.
22 Davidson, Michael. *Concerto for the Left Hand: Disability and the Defamiliar Body*. Ann Arbor: The University of Michigan Press. 2008. 1.
23 Barker and Murray, 20.
24 Siebers, *Disability Aesthetics*, 5–20.
25 Davidson, 2–4.
26 Sandahl, Carrie. "It's All the Same Movie: Making Code of the Freaks." *JCMS*, 58.4 (Summer 2019): 145–50. 145.
27 Davidson, xvii.
28 Norden, Martin. *The Cinema of Isolation: A History of Physical Disability in the Movies*. New Brunswick: Rutgers University Press, 1994.
29 Norden, 32.
30 Norden, 11.
31 Garland-Thomson, Rosemarie. Extraordinary Bodies: Figuring Physical Disability in American Culture and Literature. New York: Columbia UP. 1997. 10–11.
32 The gold standard for categorizing Shakespeare film is Jack Jorgens' *Shakespeare on Film* (Bloomington: Indiana UP. 1977). Jorgens distinguishes between three key modes of adaptation: Theatrical, Realistic and Filmic. Shakespeare film scholars including Samuel Crowl (*Shakespeare and Film: A Norton Guide*. New York: WW Norton and Co. 2008), Sarah Hatchuel (*Shakespeare, From Stage to Screen*. New York: Cambridge UP 2004) and Russell Jackson (*Shakespeare Films in the Making*. Cambridge: Cambridge UP. 2007) adopt and only topically modify Jorgens' taxonomy.
33 *Richard III*. Dir. Laurence Olivier. Perf. Laurence Olivier, John Gielgud. London Films. 1955.
34 "Richard III." *The Hollow Crown*. Dir. Dominic Cooke. BBC. 2016.
35 Qtd. in Hile, Rachel E. "Disability and the Characterization of Katherine in *The Taming of the Shrew*." *Disability Studies Quarterly*, 29.4 (2009). MLA International Bibliography. Web. May 12, 2015.
36 Garland-Thomson, *Extraordinary Bodies*, 10–11.
37 Burton, Robert. *The Anatomy of Melancholy*. Ed. Floyd Dell and Paul Jordan-Smith. New York: Tudor Publishing Co. 1927.
38 Burton, 217.
39 Hobgood, Allison P. and David Houston Wood, eds. *Recovering Disability in Early Modern England*. Columbus: Ohio State UP. 2013. 5.
40 Bearden, Elizabeth. *Monstrous Kinds: Body, Space and Narrative in Renaissance Representations of Disability*. Ann Arbor: University of Michigan Press. 2019. 16.
41 Bearden, 16.
42 Bearden, 10–12.
43 Bearden, 23–4.
44 Bearden, 25.
45 Bearden, 28.
46 Love, Genevieve. *Early Modern Theatre and the Figure of Disability*. New York: The Arden Shakespeare. Bloomsbury. 2019. 2.
47 Love, 1.
48 Davidson, 1.
49 Burton, 217.

50 Bearden, 18.
51 Doctors, legislators, activists, therapists, teachers, and laypeople all use different vocabularies to distinguish and delineate disability in context. *The Americans with Disabilities Act*, for example, uses different language to describe disability than does the American Psychiatric Association's *Diagnostic and Statistical Manual of Mental Disorders, Fifth Edition* (DSM-5), which uses different language from humanities scholars including Sujata Iyengar, Hobgood and Wood, and the writers of the *DSQ Special Shakespeare Edition* (2009). Sociologists like Garland-Thomson, Berger and Lennard Davis also use different language.
52 Garland-Thomson, Rosemarie. "Misfits: A Feminist Materialist Disability Concept." *Hypatia*, 26.3 (2011): 591–609.
53 For an early modern definition of madness, see Robert Burton's *The Anatomy of Melancholy* (Part 1, Section 1, Member 1, Subsection 4).
54 Hile, Rachel E. "Disability and the Characterization of Katherine in *The Taming of the Shrew*." *Disability Studies Quarterly*, 29.4 (2009). MLA International Bibliography. Web. May 12, 2015.
55 *Hamlet*. Dir. Laurence Olivier. Perf. Laurence Olivier. Universal-International. 1948.
56 Shaw, A. B. "Depressive Illness Delayed Hamlet's Revenge." *Medical Humanities*, 28.2 (2002): 92.
57 Lindsay Row-Heyveld, "Antic Dispositions: Mental and Intellectual Disabilities in Early Modern Revenge Tragedies" in Hobgood and Wood's *Recovering Disability in Early Modern England*, 2013.
58 Lisa Ulevich and Sonya Freeman Lofts, "Obsession/Rationality/Agency: Autistic Shakespeare" in *Disability, Health and Happiness in the Shakespearean Body*. London: Routledge. 2014.
59 Neely, Carol Thomas. *Distracted Subjects: Madness and Gender in Shakespeare and Early Modern Culture*. New York: Cornell UP. 2004. 49–50.
60 Neely, 50.
61 Row-Heyveld, Lindsay. *Dissembling Disability in Early Modern English Drama*. New York: Palgrave Macmillan. 2018.
62 Garland-Thomson, *Extraordinary Bodies*, 8–9.
63 Garland-Thomson, *Extraordinary Bodies*, 11.
64 Garland-Thomson, Rosemarie. Staring: How We Look. New York: Oxford UP. 2009. 1–3.
65 Garland-Thomson, *Extraordinary Bodies*, 9–10.
66 Norden, 3.
67 Garland-Thomson, *Extraordinary Bodies*, 9, 11; Norden, 5.
68 Berger, 27–8.
69 Samuel Crowl makes this connection in an interview, noting that after Kenneth Branagh's 1996 *Much Ado About Nothing* film adaptation was released, the next several theatre productions of *Much Ado* included either a swing or a fountain. Barbara Bogaev, host, "Episode 26: Shakespeare on Film." *Shakespeare Unlimited* (podcast), June 17, 2015, accessed December 12, 2019, https://www.folger.edu/shakespeare-unlimited/shakespeare-on-film.
70 Norden, 1.
71 "kill, v." *OED Online*. Oxford University Press, March 2018. Web. March 31, 2018.
72 Norden, 106; Barthes qtd. in Norden, 107.
73 Norden, 23–4.
74 Norden, 14–15.
75 Row-Heyveld, *Dissembling Disability*, 1–2.
76 *The Hunchback of Notre Dame*. Dir. Gary Trousdale, Kirk Wise. Perf. Tom Hulce, Demi Moore, Kevin Kline. Walt Disney Pictures. Buena Vista Pictures. 1996.

77   "The Unicorn and the Wasp." *Doctor Who*. Dir. Graeme Harper. Perf. David Tennant, Catherine Tate. BBC. May 17, 2008.
78   "kill, v." *OED Online*. Oxford University Press, March 2018. Web. March 31, 2018.
79   Norden, 106.
80   Mitchell, David T. and Sharon Snyder. *Narrative Prosthesis: Disability and the Dependencies of Discourse*. Michigan: University of Michigan UP. 2000.
81   Davidson, 15.
82   Berger, 2–3; Lennard Davis qtd. in Berger, 3; Davidson, xvii.
83   Berger, 2–3.
84   "monster, n., adv., and adj." *OED Online*. Oxford University Press. December 2020.
85   Bearden, 5–6.
86   Garland-Thomson, *Extraordinary Bodies*, 56.
87   Siebers, *Disability Aesthetics*, 3.
88   In a contrasting example, in the Star Wars saga both Anakin and Luke Skywalker lose hands during lightsaber duels, acquiring disabilities as adults.
89   OED, "monster."
90   OED, "monster."
91   The leaders in the literary reclamation of disability in an early modern context include Sujata Iyengar (*Disability, Health and Happiness in the Shakespearean Body*. New York: Routledge. 2015), Allison Hobgood and David Houston Wood (*Recovering Disability in Early Modern England*. Columbus: Ohio State UP. 2013) and the contributors to the 2009 special Shakespeare edition of *Disability Studies Quarterly*.
92   Norden, 216.
93   Berger, 7–8.
94   Garland-Thomson, *Extraordinary Bodies*, 78–9.
95   Garland-Thomson, *Staring*, 13–15.
96   Quayson, 37.
97   Davidson, 2.
98   Davidson, 2–3.
99   Mulvey, Laura. "Visual Pleasure and Narrative Cinema." *Screen*, 16.3 (1975): 6–18, 6.
100 Mulvey, 7–8.
101 Garland-Thomson, *Staring*, 3.
102 Garland-Thomson, *Extraordinary Bodies*, 9–10.
103 Garland-Thomson, *Extraordinary Bodies*, 10–11.
104 Mulvey, 6–18.
105 See Garland-Thomson (*Extraordinary Bodies*, 25), Barounis and Shildrick for an overview of the debates between sexualized and asexualized persons with disabilities.
106 Berger, 2–3; Norden, 28.
107 See Garland-Thomson (*Extraordinary Bodies*, 25), Barounis and Shildrick for an overview of the debates about sexualized and asexualized persons with disabilities.
108 Norden, 268.
109 Norden, 68.
110 Shildrick, Margrit. Dangerous Discourses of Disability, Subjectivity and Sexuality. New York: Palgrave Macmillan. 2009. 5–6.
111 *The Fault in Our Stars*. Dir. Josh Boone. Perf. Shailene Woodley, Ansel Elgort, Laura Dern. Fox 2000 Pictures, 20th Century Fox. 2014.
112 Hazel specifically uses a nasal-cannula, a small medical tube with twin protrusions that are inserted into the nostrils for the purposes of providing additional

oxygen on a day-to-day basis. Cannulas come in a variety of sizes and serve a variety of functions including giving or taking fluids intravenously, or for data collection.

113   *The Fault in Our Stars*, 2014.

114   An excellent example of this is Mike Flanagan's 2016 horror film, *Hush*.

115   Bolter, Jay David and Richard Grusin, *Remediation: Understanding New Media*. London: MIT Press. 2000. 152.

116   *Vertigo*. Dir. Alfred Hitchcock. Perf. James Stewart, Kim Novak. Paramount Pictures. 1958.

117   Gates, Philippa. *Detecting Men: Masculinity and the Hollywood Detective Film*. Albany, NY: SUNY Press. 2006. 28–9, 92.

118   For adaptation theory in general, see Linda Hutcheon and Julie Sanders. George Bluestone (*Novels into Film* (rev. ed.). Baltimore: Johns Hopkins UP. 2003), Thomas Leitch (*Film Adaptation and Its Discontents: From Gone with the Wind to The Passion of the Christ*. Baltimore: Johns Hopkins UP. 2007), and Robert Stam (*Literature Through Film: Realism, Magic, and the Art of Adaptation*. Oxford: Blackwell. 2005) address adapting literature into film, and Susan Willis (*The BBC Shakespeare Plays: Making Televised Canon*. Chapel Hill: North Carolina UP. 1991), Kenneth Rothwell (*A History of Shakespeare on Screen: A Century of Film and Television*. 2nd ed. Cambridge: Cambridge UP. 2004), and Douglas Lanier (*Shakespeare and Modern Popular Culture*. Oxford: Oxford UP. 2002) address Shakespeare film adaptation.

119   *The Duchess of Malfi*. Dir. James MacTaggart. Perf. Eileen Atkins, Michael Bryant, Charles Kay. BBC. 1972.

120   "Richard III." *The Hollow Crown*. Dir. Dominic Cooke. BBC. 2016.

121   *Richard III*, 1.3.244.

122   Acrophobia is a fear of heights. Interestingly, acrophobia is distinct from vertigo as the former is an irrational fear, and the latter is a physiological and/or neurological problem with the way balance is perceived.

123   The human sense of the body in space.

124   The clearest example of Scottie being scorned is the attitude of the judge and jurors during the investigation into Scottie's culpability in Madeleine's apparent death by suicide; we also hear from Scottie that his career was essentially ended by his initial bout of acrophobia in the beginning of the film.

125   *Hamlet*. Dir. Michael Almereyda. Perf. Ethan Hawke. Buena Vista Pictures. 2000.

126   *Richard III*, 1995.

127   Crowl, *Shakespeare at the Cineplex*, 113.

128   Quayson, 32–3.

129   Mitchell and Snyder, 49.

130   Siebers, *Disability Theory*, 23.

131   Garland-Thomson, *Extraordinary Bodies*, 8–9.

Bibliography

Barker, Claire and Stuart Murray, Eds. *The Cambridge Companion to Literature and Disability*. Cambridge: Cambridge UP. 2018.

Barounis, Cynthia. "Cripping Heterosexuality, Queering Able-Bodiedness: *Murderball*, *Brokeback Mountain* and the Contested Masculine Body." *The Disability Studies Reader*. 3rd ed. Ed. Lennard J. Davis. New York: Routledge. 2010.

Bearden, Elizabeth. *Monstrous Kinds: Body, Space and Narrative in Renaissance Representations of Disability*. Ann Arbor: University of Michigan Press. 2019.

Berger, Ronald J. *Introducing Disability Studies*. New York: Lynne Rienner. 2013.

Bolter, Jay David and Richard Grusin, *Remediation: Understanding New Media*. Cambridge, MA: MIT Press, 2000.

Burton, Robert. *The Anatomy of Melancholy*. Ed. Floyd Dell and Paul Jordan-Smith. New York: Tudor Publishing Co. 1927.

Coming Home. Dir. Hal Ashby. Perf. Jane Fonda, Jon Voight. United Artists. 1978.

Crowl, Samuel. *Shakespeare at the Cineplex*. Ohio: Ohio UP. 2003.

Davidson, Michael. *Concerto for the Left Hand: Disability and the Defamiliar Body*. Ann Arbor: University of Michigan Press. 2008.

Forbidden Planet. Dir. Fred M. Wilcox. Perf. Walter Pidgeon, Anne Francis. Metro-Goldwyn-Mayer. 1956.

Forrest Gump. Dir. Robert Zemeckis. Perf. Tom Hanks, Robin Wright. Paramount Pictures. 1994.

Garland-Thomson, Rosemarie. *Extraordinary Bodies: Figuring Physical Disability in American Culture and Literature*. New York: Columbia UP. 1997.

Garland-Thomson, Rosemarie. *Staring: How We Look*. New York: Oxford UP. 2009.

Garland-Thomson, Rosemarie. "Misfits: A Feminist Materialist Disability Concept." *Hypatia*, 26. 3 (2011): 591–609.

Gates, Philippa. *Detecting Men: Masculinity and the Hollywood Detective Film*. Albany, NY: SUNY Press. 2006.

Hamlet. Dir. Laurence Olivier. Perf. Laurence Olivier. Universal-International. 1948.

Hamlet. Dir. Michael Almereyda. Perf. Ethan Hawke. Buena Vista Pictures. 2000.

Hile, Rachel E. "Disability and the Characterization of Katherine in *The Taming of the Shrew*." *Disability Studies Quarterly*, 29. 4 (2009). MLA International Bibliography. Web. May 12, 2015.

Hobgood, Allison P. and David Housten Wood, Eds. *Recovering Disability in Early Modern England*. Columbus: Ohio State UP. 2013.

Hugo. Dir. Martin Scorsese. Perf. Asa Butterfield, Sacha Baron Cohen. Paramount Pictures. 2011.

Hutcheon, Linda. *A Theory of Adaptation*. 2nd ed. New York: Routledge. 2013.

Iyengar, Sujata, ed. *Disability, Health and Happiness in the Shakespearean Body*. New York: Routledge. 2014.

Kudlick, Catherine J. "Chapter 2 Disability History: Why We Need Another 'Other.'" *Rethinking Normalcy: A Disability Studies Reader*. Ed. Tanya Titchkosky and Rod Michalko. Toronto: Canadian Scholar's Press. 2009.

Love, Genevieve. *Early Modern Theatre and the Figure of Disability*. London: The Arden Shakespeare. Bloomsbury. 2019.

Million Dollar Baby. Dir. Clint Eastwood. Perf. Clint Eastwood, Hilary Swank, Morgan Freeman. Warner Bros. Pictures. 2004.

Mitchell, David T. and Sharon Snyder. *Narrative Prosthesis: Disability and the Dependencies of Discourse*. Michigan: University of Michigan UP. 2000.

Mulvey, Laura. "Visual Pleasure and Narrative Cinema." *Screen*, 16. 3 (1975): 6–18.

Neely, Carol Thomas. *Distracted Subjects: Madness and Gender in Shakespeare and Early Modern Culture*. New York: Cornell UP. 2004.

Norden, Martin. *The Cinema of Isolation: A History of Physical Disability in the Movies*. New Brunswick: Rutgers University Press. 1994.

Quayson, Ato. *Aesthetic Nervousness: Disability and the Crisis of Representation*. New York: Columbia UP. 2007.

Richard III. Dir. Laurence Olivier. Perf. Laurence Olivier, John Gielgud. London Films. 1955.

"*Richard III.*" *The Hollow Crown.* Dir. Dominic Cooke. BBC. 2016.

Row-Heyveld, Lindsay. *Dissembling Disability in Early Modern English Drama.* New York: Palgrave Macmillan. 2018.

Sandahl, Carrie. "It's All the Same Movie: Making Code of the Freaks." *JCMS,* 58. 4 (Summer2019): 145–150.

Scarry, Elaine. *The Body in Pain.* Oxford: Oxford UP. 1985.

Shakespeare, Tom. *Disability Rights and Wrongs Revisited.* 2nd ed. London: Routledge, 2014.

Shaw, A. B. "Depressive Illness Delayed Hamlet's Revenge." *Medical Humanities,* 28. 2 (December2002): 92.

Shildrick, Margrit. *Dangerous Discourses of Disability, Subjectivity and Sexuality.* New York: Palgrave Macmillan. 2009.

Siebers, Tobin. *Disability Aesthetics.* Ann Arbor: University of Michigan Press. 2010.

Siebers, Tobin. *Disability Theory.* Ann Arbor: University of Michigan Press. 2008.

The Duchess of Malfi. Dir. James MacTaggart. Perf. Eileen Atkins, Michael Bryant, Charles Kay. BBC. 1972.

The Fault in Our Stars. Dir. Josh Boone. Perf. Shailene Woodley, Ansel Elgort, Laura Dern. Fox 2000 Pictures. 20th Century Fox. 2014.

The Hunchback of Notre Dame. Dir. Gary Trousdale, Kirk Wise. Perf. Tom Hulce, Demi Moore, Kevin Kline. Walt Disney Pictures. Buena Vista Pictures. 1996.

The Miracle Worker. Dir. Arthur Penn. Perf. Anne Bancroft, Patty Duke. United Artists. 1962.

"The Unicorn and the Wasp." *Doctor Who.* Dir. Graeme Harper. Perf. David Tennant, Catherine Tate. BBC. May 17, 2008.

Titus. Dir. Julie Taymor. Perf. Anthony Hopkins. Fox Searchlight Productions. 1999.

"*Titus Andronicus.*" BBC Television Shakespeare. Dir. Jane Howell. Perf. Trevor Peacock. BBC. 1985.

Vertigo. Dir. Alfred Hitchcock. Perf. James Stewart, Kim Novak. Paramount Pictures. 1958.

Young Frankenstein. Dir. Mel Brooks. Perf. Gene Wilder, Peter Boyle. 20th Century Fox. 1974.

2 Physical Disabilities and the Filmic Stare in *Richard III* and *Titus Andronicus*

Progress is often conceptualized as linear as we move forward in time. It is easy to assume, however, that moving forward means improving on social and cultural systems, norms, and practices, making it easy to fall prey to the myth of progress. According to Ronald Berger, the medical model is an essentialist approach to disability as a property of the individual body rather than the social environment,[1] whereas the cultural model posits that disability can be embraced and celebrated as a group identity, a part of the broader fabric of human diversity, and as a site of resistance to socially constructed conceptions of normality.[2] As Martin Norden notes, however, films that represent physical disability as more than a hoax,[3] reason to end a life,[4] or ultimately curable plot device,[5] are unusual, and the progressive, forward-moving trend of films which provide nuanced or complex representations of disability is a collection of exceptions. This trend not only holds true for representations of disability in film adaptations of early modern films in general, but in film adaptations of *Richard III* in particular. The more contemporary the production, the less physically able Richard seems to be. Film adaptations of *Richard III* and *Titus Andronicus* also tend to create expectations on a foundation of the gaze, and then use a character's disability to subvert those expectations.

Physical (dis)ability in film is well-documented by Norden, and physical disability on film has been more widely discussed than mental disability on film because a missing limb is visible and instantly recognizable as a disability.[6] However, as noted in Chapter 1, physical disabilities are most frequently classified as being on a narrative spectrum from "accurate/empowering" to "inaccurate/offensive or belittling." My discussion will largely avoid engaging with questions of accuracy or questions of offense. In utilizing the filmic stare, I create space for a productive discussion about how the representations are constructed and subverted, and how a filmic micro-grammar affects the construction of disabilities in *Richard III* and *Titus Andronicus* from a visual rather than a narrative perspective.

To that end, I will begin this chapter with an exploration of the congenital disabilities Richard III displays in his titular production. The directors of the film adaptations of *Richard III* explore variations on the specific impairments described in the play texts, while some directors and actors see the impairments

DOI: 10.4324/9781003163374-3

as more disabling than others, and the degrees of disability are reflected in the filmic stare in interesting ways. Next, I will explore acquired physical disability in *Titus Andronicus*, and the ways in which gender affects the representation of physical disability in the mise-en-scène specifically, and the filmic stare in general. The final section of this chapter will address Yoshiko (Ophelia) in Akira Kurosawa's *The Bad Sleep Well* (1960), an adaptation of *Hamlet* that replaces Ophelia's madness with a physical disability.

The Filmic Stare and Physical Disability in *Richard III*

Kenneth Rothwell credits William Kennedy-Laurie Dickson and Sir Herbert Beerbohm Tree's 1899 excerpts of *King John* as the earliest instance of a Shakespeare play on film.[7] Not quite a decade later, Vitagraph's 1908 one-reeler version of *Richard III* is cited by Norden as the first film adaptation of that play. During the era of silent film, *Richard III* was adapted three times, with the first sound film version directed by and starring Laurence Olivier in 1955.[8] My goal in using the filmic stare to analyze physical disabilities is to move away from narrative prosthesis and explore how the representation of physical impairments affects similar characters across multiple film adaptations. *Richard III* is an excellent case study by these parameters; the Olivier, Loncraine and Cooke adaptations all explore significantly different interpretations of Richard, though the same impairments and filmic stare techniques are used. Olivier's masculine and physically active Richard gives way to Loncraine's politically savvy gangster, which in turn gives way to Cooke's isolated and relatively immobile Richard. The same filmic stare techniques are mixed with significantly different generic elements to suggest different ideas of what disability looks like. It is easy to say—and has been said by many critics, including Norden and Garland-Thomson[9]—that in Richard's case, his exterior disability mirrors interior moral failings. This interpretation fits neatly enough with the early modern worldview that any moral failing on the part of an individual, or even the fantasies/negative thoughts from the mother during pregnancy, will result in physical abnormalities.[10] It also adheres to narrative prosthesis, and even to the demands of visual shorthands so crucial for film storytelling. Through the filmic stare, however, we can explore different visual synecdoches that reveal nuances to the character which may otherwise be missed in the application of other critical lenses and explore the impact of genre on disability.

In addition to exploring the impact of different visual synecdoches on representations of physical disability, it is also important to recall that Richard is one of the only characters in Shakespeare with a congenital physical impairment; Titus Andronicus and Lavinia both have acquired physical impairments. In his discussion of casting villains with "orthopaedic impairments,"[11] Norden credits a 1912 four-reeler edition of *Richard III* for the proliferation of disabled villains, particularly what Norden refers to as the "obsessive avenger."[12] The obsessive avenger is defined as (typically) an adult male whose *raison d'etre* is revenge on those who have caused his disability or violated his moral code.[13]

For Richard, however, Norden's description is problematic because his disability is congenital. Richard (unlike the Duchess of York) does not blame anyone in particular for his physical impairments. Richard in the play text tells readers explicitly that he is simply "not shap'd for sportive tricks,/ [...] rudely stamp'd, [...] cheated of feature by dissembling nature."[14] Richard blames nature rather than his mother for his impairments, in direct opposition to Burton's understanding of the roots of congenital disability in the early modern period. The Duchess of York also eschews responsibility for Richard's impairments, telling him "Thou cam'st on earth to make the earth my hell,"[15] following Queen Margaret's conceit that Richard is something other than human, and therefore excusing the Duchess of maternal culpability for his congenital impairments as well as the crimes he commits as an adult. Margaret goes so far as to divorce the Duchess's womb from her, calling it a "kennel," from which crept a "hell-hound."[16] Ultimately, rather than blaming the Duchess of York, Richard and the women blame nature and the supernatural, respectively, acknowledging that congenital impairments, like nature and hellhounds, are outside the bounds of human control.

Recognizing that neither Richard nor the Duchess are to blame for Richard's impairments destabilizes the early modern conception that disability is a response to a moral or ethical failing, and in some ways, *Richard III* is the ultimate "overcoming" narrative. Richard tells us at the beginning of the play that he wants to be king, and despite his physical impairments, he achieves that goal. Yes, Richard is defeated by Henry VII, but fratricide and infanticide are crimes for which early modern audiences would expect to see any stage villain defeated, whether that villain is physically impaired or not. Richard's congenital disability complicates, but does not wholly inform, the political machinations inherent in the narrative. This leads to a significantly different representation on screen than do the acquired impairments of other Shakespearean characters.

Laurence Olivier, placed as he was on the leading edge of Shakespeare's transition from the theatre to the cineplex, tended to make history with his film adaptations. His *Henry V* (1944) demonstrated that Shakespeare films could be successful in commercial as well as art house cinemas,[17] and was the first Shakespeare film to be shot in colour.[18] Olivier's *Richard III* (1955) was one of the earliest instances of trans-Atlantic broadcast cinema. The film was transmitted to American television channels on March 11, 1956, the same day the film was released in British cinemas.[19] Olivier also used a combination of Technicolor and VistaVision for *Richard III*, adding to the technological spectacle of the film.[20] Rothwell argues that, although the film "lacks the cinematic complexity of Henry V," it "deserves a separate trophy for sustained acting brilliance."[21] What Olivier presents is a full, humanized integration of Richard's impairments into the character, a technique that would be abandoned in later film adaptations. Olivier plays down the visibility of Richard's limp, withered arm, and hunchback; the arm and hunch are small, and the limp could, at times, be mistaken for a cocky swagger. For Olivier, however, a minimalist approach to the visibility of the impairments works to consistently make them a visible part of Richard. Olivier composes his scenes in a consistent pattern of wide shots and medium close-ups and two shots. As a result, the limp and hunch are almost always in frame. By leaving the impairments in frame but minimizing their visual impact, the slightly canted framing is subtly highlighted, giving shots and scenes an uneasy feeling without pulling focus away from Richard's emotional arc or using the impairments as a quick and simple explanation for the angst. By allowing the impairments to be present but not overwhelming, the moments in which Richard does interact with his own impairments are stronger. The first example of this in Olivier's film is when Lady Anne is moving her father-in-law's corpse and Richard interrupts.

Richard has told the audience that he is "not shape'd for sportive tricks,"[22] and McKellen and Cumberbatch take Richard at his word—for this scene, at least. Olivier, conversely, proceeds to defeat the guard armed with a pike who challenges him. This scene is filmed in wide shots, ensuring that all of Richard's impairments are in frame. The subtlety of the impairments in the mise-en-scène creates the impression that Richard's disability troubles him not at all, and that his self-deprecation in his first monologue is hyperbole or equivocation. His hunch is barely visible, and the only indication of the limp is Richard's garter on the affected leg; he handily beats a guardsman. The overt, martial masculinity demonstrated in this scene is shaded differently in the context of Richard's discussion with the camera after he has successfully wooed Lady Anne.

Figure 2.1 Richard III defeating one of Lady Anne's retainers

Much of the critical focus on the wooing scene is on its believability; Harold Bloom argues that Richard succeeds based on "sadomasochistic seduction,"[23] Jack Jorgens dismisses Anne as "weak,"[24] and Ian McKellen himself described Anne's capitulation to Richard as "purely mercenary, a necessary step to shore up her income."[25] What is often unremarked upon is Richard's transformation immediately after Anne's exit from the scene. As I have argued, Olivier's use of martial masculinity in the film suggests a lack of sincerity to Richard's self-assessment, but after having successfully wooed Anne, Richard makes a near point-for-point refutation of his original assessment:

> Upon my life she finds (although I cannot)
> Myself to be a marv'llous proper man.
> I'll be at charges for a looking-glass,
> And entertain a score or two of tailors
> To study fashions to adorn my body:
> Since I am crept in favor with myself,
> I shall maintain it with some little cost.[26]

These lines in the play text are couched in a longer soliloquy and represent a volta in Richard's thought and emotional processes. Olivier's Richard has established that the camera is, for him, a confidant. Most Richard's soliloquies are delivered straight to camera, and Olivier's Richard invites the camera in, as you might a close friend. Olivier enhances the sense of camera as confidant in the way he cuts the speech for film as well. The text of the speech is thirty-seven lines long, but Olivier speaks only eleven of those lines, omitting Richard's recounting of his murders in the various parts of *Henry VI*, and his disdain for Anne's acquiescence to his offer of marriage. Olivier's cuts to the text in this section serve to present Richard in a more sympathetic light; when Olivier says that she finds him to be "a marv'llous proper man," it is a genuine discovery. The stare and the filmic stare can be self-reflexive; what Olivier does with his performance is recognize the power of the self-reflexive stare and then embraces his own physical appearance. Embedded in both text and performance is also the essence of the shift between the medical and social models of disability.[27] Prior to wooing Anne, Richard sees his own impairments as a deviation from the norm, and his own personal shortcomings. Insofar as early modern doctors could medicalize congenital impairments, we can look to Burton to see where the Duchess of York might be blamed for Richard's appearance:

> Great-bellied women, when they long [for another man], yield us prodigious examples in this kind, as moles, warts, scars, harelips, monsters, especially caused in their children by force of a depraved phantasy in them. She imprints that stamp upon her child which she conceives unto herself.[28]

Richard is surrounded by rhetoric that suggests his impairments are medicalized and isolated. However, in recognizing that he can be valued as he is,[29] Richard gestures toward the idea that it is the social order around him that disables him, rather than his actual impairments. My disability studies-focused reading of these two scenes also dovetails with a more political reading of the scenes. Richard's goal is to change the social order at court in his favor, and wooing Lady Anne provides not only political leverage, but confidence in his own ability to execute his plans. Olivier cuts the play text of *Richard III* so that the sword fighting, and wooing are two separate scenes in his film adaptation. In doing so, he leverages the text's political overtones, and expectations of martial masculinity to perform a Richard who is deeply nuanced, fully human and surprisingly relatable.

Olivier's performance of Richard holds much nuance, but, as Rothwell argues, the film is cinematographically less complex than the performance. In the context of the filmic stare, Olivier seems to go out of his way *not* to create a visual synecdoche for Richard. As Sarah Hatchuel notes, "In Laurence Olivier's 1955 film, Richard and Anne share the camera field. There is no particular focus on one character or the other."[30] Rothwell notices the two major motifs of the film: the crown of England and "iterative shadows" which provide "visible evidence of Richard's poisonous miasma."[31] However, neither motif fits the definition of a visual synecdoche for the filmic stare. Richard himself is insufficiently fragmented to create a disability-based synecdoche, making this film adaptation a significant exception to the filmic stare. Olivier's overarching film style is a combination of wide shots and medium close-up shots; this proved extremely effective in representing Hamlet's mental disability,[32] but is less efficient at highlighting a synecdoche for Richard's physical impairment. Olivier, however, exploits the mise-en-scène to keep the impairments in frame for much of the film without drawing undue attention to them. The filmic stare as a framework is designed to recognize and provide a context within which to analyze representations of disability; Olivier renders moot the necessity for such a framework by avoiding constructing Richard's disability as "the embodiment of corporeal insufficiency and deviance."[33] Indeed, Olivier's Richard not only finds a moment of corporeal sufficiency after he woos Anne, but his deviance is constructed primarily politically as opposed to corporeally. Simply put, by allowing Richard's disability to be a property of (primarily) the mise-en-scène, the disability is one aspect of Richard, rather than the entirety of Richard or the narrative. Olivier's Richard has moments of traditional martial masculinity unencumbered by his physical body, a romantic relationship from which he does not shy away, and a complex, nuanced relationship with his impairments. Olivier struck a unique balance with Richard and Richard's impairments, one that did not survive in future film adaptations of *Richard III*.

After 1955, the two major film adaptations of *Richard III* are the 1995 Loncraine/McKellen *Richard III* and Dominic Cooke's 2016 contribution to the BBC's *Hollow Crown Series*, "Richard III."[34] Richard Loncraine and Ian McKellen's 1995 *Richard III* is set in a fictional version of late 1930s

England, strongly evoking WWII films and—as several critics argue[35]—gangster films. In the context of Loncraine's film, the term gangster vibe suggests a sense of gleeful villainy, as well as the swagger of gangster films, which is evoked in McKellen's choice to tuck his bad arm into a pocket. The film also evokes the British political drama prior to WWII surrounding King Edward VII's abdication and potential ties to the Third Reich. McKellen's Richard is a smooth-talking villain in an SS-esque uniform.

His textually mandated impairments include a limp, a barely noticeable hunch on one shoulder, and a nerveless arm that McKellen keeps tucked into a jacket pocket, giving his Richard a saucy, gangster-esque slouch that enhances his threatening presence. McKellen's choice is the epitome of an "I could take you with one hand behind my back" attitude, and both fulfills the textually mandated impairment and suppresses the stare.

Cooke's "Richard III" is set in medieval England, and Cumberbatch as Richard looks like a villainous adaptation of Igor from Mel Brooks' *Young Frankenstein* (1974). Cooke goes so far in evoking horror elements in the film that even Queen Margaret's appearances are excuses for jump scares. Cooke's film also seems to imprison Richard to isolate him; a recurring motif is Richard socially and physically isolated in a small stone room with nothing in it but a shaft of light and a chessboard. The image takes Norden's idea of isolation and pairs it with horror and with the idea of an armchair villain, someone like Hannibal Lecter, whose greatest weapon is his mind and ability to plot.

Unlike Olivier, Loncraine and Cooke deny their Richards (to varying degrees) traditional martial and sexual masculinity and isolate them to a much greater degree. In effect, both Loncraine and Cooke use Richard's impairments to explain Richard. Their use of the filmic stare fragments actors McKellen and Benedict Cumberbatch, creating visual synecdoches which serve to excessively

Figure 2.2 Richard giving a speech reminiscent of a Nazi rally

highlight the character's physical impairments and imply that Richard is evil because he is disabled. As Norden points out, cinematic villains with ortho-paedic impairments date back to the earliest years of cinema. Norden argues that, "[n]owhere in literature are evil and disability so inextricably fused as in Shakespeare's infamous Richard Crookback, a character whose disability-informed identity is superseded only by his unremitting evil,"[36] although Oli-vier's Richard is an exception to this otherwise well-proven rule. I will now focus my discussion on a comparative reading of specific moments of isolation and denial of masculinity in the Loncraine and Cooke films, using the filmic stare as my critical scaffolding. I also argue that where Loncraine includes but visually suppresses Richard's impairments, Cooke includes and highlights the impairments.

Isolation can be many things: social, geographical, emotional. Olivier's Richard is himself often isolated from the other characters in the film, although that isolation is largely mitigated by Olivier's choice to use the camera (and by extension, the viewer) as confidant. Olivier also chose to deliver many of Richard's soliloquies direct to camera; Loncraine and Cooke follow that pat-tern. Rather than using direct address and the soliloquies to draw the viewer in, however, both Loncraine and Cooke immediately alienate the viewer. Lon-craine introduces Richard by having him directly address the camera with his sidearm.

On first viewing, audiences are unaware that this is Richard pointing a gun at them; his identity is obscured by his gas mask, and we have not yet been trained to recognize the arm with limited use tucked into a pocket as part of Richard's visual synecdoche. Richard is not moving, so we cannot see the limp, and his hunch is hidden by both posture and garments. Lon-craine has technically included all of Richard's physical impairments in this

Figure 2.3 A figure in a gas mask points a pistol at the camera

introduction but they are suppressed, alienating Richard from using the camera as confidant, and clearly demonstrating the pattern of suppressing disability that will follow. Additionally, the shot also sets up a pattern of deep focus when Richard is in frame with multiple people. Deep focus with crowds is contrasted with shallow focus when Richard directly addresses the camera in medium close-ups. Initially, in alienating Richard from the viewer, Loncraine also sets up a pattern of suppressing the filmic stare. To recognize the filmic stare in the first moments of the film, the viewer must already be aware of Richard's impairments, either because this is a second viewing or because they are familiar with the character through the film's hypotexts.

Cooke alienates his Richard through body horror, highlighting disability as opposed to violence. Cumberbatch's Richard is introduced to us first as his impairment. Cumberbatch's head is not even visible in the frame; the focus is entirely on the S-curve of the spine and the dramatic piling of flesh on his shoulder. Cooke has immediately and memorably established his Richard's visual synecdoche, and as the camera continues to track around to Richard's face, we see a wide shot that evokes filmic representations of Igor before Cooke cuts to a close-up of Richard's face while he delivers the latter half of his opening soliloquy. The chiaroscuro lighting, the focus on the impairment, and the choice to introduce a character with his impairment all evoke horror films and promote a sense of unease. Cooke's representation of Richard's impairments is explicit and reacts to Loncraine's suppression of Richard's impairments. Cumberbatch is alienated from the camera, but he is also socially and geographically isolated; he is alone in frame, alone in the room, and that pattern repeats throughout the film. The background of dimly lit stone

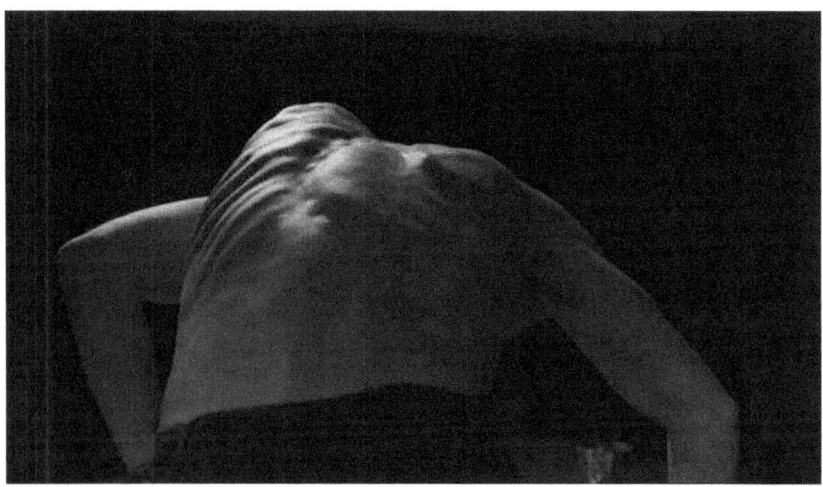

Figure 2.4 A medium shot of Richard III's physical impairment

walls leaves the viewer with nothing to focus on but the impairments. For Cooke, the geography of Richard's isolation magnifies and reflects the visual impact of the impairments. By evoking horror conventions, Cooke also cinematically ties Richard to the monstrous, without going as far as Loncraine, who included a dream sequence of a literally monstrous Richard. The dream sequence is Lord Stanley's, not Richard's, but visually constructing Richard as a "rooting, abortive hog"[37] makes Loncraine's Richard monstrous.

For Cooke and Loncraine, dehumanizing Richard by connecting him to classical monstrosity[38] makes easier the overall dehumanization and removal from any connections with martial masculinity. Both the play text and Olivier's film adaptation use Richard's confrontation with Anne and her guards to demonstrate Richard's capability with arms; he explicitly says in the scene before that he is not physically capable but proceeds to handily dispatch a soldier who comes at him with a pike.[39] For Olivier, this moment is public. He woos Anne later in the film privately, but by making the altercation with the guardsman public, Olivier ensures that he is not pigeonholed by his disability as weak or dependent. That moment is lost in the Loncraine and Cooke adaptations.

Loncraine moves Richard's meeting with Anne to a more private (and isolated) space: a morgue. Surrounded by only the dead, Richard has no need to demonstrate his physical prowess. Additionally, Richard's gift of a ring to Anne near the end of the scene serves to subtly highlight the fact that his useless arm (which is out of frame for most of the scene) is in fact useless. McKellen pulls his ring off with his teeth before using that same hand to put the ring on Anne—with her help. What is typically a tender and decidedly two-handed moment between a couple is intensely creepy. This moment also alludes to one

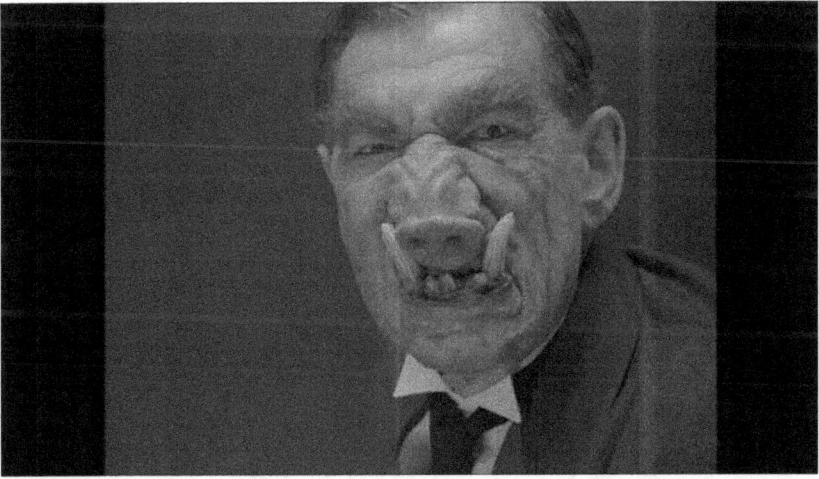

Figure 2.5 Richard in a dream sequence with a hog's face

of the very first moments of the filmic stare in the film. When Richard is delivering his "Now is the summer of our discontent"[40] speech to a crowded ballroom, the shot begins in medium close-up, and the camera slowly zooms in to an extreme close-up of Richard's lips and teeth, moving as he speaks. If Richard were a femme fatale instead of a villain, this shot would be a textbook instance of the gaze fragmenting, sexualizing, and objectifying a female subject. However, because what we are seeing is McKellen's wrinkled, off-color lips and yellowed, crooked teeth, the viewer feels discomfort and Richard is othered for audiences even more so than he was as a faceless stormtrooper in a gas mask executing an old man. The power dynamic in both these instances and in the morgue with Anne is not martially masculine, but thuggish. These incidents call into question Richard's ability to compete in a "fair fight" as a result of his physical disability.

For Cooke's Richard, a fair fight is never part of the equation. Cooke's Anne, rather than moving a body or visiting it in a morgue, sneaks out of the castle in the dead of night to visit a lone, practically unmarked grave in the middle of the woods, unaware that Richard is following her. If Cooke were directing a monster or horror film, Anne would have been dead by the end of the scene. Because of his hunch and posture, Cumberbatch is shorter than Phoebe Fox (Lady Anne). However, Anne is always shot at a high angle, and Richard is always shot at a low angle, consistently putting Anne below Richard. He is never a serious physical threat to her, and even at the battle of Bosworth Field, Richard is clearly in some trouble once the battle begins, because his impairments are relatively severe. Cooke's cinematography works to suggest that Richard has power in this scene, but that power is charisma, not physical ability, or strength. Cooke also makes sure that one of Richard's impairments is in frame whenever he is. After establishing early in the film that the hunch is Richard's visual synecdoche, Cooke uses a lot of padding and careful camera angles to make sure that in any close-up or two shot, the hunch is in the frame. Consistently throughout the film, Richard's head is canted in these shots as well, because Cumberbatch is bent in half for the entire film. These strategies ensure that viewers never have a chance to forget Richard's impairments, facilitating the filmic stare's requirement for a visual synecdoche without necessarily needing to fragment Richard in a particularly extreme fashion.

In addition to creating a visual synecdoche, close-ups function to fragment and objectify disabled characters. Normally, fragmentation and objectification are connected back to Laura Mulvey's theorization of the male gaze in "Visual Pleasure and Narrative Cinema."[41] In the context of an aesthetic approach to disability in film, however, the fragmentation, with its focus on a non-normative body, complicates Mulvey's gendered reading. Often, the fragmented and objectified body is male. In film adaptations of early modern plays, the male disabled body leads to adaptive tensions, particularly when the film adaptation of the Shakespeare play is being treated as a star vehicle. The play text dictates to the adaptor to varying degrees, and the star wants the prestige of "doing Shakespeare." As a result, the director and star are largely locked into the character's disability, but the way the character is shot places in tension active and romantic aspects of the character with the reality of being a character with a disability. Asexual objectification is a common assumption that the temporarily able-bodied make about individuals with disabilities.[42] There has been some reaction to this idea, largely in the late twentieth and twenty-first centuries,[43] but arguably the assumption in tandem with the discomfort and objectification of the stare is asexual objectification. For Richard, wooing Anne becomes a complicated cinematic sequence when directors use the filmic stare to highlight his impairments.

For Laurence Olivier, the nuanced performance that integrated Richard's disability and the rest of his life also served to largely prevent any asexual objectification that comes with the filmic stare. Arguably, Olivier also had star power helping to prevent asexual objectification; he was a well-established leading man who had already made film history with his Shakespeare film adaptations. Olivier used high-key, warm lighting and a romantic garden setting to woo his Anne. Those technical elements combined with his sincere discovery of Richard's self-liking helped to suggest that sexual desire and sexuality were just as acceptable for Richard as for any able-bodied character. That acceptability is lost in the Cooke adaptation, and actively refuted in Loncraine's film.

In Cooke's "Richard III" Anne largely disappears from the film after the wooing scene; she is peripherally involved in the coronation scene, and she is murdered on-camera, but after the wooing Richard has little to do with her. The film overall focuses on Richard as a hub of power; he is himself isolated in a room sending Catesby and Buckingham out to exercise his power in the wider world. Strikingly, Richard woos Anne by himself in the middle of the woods, and arguably that attempt pushes him further into isolation. Critics have argued that Anne's acquiescence to Richard is for socioeconomic reasons;[44] if this is how we read Cooke's Anne, then Richard himself has little power with Anne. Socioeconomic pressures are an effective mode of coercion, but are less elegant than other ruses Richard orchestrates, suggesting that Richard has no sexual appeal for or authority over the women in the play. He even seems to be actively afraid of Queen Margaret, when she appears—in a jump scare—outside of the King's bedroom to break up an argument between Queen Elizabeth, Rivers, and Richard. Cooke's film disallows Cumberbatch's Richard from engaging with women, despite the actor's star power. The lack of sexual authority with Anne suggests that in Cooke's adaptation of "Richard III" it is unacceptable for Richard to have a sex life. Cooke denies acceptability by omission rather than explicitly, as Loncraine does.

Immediately after Clarence's throat is cut, Loncraine cuts to a short, silent scene between Anne and Richard, opening with Richard having his arm and shoulder massaged. The masseur is dismissed after a small packet containing Clarence's glasses arrives. Anne then appears at the bottom of the stairs. The shot of Anne loudly announces her desire and is a classic gaze moment. The frame is composed like a painting; Anne being the central object possessing that "to be looked-at-ness"[45] upon which viewers cast their desiring gaze while listening to a smooth jazz soundtrack. Critically, this shot is objective; this is not Richard's POV. Richard himself subverts the gaze moments later. He walks up to Anne, then reaches across her body to turn out the lights before walking away from her.

Richard himself subverts the expectations of the gaze in this scene, refusing to acknowledge Anne at all. In previous scenes, Loncraine presents the two characters together in public spaces holding up the illusion of a happily married couple. The blocking reveals the lie, however, with Anne and Richard literally on different sides of the table and physically distant from each other. The attempt to convey closeness here is a simple facade for the sake of the public. In private, Richard wants nothing to do with Anne, who quietly pulls her wrap up onto both shoulders and disappears back up the stairs after she is rejected. Loncraine eloquently refutes the idea that it is acceptable for Richard to have a sexual relationship, even privately, in less than two minutes with no words spoken. The silent scene has no antecedent in the play text of *Richard III*, as Shakespeare severely limited his own use of stage directions.[46] What this scene does is actively subvert expectations surrounding the gaze. Loncraine includes a female object in a voyeuristic wide shot, something that sets up the assumed audience's expectations for Richard. The expectation is that Richard will move to possess Anne, representing a specific type of masculinity. An assumed heterosexual male viewer might identify with Richard—the protagonist of the film. The gaze often facilitates narrative suture for that assumed audience, and Loncraine and McKellen jeopardize that sense of narrative suture through both Richard's physical impairment and his refusal to engage in the typical expectations of the gaze that the silent scene with Anne sets up. In addition, because the scene opens with Richard having his bad arm and shoulder massaged, the contrast between intimate physical contact for rehabilitative or therapeutic purposes and intimate sexual contact is more starkly highlighted.

In the time between 1955 and 2016, perpetuating the illusion of progress, there have been a myriad of medical, legal, and social changes in the field of disability. However, as demonstrated by three adaptations of *Richard III*, perceptions of what is and is not acceptable for individuals with congenital physical disabilities have moved radially out from around individuals, not in a linear sense from stigma to acceptance. Olivier's Richard was more discriminated against than discriminating; his martial capabilities and sexual conquest mattered little to his impairments or vice versa. McKellen's Richard eschewed sexual intimacy but embraced a thuggish, asymmetrical martial authority. Cumberbatch's Richard was the consummate chess master, moving game pieces but having little life outside of his own impairments and isolation. These three representations all explore the same impairments, but with the filmic stare, come to different conclusions about how those impairments affect Richard.

The Filmic Stare and Physical Disability in *Titus Andronicus*

Acquired impairments in Shakespeare—blindness, amputations, and mute-ness, respectively—are all punitive, the result of political machinations within the narratives of the texts. By focusing on Lavinia's and Titus's respective representations in Jane Howell and Julie Taymor's adaptations of *Titus Andronicus*, I explore not only the representation of acquired impair-ments in both male and female characters, but also the use—or not—of prostheses. For readers unfamiliar with the play, *Titus Andronicus* opens with Titus and his sons returning to Rome after a war. Titus sacrifices the oldest son of Tamora, Queen of the Goths, and in revenge Tamora plots to ruin the Andronici family. To that end, Tamora's sons Chiron and Deme-trius murder Bassianus, Lavinia's betrothed and brother of Saturninus, Emperor of Rome. After murdering Bassianus, Chiron and Demetrius rape Lavinia and cut off her hands and tongue. They also frame two of Titus' remaining sons for the murder. Aaron the Moor, with whom Tamora is having an affair, convinces Titus to cut off his own hand to spare his son's lives, before revealing they have already been executed. Eventually, Titus captures Chiron and Demetrius, and bakes them into a pie which he serves to Tamora and Saturninus before murdering Lavinia and the dinner dis-solves into a bloodbath. Titus' son Lucius is the last man standing and is proclaimed emperor.

As I argue in Chapters 4, 5, and 6, the representation of male and female madness ultimately is not affected by gender. However, my case studies in those chapters are films directed by men; women directed the two most sig-nificant Anglophone film/TV productions of *Titus Andronicus*. Julie Taymor and Jane Howell take quite different approaches to their film adaptations. Howell was working within the larger framework of the BBC Television Shakespeare, a project that spanned the mid-1970s to the mid-1980s and was a part of the BBC's overall mission to "inform, to educate, and to entertain."[47] As a result, although Howell's production is well-respected, it follows more traditional stage conventions than cinematic con-ventions. Howell does place young Lucius at the center of the production, focusing on the generational theme that is often neglected in favor of gore in stage productions of *Titus Andronicus*. Taymor picks up on the idea of focusing on young Lucius, but Taymor's film exists in an art film modality, and therefore explores the cinematic medium through the themes of the narrative in addition to communicating the story. As a result of the different circumstances surrounding the creation of these two film adaptations, there are significant differences in the representation of disability both between the two adaptations of *Titus Andronicus*, and in the relationship between the filmic stare and the gaze in the context of Shakespeare film adaptations more generally. While both directors insist on Lavinia's humanity and resist visually fragmenting her, Howell largely follows in the tradition of repre-senting disability as disability regardless of gender, but Taymor introduces the use of prostheses to play more deeply with the representations of physical disability and gender.

In the context of the filmic stare, as with *Richard III*, the methodology for forming a visual synecdoche is different for physical impairments as opposed to mental impairments. Close-ups are good for highlighting small impairment details, affecting audience emotions, and serving as the anchor points for the construction of the stare. Medium and wide shots function in the stare to establish not only larger-scale visual impairments, e.g., a character sitting in a wheelchair, using crutches, or whose overall stature requires a point of reference to be noticeable. I discuss medium and wide shots together here because these types of shots are the most critical in terms of constructing a visual representation of impairment on screen. Close-ups might affect the audience and draw their attention to a specific impairment or prosthesis but staring insists on the visibility of the impairment in a wider frame. The medium and wide shots are also the places where the interplay between a desire to highlight or suppress disabilities is most visible. In a close-up of a non-normative body or assistive device, it is impossible not to face the visual reality of disability. Wide and medium shots allow for composing the mise-en-scène to either subtly highlight impairments and disabilities or play them down by removing them from the audience's line of sight. I will now go through several examples quite quickly. My goal is to underline the major differences in how Howell and Taymor approach visualizing physical disability. For Howell, both Titus and Lavinia's missing limbs are largely allowed to be forgotten—out of sight is out of mind. They are also visualized in the same way, regardless of gender: mere stumps. Taymor's use of prosthetics, however, genders the representation of the impairment on screen.

For physical disabilities, the medium and wide shots serve to contextualize the impairment. For example, Howell's *Titus Andronicus* (1985) composes the medium and wide shots of Titus after he loses his hand in such a way that in the medium shots the stump is not in frame. In wider shots, that arm is frequently behind a prop or another actor. Additionally, Howell's design avoids prostheses. Titus's and Lavinia's stumps are simply left at the ends of their sleeves in the brown-red color of dried blood. The color of Titus's stump nearly matches the colors of his costume, so even when the stump itself is visible in the frame, the eye slides over top of the impairment, not attending to it at all. This subtly suppresses the visibility of Titus's impairment throughout the latter half of the film. Audiences cannot stare at an impairment that is invisible either by not being in frame or as a function of the design of the film.

In contrast, Taymor provides her Titus with first a white bandage with a bright red stain, and then a dark metal cap. In terms of design, the wide shots where Titus is wearing the bandage are dark, take place in the evening and night, and Titus himself is wearing a dark costume. As a result, the bloody bandage is the brightest thing in the frame, subtly drawing attention to itself. Once Titus has the metal cap, his costumes progressively lighten, going from a light brown robe at dinner to a clean white chef's uniform, against which the metal cap is clearly contrasted. Taymor also keeps Titus' arm and bandaged/capped stump in frame and unobstructed by props or people. Further enhancing the stare, Taymor includes a medium shot of Titus filling a fountain pen from his stump.

The subtle but consistent highlighting of Titus' impairment does maintain its visibility, refusing to allow viewers to forget about or not acknowledge the impairment outside of the close-ups. The viewer's stare is therefore maintained throughout the film, not only when close-up shots thrust the impairment into the audience's face. These examples are straightforward shots, which fit neatly into narrative cinema conventions. However, Taymor exploits formal techniques more specific to an art film modality than to a more classical style, which fundamentally changes the construction of the mise-en-scène. Such a significant change to the mise-en-scène naturally changes how the wide and medium shots are interpreted in the context of the filmic stare. As an example, it is worth taking a brief look here at the "penny arcade nightmares—"[48] hypermediated, surrealist, "haiku-like" montages which reveal the "inner landscapes" of a character's mind—[49] that Taymor sprinkles throughout *Titus*. These penny arcade nightmares are an integral part of the unique space and time that Taymor sets up for her Titus to operate in, and they underscore the fact that the filmic stare, like the gaze, has no need for strict film realism to operate. Despite the fantastic and artificial nature of the diegetic world, the on-screen disabilities are to be taken seriously and have great narrative and characterological significance.

Taymor implies that some time has passed between Lavinia's assault and when she communicates the names of her attackers. As a result, the penny arcade nightmare of Lavinia's assault functions narratively as a hypermediated flashback. These shots, like the immediate aftermath of the assault itself, are mostly medium and wide. Rather than show reality, they visually associate Lavinia, Chiron, and Demetrius with images of a deer and tigers through CGI and double exposure.[50] Because the sequences use such quick cuts, it is easy to mistake the deer's hooves Lavinia is given with the stumps of her wrists. It could be argued that these images enhance and maintain the filmic stare, but as I discussed in Chapter 1, if the subject is not fully human, then they fall outside the purview of the filmic stare. Certainly, viewers are staring at this point in the film, particularly on first viewing. However, the hypermediacy Taymor employs here serves to fragment the stare in this instance, rather than maintaining it. Conversely, the hypermediated penny arcade nightmare that begins as a fireball filled with spinning marble limbs originates the filmic stare in *Titus*. While the shot itself is wide, the focus on false limbs (possibly prostheses themselves) causes the sequence to function more akin to a later tracking shot of puppet and doll limbs in the shop Young Lucius visits to procure Lavinia's prosthetic hands. The shots of prostheses function like close-ups in that they highlight Lavinia's impairment and the need of Titus and the able-bodied men in her life to undo Lavinia's disability. Prosthetics become a motif for Taymor, and a visual synecdoche for Lavinia, which also strengthens the stare.

From the first time we see Taymor's Lavinia on screen after she acquires her impairments, characters try to replace Lavinia's hands. Chiron and Demetrius tie twigs and sticks to her wrists in a cruel combination of tourniquet and prosthetic, and young Lucius procures a beautifully carved pair of hands for Lavinia. Lavinia herself, however, never interacts with her own body's impairments, is never without some kind of proxy for her hands. Conversely, Titus is the architect of his own impairment—though Aaron is responsible for misleading Titus into the act. Titus himself is constantly engaging with his own impairment, and rather than a prosthetic that is lifelike, chooses a dark metal cap that would not look out of place on the end of a club; the prosthetic itself mirrors Titus's martial background. Titus also interacts with his impairment outside of the prosthetic.

Viewers might be disturbed by Titus filling a fountain pen from his stump, but Taymor does something interesting with the sequence. Prostheses can function to make non-normative bodies look normative, restore some level of function to a limb, or some combination of both. In showing Titus interacting comfortably with his stump, and having the stump fulfill a—admittedly unorthodox—function, Taymor forces viewers to stare at Titus's stump and at his comfort with a non-normative body. It is Titus's comfort with his own body that is, in some ways, more discomfiting than the stump itself because it challenges cultural norms around aesthetic and normative levels. By "comfort" I am referring to an acceptance of Titus's impairment and a refusal to hide it from the public, members of his family, or himself. Titus's refusal to hide the impairment also by extension includes refusing to hide it from the camera and the viewer. The denotation of comfort as a lack of physical pain arguably does not apply. The sheer number of beauty magazines and academic articles on Hollywood's construction of beauty standards speaks to a standard of beauty that does not include a stump. Additionally, comfort with your own body is hard; for Titus to have that comfort with his stump is difficult to comprehend; particularly if the audience is full of twenty-somethings who have been told they are not attractive enough by artificial Hollywood beauty standards. This combined with what Garland-Thomson refers to as "ocular response to what we don't expect,"[51] really strengthens Taymor's use of the filmic stare.

Taymor herself, in the "Making of *Titus*" featurette, points out a connection in art history between beauty and horror, specifically citing artistic renderings of the crucifixion. The relationship between beauty and gore is extended throughout *Titus* and extends into the dynamics of the filmic stare as well. It is difficult to argue that Titus filling a fountain pen from his stump is a beautiful image. However, the artistry surrounding the penny arcade nightmares, the myriad on screen prostheses and run-of-the-mill disembodied artificial limbs, as well as Lavinia's use of prostheses lends a beauty aesthetic to the film that highlights the connection between beauty and horror, which functions to make the filmic stare more uncomfortable. Arguably the best example of beauty and horror enhancing the stare is the immediate aftermath of Lavinia's assault.

Kenneth Rothwell notes that in act II, scene iv, Lavinia "resembles Marilyn Monroe in *Some Like it Hot*,"[52] as she is wearing a white dress that flows around her. Sarah Hatchuel, on the other hand, notes that both Lavinia and Marcus are filmed in slow motion, which "produces an effect of contemplation, of emotional emphasis."[53] Rothwell contextualizes Taymor in the slasher film tradition,[54] whereas Hatchuel implies that Taymor is working in an art house tradition.[55] While both critics provide polarized senses of the generic and tonal qualities of the aftermath of Lavinia's assault, the mixture of horror and beauty highlights the filmic stare, but—in contrast to Rothwell's assessment that Lavinia's look echoes Marilyn Monroe—without the gaze. The scene opens with, and returns several times to, an establishing shot so wide that Lavinia herself is merely a smudge of white against a gray-brown landscape. Although Lavinia remains in virtually the same place inside the frame in the establishing shots, she almost disappears because of the shot distance. Interspersed with the extreme wide shots are close-up and medium close-up shots of Lavinia's face, sometimes with her wrists and twig prostheses in frame. The interplay of extremes in shot distance help to both establish Lavinia's visual synecdoche and to focus on her reaction and emotional state. Her visual synecdoche establishes that Chiron and Demetrius have literally fragmented her, but Taymor does not mirror the literal fragmentation with cinematographic fragmentation in this scene. Taymor shows us either Lavinia's whole body, or just her face. There is none of the fragmentation that Mulvey argues is a prerequisite for the male gaze, and even once Marcus finds Lavinia and Taymor switches to plan américain shots (a medium wide shot in which the human figure is shown in the frame from their heads to approximately their knees), there is enough distance from the camera to prevent an objectifying or eroticizing fragmentation of Lavinia.

It is with Marcus's entrance to the scene that Taymor uses slow motion so that Marcus (and viewers) can absorb what they are seeing on screen.[56] This sequence is also where Taymor really pushes the beauty and horror combination. The viewer has spent a couple of minutes at this point in the scene seeing Lavinia's missing hands and their cruel replacement; it is when Marcus entreats his niece to speak that Taymor pulls out the centerpiece of the scene.

In slow motion, Lavinia opens her mouth as though to scream, and in slow motion, a ribbon of too-bright blood falls from her lips to be carried away by the wind. The shot in Figure 2.6 is horrifying in its implications, beautiful in its execution. It also highlights Lavinia's acquired disabilities in a way that is emotionally different from how Richard III's congenital impairments are represented.

Lavinia's impairments are acquired off screen; all the viewer or Marcus sees is the aftermath. Because Taymor is mixing horror and beauty, however, the filmic stare becomes emotionally complex. Garland-Thomson argues that "[w]hen one person has a visible disability [...] it almost always

Figure 2.6 Lavinia revealing that her tongue has been cut out

dominates and skews the normate's process of sorting out perceptions and forming a reaction."[57] Lavinia's disability is not only visual, but in Taymor's film presentation, it is beautiful; beauty complicates perceptions of horror, and reminds viewers that good and bad, beauty and ugliness, all the binary oppositional structures that cultures construct for themselves, are just that: constructions. Tom Shakespeare reminds us that the disabled/abled binary is also an artificial construct,[58] and my own choice to separate mental from physical disability is an artificial construction as well. Taymor constructs an artificial time and space for *Titus* to exist in, but within that artificial construct she reminds us that the complexities of deconstructing binaries and embracing the beautiful alongside the horrific creates space for more complex reactions and analyses.

To circle back around to Lavinia's impairments, by mixing beauty and horror on her discovery by Marcus, and literally putting Lavinia on a pedestal, Taymor also evokes a freak show aesthetic[59] that is mirrored when a cart of traveling players reveals to Titus the heads of his dead sons. In Lavinia's case, however, Taymor seems to be alluding to the historical tradition of Julia Pastrana and Sartje Baartman,[60] following a function as an "inverted, parodic beauty pageant."[61] Beauty pageants and freak shows both connote management, silencing, and mediation by men,[62] which arguably fits Lavinia in this scene. She is silenced by Tamora's sons, she is managed (and ultimately killed) by the men in her family, and her story is mediated through the quill pen of a man. The break in the cycle is the mediation by Julie Taymor and her camera. To some extent, Taymor and Lavinia are trapped by the palimpsestuous nature of the Shakespearean text: Lavinia must be mediated through the men in her life. However, disobedient mediation is also a theme in *Titus*; his sons disobey Titus's order that Lavinia should marry Saturninus, Lavinia disobeys the coerced order from Chiron and Demetrius that she not reveal their names, and Titus himself disobeys the mediation of a Roman soldier trope by the chain of command when he turns on Saturninus at the end of the film. Taymor follows this theme with Lavinia into the design of the film and into the representation of Lavinia's disability. The freak show aesthetic that introduces the aftermath scene is subverted by Taymor's mixture of beauty and horror, the careful construction of a visual synecdoche with a minimum of cinematographic fragmentation, and the use of slow-motion.

For Julie Taymor's *Titus*, gender and prostheses change the representation of disability on screen. Both Titus and Lavinia engage with prostheses, but the difference is in their constancy with prosthetics and their level of comfort with their own impairments. For Jane Howell, on the other hand, a lost limb is a lost limb and needs no further emphasis; she films the representation of disability in the same manner, regardless of gender, and chooses not to include prostheses in her representation.

The Filmic Stare and Physical Disability in *The Bad Sleep Well*

In general, *Hamlet* is not a play that is overly concerned with physical disability, but Akira Kurosawa's 1960 film adaptation of the play, *The Bad Sleep Well*, significantly downplays madness for Nishi (Hamlet), and replaces it entirely with an acquired physical disability in the case of Yoshiko (Ophelia). *The Bad Sleep Well* transposes Shakespeare's *Hamlet*, a tragedy, to a noir crime mystery set in post-World War II Japan. The film focuses on the massive corruption within Japanese corporations, and Kurosawa's Hamlet is less a "prince who could not make up his mind,"[63] as Olivier framed him, and more a tragic hardboiled detective who is ultimately defeated by the very corruption he dedicated his life to revealing. Yoshiko is the daughter of the company's vice president, who is married off to Nishi by her father at the beginning of the film. Yoshiko has an unspecified orthopedic disability because her brother, Tatsuo (Laertes), accidentally injured her as a child. Although Tatsuo does attempt to resist narratives of exploitation and lesser worth when it comes to Yoshiko, she is still exploited by the men in her life throughout the film. Yoshiko herself attempts to exercise agency and help Nishi bring her father to justice, but she is ultimately unsuccessful and can only repudiate him at the end of the film.

Yoshiko is introduced at her wedding, as she walks down the aisle with a noticeable limp, and with an attendant to help her stay upright. One of the first shots of Yoshiko is a close-up on her feet, revealing that one of her Japanese sandals is triple the height of the other to accommodate a significant leg length difference. Yoshiko's impairment is the first thing viewers learn about her, and her impairment is the first thing society attributes to her. The filmic stare shows Yoshiko as a disabled bride, and the close-up on her feet and her uneven footwear highlights "disabled" far more than "bride." Even with the sandals and attendant, a short flight of stairs is enough to make the wedding venue inaccessible for Yoshiko without significant aid from her brother—something that the watching reporters refer to as "shocking."[64] She stumbles, and her stumble—framed loosely to ensure the viewer sees the reactions around Yoshiko—draws the stares of all the businessmen around her. In his speech at the wedding, Tatsuo goes as far as to call out the assumption of the businessmen in attendance that Nishi is only marrying Yoshiko in order to further his own career and insists that it is untrue. Tatsuo's speech candidly acknowledges that Yoshiko is considered damaged goods because of her physical impairment, and attempts—somewhat unsuccessfully, in the context of the scene—to resist the stereotype that a disabled person is worth less than an abled individual and the history of exploiting people with disabilities. Unfortunately, Tatsuo saying the quiet part out loud does not stop Nishi from exploiting Yoshiko, using her to get close enough to her father, Iwabuchi (Claudius) to reveal the murder of his father and the widespread corruption in Japanese companies.

For Nishi, Yoshiko is ultimately a means to an end that has absolutely nothing to do with Yoshiko as a person, and Nishi leverages her disability to get closer to Iwabuchi. After the pair are married, however, Yoshiko is isolated from him, with Nishi insisting that Yoshiko sleep separately from him. During a family cookout, Yoshiko is seated across the veranda from Nishi, as far from him as possible in the space. After Nishi kidnaps Moriyama, the pair are physically separated for political reasons. Yoshiko's isolation from Nishi not only emphasizes the fact that he is using her but also highlights the isolation that is so often par for the course for disabled people as well as the film trend of isolating characters with impairments that Norden identifies.[65]

With adaptations of *Richard III*, we can clearly see a discomfort with visible, physical disabilities; Cooke literally locks his Richard away in a tiny stone room. Julie Taymor engages with a long, complex history of representing physical disability by mixing horror and beauty. Kurosawa walks the line between discomfort with disability through the isolation of Yoshiko and attempts to problematize the assumption that disabled people are less valuable than able-bodied people. The techniques inherent to the filmic stare are largely unchanged now from when Laurence Olivier was beginning to blend cinematic and theatrical modes,[66] but the available representations of disability are, like disabilities themselves, still highly individualized, although linked with a few overarching trends. In all the extant films discussed, isolation is a key theme. That isolation, however, may manifest geographically, as with Cooke's film, or socially, as with Loncraine's and Taymor's films. Overlaying that isolation is also a set of expectations of film grammar, most prominently expectations of female fragmentation and objectification, and male looking inspired by the gaze. Disability studies already recognizes asexual objectification; therefore, for Lavinia, the gaze and filmic stare are in conflict. For McKellen's Richard, the active choice not to gaze at a proffered object subverts the strength of his look; Norden notes that characters like Quasimodo and Captain Hook are punished for exercising their power to look because both characters have physical impairments.[67] From Olivier to Taymor, however, the progression of representing physically disabled bodies in film adaptations of *Richard III, Titus*

Andronicus, and *The Bad Sleep Well* has been more a study in techniques of representation than it has been a linear progression from the medicalization of disability to a celebration of disability as an integral part of a character's identity.

Notes

1 Berger, Ronald J. *Introducing Disability Studies*. New York: Lynne Rienner. 2013. 26–7.
2 Berger, 29–30.
3 Norden (14–15) argues that the earliest example of this kind of film is Thomas Edison's 1898 film, *Fake Beggar*.
4 *Million Dollar Baby* (Eastwood, 2004) is Berger's (2–3) example of choice for this kind of film. Norden, Martin. *The Cinema of Isolation: A History of Physical Disability in the Movies*. New Brunswick: Rutgers University Press. 1994.
5 For Norden's discussion on curability, see 58–60.
6 Whether the individual missing a limb regards their impairment as a disability or simply a part of their life is a discussion that is fleshed out in disability studies texts that are patient or sociologically focused. For the purposes of this chapter, a missing limb will be considered a disability that is more easily recognized by individuals without such an impairment than a mental or other invisible disability might be.
7 Rothwell, Kenneth S. *A History of Shakespeare on Screen: A Century of Film and Television*. 2nd ed. Cambridge: Cambridge UP. 2004. 1.
8 Rothwell, 354–5.
9 Norden (32–3) argues that *Richard III* is the first major, and most famous, instance of disability and villainy combined; Garland-Thomson, Rosemarie. *Extraordinary Bodies: Figuring Physical Disability in American Culture and Literature*. New York: Columbia UP. 1997. 6, 36.
10 Burton, Robert. *The Anatomy of Melancholy*. Ed. Floyd Dell and Paul Jordan-Smith. New York: Tudor Publishing Co. 1927. 220, 221, 222.
11 Norden, 51.
12 Norden, 52.
13 Norden, 52.
14 *Richard III*, 1.1.14–19.
15 *Richard III*, 4.4.167.
16 *Richard III*, 4.4.47–8.
17 Rothwell, 47, 50.
18 Hatchuel, Sarah. *Shakespeare from Stage to Screen*. New York: Cambridge UP. 2004. 20.
19 Rothwell, 59.
20 Rothwell, 59.
21 Rothwell, 60.
22 *Richard III*, 1.1.14.
23 Bloom, Harold. *Shakespeare: The Invention of the Human*. Riverhead: New York. 1998. 65.
24 Jorgens, Jack. *Shakespeare on Film*. Bloomington: Indiana UP. 1977. 144.
25 Qtd in Rothwell, 221.
26 *Richard III*, 1.2.253–9.
27 See Berger 26–8 for an overview of the medical and social models of disability.
28 Burton, 221.
29 Whether or not Anne truly finds Richard appealing, the emotional impact of thinking she does is what triggers his reassessment of his appearance and his

emotional reaction to his own impairments. The debate about the veracity of the relationship between these two characters, although interesting, ultimately falls outside the scope of my discussion.

30 Hatchuel, 52.
31 Rothwell, 61.
32 For my discussion of Olivier's *Hamlet* and the construction of the representation of mental disability, see Chapter 4.
33 Garland-Thomson, *Extraordinary Bodies*, 6.
34 Cooke's adaptation can technically be categorized as a made-for-tv movie; however, I include it here because the film follows cinematic conventions, including typical feature-film length, and international star power. I also include this adaptation because it is a valuable film text that deserves analysis in the context of the filmic stare and disability studies. "Richard III." *The Hollow Crown*. Dir. Dominic Cooke. BBC. 2016.
35 Rothwell (220) explains the gangster elements as part and parcel of other generic quotations in the Loncraine adaptation.
36 Norden, 8.
37 *Richard III*, 1.3.227.
38 The *OED* defines "monster" as "**a.** Originally: a mythical creature which is part animal and part human, or combines elements of two or more animal forms, and is frequently of great size and ferocious appearance. Later, more generally: any imaginary creature that is large, ugly, and frightening" ("monster, n., adv., and adj." *OED Online*. Oxford University Press, June 2018. Web. August 14, 2018.) Loncraine is explicit about the human/animal hybrid with his monstrous Richard; Cooke is drawing more widely on the horror genre, but the dialogue and generic conventions suggest a possible hybridity.
39 Olivier, 1955; *Richard III*, 1.2.33–42.
40 *Richard III*, 1.1.1–40.
41 Mulvey, Laura. "Visual Pleasure and Narrative Cinema." *Screen*, 16.3 (1975): 6–18.
42 Garland-Thomson, *Extraordinary Bodies*, 25–6.
43 Barounis, Cynthia. "Cripping Heterosexuality, Queering Able-Bodiedness: *Murderball, Brokeback Mountain* and the Contested Masculine Body." *The Disability Studies Reader*. 3rd ed. Ed. Lennard J. Davis. New York: Routledge. 2010. 477; Norden, 268.
44 Bloom, 68, 71; Rothwell, 221.
45 Mulvey, 9.
46 With a few notable exceptions, including the dumbshow at the beginning of "The Mousetrap" (*Hamlet*, 3.2. Stage direction between lines 135–6) and "exit, pursued by a bear" (*The Winter's Tale*, 3.2. Stage direction between lines 58–9).
47 Willis, Susan. *The BBC Shakespeare Plays: Making Televised Canon*. Chapel Hill: North Carolina UP. 1991. 5.
48 Rothwell, 271; "Making of Featurette," *Titus*. Dir. Julie Taymor. Perf. Anthony Hopkins. Fox Searchlight Productions. 1999.
49 De Luca, Maria, Mary Lindroth and Julie Taymor. "Mayhem, Madness, Method: An Interview with Julie Taymor." *Cineaste*, 25.3 (2000): 28–31. 28.
50 "Making of *Titus*". *Titus*. Dir. Julie Taymor. Perf. Anthony Hopkins. Fox Searchlight Productions. 1999.
51 Garland-Thomson. Staring: How We Look. New York: Oxford UP. 2009. 3.
52 Rothwell, 271.
53 Hatchuel, 63.
54 Rothwell, 269.
55 Hatchuel, 30–1.
56 Hatchuel, 63.
57 Garland-Thomson, *Extraordinary Bodies*, 12.

58 Tom Shakespeare, "The Social Model of Disability." *The Disability Studies Reader*, 272.
59 See my discussion of the freak show aesthetic in Chapter 5 or Garland-Thomson, *Extraordinary Bodies*, 59, for a definition of freak show aesthetic.
60 Garland-Thomson, *Extraordinary Bodies*, 55–80.
61 Garland-Thomson, *Extraordinary Bodies*, 71.
62 Garland-Thomson, *Extraordinary Bodies*, 71.
63 Olivier, 1948.
64 Kurosawa, *The Bad Sleep Well*, 1960.
65 Norden, 1.
66 "Francis Bordat has cogently noticed that: 'Olivier seems to fear that there is not enough cinema in his theatre, while Mankiewicz is afraid there is not enough theatre in his cinema.'" Hatchuel, 20–1.
67 Norden, 100.

Bibliography

Barounis, Cynthia. "Cripping Heterosexuality, Queering Able-Bodiedness: *Murderball, Brokeback Mountain* and the Contested Masculine Body." *The Disability Studies Reader*. 3rd ed. Ed. Lennard J. Davis. New York: Routledge. 2010.

Berger, Ronald J. *Introducing Disability Studies*. New York: Lynne Rienner. 2013.

Blakemore Evans, G., *et al.* Eds. *The Riverside Shakespeare*. 2nd Ed. Boston: Wadsworth. 1997.

Bloom, Harold. *Shakespeare: The Invention of the Human*. New York: Riverhead. 1998.

Burton, Robert. *The Anatomy of Melancholy*. Ed. Floyd Dell and Paul Jordan-Smith. New York: Tudor Publishing Co. 1927.

Davis, Lennard J. *The Disability Studies Reader*. 3rd ed. New York: Routledge. 2010.

De Luca, Maria, Mary Lindroth and Julie Taymor. "Mayhem, Madness, Method: An Interview with Julie Taymor." *Cineaste*, 25. 3 (2000): 28–31.

Garland-Thomson, Rosemarie. *Extraordinary Bodies: Figuring Physical Disability in American Culture and Literature*. New York: Columbia UP. 1997.

Garland-Thomson, Rosemarie. *Staring: How We Look*. New York: Oxford UP. 2009.

Hatchuel, Sarah. *Shakespeare from Stage to Screen*. New York: Cambridge UP. 2004.

Jorgens, Jack. *Shakespeare on Film*. Bloomington: Indiana UP. 1977.

Mulvey, Laura. "Visual Pleasure and Narrative Cinema." *Screen*, 16. 3 (1975): 6–18.

Norden, Martin. *The Cinema of Isolation: A History of Physical Disability in the Movies*. New Brunswick: Rutgers University Press. 1994.

Richard III. Dir. Laurence Olivier. Perf. Laurence Olivier, John Gielgud. London Films. 1955.

Richard III. Dir. Richard Loncraine. Perf. Ian McKellan, Annette Benning. United Artists. 1995.

"*Richard III*." *The Hollow Crown*. Dir. Dominic Cooke. BBC. 2016.

Rothwell, Kenneth S. *A History of Shakespeare on Screen: A Century of Film and Television*. 2nd ed. Cambridge: Cambridge UP. 2004.

Stam, Robert. *Literature Through Film: Realism, Magic, and the Art of Adaptation*. Oxford: Blackwell. 2005.

The Bad Sleep Well. Dir. Akira Kurosawa. Perf. Toshiro Mifune, Masayuki Mori, Kyōko Kagawa. Toho. 1960.

Titus. Dir. Julie Taymor. Perf. Anthony Hopkins. Fox Searchlight Productions. 1999.

"Titus Andronicus." *BBC Television Shakespeare*. Dir. Jane Howell. Perf. Trevor Peacock. BBC. 1985.

Willis, Susan. *The BBC Shakespeare Plays: Making Televised Canon*. Chapel Hill: North Carolina UP. 1991.

3   Caliban and the Filmic Stare

In previous chapters, my discussion has focused on characters and impairments which, even using a broad critical framework, remain relatively stable and recognizable across film adaptations. In the context of disability studies, a stable impairment is defined as an impairment that either does not change over the course of the narrative, or changes in the context of either a medically recognized progression OR as required by narrative prosthesis (that is, the impairment either gets worse or resolves to further the plot and central themes of a given narrative). Stability, however, is not the only aspect of disability that is required to adapt characters with disability across media. Recognizability is also important. Recognizable is a difficult term to use in the context of disability, particularly when disability and impairments are often unique to a given individual and can be invisible. Within this discussion, however, I use the term recognizable to acknowledge that there are conventions within film regarding how a disability is represented on screen. For example, Hamlet is always "mad," and we can recognize that his deviant behaviour is representative of his madness; Richard III will always have some variation on his hunchback, limp, and bad arm, even if certain productions minimize the visual impact of these impairments.

Previously discussed characters with disabilities in Shakespeare play texts and film adaptations have been largely of higher socioeconomic status, usually (but not always) male, and white. In this chapter I will focus my discussion on a character who, across film adaptations, is unstable, often cast as an individual of colour, and a subaltern figure: Caliban, son of Sycorax, one of the antagonistic figures in Shakespeare's *The Tempest*. Caliban's representation is less stable and less recognizable in film, and in the past has crossed the boundary into classical monstrosity; that is, Caliban is often represented as not fully human. I will first briefly trace the stage history of Caliban's impairments to demonstrate a history of instability in the representation of impairment on stage, before exploring how that instability was adapted and transformed by film adaptations of *The Tempest*. Finally, I will use the filmic stare to analyze representations of Caliban in Peter Greenaway's *Prospero's Books* (1991) and Julie Taymor's 2010 *Tempest*.

In outlining the stage history of Caliban's representation, we must begin with the play text itself, and a brief overview of the narrative. Twelve years

DOI: 10.4324/9781003163374-4

prior to the events of the play, Prospero—a self-described magician—was the Duke of Milan, who was overthrown by his brother, Antonio. Antonio exiled Prospero and his three-year old daughter, Miranda, and they are shipwrecked on an island inhabited by Ariel—described as an "airy spirit"—and Caliban. Caliban was originally taken in by Prospero and raised alongside Miranda. However, on his attempted rape of Miranda, Prospero enslaves Caliban. At the opening of the play, Antonio, Alonso (the King of Naples), and Alonso's son Ferdinand are on a ship near the island, and Prospero instructs Ariel to shipwreck the passengers on different locations on the island. As a result, Miranda and Ferdinand meet, fall in love, and Prospero tests the veracity of Ferdinand's love. Caliban plots with Stephano and Trinculo (both servants of Alonso's) to murder Prospero and claim the island for themselves. Eventually, Prospero brings together all the players. Miranda and Ferdinand are handfasted, and Prospero frees Caliban and Ariel before everyone else returns to Milan. These plot events, drawing as they do on William Strachey's 1625 narrative, "True Repertory of the Wreck," which details the 'discovery' of Bermuda via the shipwreck of the Sea Venture on the way to Jamestown in 1609, present a microcosm of colonization, and are now generally read through a postcolonial lens. In addition to the shipwreck imagery, Prospero's initial survival thanks to Caliban and his subsequent assertion of authority over him also mirror the colonization of the New World and subsequent oppression of the indigenous peoples therein.

The Tempest was first performed in 1611, however the play was not printed until 1623, when it was included in the First Folio, which was compiled by John Hemminge and Henry Condell, two actors in The King's Men. Unlike *Hamlet, The Tempest* was not printed in quarto format prior to the publication of the folio, however, there is instability not only in the play text as it regards Caliban, but in the texts themselves. It is always possible that changes were made to the text between performances, or that the folio text differs from the performance texts. Additionally, *The Tempest* saw many rewrites during the Restoration, in particular the 1670 Davenant–Dryden version of the text, which includes sisters for Miranda and Caliban, and Hipolito, a young man who has never seen a woman. My discussion centers on the Shakespearean text, not the restoration text, but all these factors create a text which is inherently unstable, leading to the necessity of interpretation to create adaptations. As a result of the lengthy stage history of *The Tempest*, the proliferation of adaptations and the textual uncertainty about the specifics of Caliban's impairments, any adaptation of Caliban is built on a foundation of aesthetic choices, and the director's, designer's, and actors' interpretations of the brief, vague descriptions we get of Caliban from other characters.

The folio text introduces Caliban as "a savage and deformed slave";[1] Prospero refers to Caliban as "got by the devil himself," a "poisonous slave," and "freckled whelp [...] not honour'd with /human shape." Trinculo and Stephano call Caliban a "strange fish," and a "monster of the isle;" Antonio and Alonso respectively refer to Caliban as "a plain fish" and "as strange a thing as e're I looked on."[2] Caliban rarely even describes himself, although he gives us an oblique sense of his appearance when promising Stephano and Trinculo that "I with my long nails will dig thee pignuts."[3] These epithets and self-references are evocative, but vague in terms of concrete description. Records of Caliban's representation on stage in Shakespeare's day are unclear, but early modern theatrical tradition suggests that Caliban would have likely been an actor dressed in skins or pelts.[4] The Caliban on stage at the Globe or Blackfriars would have been recognizably human, which was not necessarily the case after the reformation, when actors and directors began to question Caliban's humanity.

In the midst of scolding Ariel, Prospero remarks that, "...Then was this Island/ (Save for the son that she did litter here,/ A freckled whelp, hag-born) not honoured with/ A human shape."[5] Morton Luce argued that this passage confirms the idea that Caliban is not, at his core, human. According to Luce, commenting on the text's ambiguity: "[i]f all the suggestions as to Caliban's form and features and endowments that are thrown out in the play are collected, it will be found that the one half renders the other half impossible."[6] In essence, Luce argues that Caliban cannot be defined as either human or inhuman, because the evidence, of which Prospero's above remarks are a significant piece, is impossibly contradictory. Alden and Virginia Vaughan argue that Prospero's description, in the context of the play as a whole, affirms rather than denies Caliban's latent humanity, arguing that, "[o]f principle importance [...] is the Folio's assertion that Caliban has a *human* form, however misshapen."[7] The argument the Vaughans make is that the lines "A freckled whelp, hag-born—not honor'd with/ A human shape"[8] have been taken out of context in Arden and Folger editions of the play through visual distortions of the syntax and editorial choices (particularly in the Oxford and Arden editions of the play) to substitute dashes for parentheses in Prospero's speech.[9] By looking at these final two lines in the context of Prospero's whole speech, and taking the first Folio's parenthetical phrase into account, Caliban's humanity is affirmed rather than denied. Simply put, Vaughan and Vaughan argue that Prospero is *excepting* Caliban from the assertion that the island was devoid of human shapes, rather than including Caliban. Caliban therefore becomes the only human on the island. I will continue to assert Caliban's humanity throughout my argument, and even with critical support for a human Caliban, it is worth considering the implications of the terms human and humanity.

Broadly, the OED defines human as " A human being, a person; a member of the species *Homo sapiens* or other (extinct) species of the genus *Homo*."[10] Metaphorically and representationally, however, this complicates some of the early stage representations of Caliban, as even the most hirsute and ape-like Calibans might potentially be a part of the genus *Homo*. In addition, the classical definition of monster requires a hybrid of human and animal, suggesting that even othered monsters are, in some way, human.[11] To be human, then, is more complex than simply being bipedal with ten fingers and ten toes. The humanities and social sciences both deal with the concept of the other; an individual who is recognized to be outside the dominant or mainstream group, and who, through the othering process might be perceived as sub- or inhuman, while still fitting the textbook definition of a member of the genus *Homo*. For the purposes of my discussion, then, hybrid Calibans who are represented as both human and animal will be omitted, as will Calibans who may represent earlier evolutionary stages of humanity. The rich history of representations of Caliban on stage bears out the implicit complexities of representing humanity on stage, if not the explicit thought processes which must necessarily be involved in designing a character.

As Vaughan and Vaughan also assert, however, "few thespians actively study literary criticism,"[12] which left stage and screen representations of Caliban questioning his very humanity. Despite Trinculo's arguably unreliable narration, many versions of Caliban take Trinculo's assessment of Caliban's fish scent and incorporate fishy elements into the character design, including scales and fins.[13] Contemporary as well as eighteenth and nineteenth century productions use this interpretation, most notably the Stratford Shakespeare Festival's 2010 production of *The Tempest*. Stratford's 2010 Caliban was more "swamp thing" than human. However, hybrid fish is not the only iteration of a non-human Caliban.

Frank Benson in 1891 played a "man monkey or monkey man" version of Caliban.[14] Benson's interpretation was influenced by and resonated with Charles Darwin's explorations of evolution, and this link was made explicit by Daniel Wilson, in his book *Caliban: The Missing Link* (1873).[15] Wilson contextualizes Caliban within "the highest stage of simian evolution,"[16] implying that Caliban is not human, but something that could, over a geological age, become human. The sense of Darwinian progress fades from stage representations of Caliban, but the "ape-like" Caliban tradition would continue with Herbert Beerbohm Tree in 1904,[17] and Tyrone Power Sr. in 1897 (not to be confused with Tyrone Power Jr., classical Hollywood star from the 1930s-1950s).[18] In the 1950s, *Forbidden Planet*'s invisible Id monster marked the end of the Darwinian ape Caliban tradition. However, despite the continuation of the non-human Caliban tradition into the twenty-first century, this particular interpretive tradition is useful primarily to contextualize some of the choices made in interpreting on screen human Calibans in the twentieth and twenty-first centuries. The filmic stare requires a human staree; it was not until the 1960s through to the 1980s that Caliban became visibly and irrefutably human,[19] and contextualized within postcolonial academic debates.

Peter Brook's 1963 production of *The Tempest* at Stratford-upon-Avon was influenced by Jan Kott's interpretation of the play—an instance of theatre and academia meeting to create an interpretation. In his book, *Shakespeare our Contemporary*, Kott argued that "Shakespeare's theatre is the *Theatrum Mundi*. Violence, as the principle on which the world is based, will be shown in cosmic terms."[20] In essence, Kott's view on Shakespeare was that, because of the plays' thematic breadth, Shakespeare will always be topically relevant, and that the topic of greatest relevance will inevitably be violence. Kott also rejects what he terms the allegorical and fairy tale traditions of *The Tempest* in performance, specifically deriding Dryden's adaptation.[21] Brook was clearly influenced by Kott's rejection of a stable and sanitized reading of *The Tempest* and used Kott's exploration of the themes of violence and power in the play text as a jumping off point to deviate from performance traditions and conventions in his exploration of power dynamics in the play. Brook's Caliban not only succeeds in raping Miranda, but his staging suggested a homosexual rape of Prospero as well, and Caliban dominating as master of his own island.[22] Brook's production was a landmark in the development of theatrical storytelling, and created, for the first time, a powerful Caliban rather than a subservient one. However, because of the highly stylized nature of the production, the question of Caliban's humanity was moot; the actor was visibly, unquestionably human, and physically normative. Roy Dotrice's Caliban was represented an as example of "emergent humanity;" a colonized figure who rebelled against subjugation and attempted to exert his own authority and power.[23]

The 1960s and 70s also saw the emergence of the tradition to either cast a colored actor as Caliban or, in the case of David Suchet's 1978 Caliban, to put an actor into blackface for the role.[24] Suchet's role in the Stratford-Upon-Avon production combined blackface with Indigenous stereotypes drawn from West India and Africa. Suchet's Caliban was something of an exception to the pattern; while Caliban does not have the rich stage history of being played in blackface that Othello does, Suchet was the first actor to racialize Caliban without also making him monstrous.[25] Calibans in this period also represented other minority and oppressed groups, including the punk rock subculture, as demonstrated by Lee Breuer's 1982 New York Production; and American Indians—this Caliban was played by Mark Del-Castillo Morante for the Globe Playhouse of Los Angeles.[26] Ultimately, as Virginia and Alden Vaughan argue in their introduction to the Arden Edition of *The Tempest*, the common thread across the many representations of Caliban is difference.[27] In spite of the instability, however, the representations of Caliban on stage tend to fall into one of two categories. Either Caliban is an inhuman monster, or Caliban is a representative of an oppressed (typically, although not always colonized) group. A representation of Caliban as human but with a physical difference that is not intended to convey primitivism is extremely rare on stage, and equally rare in film. However, in 2010 Julie Taymor's gender-swapped adaptation of *The Tempest* gave us a Caliban who can be read not only through a postcolonial lens, but also through the use of the filmic stare. Taymor's Caliban also embodies an anxiety surrounding physical disability that I argue is inherent in the text of the play and remains present in contemporary culture.

Caliban, Disability Anxiety, and Postcolonialism

Health and ability are subject to an infuriating double standard, which Richard Burton implies but does not explicitly articulate or explicate in *Anatomy of Melancholy*. Burton repeats the seemingly age-old wisdom that "No man amongst us so sound, of so good a constitution, that hath not some impediment of body or mind. We all have our infirmities, first or last, more or less."[28] On the same page, however, Burton also states that melancholy and incurable diseases are "a just and deserved punishment of our sins."[29] The implication that everyone experiences "some impediment of body or mind" suggests that disability is simply a part of life, without a suggestion of fault or wrongdoing on the disabled party. This outlook became the center of the Social Model of Disability, and points to the heart of the philosophy behind the model: if everyone experiences disability at some point in their lives, then it behooves society to shape itself around that expectation and adjust the relationship between social architecture and the individual. However, the "no fault" philosophy is often immediately abandoned when someone suddenly becomes disabled. At that point, Burton's assertion that disability is a punishment for sins committed is raised in one form or another. For Burton's audiences, that sin could be as literal as horse theft, or as ephemeral and eschatological as a continuance of God's punishment for Adam after the fall. In either case, the individual with the disability is at fault. Therefore, the double standard of disability is that disability is a no-fault state of being…until you are disabled. A primary consequence of the disability double standard being so deeply ingrained into the social and cultural consciousness is a deep anxiety about becoming disabled. Burton recognized the social and cultural double standard and its accompanying anxiety in the early 1600s, but popular film and television in the twentieth and twenty-first centuries still bear out Burton's formulation, despite the medical, sociological and advocacy progress that has been made.

Anxiety about becoming disabled manifests in films like *Avatar* (James Cameron, 2009), where Jake Sully is perceived as useless and helpless until his consciousness is transferred to a physically abled Na'vi body—which also served as a cure for his paraplegia. We also see it in popular TV series, including *Scrubs*. The episode "My Nah Nah Nah" explores a surgeon's risky decision to perform an experimental procedure on a teenager who, after a car accident, is in danger of being permanently paralyzed.[30] The teenager recovers because *Scrubs* is a sitcom; however, the anxiety about the consequences of disability (and the unspoken assumption that, should the teenager be permanently paralyzed, it will be his fault for causing the accident) drives the choice to attempt a risky, experimental procedure. Take this logic a little further, and we are once again at *Million Dollar Baby* (Clint Eastwood, 2004), in which being dead is preferable to living with a physical disability. Shakespeare's Caliban, when he is represented as human, can be subtly physically non-normative; Taymor's Caliban has webbed fingers so subtle that they are almost impossible to see on screen unless the viewer knows to look for it. Taymor's Caliban also exhibits vitiligo—an autoimmune condition in which the pigment-producing cells are damaged, causing white patches to appear on the skin. There is some debate among disability theorists as to the appropriate place for illness-related disability as opposed to disabilities which are either congenital or acquired. My view on the matter is that, if there is a substantial limitation of one or more major life activities, the presence of disease matters not at all. For example, blindness as a result of a high fever is equally as much a disability as mobility issues as a result of Rheumatoid Arthritis, and equally as disabling as the loss of a limb in combat. Such fine distinctions are necessary in the legal and advocacy branches of disability studies, but ultimately present a roadblock in the analysis of literary and film representations of disability; hence my methodology, which refrains from diagnosing characters and focuses on the representation. Taymor explains her choice to give Caliban varicolored skin as "making him a mooncalf,"[31] visually interpreting and coding Caliban's difference through his physical appearance. I will discuss Caliban's physical non-normativity in the context of the filmic stare below, but in addition to Caliban's physical body, Shakespeare also allowed his Caliban and Prospero to embody the same anxiety about physical disability that Burton described, and that we can see in twenty-first century popular film and television.

In their first interaction, Caliban curses Prospero, who then responds with a threat:

> Caliban: As wicked dew as e'er my mother brushed
> With raven's feather from unwholesome fen
> Drop on you both. A southwest blow on ye
> And blister you all o'er.
>
> Prospero: For this, be sure, tonight thou shall have cramps,
> Side-stitches that shall pen thy breath up; urchins
> Shall forth at vast of night that they may work
> All exercise on thee; thou shalt be pinched
> As thick as honeycomb, each pinch more stinging
> Than bees that made 'em.[32]

Caliban threatens with witchcraft and natural disaster; Prospero's response is specific and potentially disabling. Prospero promises physical pain, shortness of breath, and, by implication, a lack of sleep that may potentially lead to a catastrophic accident while Caliban is out collecting wood. In essence, Prospero promises torture, something early modern audiences would have had an equally real anxiety about. Torture often led to an extremely ugly execution or disability.[33] Not only does Prospero threaten Caliban in person, but Caliban is conditioned to expect it, as we see in his soliloquy prior to meeting Stephano and Trinculo:

> His spirits hear me,
> And yet I needs must curse. But they'll nor pinch,
> Fright me with urchin-shows, pitch me i'th'mire,
> Nor lead me, like a firebrand in the dark,
> Out of my way unless he bid 'em. But
> For every trifle are they set upon me:
> Sometime like apes that mow and chatter at me

And after bite me; then like hedgehogs which
Lie tumbling in my barefoot way and mount
Their pricks at my footfall; Sometime I am
All wound with adders, who with cloven tongues
Do hiss me into madness.[34]

Caliban also expects Stephano and Trinculo to harm him because he mistakes them for Prospero's spirits. The expectation that disobedience will result in physical pain aligns with the colonial oppression that tends to be read into *The Tempest*; by combining a postcolonialist reading with a disability studies reading, the othering of different groups by a majority is reinforced. As Rosemarie Garland-Thomson comments on the exhibition of native Brazilian woman Tono Maria in a London freak show: "Stripped of her own cultural context and framed by the lurid interpretations of the Englishman and his society, Tono Maria's body became a malleable image upon which her audience projected cultural characteristics they themselves disavowed."[35] Shakespeare also removed Caliban from any cultural context that might be his, and because of the ambiguity in the text, Caliban's body is malleable. Race and physical difference are the two most common visible markers of difference that film adaptations project onto Caliban. The postcolonial anxiety about racial difference is mixed with anxiety about the physical difference and perception of dependence[36] that come with disability, and suddenly Caliban is the visual representation of multiple types of social anxiety, making disability and colonization reciprocal. Caliban, the colonized, attempts to rebel against his colonizer; the punishment is pain and potential disability, which would simply other Caliban further. Worse still, a realized disability would put Caliban even more at fault because of the double standard surrounding disability blame. The logic here follows a similar line to Miranda and Caliban's exchange:

Miranda: Abhorred slave,
Which any print of goodness wilt not take,
Being capable of all ill; I pitied thee,
Took pains to make thee speak, taught thee each hour
One thing or other: when thou didst not, savage,
Know thine own meaning, but wouldst gabble like
A thing most brutish, I endow'd thy purposes
With words that made them known.
[...]
Caliban: You taught me language, and my profit on't
Is I know how to curse.[37]

Miranda's speech to Caliban implies two important assumptions: first that when Prospero and Miranda discovered Caliban, he was literally an unlettered barbarian, the savage that Miranda names him. Second, it assumes that Caliban did not know his own meaning, and therefore needs someone to come in and assign linguistic meaning to his brutish gabbling. Both these assumptions are markedly patriarchal and fit neatly into a postcolonial reading, which I will address shortly, but the imposition of language is an action that surprisingly dovetails with disability studies.

As Elaine Scarry notes in *The Body in Pain*, there is a gap between the physical experience of pain and the linguistic communication of pain to those who do not experience it: "to have great pain is to have certainty; to hear that another person has pain is to have doubt."[38] A similar gap exists in trying to communicate the lived, physical experience of a non-normative body to a normate. Given the history of representing Caliban's body as non-normative, it is instructive to consider Miranda's imposition of linguistic meaning onto the non-linguistic and non-normative body that Caliban lives in as a larger part of the kill or cure mentality that Norden references, and that I have discussed in previous chapters. If, like great pain, the experience of a physical abnormality cannot be described and understood through language, then imposing linguistic meaning and language is a way of curing (or linguistically erasing?) Caliban's non-normative body. Miranda cannot understand the experience of a non-normative body, which itself, in being represented, becomes a non-linguistic sign (something I will address in more detail in my analysis of *Prospero's Books*). Imposing language on such a body, a non-linguistic sign, inherently erases that non-linguistic experience and insists on a communicative medium that cannot adequately express the realities of the body. Admittedly, linguistic communication is far from perfect, but in a general sense, for day-to-day experiences, it is often good enough. In communicating the non-normative experiences of disabled bodies, however, language is not only insufficient, but erases the experiences. We see this not only in Miranda's imposition of language on Caliban, but in common medical parlance, particularly in terms like "the patient failed treatment x, y, or z." The language places implicit blame on the patient, but it is the medical system or specific drug that failed. Caliban, like patients with chronic illnesses or disabilities who learn medical parlance in the hopes of being better able to communicate with their doctors and specialists, quickly understood the linguistic failures at play, and as a result, can only curse.

There is a resentful tone to Caliban's use of the word curse, in addition to the typical implications of the word. Language has erased Caliban's physical experiences and has potentially implicitly blamed him for physical abnormalities that are not his fault. Being able to curse Prospero and Miranda in their own language, however, is small profit. Using the language he was given, Caliban can make it clear that his physical experiences and his body as a non-linguistic sign have been lost, but the deeper meaning and impact are inaccessible to Miranda and Prospero. Miranda and Prospero know Caliban is malcontented but cannot truly understand why.

A postcolonial reading of the exchange between Miranda and Caliban might look like this: Miranda, as a colonizer, attempts to educate a colonized figure, and, as a result, Caliban can curse. In essence, the attempts at colonization lead to rebellion, and rebellion leads to retribution, which is blamed on the colonized. Whether the retribution is massacre or disability, the additional imbalance of power and the social consequences imposed by the colonizers because of rebellion are extreme, and any visual otherness in the colonized are highlighted in order to maintain the status quo. Critical reciprocity of course goes both ways. While disability theory adds to the horror of colonization, postcolonialism provides another structural underpinning for disability studies insofar as the social—and to a lesser extent, cultural—model of disability can be described as models in which able-bodied individuals colonize and oppress individuals with disabilities. Garland-Thomson's argument that physical disability is produced by legal, medical, political, cultural, and literary narratives which comprise an exclusionary discourse gestures toward the intersection of disability studies and postcolonial studies.[39] That intersection then functions as a nexus of anxiety, within which we can contextualize Caliban via the use of the filmic stare.

Art House Caliban

In *Prospero's Books*, Greenaway and Gielgud have created an art house film that favors dense visual storytelling through intricate choreography, an exploration of the human form, and hypermediated frames to tease out elements of *The Tempest*. The viewer's first introduction to this Caliban is as a pair of hands with a knife, slashing a book to shreds. Because this adaptation of *The Tempest* focuses on an identification of Prospero with Shakespeare that many—including Trevor Nunn—choose to read into the text, the idea of Caliban defacing Prospero's preferred means of storytelling signifies both Caliban's hatred of the man who has enslaved him,[40] and the change in storytelling medium from page and stage to screen. This Caliban will not be read linguistically—either through words on a page or in the words Prospero speaks—but rather through his physical body. As a director, Greenaway was well-aware of the challenges of adapting Shakespeare to the screen, noting that, "I want to demonstrate—not only in these circumstances, but at large—that there are other vehicles of communication besides the linguistic code. But in film—as well as film theory—we are still working through that burden of textual supremacy."[41] Greenaway is gesturing towards the tradition of literary adaptation specifically aimed at Shakespeare films and the supremacy of the Shakespearean text. We see this supremacy particularly in Jack Jorgens' taxonomic structure for classifying Shakespeare film adaptations; Jorgens used fidelity to the Shakespearean text as a yardstick for determining whether a film falls into a theatrical, realistic or filmic mode.[42] Jorgens' methodology has largely been followed in Shakespeare film analysis with only slight changes, although adaptation theory has evolved to expose flaws in a fidelity model of adaptation. By creating a non-linguistic code based around the movement of the nude human body, Greenaway explores nuances in *The Tempest* that otherwise might be overlooked or subsumed by stage traditions. By casting a professional dancer to play Caliban and physically abled individuals in other nude roles, however, Greenaway's non-linguistic sign system is—likely unconsciously—underpinned by ableist assumptions.

To refer to Greenaway's film as a "freak show," in the sense of the live acts in America in the late nineteenth century that showcased physically non-normative bodies, would be to misconstrue the tone and style of the film. However, Rosemarie Garland-Thomson describes the dynamic of the presentation of the disabled body as "almost always a freakish spectacle presented by the mediating narrative voice,"[43] a dynamic which is unquestionably present in *Prospero's Books*. Shakespeare's Caliban has an extraordinary body and his own voice. Greenaway's Caliban, however, is silenced and mediated through multiple layers, including Gielgud's voiceover, functioning as Prospero the author mediating Caliban's—all the characters'—voices. Greenaway as director also mediates the mise-en-scène and framing within which Caliban exists. I am confident in referring to *Prospero's Books* as a visual spectacle, and so the only missing element from Garland-Thomson's definition of the presentation of the disabled body is disability.

Greenaway's Caliban is played by choreographer Michael Clark, who trained at the London School of Ballet, and is himself in possession of an extraordinary body; that is, a body that has been meticulously trained to be able to communicate through dance. I use the term 'extraordinary' here consciously; when Garland-Thomson titled her book *Extraordinary Bodies*, she was working to circumvent the stigma associated with disability. I use the term to underline the linguistic instability in the terms which we use to describe bodies. If extraordinary bodies are both disabled and hyper-abled, then the creation of a non-linguistic sign for Caliban largely collapses the idea of disability. If we accept James Tweedie's assertion that, "*Prospero's Books* provides a running commentary on the struggle between the book as a cultural object and the text it strives but fails to contain,"[44] then by creating Caliban as a non-linguistic sign, not only is *Prospero's Books* reacting against the idea of textual supremacy, the film is also tacitly acknowledging the overriding issues between the written records of disability (in any of a number of fields and genres) and the lived experiences of individuals with disability. This was the main criticism of the social model of disability: in the separation of impairment and disability, the real, physical bodies got lost.[45] Garland-Thomson argues that there is a fundamental difference between disability as an attribute of a literary character and the experiences of real people living with disabilities, which also underscores the inadequacy of texts—be they literary or filmic—to represent disability.[46] For Martin Norden, cinema placed the disabled body where it could be seen on screen, but isolated it, in reaction to the patterns that emerged in reaction to social attitudes about disabled bodies.[47] In all of these examples, disability is categorized as other in written and filmic texts. For Tweedie, Caliban's difference stems from a postcolonial reading, where Caliban is relegated to the lower reaches of the established hierarchical order.

Tweedie, although he does not use the terms, adds linguistic and socio-economic layers to my earlier discussion of socially projected disability. As a result, Caliban's difference is that he is a "relentlessly physical and sexual presence in a world where the body is everywhere else de-eroticized."[48] From a disability studies standpoint, then, the sexualized, non-linguistic sign that is Caliban in *Prospero's Books* must ultimately be physically abled because of the often unremarked upon asexual objectification of characters and individuals who are visibly disabled. Garland-Thomson argues that asexual objectification is a result of the stare. This assumption is so ingrained in culture, that when *Murderball* (Henry Alex Rubin and Dana Adam Shapiro, 2005) used the "normalizing powers of masculinity," specifically heteronormative, eroticized masculinity, to explore the sexuality of paraplegic rugby players, Cynthia Barounis argued that masculinity was what made the frank discussion of sexuality acceptable, rather than an idea that disability and sexuality were acceptable.[49] As I discuss in Chapter 1, there has been resistance to asexual objectification, and indeed, female characters with invisible disabilities, such as blindness or deafness, have a film history of being eroticized.[50] However, unlike Hamlet, or Richard III, Caliban lacks the socioeconomic power to overcome the taboo of a sexualized character with a disability; he is a subaltern figure. Even a physically able Caliban is subject to Prospero; therefore, in *Prospero's Books*, disability as a concept is collapsed and rendered moot with respect to the non-linguistic sign that Greenaway creates. Caliban's disability is precisely his subaltern status.

Creating a non-linguistic sign is an adaptive choice, as is using precise choreography to communicate ideas and themes. However, traditional dance styles often assume the physical ability of the dancers; ballet was not designed with missing limbs or paralysis in mind.[51] Watching Michael Clark's Caliban constantly moving, aesthetically beautiful choreography with its extensions, leaps, and intricate floor work, the question must be asked: is Caliban physically abled because the text suggests it, or because Gielgud and Greenaway required a physically abled dancer to communicate their vision? As I have discussed in this chapter, the text of *The Tempest* is itself less than exacting in its description of Caliban. Additionally, the argument can be made that Stephano and Trinculo are unreliable narrators, and that Prospero and Alonso hyperbolize the appearance of a subaltern figure. I highlight the physical ability of Greenaway's Caliban because the narrative requirements of this particular adaptation require a specific reading of Caliban which suppresses physical disability. Cinematographically, Greenaway tends to use long shots and tableau shots, deep focus, and a high depth of field, all of which lend themselves to art-historical pastiche. Greenaway's style is similar to the techniques used to show madness in *Hamlet*.[52] However, Greenaway uses these techniques to show off Caliban's choreography, particularly during the reconciliation scene, where Caliban's writhing is nearly the only movement in the frame. The imagery in the film is painterly and imperialist, even through the other layers of visual storytelling Greenaway is employing. Ultimately, the focus with Greenaway's Caliban is not the unstable textual roots of Caliban's appearance, but the power dynamics and the non-visual sign systems that Greenaway constructs. In insisting on a highly choreographed representation of Caliban, even the possibility of a Caliban with a disability becomes an impossibility.

Caliban and the Filmic Stare

As a result of the critical questions surrounding Caliban's humanity and the stage trend from the 1960s of representing Caliban as a member of an oppressed group and/or minority, many of the various film Calibans fall outside the scope of this project. These Calibans are either entirely inhuman, as in *Forbidden Planet* (Fred M. Wilcox, 1956), or the 1960 adaptation from The Hallmark Hall of Fame, featuring a puppy-faced Richard Burton as Caliban. Alternatively, they are physical normates, as in Paul Mazursky's 1980 *Tempest*, Derek Jarman's 1979 counterculture *Tempest* and Greenaway's *Prospero's Books*. While these normate Calibans are technically outside the scope of disabled subaltern figures, the instability of the text suggests a suppression of disability in these films. In terms of an intersectional Caliban who represents both postcolonial and disability anxiety, is human and has a disability, Julie Taymor's 2010 *Tempest* is the only example.

In constructing the visual synecdoche for a character who embodies postcolonial and disability anxiety while also competing with an ensemble cast for screen time and using a film style that makes extensive use of wide and extreme wide angle shots in order to capture the natural feel of the filming location,[53] Taymor minimally fragments Caliban. By far the most common shots of him are plan américain and medium shots. However, when Taymor does visually fragment Caliban, his fragmentation does not dehumanize him in the way that a series of close-ups on a prosthesis or limb stump would. There is only a single close-up in the film of Caliban's hands, and it is in the context of Russell Brand's Trinculo discovering the monster's "fins like arms."

A moment of focus on the webbed fingers and the stage tradition of taking Trinculo at his word to create fish-like creatures when designing Caliban would suggest that the webbed fingers are Taymor's Caliban's visual synecdoche. However, Taymor created Caliban as a mooncalf, and the film goes out of its way to suggest that Stephano and Trinculo are perhaps not the most reliable narrators. In addition, the webbing is extremely subtle, and without the more extreme close-up, does not read well on film, creating an additional level of invisibility for Caliban's webbed fingers: they are technically visible, but they are largely screen-invisible. What is extremely visible on screen is Caliban's vitiligo; specifically, the round patch that covers half of his face, surrounding his single blue eye.

As I have previously argued, fragmentation to create a visual synecdoche almost always excludes the face of the character with the disability, dehumanizing them. By putting the primary focus of Caliban's visual synecdoche literally around his eyes, Taymor insists on Caliban's humanity, as well as his

Figure 3.1 Trinculo examines Caliban's webbed hand

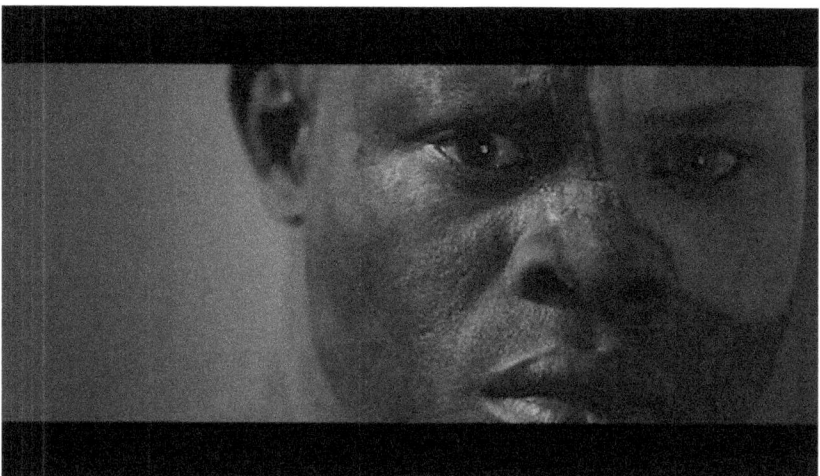

Figure 3.2 Close-up of Caliban's face with vitiligo and mismatched eyes

disability and status as a colonized individual.[54] Taymor constructs a compound visual synecdoche for Caliban; in close shots of him, both his face and his hands are visible in frame. During Caliban's first meeting with Trinculo and Stephano, his body is often out of frame, but his hands and face are in frame. Showing both Caliban's skin and webbed fingers in the same frame creates a compound visual synecdoche which acknowledges the entirety of Caliban's person, despite Garland-Thomson's assertion that literary characters lack complexity and nuance as a result of the foregrounding of their disability(ies).[55]

Because Caliban's disabilities have been historically unstable, and because Taymor constructs a human Caliban with visible physically non-normative traits, the filmic stare in Taymor's *Tempest* not only creates a visual synecdoche for the viewer, but in the wide and medium shots also highlights moments of the stare between characters.

Taymor sets up her film to reflect nature and the natural world.[56] Wide and medium shots are composed to make explicit oppositions between characters. Examples of this include the medium shot during Prospera and Miranda's conversation with Caliban, in which Caliban is almost exclusively on the left-hand side of the frame, and there is significant distance between him and the other two characters. The space between them facilitates the stares occurring between the characters within the diegesis of the film. Additionally, the distance combined with exchanged threats underlines the colonization of Caliban by Prospera, and highlights Caliban's physical difference. In this case, colonization and physical difference combine to create a unifying overlay for disability studies, postcolonial studies, and Caliban: the creation of a socially projected disability. Despite Caliban's webbed fingers and bi-colored skin, Taymor's casting underlines the visual reality that the male, physically imposing Caliban is arguably physically stronger than the two women he is facing, calling into question the use of the term physical disability. Caliban's physical difference (webbed fingers and vitiligo) may or may not in itself be a disability. Taken in combination with the social consequences of being colonized, however, Caliban's character is oppressed and stared at due to both his physical difference and because of his social/cultural differences. As a result, although Caliban's physical differences are not disabling in that a physical or mental capability is impaired—as with losing a limb or madness—but Caliban's major life activities are in fact limited by oppression and the stare. The substantial limitation of one or more major life activities as a result of a physical or mental impairment is the primary definition used by the ADA to define disability.[57] Garland-Thomson's disability-based stare is intertwined with a colonialist stare that subjugates an other because of a geographical (and often also racial) separation. I argue that, because of the combination of a visible physical abnormality and a colonialist attitude, Caliban suffers from a socially projected disability.

Socially projected disabilities function similarly to, although perhaps more strongly than, the stigma that surrounds physical and mental impairments. Stigmatization, according to Erving Goffman, is a social process.[58] Caliban, then, is socially stigmatized as a result of largely cosmetic physical abnormalities in conjunction with his status as a subaltern figure in a colonized setting. While his webbed hands and skin discolouration do not prevent Caliban from self-care, breathing, or eating, his oppression at the hands of Prospera and later at the hands of Stephano and Trinculo certainly does. Prospera and Miranda interrupt Caliban's meal in their first interaction,[59] and viewers are told in no uncertain terms that Prospera harms Caliban, preventing sleep and breath.[60] Therefore, if we understand that Caliban's physical abnormalities are entwined in his oppression, then a socially projected disability occurs as the oppressors use the subject's physical abnormalities as part and parcel of the rationale behind the oppression.

The complex interaction between the stare and colonization leading to socially projected disability is repeated at the end of the film when Caliban, Stephano, and Trinculo interrupt Prospera's reunion with the rest of the shipwrecked survivors. However, Taymor ultimately complicates the topically positive tone of the scene by once more drawing attention to Caliban's socially projected disability and the use of the filmic stare. When viewers stare at Caliban's physical difference, Taymor is facilitating a moment that mirrors the moment of mutual recognition[61] Prospera and Caliban share at the close of the film. Prospera is about to leave for Milan with her daughter, brother, and the rest, but Caliban remains. The moment encapsulates many elements. Prospera is staring at Caliban both as a colonized subaltern figure and as a physically different monster who attempted to rape Miranda. This is hardly the first time in the film that Prospera and Caliban come face to face, but this instance of the stare is active, the starer is paying attention; Garland-Thomson uses these terms to describe a stare which explicates rather than objectifies.[62] Hobgood and Wood use the term "ethical staring" to describe a productive stare which facilitates an exchange of knowledge and a recognition of difference without marginalization.[63] In Caliban's case, however, there has been objectification and marginalization. The final stare between Prospera and Caliban acknowledges previous instances of Garland-Thomson's stare between characters, which the viewers perceive through the filmic stare. Taymor constructs a self-reflexive moment of filmic staring that implicitly questions the anxiety surrounding and the attempted objectification of Caliban as a colonized subaltern figure with a visible, physical disability through the construction of a compound visual synecdoche. Prospera's final stare, and the final close-up of Caliban's white skin around his blue eye both acknowledge previous instances of stares and the filmic stare throughout the film, and simultaneously question not only the intent behind the stare, but also the willingness to stare at those who are colonized and those who are physically non-normative. As Taymor refused to wholly objectify Lavinia in *Titus*,[64] she refuses to allow the filmic stare, with its postcolonial intersection, to wholly objectify Caliban.

In complicating the filmic stare with a self-reflexive moment at end of the film, Taymor gives audiences a more complex, nuanced Caliban than a simple monster, as the stage traditions have done. As in other films that humanize Caliban, Taymor has seen fit to include some version of his textually unstable disability. Jarman and Mazursky both omit any kind of physical disability in their representations of Caliban, which is itself a suppression of disability. Despite the play text's instability and ambiguity about Caliban's physicality, the stage and film traditions have established a physically abnormal Caliban. In choosing to deviate from that tradition, Jarman and Mazursky potentially open new avenues with which to explore postcolonial and/or artistic representations. However, refusing to engage with a tradition of disability also potentially suggests that disability ought to remain in the shadows. This suggestion is strengthened when a director's storytelling methodology insists on physical ability, even to the point of requiring extraordinarily abled performers. Peter Greenaway's *Prospero's Books* (1991) takes even the possibility of a disabled Caliban off the table through his storytelling methodology and casting.

Unlike figures who are male, white, and who occupy a privileged socio-economic bracket, Caliban's relationship with disability is as unstable as the early modern text in which he was first described. Caliban is not always human in film adaptations of *The Tempest*, and when he is recognizably human, he may be physically abled or have unrecognizable—nigh invisible—impairments. Further complicating Caliban is the colonial structure of the play; within the diegetic power and social structures, Caliban is inevitably the less powerful figure. This leads to an elision of the various ways that Caliban lacks power; he is already the colonized slave and adding a socially projected disability based on cosmetic abnormalities gives oppressors another "reason" to subjugate him. Ultimately, the unstable foundation that any adaptation of Caliban is built on leads to nuance falling through the cracks. Taymor's Caliban gave subtle nods to the character's disabilities, but other productions have either gone fully monstrous, or physically normative. Greenaway goes wholly the opposite direction from Taymor, creating a mode of storytelling that actively suppresses even the possibility of an unstable impairment. As a case study, Caliban clearly underscores the wider social discomfort with disability: given the choice, it is simply easier not to even offer the option to stare at a body with a disability.

Notes

1 *The Tempest*, "Names of Actors" 1661.
2 *The Tempest*, 1.2.319–20, 282–4; 2.1.27, 65; 5.1.266, 290.
3 *The Tempest*, 2.1.168.
4 Vaughan, Virginia Mason. *The Tempest*. Manchester: Manchester UP. 2011. 9.
5 *The Tempest*, 1.2.281–4.
6 Vaughan, Alden T. and Virginia Mason Vaughan. *Shakespeare's Caliban: A Cultural History*. Cambridge: Cambridge UP. 1991. 9–10.
7 Vaughan and Vaughan, *Caliban*, 9–10.
8 *The Tempest*, 1.2.283–4.
9 Vaughan and Vaughan, *Caliban*, 10.
10 "b. n" human, adj. and n. *OED Online*. March 2019. Oxford University Press.
11 "monster, n., adv., and adj.". *OED Online*. March 2019. Oxford University Press.
12 Vaughan and Vaughan, *Caliban*, 173.
13 Vaughan and Vaughan, *Caliban*, 14.
14 Vaughan, *Tempest*, 56–7.
15 Vaughan, *Tempest*, 50–1.
16 Qtd. in Vaughan, *Tempest*, 50.
17 Vaughan, *Tempest*, 61.
18 Vaughan and Vaughan, *Caliban*, 186.
19 Vaughan and Vaughan, *Caliban*, 189.
20 Kott, Jan. *Shakespeare our Contemporary*. Trans. Boleslaw Taborski. New York: Anchor Books. 1966. 246–7.

21 Kott, 242.
22 Croyden, Margaret. *The Drama Review: TDR*, 13.3 (Spring, 1969): 125–8. 128.
23 Vaughan and Vaughan, *Caliban*, 190–1.
24 Vaughan and Vaughan, *Caliban*, 192–3.
25 Vaughan and Vaughan, *Caliban*, 192–3.
26 Vaughan and Vaughan, *Caliban*, 194–5.
27 Vaughan, Alden T. and Virginia Mason Vaughan. "Introduction." *The Tempest*. 3rd ed. Ed. Virginia Mason Vaughan and Alden T. Vaughan. London: Arden Shakespeare. 1999. 34.
28 Burton, Robert. *The Anatomy of Melancholy*. Ed. Floyd Dell and Paul Jordan-Smith. New York: Tudor Publishing Co. 1927. 119.
29 Burton, 119.
30 *Scrubs*. "My Nah Nah Nah." Season 8, Episode 11. Dir. John Putch. ABC Studios. March 18, 2009.
31 "Making of the *Tempest*" featurette. *The Tempest*. Dir. Julie Taymor. Perf. Helen Mirren. Miramax Films. 2010.
32 *The Tempest* 1.2.321–9.
33 A prominent example among early modern playwrights is Thomas Kyd, who was arrested on suspicion of libelous papers, but instead was found to be in possession of heretical texts that Kyd alleged belonged to his roommate, Christopher Marlowe. Kyd was brutally tortured nonetheless, and although he was released, he died shortly after, likely as a result of his treatment in the Tower of London.
34 *The Tempest*, 2.2.1–14.
35 Garland-Thomson, Rosemarie. *Extraordinary Bodies: Figuring Physical Disability in American Culture and Literature*. New York: Columbia UP. 1997. 55–6.
36 See Norden, Martin. *The Cinema of Isolation: A History of Physical Disability in the Movies*. New Brunswick: Rutgers University Press, 1994, 30, for a more in-depth discussion about the assumption that people with disabilities are dependent upon others for every facet of life.
37 *The Tempest*, 1.2.351–64.
38 Scarry, Elaine. *The Body in Pain*. Oxford: Oxford UP: 1985. 13.
39 Garland-Thomson, *Extraordinary Bodies*, 6.
40 And possibly a tacit nod to Peter Brook's 1968 *Tempest*, with its focus on power dynamics and overriding images of literal and metaphorical rape.
41 Stalpaert, Christel. "Interview with Peter Greenaway." *Peter Greenaway's Prospero's Books: Critical Essays*. Ed. Christel Stalpaert. Belgium: Ghent UP: 2000. 41.
42 Jorgens, Jack. *Shakespeare on Film*. Bloomington: Indiana UP. 1977. 7–9.
43 Garland-Thomson, *Extraordinary Bodies*, 10
44 Tweedie, James. "Caliban's Books: The Hybrid Text in Peter Greenaway's *Prospero's Books*." *Cinema Journal*, l 40. 1, Fall 20. 2000. *JSTOR*. 107.
45 Berger, Ronald J. "Explaining Disability." *Introducing Disability Studies*. New York: Lynne Rienner. 2013. 27–8.
46 Garland-Thomson, *Extraordinary Bodies*, 9–10.
47 Norden, 1–2.
48 Tweedie, 118.
49 Barounis, Cynthia. "Cripping Heterosexuality, Queering Able-Bodiedness: *Murderball, Brokeback Mountain* and the Contested Masculine Body." *The Disability Studies Reader*. 3rd ed. Ed. Lennard J. Davis. New York: Routledge. 2010. 443, 448.
50 See my discussion in Chapter 1 on the topic of objectifying female characters with disabilities.
51 That being said, anorexia and bulimia have been seen in dancers who are attempting to create the "perfect ballet body," and these disorders can be classified as disabilities themselves, or they can lead to co-morbidity issues that may be

classified as disabilities. So, in many ways, the idea of a dancer's body is equally as much a construct as a physically normative body. The issues of physicality in dance, while both interesting and potentially fertile academically, are unfortunately outside the scope of this project.

52 For a more detailed discussion of the cinematographic techniques used to represent Hamlet's madness, see Chapter 4.

53 "Making of Featurette," *The Tempest*. Dir. Julie Taymor. Perf. Helen Mirren. Miramax Films. 2010.

54 For more discussion of visual synecdoches that include the face of a character, see my discussion about *The Fault in Our Stars* in Chapter 1.

55 Garland-Thomson, *Extraordinary Bodies*, 12.

56 "Making of Featurette," *The Tempest*, 2010.

57 For the full text of the document, see https://www.ada.gov/pubs/adastatute08.htm.

58 Garland-Thomson, *Extraordinary Bodies*, 30.

59 *The Tempest*, 1.2.330.

60 *The Tempest*, 1.2.324–30; 2.2.3–14.

61 Helen Mirren, "Making of Featurette," *The Tempest*, 2010.

62 Garland-Thomson, Rosemarie. *Staring: How We Look*. New York: Oxford UP. 2009. 20–1.

63 Hobgood, Allison P. and David Houston Wood, eds. *Recovering Disability in Early Modern England*. Columbus: Ohio State UP. 2013. 2.

64 See my discussion in Chapter 2 on Lavinia and physical disability.

Bibliography

Barounis, Cynthia. "Cripping Heterosexuality, Queering Able-Bodiedness: *Murderball, Brokeback Mountain* and the Contested Masculine Body." *The Disability Studies Reader*. 3rd ed. Ed. Lennard J. Davis. New York: Routledge. 2010.

Berger, Ronald J. "Explaining Disability." *Introducing Disability Studies*. New York: Lynne Rienner. 2013.

Burton, Robert. *The Anatomy of Melancholy*. Ed. Floyd Dell and Paul Jordan-Smith. New York: Tudor Publishing Co. 1927.

Croyden, Margaret. "Peter Brook's *Tempest*." *The Drama Review: TDR*, 13. 3 (Spring 1969): 125–128. MIT Press. 128.

Garland-Thomson, Rosemarie. *Extraordinary Bodies: Figuring Physical Disability in American Culture and Literature*. New York: Columbia UP. 1997.

Garland-Thomson, Rosemarie. *Staring: How We Look*. New York: Oxford UP. 2009.

Hobgood, Allison P. and David Houston Wood, Eds. *Recovering Disability in Early Modern England*. Columbus: Ohio State UP. 2013.

Jorgens, Jack. *Shakespeare on Film*. Bloomington: Indiana UP. 1977.

Kott, Jan. *Shakespeare Our Contemporary*. Trans. Boleslaw Taborski. New York: Anchor Books. 1966.

Norden, Martin. *The Cinema of Isolation: A History of Physical Disability in the Movies*. New Brunswick: Rutgers University Press, 1994.

Prospero's Books. Dir. Peter Greenway. Perf. John Gielgud. Miramax Films. 1991.

Scarry, Elaine. *The Body in Pain*. Oxford: Oxford UP. 1985.

Scrubs. "My Nah Nah Nah." Season 8, Episode 11. Dir. John Putch. ABC Studios. March 18, 2009.

Stalpaert, Christel. "Interview with Peter Greenaway." *Peter Greenaway's Prospero's Books: Critical Essays*. Ed. Christel Stalpaert. Belgium: Ghent UP. 2000.

The Tempest. Dir. Julie Taymor. Perf. Helen Mirren. Miramax Films. 2010.

Tweedie, James. "Caliban's Books: The Hybrid Text in Peter Greenaway's *Prospero's Books*." *Cinema Journal*, 40. 1 (Fall 2000).

Vaughan, Virginia Mason. *The Tempest*. Manchester: Manchester UP. 2011.

Vaughan, Alden T. and Virginia Mason Vaughan. *Shakespeare's Caliban: A Cultural History*. Cambridge: Cambridge UP. 1991.

Vaughan, Alden T. and Virginia Mason Vaughan. "Introduction." *The Tempest*. 3rd ed. Ed. Virginia Mason Vaughan and Alden T. Vaughan. London: Arden Shakespeare. 1999.

4   Madness, the Filmic Stare, and Hamlet

In *Hamlet and World Cinema* (2019), Mark Thornton Burnett argues that *Hamlet* is "the world's most frequently filmed text and reveals a rich and diverse history of cinematic production reaching across the globe." For this chapter, rather than focusing on a comprehensive analysis of *Hamlet* film adaptations, I will focus on using the filmic stare to analyze the representations of mental disability in a cross-section of film adaptations of *Hamlet* from Global Cinemas, which includes adaptations from Soviet, Chinese, and Japanese cinemas as well as Hollywood, Mollywood, and Bollywood productions.

Hamlet and Ophelia are arguably two of the most well-known characters in the western canon who experience mental disability, and much of the criticism that deals with these characters and their madness directly separates the two and explores the differences between male and female madness. Additionally, the question of the legitimacy of mental disability is frequently mixed into any discussion of mental disability in *Hamlet*. In analyzing representations of madness in film adaptations of Hamlet and Ophelia in the context of disability aesthetics generally and the filmic stare specifically, however, I argue that male and female madness is represented in largely the same way, using the same techniques. By exploring madness through the filmic stare in adaptations of one of the early modern period's most well-known revenge tragedies, I position my argument within disability aesthetics, and specifically within both of Tobin Siebers's goals of making the influence of disability on modern art—in the form of film adaptations—obvious by arguing that disability is a worthy site of exploration and using it to underpin my arguments.[1] I will begin my discussion by explaining my use of the term madness before engaging with Carol Thomas Neely and her use of the term "distracted." Then I will move on to my case studies, focusing on Hamlet in this chapter, and on Ophelia in Chapter 5.

Mental disability is arguably the more elusive half of the mind–body split in disability studies, particularly in the context of cinematic adaptations of *Hamlet*. Mental disability is difficult to diagnose, and the terminology changes as science and medicine progress to more complex understandings of biology, neurology, and neurochemistry. Ronald Berger's assertion that disability studies "asks us to become more aware of the words and phrases we use [...] that demean people with disabilities"[2] in the context of the multivalent nature of

DOI: 10.4324/9781003163374-5

mental disability and its terminology complicates discussions about cinematic representations of mental disabilities. My solution to dealing with the mutable terminology that surrounds mental disability is to choose to use an anachronistic term: madness. Choosing madness as an umbrella term may be controversial; madness has specific and generally negative connotations in contemporary usage, and to refer to neuro-atypical individuals who have specific diagnoses as 'mad' can be disrespectful and inaccurate. In addition, as Carol Thomas Neely notes, "'madness' and 'melancholy' are in the [renaissance] period used diffusely and imprecisely. Both terms exist on a continuum and signify conditions either figurative or literal and ranging from mild to severe."[3] Arguments could also be made for more modern terms, depending on how Hamlet and Ophelia are diagnosed. For example, Sonya Freeman Lofts and Lisa Ulevich use autism as a diagnosis through which to explore Hamlet's behaviour in their chapter, "Obsession/Rationality/Agency: Autistic Shakespeare."[4] They argue that "[t]o read literary character is to diagnose"[5] and that "Shakespeare's plays [...] form part of a larger cultural and historical discourse that affirms neurotypical characteristics and punishes autistic ones, reading traits such as 'repetition' and 'obsession' as markers of madness."[6] However, I will not diagnose literary and filmic characters, and therefore more modern diagnostic terms would be inappropriate here. In the context of the filmic stare, the term madness is most appropriate *because* it reflects a more generalized methodology for analyzing representations of mental impairment, rather than the myriad, nuanced diagnoses that all fit under the umbrella term of mental impairment. Madness as a term is also less anachronistic in the context of Shakespeare and Robert Burton.

A contemporary of Shakespeare, Robert Burton's detailed text, *The Anatomy of Melancholy* (1621), is one of the earliest volumes to categorize and describe the many permutations of melancholy—including early descriptions of conditions that medical science would later recognize as clinical depression, lycanthropy, and rabies.[7] Burton's definition of melancholic diseases of the head includes a "division at this time [...] into those [diseases] of the body and mind—" and includes a section on diseases that he hypothesizes affect the brain itself, including "phrenzy, lethargy, melancholy, madness, weak memory, sleeping-sickness and insomnia."[8] The most pertinent definition is the definition of madness itself:

> a vehement dotage, or raving without fever, far more violent than melancholy, full of anger and clamour, horrible looks, actions, gestures, troubling the patients with far greater vehemency both of body and mind, without all fear and sorrow, with such impetus force and boldness, that sometimes three or four men cannot hold them.[9]

If Burton's definition seems familiar in theatrical and/or cinematic contexts, it is because Burton has identified the most extreme variations of behaviours that are visible to onlookers. Those behaviours, while extreme, are imitable and performable and therefore can be used on stage and in front of the camera to represent madness without the complication of trying to convey visual or auditory hallucinations, intrusive thoughts, or other inherently invisible symptoms of madness.

In addition to his definition, Burton is careful to acknowledge both the cause of these "diseases of the head" and the permeability of the human body. Burton argues through the lens of humoral theory—asserting that the "material cause" of melancholy and its assorted subdivisions is "a sort of melainia (black) chole (choler)."[10] I do not propose to subscribe to early modern medical theory to analyze the visual representation of disability in early modern film adaptations any more than I intend to use the DSM-5[11] to diagnose Hamlet or Ophelia. Nor do I intend to focus my analysis purely on language as a marker of madness, as has been done in the past.

Neely's analysis of distraction—her term for analyzing madness in early modern drama—in speech focuses on the "unshaped unsense" of language that can be "'botched' up or collected into shape by an audience's readings,"[12] and the "'quoted,' fragmentary, ritualized quality" of Ophelia's speech after she has gone mad and Hamlet's speech immediately after his encounter with the ghost.[13] Neely notes that her term "signifies how early modern subjects felt when mad; it calls up early modern attitudes toward madness as a temporary derailing, and it emphasizes that there are multiple signifiers for conditions of mental disturbance."[14] Neely's broad definition attempts to empathize with the lived experience of mad subjects, but her overall analysis genders a disability that, aside from Hamlet's assertion that his madness is feigned, differs not at all in representation in the play text.

Neely highlights the stage direction "Enter Ophelia, distracted," early in act IV, scene v of *Hamlet*. However, Shakespeare also uses the term to describe Hamlet; Rosencrantz puts the word into Hamlet's mouth, saying, "he does confess he feels himself distracted."[15] Hamlet also uses the word in act V, scene ii, explaining to Laertes that he has been "punish'd/ With sore distraction."[16] The same term is used to describe the madness of both Hamlet and Ophelia, and Hamlet claims the term himself. The egalitarian use of the word distraction (or distracted) in the play text forms the foundation for using the same tools to represent madness in a given medium, mirroring the use of cinematographic tools on film to represent madness. Neely asserts that "[Hamlet's] madness is in every way contrasted with [Ophelia's], in part, probably, to emphasize the difference between feigned and actual madness, melancholy, and distraction."[17] Ophelia sings "snatches of old tunes,"[18] but Hamlet's "words, words, words,"[19] spoken to Polonius, are equally fragmented, distracted, and thematically resonant. Taking Hamlet at his word that he is, in fact, feigning madness, is a dangerous proposition, and one that makes little sense. If Hamlet is in fact feigning madness and wants to be convincing, wouldn't his madness look more like Ophelia's madness, not less?

Linda Woodbridge notes that critics can get thoroughly tangled in the morass that is the question of the morality of revenge,[20] and summarizes the critical reactions to madness in revenge tragedies by saying "Many charge that madness deprives revengers of moral authority, tainting revenge as irrational and obsessive."[21] Her rebuttal is to argue that madness as a motif is over-emphasized, and that "[c]ritics have expanded the group by finding something mad in the act of feigning madness, and by identifying vengefulness itself with mental unbalance."[22] Woodbridge is addressing the issue of feigned madness as opposed to legitimate madness, a line which some playwrights seem to blur in characters such as Hamlet and Hieronimo (*The Spanish Tragedy*, Thomas Kyd), whereas other playwrights go out of their way to diagnose characters, as Webster does with Ferdinand in *The Duchess of Malfi*. A film example occurs in Vishal Bhardwaj's 2014 film adaptation of *Hamlet*, *Haider*, wherein a doctor explicitly diagnoses Haider with PTSD. Where I am somewhat skeptical but generally prepared to take Haider's doctor at his word on his diagnosis, I am not prepared to put forth any diagnoses myself. For a medical diagnosis, knowing if madness is real or feigned is crucial. However, in a narrative setting, the perception of madness is arguably more important than whether madness is "legitimate." Claudius is acutely aware of this; Hamlet's feigned madness is dangerous if people perceive it to be real, which is part of Claudius' rationale for sending Hamlet to England.[23]

While the question of morality in revenge tragedy is largely outside the scope of my discussion, I raise Woodbridge's point because the question of legitimacy—intimately bound up in the questions of madness and morality in revenge—is crucial to an understanding of the representation of madness in *Hamlet*. However, while Neely's arguments that female and male mad-ness manifest differently in language align with Berger's assertion at the beginning of this chapter that disability studies is about language,[24] the aesthetic turn in disability studies and its implications in analyzing film adaptations of Shakespearean drama (particularly in the context of global cinema adaptations) allows scholarship to move beyond an exclusive focus on language and an insistence that madness manifests differently in different genders.

In a film studies context, Norden documents how often people assume disabilities are faked, so the legitimate symptoms and accompanying mobi-lity aids of a disability are often assumed to be theatrically applied in sup-port of a scam in a film. As a result, legitimate and illegitimate madness are often elided in film and drama, which ultimately broadens the number of plays that fall under the revenge tragedy umbrella. As a result, madness, while not required of every single revenge tragedy, is nonetheless popularly recognized as a feature of revenge tragedy. That a mental disability is so often at the heart of a genre is significant and makes exploring the repre-sentation of that disability more crucial. By exploring representations of disability in revenge tragedies, I follow Siebers's example and make a dis-ability aesthetic one of the underpinnings of the use of the filmic stare in film adaptation of *Hamlet*, one of the most well-known revenge tragedies.

Revenge tragedy as a genre is often strictly tied to the specific time, place, and literary category with which the genre began: between approximately

1560 and 1642 in England's Elizabethan theatres. When early modern plays are adapted to film, they can be marketed in a variety of ways, but most commonly they are marketed as adaptations and retain the title of the play as the title of the film. Here it would be useful to have a definition of adaptation, but the broad definition of adaptation as the transference of narrative from one medium to another, fails to fully describe an adaptation. Linda Hutcheon uses the term palimpcestuous to acknowledge the overt relationship of one text to another.[25] Palimpcestuous also refers to a species of intertextuality wherein works are "haunted at all times by their adapting texts," and "multilaminated," or "directly and openly connected to other works" with the connection forming part of the adapted text's formal and hermeneutic identities.[26] Bolter and Grusin give us the term remediation,[27] but as a broad definition, Hutcheon's description of adaptation as an "acknowledged transposition of a recognizable other work or works[,] a creative and an interpretive act of appropriation/sharing[, and] an extended intertextual engagement with the adapted work,"[28] best fits the adaptations of early modern plays to film that I will discuss. Even when these films adapt the period in which the film is set, generally these films are still period pieces.

The myriad of available *Hamlet* adaptations underscores this point: Zeffirelli's 1990 *Hamlet* is broadly medieval, Branagh's *Hamlet* (1996) is ambiguously late-nineteenth century,[29] Olivier gives us a dark version of early modern Denmark (1946), and Gregory Doran's 2009 *Hamlet* gives audiences an ambiguously twenty-first century opulence. Michael Almereyda's *Hamlet* positions his Elsinore in 1990s New York (Almereyda, 2000), which, at the time of the film's production was contemporary, but given the advances in technology and the social and cultural changes after 9/11, the film retroactively becomes a period piece set in a pre-9/11 world.

In a more global cinema context, *Hamlet* adaptations are still largely period pieces. Akira Kurosawa's 1960 adaptation, *The Bad Sleep Well*, presents a portrait of post-World War II corporate Japan. Grigori Kozintsev's 1964 *Hamlet*, though stylized in design, has roots in the early modern period. The two *Hamlet* adaptations from Chinese cinema in 2006 are set in the tenth dynasty Tang Court (*The Banquet*, directed by Feng Xiaogang) and ancient Tibet (*Prince of the Himalayas*, directed by Sherwood Hu) respectively. Finally, Vishal Bhardwaj's 2014 adaptation *Haider* positions the family drama at the heart of *Hamlet* in 1995 Kashmir.

In terms of genre, these films are all first and foremost adaptations. Beyond being adaptations, however, critical analysis reveals how elusive genre categories are. Branagh's *Hamlet* has been compared to epics such as *Ben Hur* (Wyler, 1959) and *Dr. Zhivago* (Lean, 1965); Doran's *Hamlet* (2009) arguably falls into the category of filmed theatre (Aebisher's term) or Digital Broadcast Cinema (DBC) more than a traditional film genre; Olivier's *Hamlet* dances along the intersections of film noir and German Expressionism to largely elude being pinned down by any single genre. In contrast, films such as Ralph Fiennes's *Coriolanus* (2011) or Richard Lon-craine's *Richard III* (1995) are adaptations that fit more neatly into established Hollywood genres, war film and gangster film, respectively.

Rick Altman draws a distinction between the "classical practice of generic purity" and Hollywood's marketing strategy of combining genres.[30] From a disability studies standpoint, where impairments are more diverse than genre combinations, stepping away from the classical idea of generic purity in favor of permeability and evocations of many genres within a film allows a broader discussion of mental disability. In the context of the filmic stare, looser generic boundaries, and the Hollywood convention of combining genres offer opportunities for "the disabled or wounded body [to signal] the presence of the [disability aesthetic] itself"[31] with which directors can highlight representations of mental disability.

"Madness in Great Ones": Hamlet

Lindsay Row-Heyveld begins her exploration of mental and intellectual disabilities in early modern drama with a reiteration of Charles A. Hallett and Elaine S. Hallett's assertion that madness is both "the central symbol that binds all the motifs [of revenge tragedy] together" and "perhaps the most misunderstood revenge tragedy convention."[32] Certainly this assertion remains true to this day, and not just in the field of early modern revenge tragedies; difficulties with categorizing, diagnosing, accommodating and treating mental and intellectual impairment are exemplified in the sheer heft of the DSM-5. However, the nuance of discussing intellectual and mental impairment in film adaptations of early modern drama is amplified, as Row-Heyveld points out, by the performativity and theatricality attributed to these impairments by medical authorities in the early modern period.[33] I raise this point not to suggest that my argument will follow the thinking of early modern medical authorities, but to underline the discourse in which early modern playwrights were steeped as they wrote their own mad revengers. Playwriting in early modern England, like film production in twentieth and twenty-first century global culture, is at its core a business. Spectacle helps sell tickets, and the playhouses were competing with tours of The Hospital of St. Mary of Bethlehem,[34] arguably an early precursor to the freak shows of the twentieth-century, and the inspiration for the term bedlam.[35]

In the context of mad revengers, literary scholars (including Row-Heyveld and Woodbridge) tend to argue that madness—real or feigned—accomplishes two main functions. First, madness functions as a "literary loophole," to use Row-Heyveld's term.[36] Both Woodbridge and Row-Heyveld acknowledge the sprawling, complex legal system in early modern society, and the frustration and lack of perceived justice that came from the court system. From this context springs the argument that revengers function to enact vigilante justice,[37] "calibrat[ing] revenge to an offense."[38] In the summary collection of a "just price" or "weregild,"[39] revengers step outside legal boundaries and ethical norms. Madness is ultimately used to excuse actions that revengers take, making them commercially palatable to audiences, and circumnavigating the eyes of the censors. I argue that this logic transfers neatly from print media and live theatre performances to a film paradigm.[40]

Second, madness functions neatly in terms of Mitchell and Snyder's theory of narrative prosthesis. Narrative prosthesis argues that a disability becomes a narrative crutch on which the story turns. Essentially, the disability is introduced and metaphorically tied to the narrative's central conflict. As the central conflict is addressed and resolved, so too is the disability, either through rehabilitation and reintegration into an abled society, or through the release of the disability by the death of the disabled character. Row-Heyveld takes Mitchell and Snyder a step further, arguing that "Instead of being cured or killed, protagonists of revenge dramas appear to be cured *and* killed: they enter into the final bloodbath free of their mental impairment and then they die in the attack that they instigate."[41] The idea of madness as narrative prosthesis, or madness as spectacle, is more problematic to adapt into film than the idea of a vigilante revenger exercising (relatively) rapid and necessary justice. In early modern contexts, the idea of openly staring at an individual foaming at the mouth as he is physically restrained was largely socially acceptable; bodies as a public spectacle (through freak shows, Bethlehem Hospital Tours, executions, etc.), however, have largely been removed from the public eye. Staring at bodies in public has become far more taboo, particularly if those bodies are in some way non-normative.[42] As a result, when directors and actors adapt revenge tragedies for film, the performative and spectatorial aspects of madness that suited it so well to early modern stages becomes a sensitive point to be negotiated in the new medium.

The site of the negotiation is in the image and the use of the filmic stare. Because characters with mental impairments do not use anything as visible as prostheses to compensate for missing limbs, directors rely on the breaking of verbal and behavioural social scripts to demonstrate mental impairments. Verbal and behavioural scripts are basically the social norms that govern social interactions and manners. For example, the polite thing to do on meeting an acquaintance unexpectedly in public is smile, perhaps offer a handshake and a "How are you?" Such polite acknowledgements also function as a signal: everything is ok, this is a normal, routine interaction. When someone breaks either the behavioural or verbal script, there can be a moment of panic. We know how to respond to a polite acknowledgement, but, as Hamlet demonstrates in conversation with Polonius when he responds to a declarative statement, "The actors are come hither, my lord," with "Buzz, buzz," breaking social scripts can be both uncomfortable and funny.[43] Often the verbal breaks are in the early modern texts; play scripts are blueprints for another kind of visual medium, making the adaptation of the idea of the text more complex than a literal transposition of the words from play script to screenplay. In terms of the specifics of dialogue, verse and prose, there is much scholarship on early modern wordplay and the challenges of adapting that language to film.[44] Visually, however, the breaking of behavioural scripts is where directors frequently choose to use wide and medium shots to represent mental impairment.

Actors are, of course, a major element in the creation of a visual representation of a character with a disability. In the case of *Hamlet*, the role is designed to highlight the actor. Shakespeare was writing for his own troupe, and so Hamlet is one of the roles presumably written for Richard Burbage, the leading man who likely originated roles including Hamlet, Macbeth, and Antony.[45] After the early modern theatres closed in 1642, Hamlet remained a starring role for generations of theatre actors, including Junius Brutus Booth and Edwin Booth, Sarah Bernhardt, John Barrymore, and Christopher Plummer. Even once Shakespeare became Hollywood currency, *Hamlet* was a status symbol role. Olivier, Branagh, Ethan Hawke and Mel Gibson are the typically cited Anglophone silver screen Hamlets, to whom I will add Innokenty Smoktunovsky, Shahid Kapoor, and Purba Rgyal in my discussion of non-Anglophone Hamlets.

As Garland-Thomson and others[46] note, mental impairment carried and still carries with it a social stigma. This stigma comes into conflict with the place that Shakespeare (and *Hamlet* in particular) has come to occupy in the social and cultural consciousness. *Hamlet* represents high art, and any actor playing the role is inevitably compared with the "definitive" Hamlet not only of their generation, but with all the previous definitive Hamlets. The role itself tends to subsume discussion of mental impairment in *Hamlet*, because a tragic hero played by the star of the moment gets wrapped up in status and the star system. Even Olivier's Oedipal *Hamlet* is discussed more in the context of auteurism, and a shift from theatre to film, than representations of madness. Part of negotiating star power with the filmic stare may in fact come from the pervasive pattern of "Oscar bait" roles; the term is newer than the phenomenon. Playing Hamlet is a chance for actors to show their range; star power conflicts with but ultimately tends to overpower stigma, at least for *Hamlet*.

In adapting an invisible impairment, directors create distance between the audience and the character. That is not to say that there are no close-up shots of Hamlet; adaptation convention often dictates that Shakespearean soliloquies are spoken to the camera, and more than a few of those soliloquies are spoken to the camera in close-up. There are many places in the play where we can see Hamlet "put[ting] an antic disposition on,"[47] both in the play text and in the extant film adaptations. Hamlet's adoption of madness is the crux of the scholarly disagreement about whether Hamlet himself is legitimately mad. For exploring representations of madness, however, the legitimacy of Hamlet's madness is a moot point. Hamlet is consciously representing madness in the play text, and thereby the common early modern assumptions and stereotypes related to madness. As a result, there is still a representation of madness on the screen to analyze, foregrounding Siebers's disability aesthetic.[48] For the purposes of explicating the filmic stare in film adaptations of *Hamlet* I will focus primarily on the ghost scene, the closet scene, and the scene where Polonius first questions a "mad" Hamlet.[49] These scenes maintain a wider shot distance (and in many cases additional layers of mediation), which permits Hamlet to mirror the social scripts he is breaking with violations of conversational and behavioural norms.

The benchmark film adaptation of *Hamlet* in the western world tends to be Laurence Olivier's 1948 film. Olivier, on the cutting edge of adapting Shakespeare for film, creates a prince who "could not make up his mind."[50] Elsinore becomes the twisting, moody representation of Hamlet's psyche, a choice that supports the stare. Olivier's Hamlet is typically filmed in long shots, and in some cases extreme long shots, to allow Olivier to move in the space, highlighting his non-normative speech and behaviour. As Francis Bordat notes, "Olivier seems to fear there is not enough cinema in his theatre."[51] Bordat's observation neatly points out the structural importance of the filmic stare to the representation of madness. Olivier takes advantage of the space in a long shot to really move about the space, using it almost as he would a stage. This style is particularly well demonstrated when Olivier's Hamlet talks to Polonius.

The camera follows Hamlet as he walks along, talking to Polonius, but the focus is all on Olivier. He remains the most prominent figure in the frame, and Polonius almost disappears into the lower third, overshadowed by the set and the framing as much as by Olivier himself.

Figure 4.1 Hamlet lounges against a pillar in madness as Polonius looks on

Olivier's film style neatly lines up with the filmic stare; long shots allow us to stare as Hamlet breaks behavioral norms. Olivier marries these long shots with relatively long takes, adding a temporal element to the filmic stare. Staring is an action that takes place over time, whereas fast cutting can obscure the action in the mis-en-scène. The advantage of Olivier's combination of long shot, long take and deep focus is that viewers have the time and space to stare and be sure that they are in fact seeing the aberrant behaviours—breaking verbal scripts, physically abusing Ophelia, the extremes between lounging against pillars and sprinting across sets and upstairs—that add up to a mad Hamlet. Some later productions of *Hamlet*, including Branagh's, imitate the cinematographic combination that Olivier pioneered and used throughout his film. Other adaptations use and combine different cinematographic elements and offer a significantly different construction of the stare.

Olivier does not construct a visual synecdoche for his Hamlet, but his representation of Elsinore as a reflection of Hamlet's psychological reality largely renders moot the need for a visual synecdoche. Additionally, Olivier lacks the added layers of mediation that would come with later *Hamlet*s. Olivier does connect madness with Hamlet in a beautiful transition, however, where the Ghost seems to literally inject the memory of his murder into Hamlet's head. Olivier uses double exposure to show the scene beginning literally in his own head.

The transition and clear-cut connection between the acquisition of the Ghost's knowledge and Hamlet's madness uses classical Hollywood film techniques here in a way that future productions of *Hamlet* do not quite achieve; showing Old Hamlet's murder in flashback became a *Hamlet* trope,

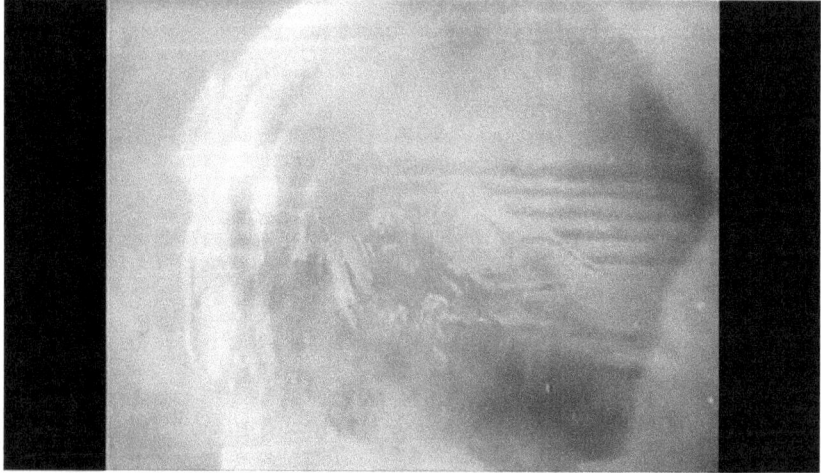

Figure 4.2 A double exposure fade transition between Hamlet speaking to the ghost of his father and the flashback to old Hamlet's death

but the explicit visual connection that Olivier achieves in this transition is mirrored in no other adaptation of *Hamlet*. Future *Hamlet* films do use other methods that facilitate the stare, however; specifically, a mirror.

"You go not till I set you up a glass/ Where you may see the inmost part of you," says Hamlet to Gertrude in the closet scene.[52] The idea that a mirror can reflect something that is inherently invisible and internal encapsulates the challenges of mediating a mental impairment. We cannot see madness with our own eyes, all we can see are the effects of madness. However, mediation—even with something as simple as a mirror—can underline and highlight the mental impairment. Different directors have chosen to mediate madness in different ways, but two trends emerge: the mirror trend and the hypermediation trend. The mirror trend likely originated with the design of Kenneth Branagh's 1996 *Hamlet*: the hall of mirrors is iconic as a set design, but the use of the mirror as the medium for the "To Be or Not to Be" speech also became one of the enduring "anchor images" of the film.[53]

Branagh uses a two-way mirror during this sequence, so we alternate between shots of Branagh in the mirror and reverse shots of Claudius and Polonius watching Hamlet. The mirror and the constant exposure to reflecting surfaces in the film help to create distance and uncertainty. There is a long tradition of using mirrors to distort as well as reflect. Mirrors, like madness, have a performative history in which they simultaneously conceal and reveal. Hamlet's impairment is mental, and his breaks with social norms are primarily (though not exclusively) verbal. Mediating speech through mirrors as well as the camera creates an additional set of images on screen (the image of Hamlet and the image of Hamlet's reflection) that create distance between the viewer and character. Branagh also chooses to begin with a wide shot, and then slowly pushes the camera dolly forward into a medium shot, maintaining the distance necessary for audiences to stare. Branagh's "To Be or Not to Be" also morphs from an objective shot, where we see both Hamlet and his reflection, into a self-reflexive shot, where we are visually aligned with Hamlet. The stage tradition creates an easy diagnosis and even easier explanation for Hamlet's madness: an Oedipus Complex. While I avoid diagnosing Hamlet in a medical context, "diagnosing" the operation of psychoanalytic tropes in a given text is always possible. The mirrors Branagh employs during the closet scene[54] and the "To Be or Not to Be"[55] soliloquy may also allude to Lacan's mirror stage, further creating a self-reflexive stare for Hamlet: Hamlet objectifies and stares at himself, prompting viewers to stare too.

The mirror tradition may have started with Branagh, but Gregory Doran and Michael Almereyda take the tradition and run with it in their respective adaptations of *Hamlet*. Both Almereyda and Doran use and then proceed to break mirrors in their productions of Hamlet, leading to some beautiful shots where characters are reflected and repeated in the broken shards of mirror. Interestingly, both directors break mirrors in the context of Polonius's death. Hawke and Tennant both shoot through mirrors to end Polonius's life, shattering the mirrored image of the actor on the bed with a sobbing Gertrude next to him.

Figure 4.3 Polonius is revealed, shot by Hamlet during the closet scene

The framing and composition choices Almereyda and Doran make closely mirror Hamlet's line to Gertrude in the scene about mirrors reflecting character interiority.[56] As a result of the critical tradition of reading *Hamlet* through an Oedipal or Freudian lens,[57] this line is often treated as an assertion that Hamlet is trying to force his mother to come to terms with her own sexual deviance in marrying her deceased husband's brother. Feminist scholars have resisted these readings, and have read against a psychoanalytic tradition,[58] however Shakespeare gives us relatively little insight into Gertrude's experiences of the events of the play. Gertrude's rationale for marrying Claudius, drinking the poisoned wine—does she know the wine is poisoned? Is she sincere in her celebration of a well-fought match?—and even her thoughts on Hamlet and Ophelia as a couple are omitted from the play text by Shakespeare. *Hamlet* as a play is characterized by what readers, viewers and characters do not know, so Hamlet's assertion that he will set up a mirror and Gertrude—and by extension Hamlet and the reader or viewer—will have some clarity and understanding. But an understanding of what? The play text suggests an understanding of character interiority, which Doran and Almereyda reflect in their choice to frame Polonius' death in mirror shots. By breaking those mirrors, however, both directors subvert Hamlet's intention. Hamlet wants those mirrors to offer clarity and answers; broken mirrors distort the images, and symbolically shatter any hope of finding answers. The shattered mirror as a film trope has also been used to represent a mind that has been "broken," or driven mad, or at least to the point of violence. Hamlet ostensibly sets up the mirror to reflect and reveal Gertrude's interiority, but Doran and Almereyda use the mirror to reflect Hamlet's loss of control and clarity.

Vishal Bhardwaj also includes a mirror in his adaptation of the closet scene in his 2014 film *Haider*, starring Shahid Kapoor as the titular Haider. *Haider* reimagines *Hamlet* in 1995 Kashmir, in which old Hamlet, Hilal Meer, disappears. Much of the first half of the film focuses on Haider's search for Hilal, and once he discovers Hilal's grave, Haider seeks revenge on his mother, Ghazala, and his uncle, Khurram. Ultimately, as both Burnett[59] and Poonam Trivedi[60] note, Ghazala becomes the avenger, not Haider, when she detonates her suicide vest. Bhardwaj sets his adaptation of the closet scene in the snowy, bombed-out wreckage of the Meer family home in Kashmir. As Ghazala crosses the threshold, the camera cuts to a shot of her face reflected twice in a cracked mirror. Haider reveals himself to be already in the house and the camera cuts to a medium shot of Haider before cutting back to the cracked mirror, but this time revealing the twinned reflections of both Ghazala and Haider. Haider is entirely focused on Ghazala, however, commenting, "My two-faced mother. Such innocence on one face, such deceit on the other."[61] Thanks to Bhardwaj's increased focus on Ghazala overall, she does not need her glass set up by Haider, she seeks it out, already looking for answers. This scene is preceded by two scenes with Haider and Ghazala in mirrors. The first is a flashback, where a young Haider kisses his mother while she is getting ready for her day, and the second is a parallel scene where Ghazala is preparing for her wedding to Khurram. Trivedi reads these scenes in the context of the Oedipal relationship between Haider and Ghazala,[62] but in the context of the filmic stare and madness, the mirror takes on a slightly different meaning. Initially cracked by the destruction of the Meer home, the cracked mirror meets its final fate at Haider's hands when he smashes it with a cricket bat before Pervez Lone—Polonius—arrives at the house. This goes beyond the reflection of Hamlet's loss of clarity and control that Doran and Almereyda set up in their closet scenes, this is Haider actively destroying clarity and control. Burnett also positions Haider and Ghazala's relationship as one that "must be repeatedly negotiated,"[63] and the breaking of the mirror, the symbol of that relationship, suggests a refusal to renegotiate again. It is difficult to separate Haider's madness from his relationship with Ghazala because, as Rachel Saltz notes, "Ghazala has such depths and mystery that she hijacks the movie, pushing Haider (Hamlet) to the sidelines in his own story."[64] However, some performative aspects of Haider's madness can be separated out and analyzed using the filmic stare.

The best example of the filmic stare in *Haider* comes when Haider is protesting in front of a crowd at the Lal Chowk intersection—one of the invocations of "To Be or Not to Be" in Bhardwaj's film.[65] The scene is composed of a combination of wide and plan américain shots, with medium close-up shots peppered in. The overall feeling of this scene is of frantic motion, and that sense comes from a combination of Shahid Kapoor's physical actions and the camera movement. The wide and medium shots allow Kapoor to move and be physically active, even as the camera itself is relatively static. The plan américain shots also tend to be low angle shots in this scene, conferring a sense of authority to Haider through his errant behavior. He might be politically powerless compared to Khurram, but by publicly breaking social behavioural and verbal scripts, Haider forces Khurram and the crowd surrounding him to take notice and react rather than act. Forcing Khurram to react confers a sense of authority and power to Haider, mirroring Neely's textual reading of Ophelia's "distracted" language speaking truth to power[66] but through visual rather than written language. The medium close-up and close-up shots of Haider's face, however, are almost always captured by a camera in motion, so that even without the visual of Haider's body moving through space, the sense of motion is unbroken, and in fact builds throughout the scene as the editing grows increasingly rapid and Haider engages the crowd in rhythmic clapping and chanting.

The frenetic movement of both Haider and the camera is in direct contrast to the shots of Khurram in this scene. Always framed in medium or medium close-up shots with a static, still camera (in contrast to the jerky handheld camera shots framing Haider) Khurram is visually separated from Haider and Haider's madness and the visual separation heightens the contrast between filmic stare and non-filmic stare moments. The interplay between the filmic stare's use of a handheld camera and frenetic editing for Haider and still shots of Khurram comes to a head near the end of her scene when both men are framed in a low-angle two shot with a handheld camera and perhaps a very slight Dutch angle. Both men are vying for authority here, but Haider ultimately acquiesces to Khurram, which is reflected in subsequent shots that are framed using the style associated with Khurram in the scene. The camera work, editing and performances all work together here to highlight the differences between Haider's madness and Khurram, subtly but insistently invoking a disability aesthetic as well as the political overtones of the scene.

While less politically fraught that Bhardwaj's *Haider*, Almereyda's *Hamlet* uses a substantially truncated text, as well as media and mediation to highlight Hamlet's madness and to privilege audio-visual media. The audience's introduction to Almereyda's Hamlet is as young man filming reporters at a press conference. For the rest of the film, Hamlet is associated with a high-tech (for 2000) world, cluttered with phones, computers, televisions, cameras, camcorders, film, editing equipment, security footage, and even physical media, including photographs, and what appears to be pages torn from books and magazines, and newspaper clippings. Bolter and Grusin note that in Classical Hollywood film, "hypermediacy is equated with dreams, mental disorder, or insanity."[67] Almereyda stuffs each frame with so many forms of media that viewers cannot help but notice that this *Hamlet* is all about technology and mediation. To that end, the visual synecdoche that becomes representative of Hawke's Hamlet is his camcorder. Hamlet himself is fragmented in this film in many shots, particularly the ones where we see him playing with his camcorder and editing material. Hamlet's hands and fingers are in frame, along with at least two screens, and various editing equipment.

Hawke is fragmented by not just the camera Almereyda is using to shoot his *Hamlet*, but also by Hamlet's own camera. The "To Be or Not to Be" section is particularly enlightening, because Hamlet is editing images of himself holding a gun to his head and reciting a speech famous for laying out the pros and cons of suicide. Hamlet's fragmented and repeated images could "not be" simply by turning off the screens. Interestingly, the speech itself appears to be coming from the image of Hamlet on the monitor, not from the actor in the frame or a traditional voiceover track. These scenes, and the shots of Hamlet's hand manipulating his camcorder, turn into his visual synecdoche for the audience. The extreme close-up as a visual synecdoche for Hamlet is unique to Almereyda's film. Previous *Hamlet*s use space in combination with breaking social and behavioural scripts to construct a visual representation of madness. Hawke's synecdoche, however, is hyper-focused on the single thing his Hamlet does have control over: mediation. This synecdoche creates tension between the artistic control Hamlet has over his own film—*The Mousetrap*—and the complete lack of control the character has over the events of the wider film, as represented by hypermediacy in the frame. This strategy is successful in separating itself from the Olivier tradition of visually representing madness, and Almereyda updates the Classical Hollywood technique of visually representing madness for a technologically savvy generation of viewers by packing the frame with media and technology.

Because of the focus on media, we get relatively few long shots, and much more fragmentation of Hamlet, leading to a unique construction of the stare. The long shots we do get are often buried under layers of mediation. For example, when Hamlet is talking to Polonius, their conversation is recorded by a security camera. We see their conversation on the screen as the camera records a bank of security monitors. The high angle long shot is canted, and the wide-angle lens of the security camera distorts perspective, producing a shot that suggests more than a few things are rotten in the state of Denmark. Ethan Hawke in this scene is a jumpy, on-edge Hamlet, who is revealed to have a half-cocked plan to shoot Claudius in his office. The shot angle and distance itself would have encouraged the audience to stare at Hamlet. By adding the extra layer of mediation, canted angle and distorted perspective, the film explicitly suggests that Hamlet is mentally impaired in some way. The additional layers of mediation also quietly allude to Hamlet's visual synecdoche, keeping viewers staring.

Particularly in Almereyda's *Hamlet*, the visual tends to overshadow the verbal, accentuated by hypermediation, and focus on families in a corporate structure of the film. Akira Kurosawa highlighted the corporatism of post-World War II Japan in his *Hamlet* adaptation, *The Bad Sleep Well* (1960). Rather than focusing on the madness of his Hamlet—Nishi, played by Toshiro Mifune—however, Kurosawa positions Nishi as possibly the only sane figure in a corporatized system that is almost designed to make those who are embroiled in it mad. This is highlighted by the fact that Nishi's father was driven to commit suicide by Vice President Iwabuchi, the film's Claudius figure. In addition, Nishi uses Wada, a disillusioned member of Public Corp to help drive Contract Officer Shirai mad to try to expose the toxic business practices that Iwabuchi is engaged in. As a result, one of the characters who highlights the disability aesthetic through the filmic stare in *The Bad Sleep Well* is not Nishi, but Shirai—a character with no clear analogue in *Hamlet*.[68]

Though clearly a result of the toxic corporate environment Kurosawa represents, Shirai's madness is highly medicalized. Throughout the film, various characters diagnose Shirai with a "nervous breakdown," "paranoia," and "acute schizophrenia" respectively, very clearly positioning Shirai's problems as individual and medical to deflect madness away from the corporate system and absolve executives of any responsibility in the (lack of) well-being of their employees. After Shirai begins experiencing madness, he is typically represented in wide and medium shots, with the occasional close-up to highlight his staring eyes. The eyes in close-up function as Shirai's visual synecdoche, and while he does not often explicitly break verbal or social scripts in those wide and medium shots, they certainly serve to visually isolate him in his madness.

Across *Hamlet* adaptations, there is a spectrum of madness in performance. Some actors, like Laurence Olivier, Kenneth Branagh, David Tennant, Shahid Kapoor, Purba Rygel, and Ethan Hawke, play a more clearly mad Hamlet, whereas Mel Gibson and Innokenty Smoktunovsky play Hamlet as more subtly mad. These variations on madness, despite the levels of subtlety the actor employs, can all still be explored through the filmic stare.

Zeffirelli's 1990 adaptation of *Hamlet* positions the family drama front and center and tends to reinforce the emphasis on the family drama by putting most scenes in private settings. Most of Hamlet's madness is exercised in relatively private spaces, the most significant exception being the play-within-a-play scene. While the entire court is present to watch the play, Zeffirelli endeavors to maintain the sense of an intimate family drama by relying on close-up shots of the royal family. However, after Claudius flees the room, the camera pulls back from intimate close-ups and moves to wide shots so that Gibson can cavort about the space, occasionally laughing boisterously and playing with the actors and musicians. This is where we see Gibson's Hamlet crack his careful, measured façade and really allow his madness free rein. However, in this scene and its immediate aftermath, the camera itself is fairly static, and Gibson and the other actors in the mise-en-scene provide the majority of the motion.

In contrast, when Hamlet and Ophelia are together before Gibson's "To Be or Not to Be" speech, Hamlet is at his most animatedly mad, and the camera reflects and amplifies Hamlet's madness by being extremely mobile and doing much of the heavy lifting for Gibson in terms of representing madness. Zeffirelli uses relatively long takes in this scene, allowing the camera to push in and out organically as Gibson moves through the space and circles Ophelia almost a full three-hundred and sixty degrees with the camera following him around her. The effect is a scene that feels frenetic, dangerous, and somewhat queasy, representing Hamlet's internal turmoil. Gibson's performance in this scene also feels somewhat shackled, as though his Hamlet is unable to express his madness effectively, and therefore the mobile camera communicates the motion and violence of Hamlet's anger and madness in the scene without Gibson yelling and screaming a la Branagh or Rygel. However, Zeffirelli owes a debt to

Olivier's version of this same scene, as the use of the stairwell and the various levels in the scene also help communicate the rise and fall of the emotional beats of the scene in addition to the wide shots and relatively longer takes. Olivier's camera was nowhere near as mobile as Zeffirelli's, but the effect of the use of the wide shots and camera movement is to highlight Hamlet's madness in this scene in a way that the viewers feel in the pit of their stomachs.

When Gibson's Hamlet interacts with Polonius in the library, however, the style of the filmic stare is slightly more traditional in that it is primarily composed of medium-wide shots that reveal the "madness signal" of Hamlet wearing only one boot. Because Hamlet is perched atop a series of bookshelves in this scene, many of the shots of Hamlet are low angle shots, reinforcing that even in madness, Hamlet is a more able wordsmith than Polonius, and, in Gibson's case, a more physically able figure as well, since he slowly and deliberately knocks Polonius off a ladder during their conversation. The filmic stare supports the sense uncertainty that comes from Hamlet very calmly and collectedly breaking with social and behavioural scripts because Gibson is extremely subdued in this scene, and the tension between his physical ablebodiedness and Hamlet's madness is palpable in his performance. It takes a specific level of physical ability to slowly knock someone off a ladder, and the combination of a physically abled and martial Hamlet who is also mad adds to the tension of this scene and contributes to the overall tension of the film. Even wearing a single boot while sitting quietly in a library, Gibson's Hamlet is physically imposing. The filmic stare helps to highlight the combination of the physicality of the actor with the madness inherent in the hypotext to lead to a Hamlet who is threatening not simply because he breaks social and behavioural scripts, but because he will break social and behavioural scripts and has the physical ability to do so in a way that could physically damage other humans. Hamlet's interactions with Polonius in this scene, read through the filmic stare, reveals an inherent tension that makes this relatively subdued Hamlet just as intimidating, if not more so, than Hamlets who are less physically imposing or actively subdue their own physicality.

Innokenty Smoktunovsky (*Hamlet*, 1964) also plays a relatively subdued Hamlet in terms of physicality and overt breaking of social scripts, but Grigori Kozintsev works with Smoktunovsky to create an aural rather than a visual synecdoche for his Hamlet. In terms of the composition of the overall film, Kozintsev and Olivier are similar in their extensive use of wide shots generally, and relatively static cameras. Additionally, Kozintsev and Olivier favor a castle by the sea for their Hamlets and use the imagery of crashing water and waves to help visually reflect the emotional and mental state of the character; particularly during their "To Be or Not to Be" speeches. However, what really serves to nail down this Hamlet's madness is the use of sound in concert with the filmic stare.

The first sign of Smoktunovsky's madness comes when the players arrive at Elsinore, and Smoktunovsky is delivering the "Oh what a rogue and peasant slave am I" soliloquy. This Hamlet is perched on a wagon and has his arm around a drum that he slowly and initially a-rhythmically begins to beat over the course of the speech, until his frustration grows to the point of yelling. However, it is the diegetic sound of the drum that begins to set up the aural synecdoche that will accompany Hamlet's madness, so viewers are prepared when the aural cues really take off during the closet scene. It is a fairly standard trope in Hamlet adaptations that when the ghost appears in the closet scene, there is usually—not always, but usually—a subjective POV shot to show that Hamlet can see the ghost. We also occasionally get subjective POV shots to underline the fact that Gertrude cannot see the ghost, but directors are often willing to let Gertrude's lines speak to the fact that she cannot see the ghost. Kozintsev omits any visual of the ghost in the closet scene entirely; even Feng Xiaogang in *The Banquet* includes "a chainmailed carapace that is empathically occupied"[69] to the point that the armor of Wu Lan's (Hamlet's) father originates a subjective POV shot. Kozintsev does not give the viewer even that much in his closet scene, instead allowing a leitmotif of descending horn notes that is associated with the ghost early in the film to fill Hamlet's ears and distract him from berating Gertrude. The horn notes in the closet scene are clearly diegetic (as were the drumbeats under the "Rogue and Peasant Slave" soliloquy) but function the same way as subjective POV shots do for other Hamlets to establish that Hamlet can hear the notes, but Gertrude cannot. The sound is part of Hamlet's subjective experience of his father's ghost and replaces the visual of the ghost appearing in the room. The aural synecdoche representing this Hamlet's madness is reinforced by the voice over of Hamlet's giggles as he drags Polonius's body out of Gertrude's room. The sound is played over shots of different locations in the castle, suggesting that the sound is reverberating throughout Elsinore. Finally, the voice of the ghost prompts Hamlet to remember him as Hamlet is aboard a ship bound for England.

The repetition of Hamlet's madness being associated with sound creates a stark contrast with the otherwise fairly reserved and subdued figure on the screen. The aural synecdoche is supported using medium and wide shots when we hear either Hamlet's giggles, drumbeats, or the voice or leitmotif of the ghost. In the context of the filmic stare, an aural synecdoche rather than a visual one helps to highlight the invisibility of madness—and mental disabilities and illnesses in general—in a primarily visual medium. For Smoktunovsky, the medium and wide shots that normally give an actor space to break verbal and behavioural norms instead allow the aurality of the synecdoche representing his madness to metaphorically fill the space. Filling space with sound to represent madness will be revisited in my discussion of Ophelia later in the chapter, but it is interesting to note that Kozintsev's *Hamlet* employs an aural rather than a visual synecdoche.

In 2006, two Chinese cinema adaptations of *Hamlet* were released: Sherwood Hu's *Prince of the Himalayas*, and Feng Xiaogang's *The Banquet*. The two films are often discussed together, despite their stylistic differences, as they both highlight the family dysfunction at the center of the *Hamlet* story and center on the female characters.[70] *The Banquet* centers on Empress Wan

(Gertrude) and the tension between her past love affair with Wu Lan (Hamlet), her stepson by her marriage to Emperor Li (Claudius). Empress Wan, like Ghazala in *Haider*, is very much the center of the film, to the point where madness—in both Wu Lan and Qing Nu (Ophelia)—is entirely omitted from the film. Wu Lan is passive and angsty, but he lacks madness, either real or feigned. Similarly, Qing Nu is emotionally distraught at times in the film, and her insistence on performing a tribute to Wu Lan before her accidental death by poisoning is perhaps politically misguided, but it is controlled and intentional, not inspired by madness. Even compared to the subtly mad Hamlets performed by Gibson and Smoktunovsky, Wu Lan and Qing Nu do not represent madness and do not invoke the disability aesthetic that is present in other *Hamlet* adaptations.

The lack of madness and disability aesthetic is particularly interesting in the context of, to borrow a phrase from Burnett, the "erotically freighted" Empress Wan and the chastity of Qing Nu.[71] While Burnett notes that "romances prevented or unconsummated have become a staple of Asian Shakespearean cinemas,"[72] it is also worth addressing the asexual objectification that Garland-Thomson identifies as a key element of staring at disabled bodies.[73] While madness is inherently invisible, and therefore can subvert that asexual objectification to some degree, madness represented on screen can still evoke a visceral reaction, as highlighted by Siebers's definition of aesthetics as tracking "the sensations that some bodies feel in the presence of other bodies."[74] Therefore, given that Xiaogang is clearly trying to highlight a female-centric sense of female sexuality, removing disability from the narrative erases both the disabled body and mind as well as the potential pitfalls of disability aesthetics and asexual objectification from the screen. The erasure of disability from *The Banquet* highlights not only a continued discomfort with representations of disability in general, but also Siebers's assertion that "disability is the master trope of human disqualification [...] because all oppressive systems function by reducing human variations to deviancy and inferiority defined on the mental and physical plane."[75] In the specific case of *The Banquet*, disability itself was disqualified, likely because of a perception that sexuality and disability cannot exist in the same space, thereby disqualifying both Qing Nu and Wu Lan from representing madness.

In contrast to the disability erasure in *The Banquet*, *Prince of the Himalayas* retains the madness from its hypotext. Hu situates the narrative in ancient Tibet and interpolates a backstory for Nanm (Gertrude) and Kulo-ngam (Claudius) that involves an extramarital affair and the family secret that Lhamoklodan (Hamlet) is not the son of Old King Tsanpo (Old Hamlet/Ghost), but rather the son of Kulo-ngam. *Prince of the Himalayas* also includes a son for Lhamoklodan and Odsaluyang (Ophelia), and a redemptive rather than vengeful arc for Lhamoklodan. Even with all these changes from the hypotext, however, Lhamoklodan maintains the disability aesthetic that is baked into *Hamlet*.

"My life is in danger. Be not surprised if I act strangely,"[76] says Lhamoklodan (played by Purba Rgyal) to Horshu (Horatio), during Nanm and Kulo-ngam's wedding. As with Hamlets from Kozintsev to Zeffirelli to Branagh, the impulse is to ask if Hu's Hamlet is truly mad or feigning madness, and as with all those Hamlets, the representation is what matters more than the legitimacy of madness in the context of the filmic stare. However, despite the multiplicity of narrative that Burnett notes in *Prince of the Himalayas*,[77] Lhamoklodan's madness has relatively minimal screen time, and he lacks an overarching synecdoche—visual or aural—to represent his madness. The lack of a synecdoche may account for the seeming elision of representations of madness and grief throughout the film. Lhamoklodan breaks verbal scripts in medium shots when addressing Polonius, but otherwise he resembles Gibson and Smoktunovsky's rather more subdued Hamlets in his interaction with Polonius. After leaving Polonius, Lhamoklodan becomes more animated in his breaking of social and behavioural scripts when he runs through the village, shedding garments as he goes and almost mischievously grabbing pelts from traders as he passes. These interactions are primarily framed as wide shots which allow for the maximum space for Rgyal to represent madness on the screen.

A similar set of wide shots are used when Lhamoklodan rejects Odsaluyang (Ophelia). Odsaluyang's lines are mostly filmed in close-up to capture her anguish at Lhamoklodan's madness, but these are intercut with wide and extreme wide shots of Lhamoklodan gamboling about and gesticulating wildly. These shots, and the relatively quick editing between them, recall the same scene in Olivier's Hamlet, but without the deep connection between Elsinore and Hamlet's psyche or a synecdoche to create any kind of continuity or distinction between scenes where Lhamoklodan is representing madness and scenes where Lhamoklodan is overcome with grief (or other strong emotions). It would be easy to say that the blurred line between these two states simply enhances the disability aesthetic of the film, but it is important not to pathologize normal, healthy emotions like grief at the death of loved ones. Because the film elides these states of being where Lhamoklodan is concerned, his self-harm in the closet scene seems abrupt and slightly out of character.

Hu's closet scene begins with Nanm reflected in her mirror, but Lhamoklodan pulls her away from the mirror rather than using the mirror in an extended way, as other *Hamlet* adaptations do. The scene also breaks with the tradition of providing the Hamlet figure with POV shots to establish that he can see the ghost, but the Gertrude figure cannot. Hu changes the lighting in the scene when the ghost appears but does not clarify visually that only Lhamoklodan can see the ghost, preferring to let Nanm's dialogue suggest that she cannot see the ghost while leaving ambiguous whether or not she notices the change in lighting that came with the ghost's presence. Like *The Banquet*, however, the ghost has a POV shot during this scene, looking at Lhamoklodan, meeting his eyes to ensure that his message gets through. The privileging of the ghost's POV over Lhamoklodan's and the immediate shift after Polonius's death and Lhamoklodan's attempt at self-harm to Nanm's and Kulo-ngam's fear for their son's life serves to highlight that Lhamoklodan the individual is not the main focus of this *Hamlet* adaptation, but rather the family unit and romance take precedence. As a result, Lhamoklodan's madness is almost an incidental inheritance from the hypotext. It is a factor in the family turbulence, but not the focus of the narrative, which may explain the overall slipperiness of the representation.

Taken together, these global film adaptations of *Hamlet* reveal that the disability aesthetic inherent to the original Shakespearean text is inherited to varying degrees through adaptation. However, they also demonstrate that while the filmic stare is flexible enough to allow some variation—the aural synecdoche of Kozintsev's *Hamlet* as opposed to a visual one, for example—it is nonetheless a pervasive, and likely unconsciously implemented, framework that can be observed across a multitude of genres, cultures, and periods. The filmic stare also allows scholarship to move beyond the purely linguistic in disability studies and allow the medium of film to add its own unique take to an overarching disability aesthetic that encompasses both language and the visual. It also reveals the palimpcestuous nature of madness as a convention of the revenge tragedy genre. Even when *Hamlet* is transposed to generic contexts beyond the early modern conception of the revenge tragedy, madness nonetheless haunts the narrative.

My discussion of madness in this chapter has focused mostly on Hamlet figures, and my discussion of Ophelia figures will occur in Chapter 5.[78] However, these two discussions are deeply connected and inform each other as well as the argument that the filmic stare is egalitarian in how it represents male and female madness on screen. Like the many Hamlets discussed in this chapter, film adaptations of Ophelia tend to be framed in wide and medium shots after they go mad. They also experience subjective realities that are often shared with the viewers, and feature synecdoches that represent madness. However, where Hamlets are largely free of the impact of the male gaze, the male gaze and the filmic stare interact and sometimes exist in the same space where Ophelia is concerned.

Notes

1 Siebers, Tobin. *Disability Aesthetics*. Ann Arbor: University of Michigan Press. 2010. 3.
2 Berger, Ronald J. *Introducing Disability Studies*. New York: Lynne Rienner. 2013. 5.
3 Neely, Carol Thomas. *Distracted Subjects: Madness and Gender in Shakespeare and Early Modern Culture*. Ithaca, NY: Cornell UP. 2004. 3.
4 Lofts, Sonya Freeman and Lisa Ulevich. "Obsession/Rationality/Agency: Autistic Shakespeare." *Disability, Health and Happiness in the Shakespearean Body*. Ed. Sujata Iyengar. New York: Routledge. 2015.
5 Lofts, 58.
6 Lofts, 59.
7 For more detail on the various "Diseases of the Head," please see Burton, Robert. "Part 1, Section 1, Member 1, Subsections 3–5." *The Anatomy of Melancholy*. Ed. Floyd Dell and Paul Jordan-Smith. New York: Tudor Publishing Co. 1927.
8 Burton, Robert. "Part One, Member 1, Subsections 1–5; Part One, Member 3, Subsections 1–3; Part One, Member 2, Subsection 1; Part One, Section 2, Member 3, Subsections 1–10." *The Anatomy of Melancholy*, 120.
9 Burton, 121.

10 Burton, 148. Gail Kern Paster explores humoral theory and pre-Cartesian ideas of the body and emotion in her book, *Humoring the Body: Emotions and the Shakespearean Stage* (Chicago: Chicago UP. 2004).

11 Fifth edition of *Diagnostic and Statistical Manual of Mental Disorders*, the benchmark text used in psychology to diagnose mental illness (Published by the American Psychiatric Association, 2013).

12 Neely, 51.

13 Neely, 54.

14 Neely, 2.

15 *Hamlet*, 3.1.5.

16 *Hamlet*, 5.2.229–30.

17 Neely, 53–4.

18 *Hamlet*, 4.7.166–83.

19 *Hamlet*, 2.2.192.

20 Woodbridge, Linda. *English Revenge Drama: Money, Resistance, Equality*. New York: Cambridge UP: 2010. 41–3.

21 Woodbridge, 42.

22 Woodbridge, 43.

23 Hamlet, 4.3.1–11.

24 Berger, 5.

25 Hutcheon Linda. *A Theory of Adaptation*. 2nd ed. New York: Routledge. 2013. 6.

26 Hutcheon, 6, 21.

27 Bolter, Jay David and Richard Grusin. *Remediation: Understanding New Media*. Cambridge, MA: MIT Press, 2000. 6.

28 Hutcheon, 8.

29 Crowl, Samuel. *Shakespeare and Film*. New York: WW Norton and Co. 2008. 132.

30 Altman, Rick. "Reusable Packaging: Generic Products and the Recycling Process." *Refiguring American Film Genres: History and Theory*. Ed. Nick Browne. Berkeley: University of California Press. 1998. 1–41. 11, 9.

31 Siebers, *Disability Aesthetics*, 19.

32 Hallet and Hallet, qtd. in Row-Heyveld, Lindsey. "Antic Dispositions: Mental and Intellectual Disabilities in Early Modern Revenge Tragedy." *Recovering Disability in Early Modern England*. Ed. Allison P. Hobgood and David Houston Wood. Columbus: Ohio State UP. 2013. 73–87. 73.

33 Row-Heyveld, 75.

34 See Row-Heyveld for additional material regarding Bedlam. See also Michael MacDonald's *Mystical Bedlam* (Cambridge: Cambridge UP. 1981), and Ken Jackson's *Separate Theatres* (Newark: University of Delaware UP. 2005).

35 *OED*, 'bedlam' 2.

36 Row-Heyveld, 74.

37 Row-Heyveld, 74.

38 Woodbridge, 15.

39 Woodbridge, 12.

40 The logical arguments for why Hamlet's behaviour is excusable are eerily similar, for example, to the DC Universe's explanations and excuses for Batman's actions. Batman's childhood trauma explains his vigilante quest to rid Gotham of a rogues' gallery that literally stems from an insane asylum. Batman's instantly visible and gratifying application of justice excuses his actions because the corruption of Gotham's legal and political systems is well-known, and powerless individuals and subaltern figures only receive justice when Batman literally punches villains in the face. Hamlet experiences the trauma of a lost parent and is both victim and vigilante. Cinematic adaptations of Hamlet as a victim and vigilante ultimately perish with Claudius, creating commercially acceptable representations of madness and revenge as well as justice.

41 Row-Heyveld, 81–2.
42 Rosemarie Garland-Thomson's *Staring: How We Look* (2009), and *Extraordinary Bodies: Figuring Physical Disability in American Culture and Literature* (1997) expand on the process through which staring went from a public event to a taboo.
43 *Hamlet*, 2.2.392–3.
44 For in-depth discussions about adapting Shakespeare to film, see Crowl, Samuel. *Shakespeare and Film* (New York: WW Norton and Co. 2008), Fischlin, Daniel, ed. *OuterSpeares: Shakespeare, Intermedia, and the Limits of Adaptation* (Toronto: University of Toronto Press. 2014), Hatchuel, Sarah. *Shakespeare from Stage to Screen* (New York: Cambridge UP. 2004), Jackson, Russell. *Shakespeare Films in the Making: Vision, Production and Reception* (Cambridge: Cambridge UP. 2007), Jorgens, Jack. *Shakespeare on Film* (Bloomington: Indiana UP. 1943), Lanier, Douglas. "Recasting the Plays: Homage, Adaptation, Parody" (*Shakespeare and Modern Popular Culture*. Oxford: Oxford UP. 2002), Sanders, Julie. *Adaptation and Appropriation* (London: Routledge. 2006), Hutcheon, Linda. *A Theory of Adaptation* (2nd ed. New York: Routledge. 2013).
45 Taylor, Gary. "Shakespeare Plays on Renaissance Stages." *The Cambridge Companion to Shakespeare on Stage*. Ed. Stanley Wells and Sarah Stanton. Cambridge: Cambridge UP. 2002. 2, 4.
46 See Lennard Davies, Ronald Berger, Robert Burton and Tom Shakespeare.
47 *Hamlet*, 1.5.171–2.
48 Siebers, *Disability Aesthetics*, 2–3.
49 These scenes fall in different places in films; in the text these scenes are as follows: Act 2, scene ii (play-within-a-play), Act 3, scene iv (closet scene), and Act 2, scene ii (Polonius questions Hamlet).
50 *Hamlet*. Dir. Laurence Olivier. Perf. Laurence Olivier. Universal-International. 1948.
51 Qtd. in Hatchuel, Sarah. *Shakespeare from Stage to Screen*. New York: Cambridge UP. 2004. 20.
52 *Hamlet*, 3.4.19–20.
53 Branagh, qtd. in Crowl, Samuel. *The Films of Kenneth Branagh*. Connecticut: Praeger. 2006. 141.
54 *Hamlet*, 3.4.
55 *Hamlet*, 3.1.
56 *Hamlet*, 3.4.19–20.
57 Thomson, Anne and Neil Taylor. "Introduction." *The Arden Shakespeare: Hamlet*. 3rd Ed. Arden: London. 2006. 29.
58 Thomson, 34.
59 Burnett, Mark Thornton. *Hamlet and World Cinema*. Cambridge: Cambridge UP. 2019. 173.
60 Trivedi, Poonam. "Woman as Avenger: 'Indianising' the Shakespearean Tragic in the Films of Vishal Bhardwaj." *Shakespeare and Indian Cinemas: 'Local Habitations'*. Ed. Poonam Trivedi and Paromita Chakravarti. New York: Routledge. 2019. 41.
61 *Haider*. Dir. Vishal Bhardwaj. Perf. Tabu, Shahid Kapoor, Irrfan Khan. UTV Motion Fictures. 2014.
62 Trivedi, 39.
63 Burnett, *Hamlet and World Cinema*, 172.
64 Saltz, Rachel. "Shakespearean Revenge in a Violent Kashmir." *The New York Times*. October 2, 2014.
65 Burnett, *Hamlet and World Cinema*, 169.
66 Neely, Carol Thomas. "Feminist Modes of Shakespearean Criticism: Compensatory, Justificatory, Transformational." *Women's Studies: An Interdisciplinary Journal*, 9.1 (1981): 3–15. 6.

67 Bolter and Grusin, 152. See also my discussion of Scottie (Hitchcock's *Vertigo*) in Chapter 1 for a more-in-depth explanation of hypermediacy in Classical Hollywood.
68 Yoshiko, Kurosawa's Ophelia figure from *The Bad Sleep Well*, also embodies a disability aesthetic in the film. However, as her impairment is orthopedic and therefore a physical rather than a mental disability, I will discuss her in Chapter 2, with other characters who have physical disabilities.
69 Burnett, *Shakespeare and World Cinema*, 129.
70 Burnett, *Hamlet and World Cinema*, 124.
71 Burnett, *Hamlet and World Cinema*, 139–40.
72 Burnett, *Hamlet and World Cinema*, 140.
73 Garland-Thomson, *Extraordinary Bodies*, 9–10.
74 Siebers, *Disability Aesthetics*, 1.
75 Siebers, *Disability Aesthetics*, 27.
76 *Prince of the Himalayas*. Dir. Sherwood Hu. Perf. Purba Rgyal, Dobrgyal, Zomskyid, and Sonamdolgar. Global Genesis Group. 2006.
77 Burnett, *Shakespeare and World Cinema*, 131.
78 My discussion of male and female madness in *Hamlet* is divided into two chapters purely for length reasons. Given the number of film adaptations covered and the number of pertinent scenes in each adaptation, it made sense to divide the discussion between Hamlet and Ophelia. The division also allows me to address Neely here, and the interaction of the filmic stare and the male gaze in Chapter 5.

Bibliography

Altman, Rick. "Reusable Packaging: Generic Products and the Recycling Process." *Refiguring American Film Genres: History and Theory*. Ed. Nick Browne. Berkeley: University of California Press. 1998. 1–41.
Berger, Ronald J. *Introducing Disability Studies*. New York: Lynne Rienner. 2013.
Bolter, Jay David and Richard Grusin. *Remediation: Understanding New Media*. London: MIT Press. 2000.
Burnett, Mark Thornton. *Shakespeare and World Cinema*. Cambridge: Cambridge UP. 2013.
Burnett, Mark Thornton. *Hamlet and World Cinema*. Cambridge: Cambridge UP. 2019.
Burton, Robert. *The Anatomy of Melancholy*. Ed. Floyd Dell and Paul Jordan-Smith. New York: Tudor Publishing Co. 1927.
Crowl, Samuel. *The Films of Kenneth Branagh*. Connecticut: Praeger. 2006.
Crowl, Samuel. *Shakespeare and Film*. New York: WW Norton and Co. 2008.
Garland-Thomson, Rosemarie. *Extraordinary Bodies: Figuring Physical Disability in American Culture and Literature*. New York: Columbia UP. 1997.
Garland-Thomson, Rosemarie. *Staring: How We Look*. New York: Oxford UP. 2009.
Haider. Dir. Vishal Bhardwaj. Perf. Tabu, Shahid Kapoor, Irrfan Khan. UTV Motion Pictures. 2014.
Hamlet. Dir. Laurence Olivier. Perf. Laurence Olivier. Universal-International. 1948.
Hamlet. Dir. Grigori Kozintsev. Perf. Innokenty Smoktunovsky, Mikhail Nazvanov, Elze Radzinya, Anastasiya Vertinskaya. Lenfilm. 1964.
Hamlet. Dir. Franco Zeffirelli. Perf. Mel Gibson, Glenn Close. Warner Bros. 1990.
Hamlet. Dir. Kenneth Branagh. Perf. Kenneth Branagh, Jack Lemon, Julie Christie, Derek Jacobi. Renaissance Films. 1996.
Hamlet. Dir. Michael Almereyda. Perf. Ethan Hawk. Buena Vista Pictures. 2000.

"Hamlet." Dir. Gregory Doran. Perf. David Tennant, Patrick Stewart. The Royal Shakespeare Company Production. 2009.

Hatchuel, Sarah. *Shakespeare from Stage to Screen.* New York: Cambridge UP. 2004.

Hutcheon, Linda. *A Theory of Adaptation.* 2nd ed. New York: Routledge. 2013.

Iyengar, Sujata, ed. *Disability, Health and Happiness in the Shakespearean Body.* New York: Routledge. 2014.

Neely, Carol Thomas. "Feminist Modes of Shakespearean Criticism: Compensatory, Justificatory, Transformational." *Women's Studies: An Interdisciplinary Journal,* 9. 1 (1981): 3–15.

Neely, Carol Thomas. *Distracted Subjects: Madness and Gender in Shakespeare and Early Modern Culture.* Ithaca, NY: Cornell UP. 2004.

Prince of the Himalayas. Dir. Sherwood Hu. Perf. Purba Rgyal, Dobrgyal, Zomskyid, Sonamdolgar. Global Genesis Group. 2006.

Row-Heyveld, Lindsey. "Antic Dispositions: Mental and Intellectual Disabilities in Early Modern Revenge Tragedy." *Recovering Disability in Early Modern England.* Ed. Allison P. Hobgood and David Houston Wood. Columbus: Ohio State UP. 2013. 73–87.

Saltz, Rachel. "Shakespearean Revenge in a Violent Kashmir." *The New York Times.* October 2,2014.

Siebers, Tobin, *Disability Aesthetics.* Ann Arbor: University of Michigan Press. 2010.

Taylor, Gary. "Shakespeare Plays on Renaissance Stages." *The Cambridge Companion to Shakespeare on Stage.* Ed. Stanley Wells and Sarah Stanton. Cambridge: Cambridge UP. 2002.

The Bad Sleep Well. Dir. AkiraKurosawa. Perf. ToshiroMifune, MasayukiMori, KyōkoKagawa. Toho. 1960.

The Banquet. Dir. Feng Xiaogang. Perf. Zhang Ziyi, Ge You, Daniel Wu. Huayi Brothers Media Asia Films. 2006.

Thomson, Anne and Neil Taylor. "Introduction." *The Arden Shakespeare: Hamlet.* 3rd ed. London: Arden. 2006.

Trivedi, Poonam. "Woman as Avenger: 'Indianising' the Shakespearean Tragic in the Films of Vishal Bhardwaj." *Shakespeare and Indian Cinemas: 'Local Habitations'.* Ed. Poonam Trivedi and Paromita Chakravarti. New York: Routledge. 2019.

Woodbridge, Linda. *English Revenge Drama: Money, Resistance, Equality.* New York: Cambridge UP. 2010.

5 Madness, the Filmic Stare, and Ophelia

Historically, Laura Mulvey's male gaze—and, by extension, feminist psycho-analytic theory—was one of the dominant critical paradigms for analyzing the representation of Shakespearean women in film. When exploring Ophelia's representations onscreen through a disability studies lens, however, the con-flicts between an aesthetic approach and a sociological approach reveal them-selves. Both Lady Macbeth and Ophelia have been decried as inaccurate and harmful representations of mental illness.[1] In medical and sociological circles, the idea of hysteria and female-specific mental illness is regarded as harmful.[2] It is useful here to briefly clarify and categorize my terms. I use the sociological approach as an umbrella term to encompass and describe the data-driven, real-world focused methodologies in those hard and social science and specifically medical subfields of disability studies. These are the double-blind controlled studies, the surveys, the medical records and case studies, and self-reported patient outcomes that are used by doctors, individuals with disabilities, advo-cates, and lawmakers to write legislation, develop treatments or prostheses, and to advocate for access and inclusion. Conversely, the aesthetic approach describes the close reading and interpretive methodologies of the literature and film sub-fields of disability studies, and dovetails with Tobin Siebers's disability aesthetic.[3] The sociological and aesthetic approaches, like many methodologi-cal categorizations, can be permeable and overlapping. Freud is a good example of this; he derived his theories from his readings of the *Oedipus Rex* and *Hamlet* and applied his methods to diagnose both Oedipus and Hamlet with Oedipal complexes. Many twentieth century stage productions of *Hamlet* took Freud's diagnosis and applied it thematically to their productions.

Laura Mulvey, by contrast, takes a psychoanalytic critical lens and trans-plants it from the sociological approach to the aesthetic approach. Mulvey shifts a data-driven model and lays it overtop the technical aspects of creating an aesthetic visual image in a specific medium that evokes emotion and a spe-cific way of looking. Essentially, by focusing on the relationship between an artistic form and its content through a psychoanalysis, Mulvey moves to work within a film's diegesis and around the cinematographic apparatus which cre-ates that diegesis, rather than applying scientific data to an imaginary world. The difference between the sociological and aesthetic approaches is ultimately

DOI: 10.4324/9781003163374-6

that the sociological approach leans toward the prescriptive, whereas the aesthetic approach is descriptive and analytic. Under the umbrella of the aesthetic approach, however, analyses of Ophelia as a cultural representation allows feminist and psychoanalytic critics to tease out gender-specific differences in representation. Aesthetic explorations in turn allow disability scholars to explore intersectional sites of disability that show similar representation, regardless of gender while also reflecting changing ideas of women's roles in society and narrative.

As a result of the critical and structural relationship between disability studies, feminist studies and film studies, a large percentage of scholarship on Ophelia and madness focuses on her body as a site of sexuality, motherhood (or its absence), submission, and subversion, or some combination thereof. Critical analyses of stage and play text also tend to focus on psychoanalytic and feminist theories. We miss the universality of human discomfort with non-normative minds and bodies as well as the disability aesthetic that is present in *Hamlet* and its adaptations by limiting our critical lens to only the male gaze or only feminist readings. Unquestionably, male and female bodies are represented differently on screen; by applying the filmic stare to on screen bodies, however, we gain an understanding of how disabled bodies of any gender are similarly depicted. I will begin my discussion with a brief exploration of the critical history surrounding Ophelia before moving into an analysis of film representations of her madness, ultimately demonstrating that film representations of madness use too many of the same cinematographic tools to construct male and female representations on screen to draw a hard dividing line between male and female madness.

Literary scholar James Mariano notes that psychoanalytic criticism of Ophelia, particularly in foundational critics like Lacan and Freud, is both sparse and so focused on Hamlet's subjectivity, that Ophelia's madness is often ignored completely.[4] Indeed, Lacan opens his essay, "Desire and the Interpretation of Desire in *Hamlet*" with the line, "As a sort of come-on, I announced that I would speak today about that piece of bait named Ophelia, and I'll be as good as my word," and then proceeds to barely discuss her.[5] If Ophelia is merely an object of Hamlet's gaze, or a displacement of Hamlet's desire for Gertrude,[6] then her mad scenes in the play text, in which Hamlet is entirely absent, must necessarily be addressed separately, if at all. Neither Freud nor Lacan address Ophelia's madness as a site of meaning within psychoanalytic theory separately from her interactions with Hamlet in either the play texts or extant film adaptations of *Hamlet*. For both, Ophelia is little more than a vessel to be filled, either by Hamlet's gaze or his displaced resentment. Ophelia has been described as "an early manifestation of an enduring female stereotype, that of the beautiful nymphomaniac, her inhibitions removed by madness."[7] Ophelia's madness is often blamed on either a lack of sexuality or an overabundance of it. For example, Olivier's and Branagh's Ophelias are overtly sexualized, with Branagh giving viewers silent flashbacks of Hamlet and Ophelia in bed, and Olivier suggesting a sexual relationship between Ophelia and Laertes through romantic kisses and a scene in which Ophelia is pawing at

Laertes's belt purse, which is worn front and center. In these cases, a sexualized Ophelia is also a deviant Ophelia. Her father and brother have both proscribed a sexual relationship with Hamlet,[8] and when Olivier suggests that Ophelia and Laertes' relationship is sexual, we have an incestuous, and therefore highly proscribed, relationship.[9] As a result, Arnold argues that Ophelia's madness *facilitates* a male, heterosexual fantasy, rather than threatening a Freudian masculinity. However, with the rise of feminist criticism in the 1960s and 70s, Ophelia was read separately from Hamlet as a marginalized voice.

Feminist criticism has separated Ophelia from Hamlet, and critics including Carol Neely and Elaine Showalter[10] have gendered madness, identifying Ophelia's mad scenes as a "powerful voice from the play's margins."[11] Neely frames her understanding of mental disability around shifts that she identifies during madness's renaissance from 1576 to 1632.[12] In particular, Neely highlights "new languages for the mad," and the gendered division in madness that emerged during this period.[13] Additionally, she further contextualizes Ophelia's madness specifically through a medicalized, although feminist, understanding "which [would] (much later) be termed hysteria," as well as through "sexual frustration, social helplessness, and enforced control over women's bodies."[14] This builds on her assertions in "Feminist Modes of Shakespearean Criticism: Compensatory, Justificatory, Transformational," in which Neely points to the tradition of reading Ophelia's madness as "revelatory" and "boldly present[ing] to the court of Elsinore images of its own corruption and of the virtues it has renounced,"[15] before asserting that Ophelia moves "from submissive daughter to mad prophet."[16] Neely highlights the strength and freedom to speak truth to an oppressive patriarchal system that is often read in Ophelia through a feminist criticism.

Gulsen Sayin Teker further argues that the lyrical, cinematic tradition of representing Ophelia's madness is a feminist representation. In her article, "Empowered by Madness: Ophelia in the films of Kozintsev, Zeffirelli and Branagh," Teker argues that Ophelia, read through the twentieth century feminist theory of Helene Cixous, exhibits madness as a unique form of female expression that is permitted by Claudius only because it is facilitated by madness and therefore outside the control of patriarchal structures.[17] Teker's reading, tied to feminist theory, is effective in that paradigm. In the context of disability studies, however, the argument becomes problematic. For Ophelia to be "freed from the Lacanian Symbolic Order/the Law of the Father and [go] back to the Pre-Oedipal/Imaginary Stage where she reconnects with the mother in the womb"[18] and to "speak with her body"[19] in her mad scenes, as Teker argues, is unquestionably to subvert and challenge patriarchal social frameworks. However, madness and mental disability come with their own social stigma that Teker—and other feminist scholars—does not consider in her reading of Ophelia. Additionally, Ophelia's death is at least partly related to her madness, as Gertrude described the event. Had Ophelia not been mad, she may not have been "[a]s one incapable of her own distress."[20] What is it to be free of patriarchal structures if stigma, a disconnection from reality and physical restraint/medicalization awaits you?

Finally, the underlying—and most harmful—assumption in Teker's argument is that madness and the performance of madness can be "said to be characteristic of 'feminine discourse.'"[21] This is a point of friction between feminism and disability studies: the desire to empower Ophelia is understandable, even laudable. However, using madness to empower female characters ultimately catastrophizes feminine discourse and perpetuates negative stereotypes about female characters with disabilities—and by extension, disabled women in the real world. It also ties Ophelia strongly to patriarchal power structures, and her madness to male characters around her. By uncoupling the representation of Ophelia's madness from the men and patriarchal power structures around her, the fragmentation so often associated with the gaze takes on a different set of meanings under the umbrella of disability studies.

The filmic stare and disability studies together tend to view disability as objectifying without sexualizing for an abled audience, whereas the male gaze assumes the sexualized objectification of the female figure for the benefit of heterosexual male spectators, creating tension between the two critical paradigms. At the center of both the gaze and the stare is fragmentation. Mulvey argues that female bodies are fragmented for the visual pleasure of a certain type of viewer;[22] I argue that fragmentation in the filmic stare permits the construction of a visual synecdoche, while also putting the focus upon a given visual impairment, if one exists. As with Hamlet, madness complicates this fragmentation because madness is not inherently visible. As I argue in Chapter 1, however, because film as a medium is visual, the filmic stare accommodates so-called invisible disabilities either by shot distance or the creation of a visual synecdoche that can be seen. An excellent example of this kind of synecdoche is the reiterated shot of Hamlet's hands manipulating camcorder controls in Almereyda's 2000 adaptation of *Hamlet*.[23] However, the visual construction of Ophelia's madness through fragmentation is in tension with the fragmentation inherent to the gaze, and the distance required by the filmic stare to visually represent madness.

In the current criticism of the play texts and stage performances, Ophelia's madness is defined in the context of the men in her life.[24] This allows analyses through Mulvey's gaze and Mitchell and Snyder's narrative prosthesis to work in those contexts, but these methods fail to allow critical space for an objective look at how madness in women is represented. Madness in women in the context of film adaptations of Shakespeare plays has been intimately tied to men. Having recognized and acknowledged the critical traditions, I will now move to examine the representations of female madness uncoupled from male figures. My intention to stay away from diagnosing characters supports this uncoupling. Because part of a diagnosis is a supposition of cause—even if the exact cause must remain unknown, often the most current theories are provided in lieu of a specific cause—then the cause of madness is irrelevant to the on-screen representation. The desire to be able to explain illnesses and disabilities is inherent in human cultures and is likely tied up in our history and enjoyment of narrative. However, in wanting to explain an illness or disability, we run into the same issues that surround narrative prosthesis: all the focus is on creating a narrative to explain (and often try to cure) the disability, and the representation of the disability itself goes unexplored as a site of meaning. Rather than look at the narrative of how Ophelia's relationship to Hamlet causes or incites madness, my analysis of film adaptations of the play will use the filmic stare to analyze the representation of on-screen madness.

Ophelia and the Filmic Stare

The major *Hamlet* adaptations I will discuss here[25] are Laurence Olivier's (1948), with Jean Simmons playing Ophelia; Franco Zeffirelli's (1990), with Helena Bonham Carter as Ophelia; Kenneth Branagh's (1996), with Kate Winslet as Ophelia; and Michael Almereyda's (2000), with Julia Stiles as Ophelia. I will also discuss Grigori Kozintsev's *Hamlet* (1964), Sherwood Hu's *Prince of the Himalayas* (2006), and Vishal Bhardwaj's *Haider* (2014). Even more so than the film adaptations of Hamlet, adaptations of Ophelia tend to follow extremely similar patterns for her on-screen aesthetic. Feminine and pretty tends to be the overarching choice, although what defines feminine and pretty depends on the period and culture the film is set in. Once on-screen Ophelias embody a disability aesthetic, however, the filmic stare reveals that even while the building blocks of the representation of madness are the same—typically wide and medium shots, occasionally with subjective POV shots, and often with an extreme wide shot in which Ophelia disappears into the background of the frame—the impact of the representation is different from film to film. I will discuss film representations of Ophelia by looking at the extreme wide shots that cause Ophelia to disappear in the frame, subjective and empathetic shots that invite the viewer into Ophelia's subjective reality, and the use of visual synecdoches.

Bhardwaj's Ophelia figure is a combination of Ophelia and Horatio[26] named Arshia Lone (played by Shraddha Kapoor), who works as a journalist in Kashmir and was a childhood friend of Haider's. She is also responsible for getting Haider released from detainment at the Kashmiri border when he is returning home at the beginning of the film and helps Haider search for his missing father in the first half of the film. After Haider shoots her father, Pervez Lone, Arshia is in tears at the funeral. After the funeral, however, it is clear that Arshia is mad. An extreme wide shot of a group of men in the foreground of the shot carrying Pervez Lone's casket cross-fades with the tiny figure of Arshia in the background, almost invisible, seated on a swing and wearing white, blending into the snow. The rest of the short scene between Ghazala/Gertrude (played by Tabu) and Arshia is shot largely in a medium close-up two-shot while Ghazala tries to explain herself to an Arshia who is singing quietly to herself and seems to be unaware of Ghazala's presence. The impact of the extreme wide shot, however, is to reflect the disappearance of Arshia into her madness through the visual language of the filmic stare. The disappearance of an Ophelia figure into the background of an extreme wide shot is a trend that is present in every adaptation of *Hamlet* that I discuss. For Arshia, the disappearance is quiet and private, with only Ghazala to see; Bhardwaj removes the public aspects of Ophelia's madness from his film text, isolating Arshia both visually and socially after she goes mad. Her isolation is also reflected in and serves to highlight Ghazala's own isolation. Despite the politically charged nature of *Haider*, Arshia's madness is something that is quiet, private, and helps to highlight the intimacy of the family dramas that are just as much a part of *Hamlet* as the political aspects. The dynamics of the Lone family are hinted at through what will become Arshia's visual synecdoche.

As Trivedi notes, "Guns and Ghazala are twinned; they bestow a purposive agency and a phallicity on an almost hysterical mother,"[27] and "innocent Arshia (Ophelia) too, handles not flowers but a pistol."[28] By tracking the presence of women and pistols throughout Bhardwaj's Shakespeare films, Trivedi argues that guns become the synecdoche for female avengers. In the context of Arshia's madness, however, a different synecdoche comes to light: Pervez Lone's red woolen muffler. We see Arshia beginning to unravel the muffler in her scene with Ghazala, and in Arshia's final scene, she is shot from a medium distance, covered in tangles of yarn while she plays with her father's gun. These two elements are inextricably intertwined in these scenes, recalling the critical arguments made by Teker about women's madness as an empowering method of female communication. Trivedi argues that all of Bhardwaj's heroines in his Shakespeare film adaptations use guns to take over the role of avenger, but Arshia's pistol is tied, as is the red wool of the muffler, to her father. The condensed nature of Arshia's scenes of madness and the two synecdoches being present together suggests that Arshia—who has, to this point in the film, been articulate and confident—has lost the threads of communication. Even during the scene with Ghazala and Arshia in which Arshia is singing to herself, her words largely fade into the background, privileging Ghazala's words and emotions rather than highlighting Arshia's words as some kind of female communication. If anything, Arshia's madness is a pathway to communication for *Ghazala*, because she can safely express her worry for Haider to this young woman who cannot report to anyone else. Arshia is ultimately caught between the synecdoche of Bhardwaj's female avengers and the synecdoche of her own madness and is silenced by the weight of conflicting expectations and realities—although Bhardwaj, unlike other directors, does not give viewers a glimpse into Arshia's subjective reality. It is notable, however, how little screen time Arshia's madness has in comparison to other Ophelias, particularly in the context of Odsaluyang/Ophelia in *Prince of the Himalayas*.

As Burnett notes, Sherwood Hu's *Prince of the Himalayas* tends to multiply the Shakespearean elements in its adaptation of *Hamlet*.[29] That multiplicity extends to Odsaluyang's (played by Sonamdolgar) madness, and she appears in several extreme wide shots after she goes mad. Most of them position Odsaluyang in the natural world of Tibet, outside the court of Kulo-ngam and

Nanm, while she wears white and has a wreath of flowers in her hair. This imagery, so similar to the western stage and film traditions of representing a mad Ophelia, reveals Hu's early training in film studies in the United States while also honoring the stunning Tibetan landscapes of Hu's transplanted *Hamlet*. Odsaluyang is also visibly pregnant in her extreme wide shots, which is a significant departure for representations of Ophelia in general, and connects Odsaluyang both to the cycle of reincarnation, forgiveness, and family that Hu foregrounds thematically in his film,[30] and to global cinema representations of Lady Macbeth, which I will focus on in chapter six. The visibility of Odsaluyang's pregnancy raises the suggestion that her madness is tied to her pregnancy, something that is often present in representations of Lady Macbeth but rarely in representations of Ophelia. Pregnancy in a mad female character is also somewhat unusual. As Garland-Thomson points out, while motherhood is often socially required for women, disabled women are either themselves infantilized, or are discouraged—historically including forced sterilization—from having children.[31] Odsaluyang, who dies in childbirth, is ultimately not responsible for parenting her child, but Kulo-ngam's reaction to Odsaluyang's pregnancy suggests that he, "like everyone else, including disabled people themselves—have absorbed cultural stereotypes"[32] and feel that Odsaluyang is unfit to reproduce because she is mad. The extreme wide shots of Odsaluyang during her mad scenes highlight her deviant behaviour, her pregnancy, and the continuation of a tradition of representing Ophelia as a smaller-than-life figure. The image of a small figure in white in the natural world representing a mad Ophelia is also present in anglophone adaptations of *Hamlet*.

Zeffirelli's Ophelia initially goes mad within the walls of Elsinore castle, and there are several moments when she visually disappears into the frame. After Bonham-Carter's Ophelia goes mad, she is frequently shot in wide and extreme wide shots. Initially she disappears into the stone of the parapets of Elsinore castle, before she sings threateningly to a guard on duty. In the extreme wide shot, Ophelia is silent, only speaking once she is in medium and medium close-up. Once she re-enters the castle, nearly half the shots of Ophelia reveal her entire body, and she dominates the conversation. This scene also reveals the stare in the film's diegesis, in which Gertrude (Glen Close) in particular is terrified of Ophelia. The fear and revulsion Gertrude betray are exactly what Garland-Thomson describes in the interaction between a starer and staree.[33] The final extreme wide shot is simple, with Ophelia running in a low ditch near the castle walls, but the figure of Ophelia is so small in frame that she might be easily missed. Unlike Odsaluyang or Arshia, who can both be heard singing softly in their wide shots, Zeffirelli's Ophelia is silent in the extreme wide shot, with only the score providing accompaniment. Some of the lack of language in the extreme wide shots can undoubtedly be attributed to a film realism; it is implied that the shot of Ophelia on the parapets might be from Gertrude's POV, and Gertrude certainly would not have been able to hear Ophelia talking at that distance. However, the points at which Ophelias have a voice—or even language—in wide shots, or not, change the way madness impacts a scene. Like Arshia and Odsaluyang, Bonham Carter's Ophelia may have a voice, but it tends to be more controlled than the Ophelias that Branagh and Almereyda bring to the screen.

Branagh has acknowledged that his *Henry V* (1998) was deeply indebted to Olivier's *Henry V* (1944), but their *Hamlet*s are less intertextually connected overall, as Olivier focuses on a psychological exploration of Hamlet and Branagh's *Hamlet* is couched in geopolitical upheaval. Almereyda is an outlier in the four anglophone *Hamlet* films, primarily because he breaks further from the stage traditions influencing Olivier and Branagh, and the heritage film tradition—big-budget costume dramas that focus on period accuracy, lush soundtracks, and literary themes—that characterizes Branagh's *Hamlet*. Almereyda brings Ophelia into the end of the twentieth century, and creates new imagery for her, while still connecting back to Olivier's imagery.

Branagh's Ophelia goes mad in a highly medicalized system and is not only isolated but incarcerated by the monarchs of Elsinore. Winslet's Ophelia is larger in frame than Bonham-Carter's, more similar to Sonamdolgar. The difference from both these Ophelias, however, is that Winslet's Ophelia is actively attempting to disappear into the white, tiled walls of a room in which she screamed as she was sprayed with water in an attempt to "treat" her madness. Unlike Zeffirelli's and Olivier's Ophelias, Winslet only loses language in this scene, not her voice entirely.

Branagh also includes a highly ambiguous flashback sequence in his *Hamlet* that should function empathetically. During Polonius's (played by Richard Briers) interrogation of Ophelia after Laertes' (played by Michael Maloney) departure for France, Branagh includes sequences of Hamlet and Ophelia together in bed. However, the film leaves ambiguous the attribution of the flashbacks, calling into question their veracity as well as their relevance to Ophelia's madness. If the flashbacks are in fact Polonius imagining that Ophelia and Hamlet have consummated their relationship, then Ophelia's madness may or may not be related to Hamlet at all. Similarly, if the flashbacks originate with Ophelia, the encounter may or may not be a figment of her imagination. The ambiguity of the origin and veracity of this flashback sequence may undermine the empathetic qualities of the sequence in isolation. However, if the flashbacks are interpreted as originating from Winslet's Ophelia, then they add to the medicalization of her madness later in the film. Whether or not the events of the flashback happened or were imagined, and regardless of their attribution, the sequence functions as a critical narrative technique in the construction of an ambiguous subjective reality that unquestionably has an effect on Ophelia and her madness.

The ambiguity of the flashback sequence reflects Burton's "Division of the Diseases of the Head," which includes diseases thought to affect the brain itself: phrenzy, lethargy, melancholy, and, most relevant to this discussion, madness.[34] Burton describes madness as "a vehement dotage, or raving without fever [...] very violent and loud, full of anger, clamour, horrible looks and actions without fear of sorrow."[35] Burton's definition certainly broadly fits the on screen representations of a mad Ophelia. However, the importance of the flashback sequence in the film's narrative arc also addresses what Burton called "The Force of Imagination."[36] To imagination, Burton grants the power to alter an unborn child's physical appearance and health, and "sometimes death itself is caused by force of phantasy."[37] Burton's assertions about the medical applications of imagination—or phantasy—give authority to the flashback sequence regardless of its relationship to the reality of Hamlet and Ophelia's relationship in Branagh's film. It also marries the medicalization of imagination—as in early modern England—with the rise of the medical model of disability. Berger defines the medical model of disability as an essentialist approach that defines disability as a property of the individual body rather than the social environment. He also references Foucault, who argues that the medical model constitutes a set of disciplinary practices aimed at producing passive individuals (docile bodies). This model has been criticized for being inherently ableist,[38] and while it is no longer the dominant model for understanding disability in North America or the UK, the medicalization of the female body—particularly a deviant or disruptive female body—nevertheless informs the mise-en-scène for Winslet's Ophelia. The medicalization of Ophelia quite literally marshals disciplinary practices to turn a deviant mind into a docile body, as represented by the straitjacketing and water shocking of Ophelia after she has gone mad. For Branagh, then, what could have been an empathetic sequence is transformed by ambiguity into a fusion of medicalized foreshadowing. The flashback sequence is arguably less to do with either Ophelia or Hamlet than it is with the creation of a world in which bodies and minds are expected to be regimented and controlled.

Wide shots and relatively loose framing are typical of Laurence Olivier's film style overall, particularly because his experiments in Shakespeare film come at a relatively early stage of Shakespeare film adaptations discovering what strengths it could retain from theatrical roots and what theatrical strengths become weaknesses on screen. Sarah Hatchuel notes that Olivier as a film director "starts with a theatrical mise-en-scène and tries to make it sometimes cinematic,"[39] which explains Olivier's pattern of leaving a static camera at a wide angle with a high depth of field, deep focus, and long takes to showcase theatrical blocking. However, Olivier's cinematographic setup, reveals that a theatrical acting style, where the actor play to the back of the house, can look overacted and exaggerated on camera. Additionally, soliloquies delivered in a long take with minimal or no editing run the risk of becoming tedious. Kenneth Rothwell points to the critical disputes about "whether [Olivier's] film is primarily 'theatrical' or 'filmic,'"[40] but does not himself reach a conclusion. I tend to conclude that it is the theatrical staging and wide shots used to highlight madness in the context of the filmic stare which Shakespeare film adaptation takes as a strength from its theatrical roots, but that a static camera and minimal editing can and may often alienate twenty-first century viewers when not employed specifically to frame madness. There is an interesting and significant graphic rhyme (as opposed to an explicit graphic match) between Olivier, Kozintsev, and Almereyda in representing a mad Ophelia; all include extreme wide shots in which Ophelia fades into the background.

Almereyda focuses in closely on Hamlet, using hypermediacy and fragmented hands to convey madness, so his departure from fragmentation in his representation of Ophelia's madness is a significant change. The depths of field and focus of figures 5.1 and 5.2, as well as the geometric repetition of the fluid and concentrically circular architecture in the mise-en-scène, and the small size

Figure 5.1 Olivier's Ophelia looks down a hall through a set of archways

Figure 5.2 Ophelia screams in the Guggenheim Museum

'To-morrow is
Saint Valentine's day

Figure 5.3 Kozintsev's Ophelia is framed in arches

of the human figure(s) demonstrate that Ophelia's madness is simultaneously dwarfed by and yet fills these spaces. Male protagonists who go mad typically overpower the spaces they find themselves in; the wide shots of the filmic stare that capture male madness leave them space to physically flail about the frame, physically and behaviorally filling the space. Hamlet's madness is publicly displayed in the play-within-a-play scene,[41] surrounded by the travelling players and the court of Denmark. Hamlet dominates and controls his space, whereas Ophelia is a tiny figure within the frame. Simmons is silent in these extreme wide shots, but Stiles screams, literally filling the space with sound as she visually disappears in it before being hurriedly silenced by Claudius.

Claudius's silencing of Ophelia also highlights Olivier's and Almereyda's choice to center the focus of their films on the royal family and court of Denmark, largely eliminating the wider political subtexts of the play. Olivier eliminates Fortinbras, Rosencrantz, and Guildenstern from his screenplay, focusing on the psychological reality of Elsinore as Hamlet and Ophelia both engage with madness. The geopolitical issues with Norway and the sketchy internal politics of succession are also largely eliminated in Olivier's adaptation. Almereyda nods to the wider political issues, but the focus on corporate corruption and Hamlet as a struggling, affluent, aspiring student filmmaker again focuses the film more on Hamlet's psychological state than on politics. Ophelia's madness (like Hamlet's) is a family matter, and the family deals with her by enveloping her and her madness in the geometry and repetition of the mise-en-scène, to the point where Ophelia herself is almost lost in the frame. It is at this point of near-visual loss that Ophelia begins to fill the space. Stiles as Ophelia literally screams into the void, filling it with sound. Simmons' silent Ophelia does not physically or aurally fill the space, but the loss of the expected control of her own mind creates in itself a kind of chaotic control. Ophelia may not be consciously controlling her space and actions, but the chaos she is at the center of is its own kind of control, forcing the rest of the court of Denmark not to act, but to react. In inciting the reactions of other characters, even if she cannot control those reactions, Stiles' Ophelia is in control of events to a larger extent than Simmons' Ophelia. Conversely, actors in the role of Hamlet are reacting as opposed to acting from the beginning of the film, reflecting Hamlet's overall lack of control throughout the narrative. Given that a lack of bodily control is consistently cited as one of the hallmarks of a disability,[42] a mad Ophelia inciting responses from those around her represents a subversive version of control. It is clear that Gertrude and Claudius cannot control Ophelia, any more than they could control Hamlet. However, where Claudius can send Hamlet away from court, he cannot seem to banish Ophelia. Through her lack of control over her own madness, Ophelia gains an even more powerful, if somewhat imprecise, form of control over the king and queen.

Although Kozintsev's framing of Ophelia strongly evokes Olivier's in this context, where Olivier silences Ophelia, Kozintsev has her speaking in voice-over. Despite the public nature of Ophelia's (played by Anastasiya Vertinskaya) madness, neither Claudius nor Gertrude seriously attempts to silence her despite the public nature of her madness. As we see with Almereyda's Ophelia, Kozintsev's goes mad in a public place, in front of the entire court. However, where Stiles screams, Vertinskaya speaks softly and musically, and almost appears to be sleepwalking, especially in her first mad scene, when she is wearing a black dress and veil over iron foundation garments. In her second scene, Vertinskaya must literally pick her way through a crowded room as she hands out small twigs. In both scenes other characters recognize that Ophelia is mad, but Vertinskaya's Ophelia seems not to require an immediate, violent reaction the way Stiles' does. The discomfort of the diegetic stare is present in both cases, but where Kyle MacLachlan's Claudius reacts to piercing shrieks violently, the court of Kozintsev's Elsinore is almost entranced by Ophelia's madness as they stare at it.

Kozintsev, unlike Olivier, maintained the political aspects of *Hamlet* in his adaptation, implying that Ophelia's madness is not simply the individual purview of one body, but rather that madness, like politics, like family, is positioned within, and must be addressed by, the society. The well-known image of Ophelia being strapped into an iron corset and farthingale might suggest the imprisonment and restraint of the individual body, but it is clear from the framing of Ophelia in the long shot that the restraint of the individual does not prevent the public display of madness. Unlike Olivier, Kozintsev's framing of Ophelia's madness in terms of both her body and wide shots complicates the idea that madness is individual, medicalized, and private. Also unlike Olivier, but similar to the tactics Almereyda would use to represent his Ophelia, is the treatment of her body, and the choice to manipulate and/or fragment the female body in order to address madness.

Simmons is unequivocally fragmented the closer she comes to madness. When we first meet Simmons' Ophelia, she is modestly attired, and her face is always visible in frame. During the nunnery scene,[43] however, Simmons' face is obscured when Olivier's Hamlet throws her face down on a stone staircase. This series of shots, where all we see of Ophelia is hair and white gown, is mirrored during Ophelia's mad dissemination of flowers. In that scene, however, Ophelia's exposed leg (and the sudden appearance of cleavage) is the focus. Ophelia is literally objectified in these shots; however, the latter is a departure from the former in that a sane Ophelia is less a sexualized figure than mad Ophelia is. Olivier goes out of his way to suggest that his *Hamlet* is set in a Freudian universe; it then follows that Ophelia's sexual repression breaks its bonds and is expressed through madness. Her body becomes doubly objectified, through the gaze and through the stare. In Olivier's case, the gaze and the stare work together to objectify Ophelia as a female figure and as a disabled figure. Crucially, however, in Simmons' case the only person manipulating Ophelia's body is Simmons.

Stiles' Ophelia is less sexually charged, and her body is manipulated by almost everyone but her over the course of the film. Bill Murray's Polonius frequently manhandles Stiles' Ophelia, in scenes that range from the quietly touching, where a frustrated and distracted parent ties his daughter's shoelaces for her, to the uncomfortable background action of Polonius wiring Ophelia for sound so he and Claudius can spy on Hamlet—a scene not unlike Kozintsev's Ophelia being strapped into her iron foundation garments. After Polonius's murder, Ophelia is mad, and her body is still not her own. It takes Claudius, Gertrude, a host of bodyguards and Laertes to attempt to physically restrain Stiles' Ophelia. Almereyda (like Kozintsev) does not fragment Ophelia as much as Olivier or Branagh do, and the suggestion of a sexual relationship between Hamlet and Ophelia *remains* just that, a suggestion; their sex life is not the focus of the narrative. Stiles' Ophelia's madness is arguably more related to her lack of agency and lack of voice than it is to any kind of relationship with Hamlet himself. Almereyda creates distance between the representations of male and female madness, and in doing so creates distance between Ophelia's madness and Hamlet's actions. Hamlet's madness may originate in his own mind, but the representation of that madness is hypermediated and fragmented across the various media. Ophelia's madness encompasses her physical body, suggesting that, at least in Almereyda's film grammar, madness can be fragmented outside of the self, but when it is represented by the physical body as opposed to formal hypermediacy, that fragmentation gives way to shot distance. However, even a wider shot distance does not necessarily solve the issue of trying to represent a subjective reality.

Almereyda's big-city *Hamlet* includes a sequence in which Stiles' Ophelia imagines leaping into a pool in embarrassment while her father reads Hamlet's letter to her out loud. The sequence functions as both empathetic and self-reflexive,[44] demonstrating the depth of Ophelia's disquiet and inviting viewers to share in the familiar feelings. However, like Branagh's flashback, this sequence comes *before* Ophelia's madness. Additionally, this sequence is clearly a representation of Ophelia's subjective emotional state, so it does not have the ambiguity to attribute it to someone else the way Branagh's sequence does.

This sequence is much more empathetic, and functions as an instance of fore-shadowing. Olivier and Kozintsev largely exclude any sequences that give a glimpse into Ophelia's subjective reality, preferring instead to focus on Hamlet's relationships and emotional trajectory.

Winslet's, Stiles', and Simmons' Ophelias all have scenes with water that foreshadow their eventual drowning. However, in addition to foreshadowing, these scenes also suggest an acknowledgement that minds and bodies can be out of explicit control of the embodied subject, but that that lack of control is ultimately unacceptable in a patriarchal, able society. As a result, Ophelia is marginalized, isolated, humiliated, and eventually loses her life because of the jarring disjuncture between her embodied experience and the social and cultural conventions of Elsinore's court. The significant differences between the Almereyda and Olivier productions—cinematographic style, thematic content, period, etc.—serve to highlight the fact that anywhere can potentially be Elsinore for individuals who experience disability. Stiles and Simmons' performances represent a microcosm of a disjuncture between disability and society, as well as the gendered and social consequences of deviating from the socially accepted norm in general.

What we can take away from the patterns emerging in this cross-section of global cinema adaptations of *Hamlet* is that there are significant tensions between the male gaze and the filmic stare in terms of visually representing Ophelia, particularly after she goes mad. Where the male gaze assumes the fragmentation of the female subject for the voyeuristic and scopophilic pleasure of the male spectator, the filmic stare represents madness through wide shots of the full body (regardless of the gender of the subject), deviant behaviour, and often a visual synecdoche. The same building blocks go into the representation of a mad Ophelia that go into the representation of a mad Hamlet. Both characters are framed in wide shots and have visual synecdoches associated with their madness, and representations of Ophelia after she is mad tend not to be fragmented. As many scholars note, disability (outside of arenas like amputee pornography) tends to lead to asexual objectification, which inherently complicates a female figure's visual representation when that female figure is mad unless the film actively works against asexual objectification. All these factors exist in tension with feminist psychoanalytic theory, which is often the critical lens through which Ophelia is analyzed.

These tensions also reflect larger, ongoing tensions between disability studies and feminism, as well as the tensions that Garland-Thomson explicates between femininity and disability.[45] There is a desire, evident in the patterns of imagery that persist in the representations of Ophelia and the critical patterns of denoting female speech/language/expression, to present Ophelia as a feminine figure whose patriarchally-defined role in society is either thwarted by or subverted in a feminist manner by madness. Given the persistent interest in Ophelia's madness by artists, scholars, critics, and filmmakers, it goes without saying that Ophelia embodies a disability aesthetic. However, the disability aesthetic is also bound up with changing ideas of femininity and women's roles in society and narrative, which ultimately means that the aesthetic and sociological approaches will need to work together as opposed to in opposition.

The strength of the filmic stare in exploring film representations of Ophelia and Hamlet is that it reveals that madness, which is so often gendered, is ultimately a human experience rather than a male or female experience. The filmic stare also potentially opens the critical door to future adaptations of *Hamlet* that may include genderfluid, non-binary, or transgender Hamlets and Ophelias, all of whom would experience madness. Such adaptations will require a more flexible framework with which to understand disability in these bodies *without* pathologizing them.

Notes

1 Garland-Thomson, Rosemarie. *Extraordinary Bodies: Figuring Physical Disability in American Culture and Literature*. New York: Columbia UP. 1997. 27, 29; Neely, Carol Thomas. *Distracted Subjects: Madness and Gender in Shakespeare and Early Modern Culture*. Ithaca, NY: Cornell UP. 2004. 49, 52.
2 Garland-Thomson, *Extraordinary Bodies*, 26, 29.
3 Siebers, Tobin, *Disability Aesthetics*. Ann Arbor: University of Michigan Press. 2010. 2–3.
4 Mariano, James. "Ophelia's Desire." *EHL*, 84.4 (Winter 2017): 818–20. 820.
5 Lacan, Jaques. "Desire and the Interpretation of Desire in *Hamlet*." *Yale French Studies*, 55/56 (1977): 11–52. 11.
6 Mariano, 817, 819.
7 Arnold, Catharine. *Bedlam: London and Its Mad*. Simon and Schuster: London. 2008. 49.
8 *Hamlet*, 1.3.90–135; *Hamlet*, 1.3.5–44.
9 Rothwell, Kenneth S. *A History of Shakespeare on Screen: A Century of Film and Television*. 2nd ed. Cambridge: Cambridge UP. 2004. 56–7.
10 Showalter, Elaine. "Representing Ophelia: Women, Madness, and the Responsibilities of Feminist Criticism." *Shakespeare and the Question of Theory*. Ed. Geoffrey H. Hartman and Patricia Parker. New York: Methuen. 1985. 77–94. 78.
11 Mariano, 821; Neely, 52.
12 Neely, *Distracted Subjects*, 1.
13 Neely, *Distracted Subjects*, 2.
14 Neely, *Distracted Subjects*, 52.
15 Neely, Carol Thomas. "Feminist Modes of Shakespearean Criticism: Compensatory, Justificatory, Transformational." *Women's Studies: An Interdisciplinary Journal*, 9:1 (1981): 3–15. 6.
16 Neely, "Feminist Modes", 10.
17 Teker, Gulsen Sayin. "Empowered by Madness: Ophelia in the films of Kozintsev, Zeffirelli and Branagh." *Literature Film Quarterly*, 34(2): 113–19. 116, 118.
18 Teker, 116.
19 Teker, 118.
20 *Hamlet*, 4.7.178.
21 Teker, 118.
22 Mulvey, Laura. "Visual Pleasure and Narrative Cinema." *Screen*, 16.3 (1975): 6–18. Since Mulvey's original article, feminist film criticism has evolved. Mulvey herself wrote a follow-up to "Visual Pleasure and Narrative Cinema" in 1981,

"Afterthoughts on 'Visual Pleasure and Narrative Cinema' Inspired by 'Duel in the Sun,'" addressing the questions of the female spectator and female protagonist. As I note in Chapter 1, the filmic stare works with an assumed, rather than ethnographic, audience, so the question of the abled film audience in the real world is, unfortunately, outside the bounds of this study. In terms of the question of a female character taking center screen and how the gaze (and filmic stare) change in that context, Shakespeare film adaptation is perhaps not the most effective location for that discussion, as the female characters discussed herein are not the protagonist, even if they are significant to the work as a whole. Ophelia, Lavinia, and Lady Macbeth are all upstaged by the male titular characters of their plays, and that often occurs in subsequent film adaptations as well. In some non-anglophone adaptations of *Hamlet*, Gertrude takes center stage as a character, but Gertrude does not experience any disabilities, so conversations about her are best left to other locations, particularly Poonam Trivedi's chapter about the female avenger in *Shakespeare and Indian Cinemas: Local Habitations*.

23 See Chapter 4 for an in-depth discussion of Almereyda's construction of Hamlet's visual synecdoche.

24 Mariano, 819.

25 Akira Kurosawa's *The Bad Sleep Well* (1960) might reasonably be expected to be discussed here, as it is an adaptation of *Hamlet*. However, because Kurosawa refigures Yoshiko's (Ophelia's) disability to be an orthopedic impairment, the film is included in the discussion of physical disabilities in Chapter 2.

26 Noted by Trivedi and Chakravarti, *Shakespeare and Indian Cinemas: 'Local Habitations'*. Ed. Poonam Trivedi and Paromita Chakravarti. New York: Routledge. 2019. 40, and Burnett, Mark Thornton. *Hamlet and World Cinema*. Cambridge: Cambridge UP. 2019. 172.

27 Trivedi, Poonam. "Woman as Avenger: 'Indianising' the Shakespearean Tragic in the Films of Vishal Bhardwaj." *Shakespeare and Indian Cinemas: Local Habitations*. Ed. Poonam Trivedi and Paromita Chakravarti. New York: Routledge. 2020. 37.

28 Trivedi, 25.

29 Burnett, Mark Thornton. *Shakespeare and World Cinema*. Cambridge: Cambridge UP. 2013. 131.

30 Burnett, *Hamlet and World Cinema*, 141, 145.

31 Garland-Thomson, *Extraordinary Bodies*, 26.

32 Garland-Thomson, *Extraordinary Bodies*, 26–7.

33 Garland-Thomson, Rosemarie. *Staring: How We Look*. New York: Oxford UP. 2009. 3–4.

34 Burton, Robert. *The Anatomy of Melancholy*. Ed. Floyd Dell and Paul Jordan-Smith. New York: Tudor Publishing Co. 1927. 120.

35 Burton, 121.

36 Burton, 139.

37 Burton, 220–2.

38 Berger, Ronald J. *Introducing Disability Studies*. New York: Lynne Rienner. 2013. 26–7.

39 Hatchuel, Sarah. *Shakespeare from Stage to Screen*. New York: Cambridge UP. 2004. 20–1.

40 Rothwell, 55.

41 *Hamlet*, 3.2.90–7, 108–24, 230–7.

42 Garland-Thomson, *Extraordinary Bodies*, 37.

43 *Hamlet*, 3.1.

44 See Chapter 1 for explanations of these terms.

45 Garland-Thomson, *Extraordinary Bodies*, 27–9.

Bibliography

Arnold, Catharine. *Bedlam: London and Its Mad*. London: Simon and Schuster. 2008.

Barounis, Cynthia. "Cripping Heterosexuality, Queering Able-Bodiedness: *Murderball, Brokeback Mountain* and the Contested Masculine Body." *The Disability Studies Reader*. 3rd ed. Ed. Lennard J. Davis. New York: Routledge. 2010.

Berger, Ronald J. *Introducing Disability Studies*. New York: Lynne Rienner. 2013.

Burnett, Mark Thornton. *Shakespeare and World Cinema*. Cambridge: Cambridge UP. 2013.

Burnett, Mark Thornton. *Hamlet and World Cinema*. Cambridge: Cambridge UP. 2019.

Burton, Robert. *The Anatomy of Melancholy*. Ed. Floyd Dell and Paul Jordan-Smith. New York: Tudor Publishing Co. 1927.

Garland-Thomson, Rosemarie. *Extraordinary Bodies: Figuring Physical Disability in American Culture and Literature*. New York: Columbia UP. 1997.

Garland-Thomson, Rosemarie. *Staring: How We Look*. New York: Oxford UP. 2009.

Haider. Dir. Vishal Bhardwaj. Perf. Tabu, Shahid Kapoor, Irrfan Khan. UTV Motion Pictures. 2014.

Hamlet. Dir. Laurence Olivier. Perf. Laurence Olivier. Universal-International. 1948.

Hamlet. Dir. Grigori Kozintsev. Perf. Innokenty Smoktunovsky, Mikhail Nazvanov, Elze Radzinya, Anastasiya Vertinskaya. Lenfilm. 1964.

Hamlet. Dir. Franco Zeffirelli. Perf. Mel Gibson, Glenn Close. Warner Bros. 1990.

Hamlet. Dir. Kenneth Branagh. Perf. Kenneth Branagh, Jack Lemon, Julie Christie, Derek Jacobi. Renaissance Films. 1996.

Hamlet. Dir. Michael Almereyda. Perf. Ethan Hawk. Buena Vista Pictures. 2000.

Hatchuel, Sarah. *Shakespeare from Stage to Screen*. New York: Cambridge UP. 2004.

Lacan, Jaques. "Desire and the Interpretation of Desire in *Hamlet*." *Yale French Studies*, 55/56 (1977): 11–52.

Mariano, James. "Ophelia's Desire." *EHL* 84. 4 (Winter2017): 818–820.

Mulvey, Laura. "Visual Pleasure and Narrative Cinema." *Screen*, 16. 3 (1975): 6–18.

Neely, Carol Thomas. "Feminist Modes of Shakespearean Criticism: Compensatory, Justificatory, Transformational." *Women's Studies: An Interdisciplinary Journal*, 9. 1 (1981): 3–15.

Neely, Carol Thomas. *Distracted Subjects: Madness and Gender in Shakespeare and Early Modern Culture*. Ithaca, NY: Cornell UP. 2004.

Prince of the Himalayas. Dir. Sherwood Hu. Perf. Purba Rgyal, Dobrgyal, Zomskyid, Sonamdolgar. Global Genesis Group. 2006.

Rothwell, Kenneth S. *A History of Shakespeare on Screen: A Century of Film and Television*. 2nd ed. Cambridge: Cambridge UP. 2004.

Showalter, Elaine. "Representing Ophelia: Women, Madness, and the Responsibilities of Feminist Criticism." *Shakespeare and the Question of Theory*. Ed. Geoffrey H. Hartman and Patricia Parker. New York: Methuen. 1985: 77–94.

Siebers, Tobin. *Disability Aesthetics*. Ann Arbor: University of Michigan Press. 2010.

Teker, Gulsen Sayin. "Empowered by Madness: Ophelia in the films of Kozintsev, Zeffirelli and Branagh." *Literature Film Quarterly*, 34. 2: 113–119.

Trivedi, Poonam. "Woman as Avenger: 'Indianising' the Shakespearean Tragic in the Films of Vishal Bhardwaj." *Shakespeare and Indian Cinemas: 'Local Habitations'*. Ed. Poonam Trivedi and Paromita Chakravarti. New York: Routledge. 2019.

Trivedi, Poonam and Paromita Chakravarti, eds. *Shakespeare and Indian Cinemas: 'Local Habitations'*. New York: Routledge. 2019.

6 Madness, the Filmic Stare, and *Macbeth*

Actress Sarah Bernhardt holds the dual distinctions of being the first woman to play Hamlet on film in 1900 at the Paris Exposition, and to be one of the earliest women to pass as abled on stage and screen after the loss of her right leg to gangrene in 1915, to her death in 1923. Bernhardt had played Lady Macbeth in 1884, Ophelia in 1886, and played Hamlet onstage at the Theatre Sarah Bernhardt (formerly the Theatre des Nations) in France to mixed—leaning to negative—reviews, but as a singular figure, Bernhardt is uniquely positioned at the intersection of madness and disability studies, particularly in *Hamlet* and *Macbeth*.

Bernhardt largely left Shakespeare behind after 1900, and her initial leg injury occurred in 1905. Improper healing and subsequent re-injury to the same leg however, meant that by the time *La Dame aux camélias* (1911) and *Les Amours de la reine Élisabeth* (1912) were shot and released, Bernhardt could not walk unaided. Norden remarks that the fact that the star of the film that opened the feature film era in the United States was disabled went largely unnoticed. In fact, Bernhardt went out of her way to prevent the general population from understanding the extent of her injury and subsequent disability. In 1912 she released *Sarah Bernhardt at Home*, a two-reeler showing her playing tennis, and after her leg was amputated in 1915, she carefully blocked stage and screen performances to conceal her missing leg. Her success in passing as able-bodied was mixed. Louis Verneuil, a collaborator and friend of Bernhardt's, said "She was so prodigiously clever, with so much skill and grace at the same time, that nobody in the audience could suspect the incredible effort she had to make in order to seem as if she were walking in a normal fashion."[1] Conversely, Terry Ramsaye assessed Bernhardt thusly: "In this picture [Mères françaises] Bernhardt, crippled and enfeebled, is a sad relic of herself as the personification of Gallic emotion, sat through her scenes in a chair."[2] All of this effort to conceal a physical disability in an actress, and yet Bernhardt embraced representing madness in Ophelia, Hamlet, and Lady Macbeth. This seemingly oppositional position on representing vs experiencing disability is still seen in celebrities today, but under the aegis of disability studies is hardly a new phenomenon.

To my knowledge, it has not previously been explicitly argued that hierarchies of representation exist in representations of disabilities. However, I

DOI: 10.4324/9781003163374-7

argue that Bernhardt's story, in combination with cultural phenomena like the American freak shows of the late nineteenth and early twentieth centuries, and the penchant for casting abled actors to play disabled roles—or to deride disabled actors who play roles that reflect their own disabilities as "not really acting"—all come together to reveal an inherent hierarchy. This hierarchy privileges the representation of a character with a disability—Lady Macbeth, in this case—played by an able-bodied actress over an actress with a disability playing a character with a similar disability. Aesthetics also contribute to the hierarchy.

Deaf Actress Marlee Matlin has an invisible disability, and as an attractive white woman, she is respected as an actress—and rightly so, her performance as Joey Lucas in *The West Wing* was nuanced and funny, and she earned an Academy Award for Best Actress for her work in *Children of a Lesser God* (1986)—whereas figures like Sartje Baartman and Julia Pastrana were relegated to those American freak shows because they did not fit into a white western aesthetic of disability or beauty.[3] A hierarchy of representations of disability also helps to explain Bernhardt's efforts to pass as physically abled. As a white, abled actress, she could—and did—gain popularity and status by representing famous, mad, literary characters. However, as a disabled woman at the turn of the century, she risked marginalization and enfreakment—the process by which a non-normative or disabled body is othered to the point of seeming non-human in its display. Bernhardt's choice to pass as abled and her continuation of her acting career after acquiring her disability has all the makings of an overcoming narrative. However, as many disability studies scholars have argued, overcoming narratives perpetuate unrealistic expectations, and I would add that they often overlook the material realities of being disabled in a world that expects people to keep up or fall away. The varying hierarchies of ability, the status gained for playing mad Shakespearean characters, and the stigma of acquiring a physical disability all influenced Bernhardt's choices as an actress, as well as the traditions in which many actresses would walk in their portrayals of Lady Macbeth.

Both Lady Macbeth and Macbeth experience madness in Shakespeare's play, and both also experience madness—as mediated by the filmic stare—in film adaptations of the *Macbeth*. In this chapter, I will first explore the progressive (in the sense of something continuing uninterrupted rather than in the sense of reform or new/liberal ideas) representation of Lady Macbeth's madness before moving on to discuss the episodic representation of Macbeth's madness. Both representations use similar building blocks of the filmic stare, leading once again to a largely egalitarian representation of madness. Directors tend to show both Macbeth and Lady Macbeth's subjective realities through the filmic stare, and both characters have visual synecdoches connected to their madness. For Macbeth, Banquo's ghost is the visual synecdoche of his madness.

Lady Macbeth's visual synecdoche is often constructed around her hands, and this visual synecdoche may seem to conflict with the argument that Lady Macbeth's madness is not gendered, particularly because the films that use hands as Lady Macbeth's synecdoche often suggest that Lady Macbeth's madness is centered around themes of pregnancy and thwarted motherhood. However, conflicting themes and visual synecdoches highlight the use of the filmic stare and encourage viewers to rethink their assumptions about the ways in which themes—in this case parenthood—and disability intersect. Especially since the inclusion of a child for the Macbeths in film adaptations tends to hinge on a notoriously enigmatic—to use Stephanie Chamberlain's term[4]—line from the play:

> I have given suck, and know
> How tender 'tis to love the babe that milks me;
> I would, while it was smiling in my face,
> Have pluck'd my nipple from his boneless gums,
> And dash'd the brains out, had I so sworn...[5]

Lady Macbeth's line is, according to Chamberlain, traditionally read as an attempt to goad her husband rather than a literal admission of infanticide or a specific confirmation that the Macbeths have had children who do not appear at any other point in the play text.[6] However, the fact that film directors use the filmic stare in such similar ways to represent both Macbeth and Lady Macbeth's madness supports my argument that the filmic stare is used in an egalitarian way, and that the use of the filmic stare creates space for scholars and casual viewers of the films to reevaluate their preconceptions of disability.

"Out, Damn Spot:" Lady Macbeth and the Filmic Stare

In popular culture, at least in North America, Lady Macbeth has in many ways become an excuse for men in power to transgress without taking blame or responsibility for their actions. Arguably the most famous example of this is Hillary Clinton, named "The Lady Macbeth of Little Rock" by *The American Spectator* in 1992[7] and again in 2015,[8] who was often cited as a factor in decisions her husband made that were unfavorable to both opponents and the political base. Likewise, Lady Macbeth has historically been blamed for Macbeth's atrocities.[9] The Hillary Clinton example demonstrates how closely women are still tied to the actions of the significant men in their lives. The stage tradition of a Macbeth who is incited to murder and beyond by a powerful wife began with David Garrick's 1748 stage production,[10] but actresses Helen Faucit and Ellen Terry played her as motivated by "wifely ambition for her husband's success,"[11] complicating the character and the question of her share in the blame for his actions. Ambitious stage Lady Macbeths are often read in a Freudian context, focusing on gendered speech and phallic symbolism throughout the play, particularly with reference to the daggers. A threatening Lady Macbeth comes directly from the stage tradition, as theatre historian Tanya Pollard points out. Pollard describes an 1830s Charlotte Cushman as a strong, almost bullying Lady Macbeth; an 1880s Sarah Bernhardt as a hypersexualized Lady Macbeth; and finally in 1937 a vampiric Lady Macbeth played by Judith Anderson at the Old Vic.[12] However, the 2010 Cheek by Jowl Theatre Company's production of *Macbeth* took a different approach to Freud and *Macbeth* by interpreting the couple as a single consciousness and including a ghostly Lady Macbeth in scenes occurring after her death.[13] These stage representations laid the foundation for a series of Lady Macbeths on film who largely follow these trends.

In this section, I will explore the filmic stare in seven film adaptations of *Macbeth*: Orson Welles's *Macbeth* (1948), with Jeanette Nolan as Lady Macbeth; Akira Kurosawa's *Throne of Blood* (1957), starring Isuzu Yamada as Asaji; Roman Polanski's *Macbeth* (1971), starring Francesca Annis as Lady Macbeth; Vishal Bhardwaj's *Maqbool* (2004), starring Tabu as Nimmi; Rupert Goold's *Macbeth* (2010) with Kate Fleetwood playing Lady Macbeth; Justin Kurzel's *Macbeth* (2015) with Marion Cotillard as Lady Macbeth; and Jayaraj's *Veeram* (2016), with Divina Thakur as Kuttimani. Polanski, Goold and Jayaraj address Lady Macbeth's madness in similar ways, specifically through a visual synecdoche that centers on Lady Macbeth's hands. Goold and Polanski also include subjective shots of the blood she cannot escape after Duncan's murder, signifying an invitation to the viewer into Lady Macbeth's madness; Jayaraj does not explore Kuttimani's subjective reality after she goes mad. While Goold and Polanski adapt the text of Shakespeare's *Macbeth* to vaguely 1960s Romania and medieval Scotland respectively, Jayaraj mobilized Mollywood (Malayalam cinema) and the *Vadakkan Pattukal* (Northern Ballads) of the North Malabar region in India to weave together Shakespeare's *Macbeth* and the story of Chandu Chekavar (played by Kunal Kapoor) and his wife Kuttimani into a distinctly Malayalam *Macbeth* set in thirteenth-century Malabar.

Like Jayaraj, Orson Welles devotes a relatively small percentage of the overall run time of his film to Lady Macbeth's madness. Unlike Jayaraj, who uses the filmic stare with precision to highlight Kuttimani's madness, Welles omits a visual synecdoche for Lady Macbeth, preferring to frame her in predominantly plan américain shots as she descends a stairwell and walks toward the camera, which subtly moves away from her, almost matching step for step. For Welles, the wide shots of the filmic stare and a mobile camera combine to replicate the almost instinctive step back humans take when they are uncomfortable. Because Lady Macbeth is walking directly toward the camera, Welles has placed the viewers in the position of starer, as though to attempt to remove the mediation of the camera and to highlight the discomfort that Garland-Thomson identifies in the stare that occurs between two people in the real world.[14] Ultimately, Welles returns viewers to the diegesis quickly, as Lady Macbeth falls into Macbeth's arms for an embrace before seeing him, screaming, and sprinting away off-camera.

Kurzel explores a different side of Lady Macbeth and shifts the construction of her visual synecdoche slightly. As Lady Macbeth, Cotillard's hands are visually connected not with Duncan's blood, but with the daggers used to kill him. In addition, Kurzel's subjective shots link Cotillard's Lady Macbeth more closely to the tradition of madness we see in Hamlet, through the appearance of ghostly apparitions, rather than the patterns of madness seen in Ophelia, with the exception of Odsaluyang. Kurzel strongly links Lady Macbeth's madness with thwarted motherhood, choosing to open the film on the funeral of the Macbeth's young child.

Kurzel's choice evokes the connection between motherhood and madness that both Bhardwaj and Kurosawa explore in their respective adaptations of *Macbeth* as well. The 2004 *Maqbool* transposes Shakespeare's *Macbeth* from ancient Scotland to late twentieth-century Mumbai. Rather than a monarchy, the film focuses on the reign and overthrow of Abbuji (played by Pankaj Kapur), the head of the organized crime in Mumbai. Miyan Maqbool (played by Irrfan Khan) is Abbuji's right hand, and Nimmi is Abbuji's mistress who takes it upon herself to seduce Maqbool and help him murder Abbuji and take over the criminal empire. Ultimately, they are unsuccessful; Nimmi dies of complications due to childbirth and Maqbool is shot outside the hospital. Nimmi's madness is not tied to her hands, they are busy holding pistols and signifying, as Poonam Trivedi argues, a female avenger.[15] However, we do see the filmic stare in Nimmi's subjective reality as she feels Abbuji's blood on her face, and Nimmi herself reports an aural synecdoche—her fetus wailing.

The 1957 *Throne of Blood* positions *Macbeth* in feudal Japan, and substitutes Shakespeare's three witches for a single wood spirit who serves the same role. Also added is a pregnancy and stillbirth for Lady Macbeth, but otherwise Kurosawa retains the broad strokes of Shakespeare's plot. Kurosawas's Lady Macbeth figure, Asaji, uses hands as one part of the visual synecdoche for her madness. However, unlike Kurzel and Bhardwaj, Kurosawa does not share Asaji's subjective point of view (POV) with viewers, and even Asaji's pregnancy and subsequent stillbirth are told, not shown. The context of the pregnancy and madness, however, position Asaji with Nimmi and Cotillard's Lady Macbeth in terms of tying the representation of madness through the filmic stare to pregnancy and thwarted motherhood.

Despite these differences in the construction of Lady Macbeth's madness and visual synecdoche, directors adapting *Macbeth* all create a Lady Macbeth who is intelligent and domineering. However, even presenting a strong female character who slides into madness might, in a disability studies context, be considered a negative representation. Certainly, Lady Macbeth is killed, not cured, and narratively her death is presented as a punishment, as surely as the lopping of limbs is in *Titus Andronicus*. Nonetheless, these representations are worthwhile sites of analysis. Rarely do women who wield the power of Lady Macbeth admit to experiencing mental disabilities, and Lady Macbeth is a useful case study in both the filmic stare as a medium-specific way of constructing a representation of a disabled mind, and in the broader assumptions about madness and gender that disability studies and culture hold about women who experience mental disabilities.

Lady Macbeth is, narratively, the driving force behind Macbeth's murder of Duncan, and as such establishes herself as a dominant figure. Lady Macbeth's textual/subtextual dominance, and the Freudian nature of the visual synecdoche that is created for her, lead to a female figure that is ultimately threatening. In film adaptations, Lady Macbeth tends to have one clear visual synecdoche, built into the play by Shakespeare. The famous exhortation "Out, damned spot; out I say,"[16] in combination with the doctor telling the audience that Lady Macbeth rubs her hands, suggests an intensive focus on those appendages. Filmmakers have taken ample advantage of this textual detail, and frequently build referential and focal moments in the films that build a visual synecdoche for Lady Macbeth's madness. Both Goold and Polanski in particular frequently use close-ups of Lady Macbeth's hands throughout their films. They introduce us to Lady Macbeth through shots of her hands as she reads Macbeth's letter.

Polanski mirrors his initial shot of Lady Macbeth with a shot just prior to her death, in which Lady Macbeth's hands again hold a letter. The difference is that this Lady Macbeth has gone mad, and this is the last time she will be in frame alive.

Polanski's Lady Macbeth is very much a prop in the film; we see more of the back of her head and her hands than her face. However, the fragmentation of Lady Macbeth to create the synecdoche of the hands is present across most major adaptations of the play.

A more minimal but still present example of fragmenting Lady Macbeth to highlight her hands as a synecdoche for her madness is in Jayaraj's *Veeram*.

Figure 6.1 Close-up of Lady Macbeth's hands as she reads a letter from Macbeth

Figure 6.2 Close-up of Lady Macbeth's hands as she reads a letter from Macbeth

Figure 6.3 A mad Lady Macbeth rereads a letter from Macbeth

After Chandu has murdered Aromal (King Duncan), there is a two shot of Chandu and Kuttimani's faces, with Chandu's bloody hands holding the murder weapon centered in the frame between their faces. While the focus here is technically on Chandu's bloody hands, the composition of the mis-en-scène—their faces being nearly on the same level, the bloody hands and metal implement equidistant between the two, and Kuttimani's hand in frame on her staff before she grabs for the implement—suggests a *shared* synecdoche, highlighting that both Chandu and Kuttimani are equally responsible for not only the murder of a friend and ruler, but the madness that each will experience.

This shared synecdoche is cemented over the next minute of the film, when Kuttimani covers her own hands and Aromal's guards' hands in Aromal's blood. Once she is finished framing the guards, Kuttimani and Chandu's faces reappear together as reflections in water as they raise their hands above it. Then their hands come into frame from above, and we see Kuttimani's extremely bloody hands begin to wash Chandu's less bloody ones. The camera here is objective rather than subjective, keeping viewers in the diegesis of the film without any visual suggestion of madness yet. Kuttimani's bloody hands are evoked later in the film, when Kuttimani has gone mad, and she is pantomiming washing them in a wide shot under the watch of an attendant and a doctor. However, after Kuttimani goes mad, Jayaraj does not offer the viewers a glimpse into her subjective reality.

Where madness exists in male protagonists, filmmakers have gone out of their way to try to visually express the subjective reality of that protagonist. The trombone shot from Hitchcock's *Vertigo* (1958), the penny dreadful vision of Tamora and her sons dressed as Murder, Rape and Revenge in Taymor's *Titus* (1999), and the visions that the Olivier (1948) and Branagh (1996)—but interestingly not the Almereyda (2000)—Hamlets see of Claudius murdering Old Hamlet all work to elicit empathy and understanding for a character's subjective, mad reality. Hamlet's madness, the legitimacy of which is often questioned by critics, is nonetheless shared with the viewer by the film and thereby Hamlet's subjective reality is imparted with a certain level of authority. The authority conferred by sharing a subjective reality and confirming that a character really is experiencing something different than what might be considered "normal" is typically not given to Ophelia, with exceptions in the Branagh and Almereyda adaptations. Viewers do, however, often have a chance to share the experience of Lady Macbeth's subjective reality, just as they do with Hamlet and Titus.[17] In film terms, this neatly side-steps the problem of representing an invisible disability in a visual medium. By allowing viewers to see what Lady Macbeth sees, madness becomes less unknowable, and seeing her subjective reality adds legitimacy to the madness.

Polanski and Goold include POV shots of what Lady Macbeth sees in her madness. For Polanski, the shot serves double duty, reinforcing Lady Macbeth's visual synecdoche as well as creating an empathetic moment in which Lady Macbeth's subjective reality can be shared. Goold leaves out the hands, but again creates a sense of empathy; seeing things that are not really there is uncomfortable. By using a POV shot that is not focused on hands, Goold momentarily takes gender out of consideration. Lady Macbeth sees blood come out of the faucet in a POV shot that mirrors similar shots from mad male protagonists, conferring a level of authority on Lady Macbeth that is less prevalent in the Polanski adaptation of *Macbeth*.

Hands become the sign of Lady Macbeth's madness in film adaptations, and this synecdoche—with its oft-associated subjective reality—can be interpreted in a variety of ways. Fragmentation of the female body is a key

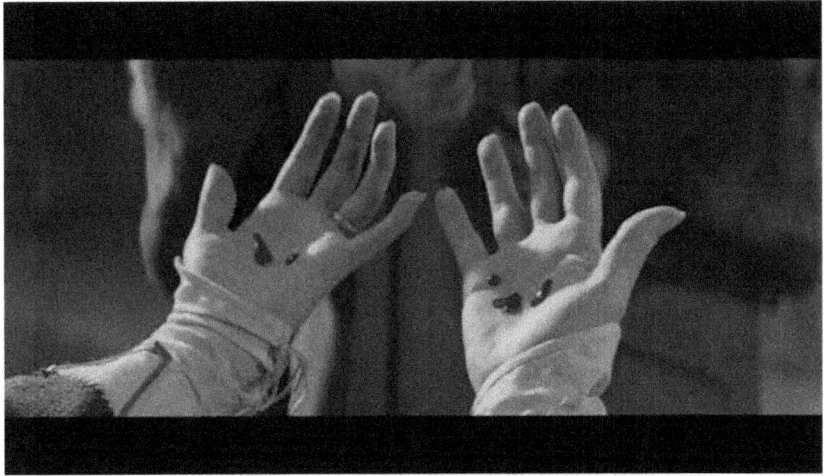

Figure 6.4 Subjective shot of Mad Lady Macbeth seeing blood on her hands

Figure 6.5 Subjective shot of a mad Lady Macbeth seeing a sink run with blood

point in Mulvey's construction of the gaze. In the Freudian tradition of psychoanalysis and the subsequent feminist psychoanalytic theories that evolved, both knives and fingers can be phallic symbols. The multiplication of phallic symbols—two knives, five or more fingers—as Freud argues, "is a confirmation of the technical rule according to which a multiplication of penis symbols signifies castration."[18] Based on a psychoanalytic visual synecdoche, Lady Macbeth is both a threatening and alluring figure. Even looking at Lady Macbeth's hands in the context of Mitchell and Snyder's narrative prosthesis, the madness is intimately bound up in Macbeth and

Lady Macbeth's relationship (and the power dynamics thereof) as well as Duncan's murder. A reading of *Macbeth* through narrative prosthesis might look like this: Lady Macbeth's insistence on killing Duncan is introduced, and her reaction to seeing his murdered body arguably is the first spark of madness. Then as the plot progresses, Lady Macbeth's madness drives Macbeth on, and her death (the "kill" half of kill or cure) eliminates both her madness and the last of the drive that keeps Macbeth moving forward. His eventual defeat and his acknowledgement to MacDuff that he went too far are a reversal of his character because Lady Macbeth is no longer there to goad him forward. Mitchell and Snyder's methods of analysis leave Lady Macbeth, as Mulvey argues, "the bearer, not maker, of meaning."[19] As a visual synecdoche for the filmic stare, however, Lady Macbeth's hands function differently.

Until and unless we lose the use of our hands, we tend to forget that hands are one of the principal ways we interact with the world. Hands are largely how we exercise our agency; we use them to vote, to write, to wield a sword, and to manipulate a lover's body. Lady Macbeth uses her hands in combination with her verbal attacks on her husband's masculinity[20] to goad him into regicide, and then she uses her own hands to put the daggers back and smear the grooms with blood to frame them.[21] Lady Macbeth's hands begin as a sign of power and agency, and, once she has gone mad, the synecdoche signifies not only the strength of the mind-body connection (in an inversion of the mind-body split that characterizes the largely artificial divide between mental and physical disability) but also that Lady Macbeth's agency has been subverted by her madness. The hands that were once in her control are now a focal point for her lack of control. Garland-Thomson argues that a major social expectation is that individuals can and must control their bodies and minds; this assumption is partly responsible for the stigma that particularly surrounds mental illness and leads to statements like "have you tried not being depressed?"[22] Lady Macbeth, who has demonstrated self-control and even control of Macbeth for the first half of the play and film adaptations, loses control of her mind and her hands. Beyond her narrative function, the visual synecdoche constructed by Lady Macbeth's hands speaks eloquently to the largely unspoken social expectations around maintaining control over the body and the mind alike. The visual synecdoche of Lady Macbeth's hands in Goold's, Polanski's, and Jayaraj's films represents both complete control and a complete lack of control, uncoupled from a narrative.

In the context of the filmic stare, there is sufficient shot distance to see behavioural changes in the Polanski, Jayaraj, and Goold *Macbeth*s, as well as Lady Macbeth's bloody subjective reality in Goold and Polanski's adaptations. The use of hands as a synecdoche for Lady Macbeth's madness is also well-documented. However, hands are not the only extant synecdoche that applies to representations of Lady Macbeth. Kurzel, Bhardwaj, and Kurosawa all tie Lady Macbeth's madness to the theme of thwarted motherhood—thwarted either by infant/child or maternal mortality in these cases. Kurzel and Bhardwaj do so through the use of subjective realities, to which Bhardwaj also adds an aural synecdoche. Kurosawa, like Welles, relies primarily on shot distance to communicate madness through the filmic stare.

In his 2015 adaptation of *Macbeth*, Kurzel nods to the tradition of using close-ups on Lady Macbeth's hands to create a visual synecdoche, but he chooses a different method for engaging with madness through the filmic stare. For Kurzel, the sign and arguably the instigation of madness is dead children. The film opens on a funeral, with Macbeth (Michael Fassbender) and Lady Macbeth cremating their child.[23] In the early battle sequences of the film, many of the soldiers are young boys, who Macbeth prepares for battle.[24] The soldiers surrounding Macbeth and MacDuff in films are generally men in their prime or grizzled older soldiers. The use of boys in Kurzel's film underlines the theme of parenthood in the film text, positions the film more closely to the play text tradition of surrounding Macbeth with young men and boys rather than old soldiers, and creates an interesting parallel between Lady Macbeth's madness and Macbeth's actions. Ultimately, the boy we see Macbeth so paternally prepare is slain, but the boy's ghost is at Macbeth's shoulder throughout the rest of the film. The ghost of this unnamed boy sets up and resonates with Lady Macbeth's non-sleeping sleepwalking scene in the film.

Rather than sleepwalk somewhere deep in Dunsinane Castle, Cotillard's Lady Macbeth returns to the chapel in the small village in which we meet her when she is reading Macbeth's letter to her. There is a high degree of relative distance between Cotillard's Lady Macbeth and the camera in this scene. Typically, mad characters need the space a wide shot provides to cavort in madness and provide a site for the filmic stare. Not so for Kurzel's Lady Macbeth in the chapel. Once she leaves the chapel and goes to the witches on the heath, we see a wide shot that creates space for mad movement. In the chapel, however, the feeling is one of stillness and of distance. Lady Macbeth sits alone in the center of the floor and delivers her lines. The distance and stillness are more eerie than any wild gesticulations or headstands that a Hamlet might perform to signify madness. Kurzel also uses the distance and the stillness to give viewers an empathetic shot of Lady Macbeth's reality in this moment. The shot of Lady Macbeth alone in the chapel is closely mirrored by a shot of Lady Macbeth accompanied by the ghost of her dead son.

At this point in the film, Lady Macbeth has seen Macbeth burn Lady Mac-Duff and her children at the stake, has cremated her own son, and Macbeth has been haunted by a dead child soldier. Kurzel's representation of Lady Macbeth's subjective reality is not entirely divorced from Martin Norden's *Cinema of Isolation*, however.[25] Lady Macbeth is literally alone in an empty chapel in an abandoned village when we gain access to her subjective reality and the ghost of her son. She is isolated socially, geographically, and in terms of her subjective vs her objective reality. The attempt at empathy is counterbalanced by an acknowledgement of the reality of isolation as a result of disability. Throughout the film, Kurzel shows not only the objective reality of the funeral

Figure 6.6 Mad Lady Macbeth subjective shot of her ghostly child

and battle, but also the subjective realities of the ghost children only Macbeth and Lady Macbeth experience. For Kurzel, battle is frenetic, not madness. Kurzel exemplifies madness through stillness and ghosts, in a way that evokes Hamlet's struggles with his own ghosts and antic disposition. Comparing Hamlet and Macbeth makes a certain level of poetic sense; both are male protagonists and connecting them through one of their goads to action lends Macbeth a sense of masculinity that can be a little lost under the sheer power of Lady Macbeth before her madness.

Bhardwaj sets up a twist on Lady Macbeth's bloody subjective reality for Nimmi. When Maqbool shoots Abbuji, Nimmi is in bed next to him, and her face is spattered with Abbuji's blood. To cover up the murder, Nimmi fires a shot into the air, summoning a guard who Nimmi then shoots and frames for Abbuji's death. Later Nimmi is startled out of sleep, presumably by the sensation of Abbuji's blood on her face, a subjective, sensory reality for Nimmi that is shown visually to the viewers, but with an objective camera rather than a subjective POV shot in a mirror. Maqbool's face comes into frame over Nimmi's shoulder as he and the viewers watch her try to clean blood—that has now disappeared from the screen—from her face. Bhardwaj makes a point of visualizing a sensory subjective reality for the viewers but uses an objective camera to do so. This is a shift from Goold and Polanski, who both allow Lady Macbeth to actively look and see her subjective reality. It is clear that Nimmi can see the blood on her face once she wipes her hand across it, but we are not optically aligned with Nimmi when she does so. A similar instance comes toward the end of the film when Nimmi insists she can see Abbuji's blood on the walls and sheets of the bedroom, although at the end of the film the blood of Nimmi's subjective reality is not made visual for the viewers. Bhardwaj does not endow Nimmi with what Norden calls the "power of the look"[26] the way that Goold and Polanski do for their Lady Macbeths. Norden notes that for a disabled character, looking—usually through a POV shot—has traditionally been forbidden to them, although some film adaptations of *The Hunchback of Notre Dame* and *Peter Pan* have allowed Hook and Quasimodo to originate subjective POV shots, but both are punished for doing so.[27] Annis and Fleetwood's Lady Macbeths are certainly both punished for looking, and seeing Duncan's blood is usually the site for both looking and foreshadowing punishment for looking. For most Lady Macbeths, the blood she cannot wash off is the only subjective reality we see. However, Nimmi has a second instance of a different but related subjective reality.

Nimmi becomes pregnant shortly after Abbuji's death. Trivedi notes that this pregnancy comes at a poor time for Maqbool, who is facing shaky and shifting loyalties in Abbuji's gang and yet is "preoccupied, nursing the pregnant but distracted Nimmi."[28] Part of Nimmi's distraction—Trivedi's use of the term distraction recalls Neely's use of the term to characterize madness in *Hamlet, Macbeth,* and *King Lear*—is a sound that Nimmi insists she can hear: the wailing of her unborn baby, which is preventing Nimmi from sleeping. Nimmi does not sleepwalk as Lady Macbeth, so the sound of the baby crying becomes an aural synecdoche for her madness that works alongside her subjective reality to communicate madness. The two components of the filmic stare—Nimmi's subjective reality and her aural synecdoche—seem at first to be signifying madness as a result of her role in Abbuji's murder, especially because the paternity of the child is unclear, and the child could be Abbuji's rather than Maqbool's. Nimmi even tries to explain the wailing she is hearing by telling Maqbool that the pair murdered the baby's father. However, the implication of the infant's complicated paternity, the objectivity of the visualization of Nimmi's subjective reality, and the use of an aural rather than a visual synecdoche all ties Nimmi's madness closer to thwarted motherhood than murder. Nimmi is never shown on screen with her child after it is born, and her death as a result of complications from labor and delivery seals the lack of agency in looking that we find in other film representations of Lady Macbeth. Nimmi only hears her unborn child's cries, creating an aural rather than a visual synecdoche, and she does not have any subjective POV shots of the blood on her face. Bhardwaj combines a lack of looking, a lack of sight for Nimmi with the filmic stare to highlight madness and to tie that madness closely to motherhood, perhaps as a way to explain Nimmi's madness beyond her role in Abbuji's murder. Blair Orfall notes that the "appearance of a child" is the factor that most strongly ties Bhardwaj to Kurosawa's adaptation of Macbeth, *Throne of Blood.*[29] However, the lack of looking surrounding Asaji, Kurosawa's Lady Macbeth, is also extremely similar to the way Bhardwaj constructed his representation of Nimmi's madness.

Before Kurzel and Bhardwaj, Kurosawa's *Throne of Blood* (1957) was one of, if not the earliest adaptation of *Macbeth* to include a child for the Macbeths. Unlike Kurzel and Bhardwaj, however, Kurosawa never actually shows the child onscreen, and minimizes Asaji's madness in terms of total screen time.

Additionally, while Kurosawa's film tends to rely on medium and wide shots, there are a few strategic close-up shots that allude to Lady Macbeth's hands becoming the visual synecdoche for her madness.

Asaji's pregnancy does not really exist in the mis-en-scène of *Throne of Blood* in the way that Nimmi's pregnancy is visible and highlighted in *Maqbool*. Asaji simply tells Washizu (Macbeth, played by Toshiro Mifune) that she is pregnant (presumably at a relatively early stage of pregnancy because she is not visibly pregnant), after which her pregnancy is not addressed again until a midwife reports to Washizu that the child was stillborn. Almost immediately on the heels of this news is the news that the First and Second Fortresses have been lost, so Asaji is left offscreen until very nearly the end of the film. Washizu is interrupted by female screams while conferring with his commanders and goes to Asaji to find her sobbing as she washes her hands and crying that the bloodstains and the smell of blood will not come out. Once again, there is no visible sign that Asaji recently delivered. However, the scene does include a close-up on Asaji's face with her hands in front of her. The close-up in this scene recalls the close-up of Asaji's and Washizu's hands after Washizu has killed Kunimaru (Duncan). Asaji literally pulls her husband's bloody fingers one by one off the spear so she can use it to frame a soldier for the murder. After returning the spear, Asaji goes to clean her own hands, and the framing and mis-en-scene when Asaji washes her hands after the murder and in madness after her stillbirth are extremely similar. For Asaji, pregnancy, although a new development in adapting *Macbeth* to film, ultimately has less to do with madness than it does with giving Washizu a reason to kill Miki (Banquo).

Feminist criticism has, for many years, attempted to reclaim Lady Macbeth as something other than an ambitious monster who helps bring about the downfall of a great man. Coppelia Kahn explores the role of the patriarchal society in the creation of women's fantasies and desires about masculinity without blaming Lady Macbeth for Macbeth's atrocities.[30] Janet Adelman takes a psychoanalytic feminist approach and explores the play's movement towards a "radical excision of the female site of origin."[31] Trivedi argues that, "feminist criticism, while not able to exactly 'save' her, has succeeded in humanizing her," especially by making Lady Macbeth a maternal figure.[32] It is almost deceptively easy to explain madness through thwarted pregnancy in the *Macbeth* adaptations of Kurzel, Bhardwaj and Kurosawa, particularly in the context of current critical constructions of a maternal Lady Macbeth. After all, Nimmi claims to hear her child cry in utero, and Asaji and Cotillard's Lady Macbeth both experience madness after the loss of a child. However, what the filmic stare highlights in closely examining the visual synecdoches and subjective realities that are consistent throughout all the adaptations of *Macbeth* I discuss here is that motherhood is still largely secondary to Lady Macbeth's madness. Only Kurzel's Lady Macbeth has a subjective reality so tightly tied to thwarted motherhood that it is almost impossible to extricate murder and motherhood from each other. For Asaji and Nimmi, thwarted motherhood is contextualized within the power struggles inherent to the films' hypotext, not a cause of madness in and of itself.

The filmic stare also helps reveal the fact that a maternal Lady Macbeth is another point of friction between feminist studies and disability studies. Inherent in the assumption that "humanizing" Lady Macbeth involves making her more maternal are social tensions about female disabled bodies, and the fact that female disabled bodies are so often "denied or discouraged" reproduction.[33] Garland-Thomson goes further still, to point out that "feminist abortion rationale seldom questions the prejudicial assumption that 'defective' fetuses destined to become disabled people should be eliminated."[34] The tensions between the female disabled body and reproduction are further heightened by Lady Macbeth's death in both Shakespeare's text and the film adaptations. In addition to thwarting motherhood for the female disabled body, Lady Macbeth is ultimately isolated and killed rather than cured, reproducing patterns that Norden identified as foundational to Hollywood representations of disabled bodies.[35] Explaining Lady Macbeth's madness away as pregnancy-related or as a result of thwarted motherhood ultimately pathologizes Lady Macbeth, and undoes any attempts to "humanize" her when those attempts are critically evaluated through a disability studies lens. Lady Macbeth's hands as a visual synecdoche for her madness and the subjective reality she experiences when she cannot stop feeling and smelling Duncan's blood are present across adaptations, and the filmic stare reveals the disconnect between madness and motherhood.

"Never Shake Thy Gory Locks at Me:" Macbeth and the Filmic Stare

Unlike the fame that surrounds Lady Macbeth's descent into madness and her sleepwalking scene, Macbeth seeing Banquo's ghost during the banquet scene garners less attention as a representation of madness in Shakespeare studies and is most often discussed in the context of Shakespeare's ghosts. Categorizing Banquo's ghost as a scene of the supernatural rather than madness may simply be because of how memorable Lady Macbeth's madness is, or it could be because Macbeth seems to "shake off" or "snap out of" his madness in a way that Lady Macbeth does not. Like Ophelia, once Lady Macbeth goes mad, she remains mad until her death. And like Hamlet, Macbeth's madness seems to be episodic, with periods of relative lucidity surrounding moments of madness. However, even though Macbeth's madness is episodic, and Lady Macbeth's is more linear, the filmic stare is used to construct representations of both. For Macbeth, seeing Banquo's ghost is a moment of subjective reality that is constructed using the same tools of the filmic stare that are used to construct Lady Macbeth's subjective reality.

In an interview for the Folger Shakespeare Library's podcast, *Shakespeare Unlimited*, about her memoir, *Shakespeare Saved My Life: Ten Years in Solitary with the Bard*, Laura Bates recalls asking both her university and her prison students a pair of questions: Why does Macbeth see the ghost of Banquo? Why does he not see the ghost of Duncan?[36] Bates's prison students theorized that Macbeth sees the ghost of Banquo because where Macbeth personally killed Duncan, Banquo was killed by hired murderers and Macbeth needs reassurance that Banquo is in fact dead.[37] Whether seeing a ghost is actually reassuring or not, it is fair to say that seeing the ghost is disabling for Macbeth in the banquet scene because his subjective reality is so significantly different from, and cannot be explained to, others in the room. The extent to which the episode is disabling for Macbeth is evident in his language, the reactions of other characters around him, and, in film adaptations, the disability aesthetic the filmic stare reveals in the scene.

Broadly speaking, the initial moments of Macbeth seeing Banquo's ghost tend to involve medium close-up shot-reverse-shots, sometimes with a bait-and-switch wherein the second time Macbeth looks at Banquo's empty seat, the ghost will not be there, causing Macbeth to question if he saw the ghost the first time. Then when Macbeth next looks back, Banquo's ghost is there with a vengeance, and often a plethora of blood. Once the presence of Banquo's ghost has been firmly established, the shots become wider to allow Macbeth, Banquo's ghost, or both to react and break behavioural and verbal social scripts. Depending on how much of Shakespeare's text is retained in the film adaptation, this section may be shorter or longer. The pattern of showing Macbeth's subjective reality, often with POV shots for Macbeth contrasted with an objective camera showing an empty seat, holds largely true for Welles, Polanski, Goold, and Kurzel, and is extremely similar to the construction of Lady Macbeth's subjective reality involving her hands and Duncan's blood. Kurosawa, Bhardwaj, and Jayaraj, however, construct Macbeth's madness during his encounter with Banquo's ghost with slightly different uses of the elements that comprise the filmic stare.

Kurosawa's *Throne of Blood* is largely characterized by a relatively static camera with wide and medium shots. The inclusion of close-ups highlighted Asaji's visual synecdoche because of the sharp contrast between shot styles. For Washizu, the contrast is in the mobility of the camera and the length of the take to highlight his madness. Kurosawa does include a shot-reverse-shot POV to establish that Washizu is seeing the ghost, but that occurs after a long take. The nearly two-and-a-half-minute take begins by revealing Washizu sitting on a low platform in the background with Miki's (Banquo's) empty seat in the foreground. Then the camera pushes in on Washizu, allowing Miki's seat to fall out of frame. Suddenly, Washizu reacts to seeing a ghost out of frame, and the camera pulls back out to reveal Miki's ghost. Then the camera tracks with Washizu as he moves away from his seat, allowing Miki's ghost to fall out of frame and include some members of the court and Asaji in the shot. Asaji tries to explain away Wasizu's behaviour as drunkenness, but as Washizu moves back to his seat and Miki's seat comes back into frame, Miki's ghost is gone again. In this case, Washizu's madness is reflected in the mobility of the camera as it follows his movements around Miki's ghost. The long take and mobile camera also highlight the episodic nature of Washizu's madness because Miki's ghost appears and disappears during the long take and reframing due to the mobile camera. In this case, Washizu first seeing the ghost via on objective rather than subjective camera—particularly with the subjective POV shots afterward to solidify that yes, Washizu's subjective reality is different from the reality of others in the room—is effectively used to communicate Washizu's altered reality, its nature, and the reactions of everyone else in the room highly effectively.

Jayaraj also combines the conventional representation of Chandu seeing Kelu's (Banquo) ghost through his own POV shot-reverse-shot with a more unique construction of madness, but where Kurosawa uses both the traditional and nontraditional techniques in the same scene, Jayaraj includes two separate scenes with Kelu's ghost, and connects them with an extremely specific sound effect. The first scene positions Kelu's ghost seated in a circle as Chandu meets with other men, and Kelu's ghost almost seems to challenge Chandu to look and see him, which of course Chandu does. Chandu then attempts to murder Kelu's ghost with his sword, and Kuttimani must talk him down. The second scene occurs after the second time Chandu visits the witches, and he is walking alone. Suddenly an orange-clothed figure who is screaming and waving a sword is running toward Chandu. Chandu looks away, but when he looks back, there are three figures instead of one. Every direction Chandu looks the same figure is multiplied, screaming, armed, and running toward him in extreme wide shots. These shots are contrasted with medium close-ups of Chandu surrounded by the bloody, screaming faces of Kelu. The cacophony builds and the editing speeds up as Jayaraj cuts between wide and close-up shots until the cacophony ceases and Kelu's ghosts suddenly disappear. After both scenes, however, Chandu appears to simply shrug off the aftereffects of madness. Both scenes use the filmic stare to frame Chandu's episodic madness, but Jayaraj uses both traditional (shot-reverse-shot subjective POV shots) and nontraditional shot constructions within the filmic stare to communicate Chandu's subjective reality.

Bhardwaj's approach to the banquet scene, and to the idea of a ghost in general, highlights Bates's prison students' supposition that Banquo's ghost is a confirmation for Macbeth that Banquo is in fact dead because Maqbool is confronted with Kaka's (Banquo's) dead body directly. Kaka's body is brought to Maqbool by corrupt police inspectors Pandit and Purohit, who represent Bhardwaj's interpretation of the weird sisters. Maqbool crouches next to the body, and turns Kaka's head toward him, a gesture that presumably reads as grief to those around Maqbool but physically and emotionally confirms for Maqbool that Kaka is dead, even though his death was contracted out. Confirms, that is, until Kaka's eyes open in an extreme close-up. Maqbool's violent recoil is captured in an extremely high angle wide shot, as he screams for someone to take Kaka away, that he is alive. Nimmi talks Maqbool down, and this ends up being one of the shortest "ghost" scenes in the adaptations of *Macbeth* so far discussed. Despite the short duration, however, the filmic stare is still evident in Maqbool's brief moment of madness when he believes that Kaka is still alive.

Film adaptations of *Macbeth* clearly demonstrate that regardless of how directors attempt to explain away madness because of grief or pregnancy, or to separate male and female madness through different progressions, the egalitarian nature of the filmic stare ultimately fails to support gendered explanations for madness. Rather, the filmic stare represents disability as a state of existence that does not discriminate based on gender. Both Macbeth and Lady Macbeth experience subjective realities that are significantly different from the reality of those around them, and both are prevented from fully participating in social events and are stared at in the film's diegesis as a result of madness. Despite the difference between continuously progressing madness and episodic madness—something reflected in *Hamlet* as well as *Macbeth*—when Macbeth does experience madness and sees Banquo's ghost, the representation of that subjective reality is constructed on film in the same manner as Lady Macbeth's subjective reality.

Part of attempting to hierarchize representations of disability is deeply tied to existing hierarchies of gender, race, and class, and the history of hierarchizing disability can be largely tied to the histories of the freak show and of attempts to pass as abled. Just as Sarah Bernhardt did in the early twentieth century, Macbeth and Lady Macbeth go to great lengths to hide their impairments and to pass as abled, until the point that passing is simply impossible. At that point, the stare exists in the diegesis of the film, largely unaffected by the gender of either starer or staree. The filmic stare is also unaffected by the gender of the impaired character, and so the gendered hierarchy that is still so prevalent in film representations of humans is disrupted by the presence of disability.

Notes

1 Qtd. in Norden, Martin. *The Cinema of Isolation: A History of Physical Disability in the Movies*. New Brunswick: Rutgers University Press. 1994. 69.
2 Qtd. in Norden, 69.
3 Garland-Thomson, Rosemarie. *Extraordinary Bodies: Figuring Physical Disability in American Culture and Literature*. New York: Columbia UP. 1997. 70–1.
4 Chamberlain, Stephanie. "Fantasizing Infanticide: Lady Macbeth and the Murdering Mother in Early Modern England." *College Literature*, 32.3 (Summer 2005): 72–91. 72.
5 *Macbeth* 1.7.54–8.
6 Chamberlain, 72.
7 Wattenberg, Daniel. "The Lady Macbeth of Little Rock." *The American Spectator*. August 1992. 25–32.
8 Wattenberg, Daniel. "The Lady Macbeth of Little Rock." *The American Spectator*. November 20, 2015. Web.
9 Clark, Sandra and Pamela Mason. "Introduction." *The Arden Shakespeare: Macbeth*. 3rd ed. London: Bloomsbury. 5.
10 Clark and Mason, 104.
11 Clark and Mason, 109.
12 Tanya Pollard, in an interview in "Macbeth." *Shakespeare Uncovered*. Dir. Richard Denton, Nicola Stockley. Perf. Ethan Hawke. PBS. 2012.
13 Clark and Mason, 111–12.
14 Garland-Thomson, Rosemarie. *Staring: How We Look*. New York: Oxford UP. 2009. 3–4.
15 Trivedi, Poonam. "Woman as Avenger: 'Indianising' the Shakespearean Tragic in the Films of Vishal Bhardwaj." *Shakespeare and Indian Cinemas: 'Local*

Habitations'. Ed. Poonam Trivedi and Paromita Chakravarti. New York: Routledge. 2019. 24.
16 *Macbeth*, 5.1.30.
17 See Chapters 2 and 4 for my discussions about Titus and Hamlet.
18 Freud, Sigmund. "Medusa's Head." *The Critical Tradition: Classic Texts and Contemporary Trends*. 3rd ed. Ed. David H. Richter. Boston: Bedford/St. Martin. 2007. 533
19 Mulvey, Laura. "Visual Pleasure and Narrative Cinema." *Screen*, 16.3 (1975): 6–18.
20 *Macbeth*, 1.7.35–72.
21 *Macbeth*, 2.2.45–62.
22 Garland-Thomson, *Extraordinary Bodies*, 37.
23 This funeral is not present in any of the extant play texts of *Macbeth*, nor is it present in any other film adaptations of the play.
24 Kurzel draws an interesting parallel to Kenneth Branagh's 1989 *Henry V* and Thea Sharrock's 2012 *Henry V* with the use of boy soldiers. In *Henry V*, the murder of the boys behind the English lines at Agincourt is seen as a piece of French brutality, which spurs Branagh's Henry on to fight, and is counterbalanced by Hiddleston's Henry's execution of the French prisoners. The horror of the loss of young boys in war is not typically seen in film adaptations of *Macbeth*.
25 Recall that Norden argues that, historically, characters with disabilities were geographically and socially isolated, and that isolation was visually represented on screen as part of the filmic experience of being disabled.
26 Norden, 100.
27 Norden, 100.
28 Trivedi, 31.
29 Qtd. in Trivedi, 31.
30 Kahn, Coppelia. *Man's Estate: Masculine Identity in Shakespeare*. Berkeley: University of California Press. 1981. 76–8.
31 Adelman, Janet. *Suffocating Mothers: Fantasies of Maternal Origin in Shakespeare's Plays*, Hamlet *to* Tempest. New York: Routledge. 1992. 139.
32 Trivedi, 28.
33 Garland-Thomson, *Extraordinary Bodies*, 26.
34 Garland-Thomson, *Extraordinary Bodies*, 26.
35 Norden, 1, 106.
36 Barbara Bogaev, host, "Shakespeare Unlimited: Episode 58 Shakespeare in Solitary," *Shakespeare Unlimited* (podcast), October 4, 2016, accessed January 22, 2021, https://www.folger.edu/shakespeare-unlimited/solitary-prison.
37 Barbara Bogaev, host, "Shakespeare Unlimited: Episode 58 Shakespeare in Solitary," *Shakespeare Unlimited* (podcast), October 4, 2016, accessed January 22, 2021, https://www.folger.edu/shakespeare-unlimited/solitary-prison.

Bibliography

Adelman, Janet. *Suffocating Mothers: Fantasies of Maternal Origin in Shakespeare's Plays, Hamlet to Tempest*. New York: Routledge. 1992.

Chamberlain, Stephanie. "Fantasizing Infanticide: Lady Macbeth and the Murdering Mother in Early Modern England." *College Literature*, 32. 3 (Summer2005): 72–91.

Clark, Sandra and Pamela Mason. "Introduction." *The Arden Shakespeare: Macbeth*. 3rd ed. London: Bloomsbury.

Freud, Sigmund. "Medusa's Head." *The Critical Tradition: Classic Texts and Contemporary Trends*. 3rd ed. Ed. David H. Richter. Boston: Bedford/St. Martin. 2007.

Garland-Thomson, Rosemarie. *Extraordinary Bodies: Figuring Physical Disability in American Culture and Literature*. New York: Columbia UP. 1997.

Garland-Thomson, Rosemarie. *Staring: How We Look*. New York: Oxford UP. 2009.

Kahn, Coppelia. *Man's Estate: Masculine Identity in Shakespeare*. Berkeley: University of California Press. 1981: 76–78.

Macbeth. Dir. Roman Polanski. Perf. Jon Finch, Francesca Annis. Columbia Pictures. 1971.

Macbeth. Dir. Rupert Goold. Perf. Patrick Stewart, Kate Fleetwood. PBS: Illuminations. 2010.

Macbeth. Dir. Justin Kurzel. Perf. Michael Fassbender, Marion Cotillard. The Weinstein Company. 2015.

Macbeth. Dir. Orson Welles. Perf. Orson Welles, Jeanette Nolan. Republic Pictures. 1948.

"Macbeth." *Shakespeare Uncovered*. Dir. Richard Denton, Nicola Stockley. Perf. Ethan Hawke. PBS. 2012.

Maqbool. Dir. Vishal Bhardwaj. Perf. Irrfan Khan, Tabu. Kaleidoscope Entertainment Pvt. Ltd. 2004.

Mulvey, Laura. "Visual Pleasure and Narrative Cinema." *Screen*, 16. 3 (1975): 6–18.

Norden, Martin. *The Cinema of Isolation: A History of Physical Disability in the Movies*. New Brunswick: Rutgers University Press. 1994.

Throne of Blood. Dir. Akira Kurosawa. Perf. Toshiro Mifune, Isuzi Yamada. Toho. 1957.

Trivedi, Poonam. "Woman as Avenger: 'Indianising' the Shakespearean Tragic in the Films of Vishal Bhardwaj." *Shakespeare and Indian Cinemas: 'Local Habitations'*. Ed. Poonam Trivedi and Paromita Chakravarti. New York: Routledge. 2019.

Veeram. Dir. Jayaraj. Perf. Kunal Kapoor, Divina Thakur. Chandrakala Arts. 2016.

Wattenberg, Daniel. "The Lady Macbeth of Little Rock." *The American Spectator*, August1992: 25–32.

Wattenberg, Daniel. "The Lady Macbeth of Little Rock." *The American Spectator*, 20 November2015. Web.

7 The Filmic Stare and Digital Broadcast Cinema

Thus far, my discussions of the filmic stare have been restricted to cinema, and cinematic adaptations created for television. These parameters include a great many valuable adaptations of early modern dramatic works, but one of the major ways that Shakespeare is disseminated in the late twentieth and twenty-first centuries is through Digital Broadcast Cinema (DBC). Paul Heyer argues that DBC "can be said to include the broadcast into movie theatres, either live or recorded, of various arts and entertainment productions that, like cinema, have a narrative format."[1] I will also include—as do Aebischer, Greenhalgh, and Osborne[2]—the creation and distribution of DVD, Blu-Ray, and digital downloads of these broadcasts in my discussion of the filmic stare in DBC productions of early modern drama. DBC functions—particularly for institutions like The Stratford Shakespeare Festival (Stratford, Ontario, Canada), The Royal Shakespeare Company (Stratford-upon-Avon, Warwickshire, England, UK) and The Globe Theatre (London, England, UK)—as both a medium and a methodology. The medium has been praised for connecting theatre to larger audiences than any playhouse could ever accommodate, and for combating the social class stratifications that may bar interested populations from live theatre. The 2018 collection, *Shakespeare and the 'Live' Theatre Broadcast Experience*, positions Shakespearean DBC economically, through cultural access, in terms of place and space, and through the experience of 'liveness' for the digital audience.[3] As a methodology, DBC artificially marries theatre techniques and staging with cinematography and editing to create a chimeric experience of both theatre and cinema. DBC also circumvents many of the marketing issues that plague film adaptations of lesser-known early modern dramas: the target audience for popular cinema will not be interested in film adaptations of Shakespeare's lesser known plays or plays by early modern playwrights who are not part of the contemporary zeitgeist, but theatre audiences bring that interest with them. Therefore, DBC has a far wider extant library of early modern dramatic texts than traditional cinema or television adaptations do, making DBC a valuable resource. For example, plays like Kyd's *The Spanish Tragedy* have been recorded, as have Webster's *The Duchess of Malfi*, and Shakespeare's *The Winter's Tale* and *Titus Andronicus*, which I will discuss later in this chapter. Additionally, DBC thrusts Jack Jorgens' taxonomies for classifying Shakespeare film back into the conversation.[4]

DOI: 10.4324/9781003163374-8

Jorgens was taxonomizing the levels of adaptation around Shakespeare film in the late 1970s, and he defines the 'Theatrical Mode' as using film as a transparent medium which "can encapsulate any of the performing arts and render it in a film transcription," but critically the theatrical mode looks and feels like a performance for a static theatrical space and live audience.[5] Jorgens further argues that "most films in the theatrical mode fail because they were never good theatre in the first place."[6] Jorgens' categorization and line of argument is in response to the post-WWII changes in Britain, including the creation of the Arts Council in 1946, and the subsidization of public theatres, which grew into the second period in the 1960s in which stage-derived Shakespeare films were frequently produced.[7] When theatre is captured on film, the question that naturally arises is how to separate archival footage from a discrete work in its own right. Jorgens acknowledges the complexity of hybrid media, arguing that his own divisions "conceal much more than they reveal, perpetuating as they do the largely artificial division between the disciplines of literature, theatre and film."[8] However, Jorgens offers no potential solution to the archival vs work question of hybridity—whether to classify a theatre production captured on film as a simple record, or as a new form. Bolter and Grusin's argument that remediation constitutes a "transparent 'representation of one medium in another'"[9] can suggest an archival quality to DBC, as the theatrical 'experience' is captured on film. Aebischer, Greenhalgh, and Osborne rebut this reading of DBC, however, arguing that,

> When [...] a theatrical production like the Donmar *Caesar* is considered as a 'work,' it can be seen to encompass all the distinct live performance events in the course of its run as well as their production and consumption through audio and theatre broadcasting. A theatre broadcast is therefore both an original performance in its own right and a component of the overarching work.[10]

Unlike Jorgens, Aebischer et al. move to define the hybridity of DBC, and further break down the categories under the purview of the umbrella term. Like Jorgens' modes of Shakespeare film adaptations, Aebischer et al. outline three distinct modes of DBC.

The first mode is 'Live' Theatre Broadcasts, which may also be referred to in other texts as simulcasts. These broadcasts are live-mixed during capture (or, to use Heyer's term, in-camera editing),[11] and are distributed simultaneously through television, cinemas or online, and may also be accessed as 'delayed live' to account for different time zones. An example of this kind of live theatre broadcast was Kenneth Branagh's livestream from the Garrick Theatre in 2015–16. *The Winter's Tale* and *Romeo and Juliet* were broadcast to theatres across the UK and North America, taking time zones into account.[12] These casts may also be presented as 'encore' days, broadcast days, months, or years after the theatrical performance.[13] This particular methodology creates challenges which are not present during principal photography on a film. In cinema, directors have time to compose and frame shots, and principal photography on a film allows space and time to shoot the same scene over and over (within budgetary limitations) until the scene is cinematographically and compositionally correct. Stage productions inherently do not allow for these types of reshoots, and multiple cameras in different positions mimic, but do not replace, the ability to shoot a scene in multiple takes. So, if a cameraman gets a shot of an actor's backside in DBC from one camera, the editor potentially has the option to edit in-camera and switch to a different camera, but that means changing shot distance, direction, and angle. If a stage production is not designed to be filmed, or is not re-blocked to accommodate filming, then the in-camera editing is far less controlled by the editor than a traditional film. James Monaco argues that "we watch a play as we will; we see a film only as the filmmaker wants us to see it."[14] Heyer jumps off this argument to discuss the roles of the dual audiences—the audience watching the play in the theatre and the audience watching the broadcast—but I address Monaco's argument from a production standpoint: if during the play-within-a-play scene in *Hamlet* there is no camera covering Ophelia, then the editor is limited even beyond what he or the director wants the broadcast audience to see. If the cameras misses a reaction, then so too does the broadcast audience, at least for simulcasts.

The second mode of DBC, Theatre broadcasts, have more opportunities to edit captured footage of theatre productions because they have a post-production phase. Theatre broadcasts are typically captured with multi-camera setups, often over two or more performances with live audiences, and are edited together in post-production before being broadcast.[15] The Stratford HD series falls into this category, as the performances recorded in the Festival and Patterson theatres are not broadcast until months after the season closes. This methodology allows more precision in editing than live theatre broadcasts do, although there is still a limit to the number of shot options based on the placement of the cameras and the actors' blocking.

Theatre broadcasts have a nearly identical methodology to the third mode of DBC, recorded theatre. Recorded theatre is captured by a multi-camera setup over multiple performances, and edited in post, but rather than being broadcast to cinemas or television, these mixes are released directly to DVD or the web.[16] Aebischer, Greenhalgh, and Osborne acknowledge that these categories—much like Jorgens'—are highly permeable, since captured footage can be stored, played on multiple platforms years after the fact, or even re-mixed to create new works entirely.[17] Additionally, DBC differs from cinema in that the cinematic apparatus is not always invisible, even in the theatre broadcast and recorded theatre modes, because cameramen often capture each other as they capture the performance.[18] The use of live audience reaction shots also serves to highlight the distance between the broadcast audience and the live performance, and draws attention to the hybridization of the medium.

In terms of the filmic stare, however, DBC's hybrid nature creates some interesting changes. Critical discussions of DBC tend to focus on production and reception and highlight the hybridity of the medium itself. That hybridity also extends to the filmic stare. The filmic stare posits that the network of cinematographic techniques used by directors highlights or suppresses disability in the frame; the first and most fundamental hybridization that happens with DBC is that instead of one director thinking in film grammar, there are two directors. One is a stage director, working with any of a variety of stage configurations—at the Stratford Shakespeare Festival, for example, Shakespeare productions might be staged on a thrust stage, in the round, or on a black box stage or even on a traditional proscenium stage. The other director is a DBC director, who functions first and foremost as a bridge between media, negotiating between the stage director's vision of the play, and the needs of a film production. On the Stratford HD On Demand web page, each DBC production credits both a stage director and a film director; for example, *Macbeth* (2016) credits Antoni Cimolino as stage director, and Shelagh O'Brien as film director. Even in cases where actors are instructed not to change their performances for the cameras, the presence of the cameras changes the dynamic of the performance, and therefore what is captured on film.[19] What is captured on film, however, is only a small part of constructing the filmic stare.

In terms of the hybrid medium that is ultimately transmitted to a broadcast audience, Aebischer draws on Michel de Certeau to differentiate between place and space. Certeau defines place as a physical location, but space "takes into consideration vectors of direction, velocities, and time of mobile elements. [...] Space occurs as the effect produced by the operations that orient it, situate it, temporalize it...in short, space is a practiced place."[20] In essence, Aebischer is arguing that the individual theatres are places, but DBC productions create virtual spaces that transcend the physical place, allowing both audiences—the physical one in the theatre where the play takes place and the one viewing the digital representation—to enjoy it. Spaces, then, are not physical locations, nor are they strictly diegetic worlds. The virtual space is created in cinemas, where audiences watch live streams, and in personal homes, when individuals watch DVDs of DBC productions or YouTube livestreams. In the context of my discussion, place is where the stare exists, whereas the filmic stare exists within or adjacent to the virtual space created by DBC in which the stare and filmic stare can interact, creating the meta-stare, which I will discuss below. Place and space affect the filmic stare in DBC productions but editing influences the filmic stare as well. In that respect, the changes in the editing, or in the case of simulcasts, mixing, change how the filmic stare exists in DBC productions. These factors primarily affect the filmic stare's fundamental unit: the visual synecdoche.

Do You See What I See? The Meta-Stare and DBC

In previous chapters, I have explored the construction of visual synecdoches for Lady Macbeth (her hands), Lavinia (disembodied hands), and Caliban (his bi-colored skin, particularly around his eyes) across as many extant cinematic films as possible. The visual synecdoche in all these cases, however, relies on the intimacy that a close-up or extreme close-up in a cinematic film—or TV movie, as the case may be—can bring. Multiple close-ups of hands (or stumps) are affective, and they can be used repeatedly as a narrative motif as well as a visual synecdoche for the filmic stare. DBC productions are, as Aebischer points out, focused on transmitting an experience in a specific space.[21] The focus on the space and the theatrical experience changes the dynamics of the filmic stare because it is extremely rare to have close-up shots, and extreme close-up shots are even rarer. Typically, when a character is delivering a soliloquy, the editor might choose to use a medium shot, so while the *theatre* audience is still seeing the whole stage and whole actor, the *broadcast* audience is seeing only the actor in a medium or medium close-up shot. This particular shot construction is common in DBC productions of *Hamlet*, and it carries over into productions of other plays, including *The Duchess of Malfi* and *Titus Andronicus*. In hybridizing two media to transmit a 'live' experience in a particular place and space, wider shots and looser framings are used overall in order to include not only actors' performances, but also the stage and the theatre audiences. As the camera zooms out, so must the filmic stare. An intense, close-up focus on hands or a small prop simply does not play to the back of the house to become a production motif, ergo it will be extremely rare in DBC productions as a visual synecdoche. As the cameras zoom out to capture live theatre performances, so too does the filmic stare zoom out; the filmic stare also gains a new meta level, as broadcast audiences stare at theatrical audiences staring at characters with disabilities.

In directly addressing the theatre audience—and in some cases directly interacting with audience members, depending on the theatre—characters with disabilities create a specific environment for the stare to exist in. For broadcast audiences, however, rather than being in a position to be a direct starer, they are positioned to stare at both the character with the disability, and the audience member(s) the character is addressing and/or interacting with. A level of discomfort is generated when a broadcast audience member stares at both character and theatre audience and recognizes the discomfort of a non-normative mind and/or body that is breaking not only the social scripts implicit in the world of the play but also the social scripts governing the interactions of actors and audience members during a live performance. The discomfort is recognizable as secondhand embarrassment, but the discomfort also recognizes the affective reaction that the stare implies: the gut-level discomfort with disabilities. In watching a theatre audience member, it is hard not to think "what would I do in that situation?" That self-reflection creates a meta-stare; by watching the stare in action through a DBC production, even the presence of a weaker filmic stare is fortified by the self-reflexivity inherent in the medium. However, widening the cinematic frame to include the theatre audience and therefore the meta-stare tends to come at the cost of a weakened filmic stare, partially due to the differences between the functional realities of cinematic film productions and DBC productions.

The weakening of the filmic stare is particularly noticeable in representations of madness.

Dominic Dromgoole's production of John Webster's *The Duchess of Malfi*[22] at the Globe Theatre's Sam Wanamaker Playhouse[23] was filmed in 2014 and distributed digitally and on DVD. The production used seventeenth century staging and costumes, and, like the TV movie version from the 1970s,[24] includes scenes of Ferdinand experiencing lycanthropy (Webster's diagnosis, not mine). Like MacTaggart, Dromgoole also loosely frames Ferdinand's lycanthropy in a combination of wide and medium shots, in a deep field. The difference, however, is that Dromgoole does not construct a visual synecdoche around which to anchor the wider shots of Ferdinand. As a result, the filmic stare is weak; Ferdinand is clearly mad, but the camera merely gives the actor space to portray the physicality of madness, rather than shaping the broadcast audience's perspective through cinematographic techniques. This point illustrates rather well Aebisher's argument that transmitting place and space is the foundational purpose of DBC. However, unlike cinema or cinematic television adaptations of early modern drama, in capturing the theatrical experience and focusing on transmitting place and space, the stare itself is included in DBC. Madness in the theatre is rarely intimate; even when characters are alone on the stage, their madness is largely uncontained by—depending on the theatre—the illusion of the fourth wall provided by the proscenium, or the physical space between actor and audience. An example of madness crossing distance is in the Royal Shakespeare Company's 1999 production of *The Winter's Tale*,[25] when Leontes is explaining that he "has drunk and seen the spider,"[26] which he uses to explain why knowledge of Hermione and Polixenes' affair (entirely fabricated in Leontes' mind) has driven him to madness.

Sher's Leontes directly addresses the audience, removing the contemporary polite fiction of a barrier between character and audience. This Leontes is implicating the audience in his madness and making himself a staree. The wide shot and inclusion of the audience in nearly a full third of the frame present an experiential image of the stare in action, as the audience recognizes the madness of Leontes, is discomfited by it, but is nonetheless visually engaged. The distance between audience and actor, however, came about in the Restoration, when the theatres in England reopened after the English Civil War. During the Elizabethan and Jacobean eras of playgoing, however, the theatre was a rowdier, louder place where audiences were vocally engaged with actors during the course of the play.[27] Wealthy playgoers could even pay a little extra to sit on stools on the edges of the stage itself, literally in the action.[28] The effect of the lack of separation between audience and actors in the early modern playhouses was an energetic and immediate form of feedback and criticism, and it meant that audiences were arguably complicit in the action of the play.

Rarely do RSC, Globe Theatre, or National Theatre productions allow early modern levels of audience participation, but the Sam Wanamaker theatre allows for a more intimate interaction between actors and audiences than a proscenium or apron theatre, and the intimacy helps to recapture some of the radicalization of interactive theatre techniques both in the theatre itself and in DBC versions of productions, such as that of the *Duchess of Malfi*. Amid the confusion of the Cardinal attempting to remove a body with Bosola's help, for instance, there is a brief, quiet moment where Ferdinand contemplates strangling as a murder method. His question "What say to that?" is directed to an audience member who is seated behind a short barrier, but right next to the stage. Ferdinand's candle is the only light in the room at this moment, so all eyes are following the light source and madman as he interrogates an audience member. Dromgoole begins this section in an extreme wide shot, before cutting to a medium shot.

Here again, the cinematography is capturing the stare in action, rather than framing a constructed filmic stare. Ferdinand as a staree and as bearer of the only source of light in the room, commands the stares of the theatre audience, particularly the woman he is interrogating. The cinematography is simple, the lighting is simple, and the filmic simplicity allows the power of the stare to be captured on camera. All eyes in the theatre audience are on Ferdinand, whose mind is not under control, and who is promoting behaviour that breaks the social script expectations in the play, and in the contemporary expectations of playgoing. Actors in the twentieth and twenty-first centuries are, by and large, not expected to acknowledge the audience directly, and certainly getting in an audience member's face is—outside of parodies and some styles of comedies— something to stare at. By engaging so closely with a single audience member, Ferdinand has taken the early modern ideas about lycanthropy and madness and transmuted them to the present; suddenly he is the aggressive gentleman with a mental impairment on the subway. That level of discomfort with deviant minds and/or bodies is still immediate, and the fact that Ferdinand is mad, not drunk, adds yet another level of discomfort. The filmic stare constructs a

Figure 7.1 Ferdinand interrogates an audience member

cinematic version of what DBC productions simply capture on film: the meeting of eyes and the intense discomfort that disability can engender. Of course, in the case of Ferdinand (and to a lesser degree Leontes), the disability in question is mental; there is nothing to see except the behavioural deviation from broken social scripts.

For mental disability in DBC productions, transmitting the experience of the stare in a given place takes the place of the filmic stare. Place does make a difference in DBC productions, and for *Titus Andronicus*, which combines mental and physical disability in one play, the interplay between the meta-stare, representing mental impairments, and the filmic stare representing physical disability—the difference between the Globe's DBC production and The RSC's production—is fascinating. *Titus Andronicus* illustrates not only the meta-stare, but also how physical disability is constructed via a zoomed-out version of the filmic stare. The two productions, from 2014[29] and 2017,[30] respectively, explore the meta-stare through Titus's madness and the filmic stare through the loss of Lavinia's and Titus's hands.

As the examples with Leontes and Ferdinand above show, and as Aebischer et al. underline, the meta-stare is strengthened or weakened by the design of the physical place in which the filmed production took place. Both the Globe Theatre and The Royal Shakespeare Theatre have thrust stages; the Globe Theatre also incorporates the pit design for the groundlings to stand in that was a part of the original Globe Theatre, where the Lord Chamberlain's Men (later the King's Men) played in the sixteenth and seventeenth centuries. In contrast, The Royal Shakespeare Theatre does not use a pit, but does include raised walkways that extend past the thrust to the back and sides of the house, allowing actors to use them not only as exits/entrances but also as playing space. As a result, the designs of these two places naturally encourage a breakdown of that fourth wall, even for characters who are not mad. For example, the RSC's Lucius physically hands Aaron's child to an audience member at several points during his interrogation of Aaron, leading to an awkwardly funny emotional moment as the audience member is implicated in the threat to the life of the child, but also has become a prop in the scene; a human cradle. For an audience member, being confronted by a non-normative mind is potentially quite shocking.

The RSC's Titus mirrors the meta-stare in the above Leontes example. Although he is physically closer to the audience than Leontes and not restrained by a proscenium, the actor is physically above an unlit audience, and the shot is wide.

The meta-stare is weaker here than in the Ferdinand example because the frame highlights the mad character, not the audience's reaction to the character. Additionally, the physical distance between actor and audience still provides a sense of separation, so the discomfort associated with the stare is diluted in the place and the meta-stare is diluted in the space of the DBC production. This Titus might be mad, and he might be talking to the theatre audience, but because of the physical distance and the darkness provided by

Figure 7.2 Titus addresses the audience from the stage

turning off the house lights in the theatre, the possibility of denial—that sense of "he's not talking directly to me"—permeates both the stare and meta-stare. The meta-stare refers purely to the DBC version of these productions; that is, the DBC treatment of a live production adds the meta-stare to a filmed production, an added filmic value to a live experience that also adds a layer of meaning that is not otherwise in the production.

In contrast, however, the Globe Theatre lights the audience in the evenings when natural light fades, and their production of *Titus Andronicus* uses the pit as part of the performance area. The production establishes the pit as part of the action at the very beginning. Both Saturninus and Bassianus perform their opening lines from mobile steel scaffolding platforms located amid the groundlings, and the Roman triumph that heralds the return of Titus parades throughout the pit before climbing to the stage. Already the production is very much in the viewer's faces, and they must frequently physically step aside to allow actors and set pieces to pass. By the time Titus has gone mad and is conspiring with his extended family to shoot arrows appealing to the gods for help, the groundlings are well aware that they are in what might be considered a "splash zone," both literally—as a character splashes wine onto audience members at several points—and figuratively, in the context of emotional and performative spillover as the actors inhabit a place that, in the twenty-first century, is typically reserved for spectators. However, that knowledge does little to alleviate the stares and discomfort when a mad Titus invades the pit.

The faces of the four women at whom Titus is yelling speak volumes: this encounter is too familiar, as a large male figure with questionable control over his mind and body yells at you in a crowded public space. Many, if not most women recognize this way of breaking social scripts, and even the presence of Publius to rein Titus in is little comfort. The discomfort both

Figure 7.3 Titus yelling at the audience while among them in the pit

with the situation and the mental impairment that is arguably causing the situation are writ large for the theatre audience to see and are captured on film for the broadcast audience to see. Broadcast audiences are staring at Titus and the theatre audience around him and recognize the stares and the affective experience of fear and discomfort that comes with the stare. In the context of this specific production, it is important to remember that, although this moment is tightly knit to broader social issues with gender relations, the meta-stare exists because of Titus' madness. The audience knows Titus is mad because his family members have made a point of highlighting it, and the fear is not just that of a potentially violent person who is physically larger and stronger than most women. The meta-stare taps into the fear of disabled minds/bodies; the lack of understanding a given disability, the fear that it could be you someday, and the uncertainty with how to address the disability that is in front of you. If Titus were simply angry and aggressive, this example would not fall into the purview of the discussion. Because he is mad in addition to being angry and aggressive, however, it is crucial to note that the meta-stare is tied up with other gendered concerns about breaking social scripts that may not be inherent to disability. The production produced a feeling of how crowd moods can shift and change, so the meta-stare is a component of that sense overall.

In a technical sense, this shot is still wide and high angle, and we see little more of Titus than a head and shoulder, so it is significantly different from the RSC's Titus, and even from the Leontes and Ferdinand examples, where we see an actor directly addressing an audience member. The crowd aspect of the Globe's production and this specific instance of the meta-stare taps into the wider social atmospheres from which, according to Garland-Thomson, the stare emerges, leading to a strong moment of the meta-stare for the broadcast audience. The immediacy of surrounding actor with audience in a moment of madness and allowing the broadcast audience to see the theatre audience creates an immensely poignant space for the meta-stare.

The examples so far discussed are significant because while addressing soliloquies to the audience is a relatively common technique in Shakespeare theatre and film productions, once characters have acquired madness, their audience interactions are more complex, layered, and potentially uncomfortable. In short, confronting an audience member as a mad character is a technique that seems to be used sparingly. Ultimately, the technique of closely confronting audience members shatters the comfortable, passive barrier between audience and production, and in some cases might take audience members right out of the production because they recognize the fear and discomfort from real life. Certainly, it has been said that art imitates life, and after Vice President Pence walked out of a production of *Hamilton*, theatre fans were reminded that theatres have a history of being spaces of subversion, spaces where uncomfortable topics are brought into the light and addressed. For madness in Shakespeare, however, maintaining the comfort of the fourth wall is as important as breaking it. *Malfi, Titus* and *Winter's Tale* all have moments where the fourth wall is broken, and those moments serve to highlight the discomfort inherent in the stares of the theatre audience, potentially serving to create an even greater contrast between men who are mad and men who are not. For the theatre audience, breaking the fourth wall inflames unconsciously held discomfort with disabilities by putting the disability literally in the spotlight, then gives a specific audience member little choice but to interact with the character with a disability. Breaking the fourth wall also signifies, in a theatrical sense, the breaking of an assumed social script specific to the theatre: actors are not supposed to acknowledge the audience. This underpins the more overt breaking of behavioural and verbal scripts within the world of the play, and, again, highlights the discomfort.

For the broadcast audience, the actor is mediated through a screen, separated through time, space and place. Because the cameras capture the stare between theatre audience member and actor, however, the interactive theatrical technique becomes a way for the broadcast audience to empathize with the theatre audience and symbolically share the "audience space" even though the broadcast audience might be watching the production in their bed on a smartphone. Sharing the audience space means that the broadcast audience is emotionally affected in similar ways to the theatre audience when interactive strategies are used to highlight madness as a disability.

Overall, the meta-stare in DBC productions is possible because of interactive theatre techniques used in the theatre productions being filmed, and it functions to close the emotional distance between theatre audience and broadcast audience. Under the aegis of disability studies, the meta-stare fundamentally functions to highlight an audience's reaction to mental disability, not just in the world of the play, but in their own lives and experiences. Any woman understands the fear and discomfort of a physically and/or mentally uncontrolled man in her space, but when the underlying reason for the lack of control is a disability, hopefully the meta-stare creates enough space to engage with a more intellectual reaction, allowing broadcast audience members to understand and empathize with the reactions of the theatre audience, but also to reevaluate those reactions, and consider their own reactions to disabilities.

The Gendered Representation of Physical Disability in *Titus Andronicus*

What both productions of *Titus Andronicus* share in terms of the filmic stare overall is a lack of a visual synecdoche for Titus' madness. Unlike Taymor's cinematic *Titus*, where the intensive repetition of penny arcade nightmares functioned as a synecdoche for Titus' madness,[31] the theatre productions rely on the actor's choices to convey madness, and the DBC productions lean heavily on shots that create space around the meta-stare to reinforce madness. Madness, as I have previously argued, is difficult to represent on screen because it is ultimately invisible, aside from the changes in behaviour and the breaks in social scripts. Not so with physical disabilities, particularly in *Titus Andronicus*, because a missing hand is quite visible. Unlike the cinematic films discussed in previous chapters, where the filmic stare can focus so intently on the visual synecdoche that the humanity of the character with the disability disappears behind the impairment, DBC productions that focus on the loss of hands for Titus and Lavinia seem to favor affective shots of the performer's face. DBC as a form highlights affect and the humanity of the characters in a way that cinematic films tend to have to actively go out of their way to accomplish, at least for amputee characters. What we see with both Titus and Lavinia as a result is a relative lack of visibility of the physical impairment for the broadcast audience, but a greater focus on the emotional content of the scenes.

In terms of the visibility of Titus and Lavinia's stumps after they lose their hands, Taymor and Howell represent the two methodologies: Taymor uses the mise-en-scène to highlight the impairment in frame by making the impairment stand out, whereas Howell minimizes the visual impact by making bandages the same color as long sleeves. For their respective DBC productions, the Globe follows the minimization method, wherein both Titus and Lavinia are dressed in white garments that evoke bandages, which allows the white bandages covering their respective stumps to blend into the garment, becoming part of a physical and visual line and masking the loss of a hand, particularly to the theatre audience who are a greater distance from the characters than the broadcast audience.

In addition to minimizing the visibility of the impairments through design choices, the Globe's production makes a point of using very few close-ups of Titus's stump. In fact, the two major close-ups of his stump in this production are restricted to a close-up of Titus writing with his own blood, and a close-up of Titus serving the pie to Tamora and Saturninus. In both shots, Titus's bandaged stump is centrally placed in the frame, highlighting the impairment and, particularly in the shot serving the pie, thematically resonating with revenge. These shots also highlight Titus's *ability*. He can still effectively serve at dinner and can still write. We are even treated to a scene in which Titus shoots a longbow with the use of both feet and his one hand, highlighting the fact that, while the loss of his hand was certainly traumatic and ultimately a cruel trick of Aaron's, the visual minimization of the impairment suggests that it functions as a goad for Titus' revenge—disability becomes renewed ability. The treatment of Lavinia's amputation, however, is different in the context of the filmic stare, if not in the context of the design choice which leads to a visual minimization.

For the broadcast audience, Lavinia's double amputation is largely lost as a visual synecdoche, in comparison to the way the Globe DBC production creates a weak but present synecdoche for Titus' amputation. For the theatre audience, Lavinia's bloody bandages blend in with her dress, and her white bandages are completely lost in her white dress. In moments where the focus is on Lavinia, however, even in medium and medium close-up shots, her stumps tend to be in the lower third of the frame, and typically they are just barely in frame at all. Central in the frame, however, is Lavinia's face. Again, in the context of the filmic stare in cinematic film adaptations of *Titus*, often directors must go out of their way to include faces in shots which highlight physical impairments, and when faces are not included, humanity is lost to the characters. The visual synecdoche in cinematic film often comes at the cost of humanizing characters. For the Globe's DBC production, however, the face and performance, the insistence on the humanity of Lavinia despite her impairment, comes quite naturally from the medium shots that dominate the scenes immediately after she is raped. This cinematographic choice is also underlined by the play text itself. Marcus, on finding Lavinia, insists that he and the family will "mourn with you,"[32] and Titus sharply corrects Lucius when he would turn away from his sister, saying "look upon her."[33] The Globe production puts the filmic stare and affect in competition here, but also reflects the insistence Titus and Marcus carry from the text of the play that Lavinia will be seen and recognized as human. Recognizing a survivor of rape and mutilation as human may seem obvious to a twenty-first century audience, but the loss of chastity in an early modern context was serious. Titus and Saturninus, however, highlight the tension between the idea that the "girl should not outlive her shame,"[34] as Saturninus says, and the shock of watching a father murder a daughter who has been raped. Similarly, the loss of physical or mental ability is a complex phenomenon; the value of an individual does not diminish due to disability, but Hollywood's history of isolating characters with disabilities, the fears surrounding disability, and a kill or cure[35] mentality certainly suggests a diminishment of the social value of the individual. It is tricky to tease out the separate threads of trauma and rape survival with the effects of an acquired disability in Lavinia's case. Lavinia's inherent humanity, insisted on by both Titus and Marcus, as well as the cinematography creates a version of the filmic stare that exists in reaction to the diminishment of a character with a disability to merely the visual of the impairment.

In contrast to the Globe production, the RSC production highlights Lavinia's missing hands with stark white bandages at the end of dark grey sleeves. The RSC's Titus, however, simply has a rolled sleeve, rather than a kind of wrap or bandages. The RSC's production is the first of the productions so far discussed that differentiates between the representation of Titus's physical disability and Lavinia's, although both acquire physical impairments.

In terms of design, both Lavinia and Titus wear jackets of nearly the same color, but Lavinia's white bandages visually stand out in the frame to a greater degree in contrast. In terms of the construction of the filmic stare, the broadcast audience for the RSC production sees a loose construction of a visual synecdoche for Titus that centers around severed hands. In the immediate aftermath of Titus' hand being severed, Aaron is in the foreground at a medium distance of the next several shots, manipulating and stroking the severed hand. During the scene with Tamora impersonating Revenge, Titus has gotten hold of his severed (now rotting) hand and waves it for emphasis in a rare close-up. While less dense than Taymor's cinematic construction of a visual synecdoche in a cinematic film, the RSC production uses similar techniques to highlight the severed limb rather than the impairment to Titus' body as a whole. The combination of the minimalist visual presence of the stump and the highlighting of the severed limb function to distract the focus from the physical disability. By distracting both theatre and broadcast audiences from his physical disability, Titus avoids

Figure 7.4 Andronici family dinner

some, though not all, of the feminization that Garland-Thomson argues is inherent in the acquisition or experience of physical disability.[36] For Lavinia, however, being female and having her physical disability highlighted creates a significantly different dynamic.

Unlike Titus, Lavinia's amputated extremities make no reappearance on stage; the visual that both theatre and broadcast audiences are left with is the white bandage at the end of the dark sleeve. In contrast to the Globe's DBC production too, the RSC tends to center Lavinia's bandages, both in frame and in the action of the scene, so that they are consistently highlighted. Rather than separate the disability from the body as we see with Titus, Lavinia's impairment is always connected directly to her body. As I have previously argued,[37] the filmic stare in cinematic film adaptations of *Hamlet* is egalitarian in its representation of disability; male and female madness are represented in visually similar ways. Taymor's *Titus* and the Globe's *Titus Andronicus* both used similar techniques to visually represent Titus and Lavinia's physical disability too, following in that egalitarian mode. The RSC's choice to represent physical disability based on gender is significantly different from other adaptations of the play. The two different representations of physical disability also dovetail with the social and cultural models of disability. Titus' impairment is separated from his physical body through the creation of a visual synecdoche centered on the severed hand rather than the stump; we can see from the social model[38] influencing the thematic tie-in that it is the socio-political factors surrounding Titus that inform the death of four of his sons in Rome, and the disintegration of the Andronici family unit throughout the play. Titus himself is socially (and ultimately physically and mentally) disabled by Roman politics and the machinations of Saturninus.

Lavinia, however, has her visual synecdoche fully integrated with her body; as Jonathan Bate notes, Lavinia is "a 'speechless complainer' but a bodily presence."[39] Her identity and her physical experience shifts as a result of her impairment. Some critics, including Emily Detmer-Goebel,[40] have argued that Lavinia is herself a site of resistance in that she is an active part of communicating who raped and mutilated her. From a disability studies standpoint, Lavinia learning to communicate might be read as an embrace of her "new normal," after she has acquired her disability. The connection admittedly falls apart in the context of Titus' murder of his daughter in a classic example of kill or cure; but Lavinia's integration of her impairment into her physical experience and the sheer visibility of the impairment—particularly in contrast with Titus' visibly minimized impairment—suggests that Lavinia's body and impairment are a site of resistance to "socially constructed conceptions of normality."[41] It would be anachronistic hyperbole to argue that Lavinia celebrates her disability as a part of a group identity, as the cultural model posits, but her identity, highlighted by the production design and editing choices that construct the filmic stare around her, places Lavinia in conversation with the cultural model of disability and with women who experience physical disabilities—with all the complexities inherent therein.

As a hybrid medium, DBC productions are unique in the ways in which they interact with disability. The meta-stare and its potential for distancing as well as empathy would be impossible without the theatre audiences. In particular, the theatre audience is critical for the radical, interactive theatre techniques brought to bear when characters with mental disabilities take direct address a step past the fourth wall. Still a relatively new player on the popular Shakespearean stage, DBC productions will surely continue to evolve and change, and more scholarly attention deserves to be paid to DBC productions. DBC productions of Verdi's *Otello* come to mind as a potentially interesting site for research, as do DBC productions of contemporary Broadway shows that explore disability. However, those explorations must wait for future studies, as gendered patterns in the representation of physical disabilities in DBC productions seem to follow patterns identified in earlier chapters on cinematic and televisual film adaptations of early modern plays. Those threads will be pulled together in the concluding chapter.

Notes

1   Heyer, Paul. "Live from the Met: Digital Broadcast Cinema, Medium Theory, and Opera for the Masses." *Canadian Journal of Communication*, 33 (2008): 591–604.
2   *Shakespeare & The 'Live' Theatre Broadcast Experience*. Ed. Pascale Aebischer, Susanne Greenhalgh, and Laurie E. Osborne. New York: The Arden Shakespeare. 2018. 4.
3   Aebischer, Pascale and Susanne Greenhalgh. "Introduction." *Shakespeare & The 'Live' Theatre Broadcast Experience*. Ed. Pascale Aebischer, Susanne Greenhalgh, and Laurie E. Osborne. New York. The Arden Shakespeare: 2018. 1–16. 7.
4   Jorgens, Jack. *Shakespeare on Film*. Bloomington: Indiana UP. 1977.
5   Jorgens, 7.
6   Jorgens, 8.
7   Greenhalgh, Susanne. "The Remains of the Stage: Revivifying Shakespearean Theatre on Screen, 1964–2016." *Shakespeare & The 'Live' Theatre Broadcast Experience*. Ed. Pascale Aebischer, Susanne Greenhalgh, and Laurie E. Osborne. New York: The Arden Shakespeare. 2018. 19, 21–2.
8   Jorgens, 15.
9   Qtd. in Aebischer, Greenhalgh, and Osborne, 5.
10   Aebischer, Greenhalgh, and Osborne, 6.
11   Heyer, 593.
12   Brown, Mark. "Kenneth Branagh's Garrick Productions to be Shown Live in Cinemas Worldwide." *The Guardian*. September 10, 2015. Web.
13   Aebischer, Greenhalgh, and Osborne, 4.
14   Qtd. in Heyer, 594.
15   Aebischer, Greenhalgh, and Osborne, 4.
16   Aebischer, Greenhalgh, and Osborne, 4.
17   Aebischer, Greenhalgh, and Osborne, 4.
18   Heyer, 593.
19   Sharrock, Beth. "A View from the Stage: Interviews with Performers." *Shakespeare & The 'Live' Theatre Broadcast Experience*. Ed. Pascale Aebischer, Susanne Greenhalgh, and Laurie E. Osborne. New York: The Arden Shakespeare. 2018. 99.
20   Aebischer, 116–17.
21   Aebischer, Greenhalgh, and Osborne, 2, 115–17.

22 *The Duchess of Malfi*. The Globe Theatre. Recorded Theatre Production. Dir. Dominic Dromgoole. 2014.
23 This theatre recalls, although it is not an exact reproduction of, an indoor Jacobean theatre, Blackfriars. The Wannamaker theatre is an indoor theatre affiliated with the Globe Theatre replica. *The Duchess of Malfi* was the theatre's first production.
24 See discussion in Chapter 4.
25 *The Winter's Tale*. Dir. Gregory Doran and Robin Lough. Perf. Antony Sher, Alexandra Gilbreath. Kultur. 1999.
26 *The Winter's Tale*, 2.1.45.
27 Gurr, Andrew. *The Shakespearean Stage 1574–1642*. 3rd ed. Cambridge: Cambridge UP: 1992. 222–9. 223.
28 Gurr, 214.
29 "William Shakespeare's *Titus Andronicus*." Dir. Lucy Bailey and Ian Russell. Perf. William Houston, Obi Abili, Indira Varma. Opus Arte. 2014.
30 "Titus Andronicus." Directed for the stage by Blanche McIntyre. Directed for film by Matt Woodward. *Live from Stratford-Upon-Avon*; Opus Arte. 2017.
31 See my discussion of *Titus* in Chapter 2.
32 *Titus Andronicus*, 2.4.56.
33 *Titus Andronicus*, 3.1.65.
34 *Titus Andronicus*, 5.3.41–2.
35 Norden, Martin. *The Cinema of Isolation: A History of Physical Disability in the Movies*. New Brunswick: Rutgers University Press. 1994. 7, 107.
36 Garland-Thomson, Rosemarie. *Extraordinary Bodies: Figuring Physical Disability in American Culture and Literature*. New York: Columbia UP. 1997. 9.
37 See my introduction for an explanation of the egalitarian representation of madness.
38 Berger, Ronald J. "Explaining Disability." *Introducing Disability Studies*. New York: Lynne Rienner. 2013. 27–8.
39 Bate, Jonathan. "Introduction." *Titus Andronicus*. 3rd ed. Ed. Jonathan Bate. London: The Arden Shakespeare. 2018. 35.
40 Detmer-Goebel, Emily. "The Need for Lavinia's Voice: *Titus Andronicus* and the Telling of Rape." *Shakespeare Studies*. 2001.
41 Berger, 29–30.

Bibliography

Aebischer, Pascale, Susanne Greenhalgh, and Laurie E. Osborne, Eds. *Shakespeare & The 'Live' Theatre Broadcast Experience*. New York: The Arden Shakespeare. 2018.

Bate, Jonathan. "Introduction." *Titus Andronicus*. 3rd ed. Ed. Jonathan Bate. London: The Arden Shakespeare. 2018.

Berger, Ronald J. "Explaining Disability." *Introducing Disability Studies*. New York: Lynne Rienner. 2013.

Brown, Mark. "Kenneth Branagh's Garrick Productions to be Shown Live in Cinemas Worldwide." *The Guardian*, September 10, 2015. Web.

Detmer-Goebel, Emily. "The Need for Lavinia's Voice: *Titus Andronicus* and the Telling of Rape." *Shakespeare Studies*. 2001: 75.

Garland-Thomson, Rosemarie. *Extraordinary Bodies: Figuring Physical Disability in American Culture and Literature*. New York: Columbia UP. 1997.

Greenhalgh, Susanne. "The Remains of the Stage: Revivifying Shakespearean Theatre on Screen, 1964–2016." *Shakespeare & The 'Live' Theatre Broadcast Experience*.

Ed. Pascale Aebischer, Susanne Greenhalgh, and Laurie E. Osborne. New York: The Arden Shakespeare. 2018. 19, 21–22.

Gurr, Andrew. *The Shakespearean Stage 1574–1642*. 3rd ed. Cambridge: Cambridge UP. 1992.

Heyer, Paul. "Live from the Met: Digital Broadcast Cinema, Medium Theory, and Opera for the Masses." *Canadian Journal of Communication*, 33 (2008): 591–604.

Jorgens, Jack. *Shakespeare on Film*. Bloomington: Indiana UP. 1977.

Norden, Martin. *The Cinema of Isolation: A History of Physical Disability in the Movies*. New Brunswick: Rutgers University Press. 1994.

Sharrock, Beth. "A View from the Stage: Interviews with Performers." *Shakespeare & The 'Live' Theatre Broadcast Experience*. Ed. Pascale Aebischer, Susanne Greenhalgh, and Laurie E. Osborne. New York: The Arden Shakespeare. 2018.

The Duchess of Malfi. The Globe Theatre. Recorded Theatre Production. Dir. Dominic Dromgoole. 2014.

"*Titus Andronicus*." Live from Stratford-Upon-Avon. Dir. Blanche McIntyre and Matt Woodward. Perf. David Troughton. Opus Arte. 2017.

The Winter's Tale. Dir. Gregory Doran and Robin Lough. Perf. Antony Sher, Alexandra Gilbreath. Kultur. 1999.

William Shakespeare's Titus Andronicus. Dir. Lucy Bailey and Ian Russell. Perf. William Houston, Obi Abili, Indira Varma. Opus Arte. 2014.

Conclusion

Ronald Berger argues that disability studies "asks us to become more aware of the words and phrases we use [...] that demean people with disabilities."[1] Berger's assertion makes two primary assumptions: first that words and phrases—be they spoken or written—are the only and/or primary way that people with disabilities are demeaned. Second, that the end goal of using specific words and phrases—or, in the case of cinematic representations, embodiments of those words and phrases—is to demean people with disabilities. The English language certainly does possess built-in biases and phraseology that is demeaning; however, in an image-saturated late twentieth and twenty-first century, still images and cinematic representations have been subject to the same reactions as demeaning words or phrases. For example, the word "cripple" has a storied history of first being the term for people with disabilities, then being banned for being dehumanizing and demeaning, before being reclaimed and—to use an equally fraught term—rehabilitated by people with disabilities as an expression of self-representation. Robert McRuer's 2006 book, *Crip Theory: Cultural Signs of Queerness and Disability*,[2] reflects the full return to reclaiming and celebrating a term that had once been dehumanizing and demeaning. McRuer focuses on disability theory and cultural studies, and Tobin Siebers, Ato Quayson, and other scholars or disability aesthetics provide a framework to see the potential for a similar developmental curve in the critical theory surrounding disability film studies. Ultimately, understanding representations of disability through the filmic stare will require a synthesis of both linguistic and aesthetic disability studies, just as understanding the specific representations of disability in Shakespeare film requires as synthesis of literary and film knowledge.

At this point in the development of disability film studies, the existing frameworks for assessing representations of disability in cinema have primarily come from English, Cultural Studies, and Sociological backgrounds. The main examples include the medical, social and cultural models of disability which come from cultural and sociological backgrounds;[3] Mitchell and Snyder's narrative prosthesis, which comes from a literary background;[4] and Martin Norden's *Cinema of Isolation*, which seeks to create a genre-based methodology for identifying physical disability in the movies.[5] These models

DOI: 10.4324/9781003163374-9

and methodologies are careful to pay attention to the words and phrases they use, and to identify inspiration porn and overcoming narratives as harmful, but none address the cinematographic building blocks of the representations they explicate.

The foundational critical-theoretical framework that does address the cinematographic building blocks of representations of disability on screen is the filmic stare. The filmic stare functions to create a visual synecdoche for the character with a disability, exploring the cinematographic techniques used to highlight or suppress disability in each frame of film. It also argues that, ultimately, while male and female bodies are often represented differently on camera, the building blocks of cinematography that compose a visual representation of disability are the same regardless of gender. Therefore, on a "sentence-level" analysis of visual representations of disability, masculine and feminine representations, particularly of madness, but of physical disability to a degree as well, are too similar to draw a hard dividing line between male and female representations of disability.

Of the film adaptations and DBC productions I have discussed throughout this book, the cinematographic techniques that form the filmic stare are consistently deployed across gender. The gendered *difference* is in whether a disability is highlighted or suppressed. Additional factors in the gendered split between suppression and highlighting include whether an impairment is mental or physical, and the genre of the cinematic film or made-for-TV movie. Typically, in film adaptations of early modern plays—although exceptions do exist for each of these arguments—mental disabilities are highlighted in female characters through more liberal uses of empathetic subjective shots, but in male characters the highlighting comes mostly through wide and extreme wide shots which showcase the breaking of verbal and behavioural scripts. For physical disabilities, on the other hand, genre is the primary determinant as to whether a male character's impairment is highlighted or suppressed, and for Lavinia—Shakespeare's only female character with an immediately visible physical disability—the existence of a visual synecdoche determines whether her impairment is highlighted or suppressed. It is important to note here that my discussion in this chapter, unlike my broader discussion of the filmic stare in Chapter 1, is focused explicitly on film adaptations of early modern drama, not on the applicability of a gendered divide between highlighting and suppressing disability across all of film studies. Certainly, a film like *The Fault in Our Stars* (2014) or *Million Dollar Baby* (2004) might deviate from the gendered divide I will discuss. Shakespeare films, however, adhere to a gendered divide in highlighting/suppressing impairments more than they do not. I will begin my discussion of a gendered divide in representation by focusing on mental disabilities in cinematic film, made-for-TV movies and (DBC) before moving to physical disabilities in those same media.

Madness, as I have previously argued, is an inherently invisible disability which is represented on screen through the filmic stare using six key cinematographic techniques: wide/extreme wide shots, physically disheveling previously neat characters, the construction of a visual synecdoche, self-reflexive shots, empathetic shots, and breaking verbal/behavioural social scripts. In terms of a gendered highlighting of madness, however, film-makers seem to take male madness at its representation via wide shots, whereas there is a need to prove female madness through shots of the female character's subjective reality while she is mad. The underlying—uncon-scious?—assumption of these techniques is that when female characters experience mental disabilities, they experience a subjective visual reality that is significantly different from the visual reality of characters who do not experience a mental disability. Conversely, male characters who experience mental disabilities do not experience a significantly altered visual reality.

For example, when Polonius asks Hamlet, "Do you know me, my lord?" and Hamlet responds "Excellent well. You are a fishmonger,"[6] no extant film version of *Hamlet* cuts to a subjective shot from Hamlet's point of view wherein Polonius is dressed like a fishmonger or surrounded by fish. Ham-let's madness is typically represented on film as a synaptic misfire in his comprehension or his memory, not as an explicitly visual hallucination. That Hamlet cannot "wield the gaze" in his madness is largely in keeping with the pattern that Martin Norden identifies—that characters with dis-abilities cannot look without being punished.[7] Norden is discussing physical disability, but at least in terms of male characters who experience mental disabilities, the pattern seems to hold true.

Female characters with mental disabilities are characterized—in Shakespeare films—by subjective and empathetic subjective shots of the visual reality they experience because of their impairment. Olivier and Branagh both include empathetic shots of Ophelia seeing herself reflected in the water before she drowns, and Almereyda takes those empathetic shots and uses them to create a watery motif associated with Ophelia in what is otherwise a highly technology-oriented *Hamlet*. Almereyda's Ophelia not only sees her reflection in water, but her subjective reality includes jumping into a pool to avoid the embarrassment of her father reading a letter Hamlet wrote to her in front of Claudius and Gertrude. In Ophelia's case, these shots ultimately seem to ask for sympathy; Ophelia, like Hamlet, has little control over events.

For Lady Macbeth, however, subjective shots of bloodied hands serve as a stark reminder that Lady Macbeth pushed her husband into murder; they are almost a badge of blame. However, they also reflect the agency Lady Macbeth shows because, even after she goes mad, she is allowed subjective looks in film. Polanski and Goold construct Lady Macbeth's visual synec-doche around her hands, and both directors focus their subjective shots around hands as well. Kurzel, on the other hand, expands Lady Macbeth's subjective reality to include an interaction with the ghost of her dead son. Having moved from their village to Dunsinane, Lady Macbeth in her mad-ness returns to the village and confronts his ghost, linking Lady Macbeth to Hamlet. It is interesting to note that Gertrude never sees the ghost of Old Hamlet, so in allowing Lady Macbeth to see the ghost of her dead child in her madness, Kurzel creates a link to madness and ghosts across a gender boundary.

Ultimately, mental disabilities are represented on screen using the same tools of the filmic stare but are employed differently for male and female characters. Using wide shots and limiting or eliminating subjective and empathetic shots for mad characters who are male suggests a different experience of madness than does highlighting subjective shots and visually different subjective realities for female madness. Although these approaches highlight different lived experiences of madness, the tools with which they are represented on screen are foundationally identical. The use of identical techniques to represent madness in both male and female characters on screen is itself radical; gendered representations to this day create controversy, but when disability enters the frame, the typical gendered othering that occurs falls away and the grammar of the filmic stare is applied with a relatively egalitarian brush. Directors might favor certain filmic stare techniques over others, but exceptions are not uncommon, and the connections made through those exceptions clearly demonstrate that representations of mental disability on screen are nearly as gender blind as instances of mental disability are in the real world.

In the context of physical disability and Shakespeare film, there are three major factors that affect the filmic stare and gender. The first is that, while Lady Macbeth and Ophelia go mad differently for different narrative reasons, in the Shakespearean canon only one female character has a textually unambiguous physical disability: Lavinia. Such a small sample size ultimately means that, while Lavinia is an extraordinarily interesting site for analysis, the filmic stare as a critical theory needs a broader application beyond film adaptations of Shakespeare's plays to really explore female physical disability in cinema. The second factor is that the two major twentieth century film adaptations of *Titus Andronicus*[8] were directed by women. Julie Taymor and Jane Howell both constructed their films to avoid explicit instances of the gaze and the typical fragmentation and objectification of women on film. Avoiding the gaze had a significant impact on the relationship of the gaze and the filmic stare in addition to humanizing Lavinia as more than a prop in the familial and political machinations in Rome.

The third and final major factor affecting physical disability in film adaptations of Shakespeare plays and the filmic stare is genre. Adaptations of *Titus Andronicus* and *Richard III* tend to fall into one of two genres: horror films and war films. For Titus and for Richard, horror adaptation tends to highlight physical disabilities, whereas war film adaptations tend to suppress them. In all cases, however, the foundational elements of the filmic stare remain the same. Crucially, Lavinia's representation also follows this war film/horror film split. Kenneth Rothwell categorizes Taymor's *Titus* as a slasher film,[9] and Lavinia's impairments are accordingly highlighted through the motif of severed limbs and prosthetic limbs throughout the film. Howell's war film adaptation of *Titus Andronicus*, however, goes out of its way to suppress Lavinia's—and Titus'—impairments in the frame, focusing the film's attention on the politicization of bodies rather than the physiological bodies. This same pattern of genre affecting highlighting and/or suppression can be seen across the adaptations of *Richard III* as well. McKellen's savvy gangster Richard highlights the political pre-war tensions of late 1930s Britain and, in doing so, suppresses the visibility and corporeal impact of Richard's impairments. Conversely, Cumberbatch's Igor-esque hunch and body horror money shots make it impossible to downplay his impairments, and while *Richard III* does end in the battle of Bosworth Field, director Dominic Cooke highlights horror aspects including jump scares and creepy meetings in the woods at midnight. Hence, horror is the predominant genre under which I classify his *Richard III*. Lavinia's mirroring of the split between genre and highlighting and/or suppressing disability in *Richard III* and other male characters in Titus Andronicus is critical, because not only are male and female physical disabilities reflected by genre in a similar fashion, but the filmic stare, as discussed in depth in Chapters 2 and 4, provides a critical framework for describing and categorizing the shot-by-shot and sequence-by-sequence construction of representations of disability in each of the films using the same techniques. Representing disability using the same techniques across gender is unusual for film cinematography, particularly in the context of the gaze and the tradition of literary criticism separating male and female disability.

Where physical disability is concerned, however, there is a change to the filmic stare insofar as empathetic subjective shots seem to disappear from the visual grammar. Likely this is because film can communicate differences in subjective visual reality easily, as we saw with Lady Macbeth example above. However, differences in a proprioceptive subjective reality are immensely challenging to visually represent from the perspective of the character with the disability. The example that comes to mind is not a Shakespearean one; perhaps the best example of visually representing a proprioceptive subjective reality comes from *Vertigo*, in Hitchcock's dolly zoom shot as Scottie looks down from the stairs in the bell tower.[10] For a viewer who has never experienced vertigo, the dolly zoom shot provides a clear representation of the stomach-twisting, dizzying, proprioceptive change Scottie experienced. Cumberbatch's Richard III does catch a glimpse of his own reflection in the blade of a dagger, but because the shot is static and close-up, and while a certain level of positional empathy is gained by viewers as a result of this shot, there is no sense of what it is to experience Richard's balance being affected by his impairments. Richard tells us in the play text after he woos Lady Ann that he will "be at charges for a looking glass,"[11] but no extant film adaptation takes Richard at his word, turns the camera, and gives viewers a subjective shot of Richard looking at himself. It seems that if a character has a visible, physical disability, the character's ability to look at—or reflect on—their self is ignored, and the camera's (and the viewer's) look is privileged.

Privileging the camera's looking in the case of physical disability is also reflected in Lavinia and in Caliban. Neither Howell nor Taymor allows Lavinia any subjective or subjective empathetic shots with which to look at her own body and impairments, regardless of the film's genre. Interestingly, however, it is Taymor's insistence on the humanity of her disabled characters within the grammar of the filmic stare that connect her Lavinia and her Caliban. Neither is granted subjective or subjective empathetic shots, but in many of the shots in which their impairments are highlighted, their faces are included in the frame. If Lavinia and Caliban cannot look at their own physical impairments, then Taymor goes out of her way to remind viewers of these characters' humanity. Privileging the humanity of characters with disabilities is a significant step from the days of the 1970s when America still had "Ugly Laws" on their books,[12] or the days of the popularity of American Freak Shows. It also builds on a history of physical disability in cinema that dehumanized, infantilized, and ultimately othered characters with disabilities through the kill or cure paradigm. In the kill or cure context, Caliban might be the most significant departure; Lavinia is killed by Titus, but Caliban is simply released—admittedly into isolation on the island, but hey, baby steps—by Prospero without killing or curing the impairments. To simply allow Caliban to exist with his impairments, even in isolation, is unusual in films that feature characters with disabilities, regardless of genre.

In addition to genre, production can also be a factor in the filmic stare, particularly when it comes to digital broadcast cinema. Where film and television always have separate, dedicated photography and editing phases in their productions, DBC productions may in fact shoot and edit simultaneously. Not only may the editing and photography phases of production be elided in DBC, most often these productions are attempting to capture a specific stage production, and the theatrical experience, which means being aware of other audience members and the theatrical atmosphere. The design of the theatre in which filming takes place can affect the prominence of the theatrical audience; a proscenium theatre might minimize the amount of the theatre audience the cameras capture, whereas the Globe Theatre often utilizes the pit as playing space, so the actors are in amongst the groundlings and the experience of the theatre audience is unique to them and to the broadcast audience. As a direct result of including a theatrical audience in the DBC frame, the filmic stare gains an element: the meta-stare.

The meta-stare describes the broadcast viewer watching the theatrical audience react to a character with a disability, and the instinctive, distancing effect of the broadcast audience watching theatrical audiences react and considering how they, the broadcast audience, might react in similar circumstances. At its core, the meta-stare is a mediated, multi-layered version of Garland-Thomson's stare, and the mediation and multiple layers of viewers means that, in many ways, the actual body with the disability on the stage becomes somewhat lost in the layers of (presumably) abled audience members watching each other out of one eye and the character with a disability from the other. The disconnection between the disabled body and the abled viewer looking mirrors the social model of disability in an interesting way. The social model has been criticized for focusing so much on the relationship between the individual and society, culture, architecture, etc., that the actual impairment and the actual body tends to be lost in the semantics of discussing the relationship.[13] The layers of mediation and the audiences involved in the meta-stare function the same way. The danger of using the meta-stare is to move so far from the actual bodies on the stage that the filmic stare and the cinematic building blocks creating the on-screen representation of disability is itself usurped in discussion by social anxiety and/or secondhand embarrassment. Despite this pitfall, however, the meta-stare when analyzed in conjunction with the filmic stare, can add nuance to an analysis of an on-screen representation of disability, while heightening the broadcast audience's awareness of the unconscious power of the stare. Pedagogically, the meta-stare and DBC productions may be an even more solid foundation from which to teach students about the stare, because, rather than putting students on the (possibly extremely uncomfortable) spot by asking them what their reaction is to seeing a person with a disability, they can analyze their own reactions to the theatre audience of a DBC production and the discussion can include the stare and the meta-stare in order to make students more aware of how much impact the unconscious social assumptions we might make can affect/influence our own work and lives.

Becoming more aware of the unconscious social assumptions we make is really the film studies answer to Berger's assertion that disability studies asks us to look at the words we use.[14] Dialogue and physical scripts are important in the context of words, but in the context of cinema as a visual medium, becoming aware of how we see images of disability—or how we compose images of disability—is key. The creation of a visual synecdoche for a character is to create a shorthand for a given impairment, for quick, nonverbal recognition. The specific use of framing and shot scale, as well as the use of subjective POV and subjective empathetic shots,[15] creates tension within the film around the visual synecdoche, making the visual representation of disability more complex. The relationship of the overall construction of a representation of character with a disability to the film's narrative then must necessarily be more complex than the binaries accurate/not accurate, or positive/negative.

The strength of the filmic stare in terms of the intersection between film studies and disability studies is that it provides a specific, film-studies based language with which to describe, categorize and discuss representations of mental and physical disabilities in cinema without relapsing into the recursive and limiting trap of applying sociological, medical or even narratological frameworks to a visual medium and expecting real-life, medically-accurate representations, and, when those expectations go unmet, shutting down any discussion by dismissing the representation as inaccurate and/or negative. The filmic stare creates a visual grammar, and that visual grammar allows scholars to explore the nuances more specifically and clearly in the representations of disability, finding patterns that might be surprising—potentially even positive overarching patterns; for example, the pattern of representing male and female bodies with disabilities in similar ways. It is still radical to see abled female characters represented in similar ways to male abled characters on screen; the fact that male and female characters with disabilities are presented on screen using the same techniques has significant potential to be read through feminist theoretical lenses.

In its current iteration, however, the filmic stare helps fill a gap in current film studies explorations of representations of disability studies. The creation of a visual synecdoche, the use of specific shot scales and the use of subjective empathetic shots, combined with the refusal to diagnose literary characters, invites discussions that have previously been recursive, stifled, or silenced completely.

Notes

1 Berger, Ronald J. *Introducing Disability Studies*. New York: Lynne Rienner. 2013. 5.
2 McRuer, Robert. *Crip Theory: Cultural Signs of Queerness and Disability*. New York: New York UP. 2006.
3 Berger, Ronald J. *Introducing Disability Studies*. New York: Lynne Rienner. 2013.
4 Mitchell, David T. and Sharon Snyder. *Narrative Prosthesis: Disability and the Dependencies of Discourse*. University of Michigan UP: Michigan. 2000.
5 Norden, Martin. *The Cinema of Isolation: A History of Physical Disability in the Movies*. New Brunswick: Rutgers University Press. 1994.
6 *Hamlet*, 2.2173–4.
7 Norden, 45–6, 100.
8 *Titus*. Dir. Julie Taymor. Perf. Anthony Hopkins. Fox Searchlight Productions. 1999.
   "Titus Andronicus." *BBC Television Shakespeare*. Dir. Jane Howell. Perf. Trevor Peacock. BBC. 1985.
9 Rothwell, Kenneth S. *A History of Shakespeare on Screen: A Century of Film and Television*. 2nd ed. Cambridge: Cambridge UP. 2004. 269.
10 *Vertigo*. Dir. Alfred Hitchcock. Perf. James Stewart, Kim Novak. Paramount Pictures. 1958.
11 *Richard III*, 1.2.255.
12 Garland-Thomson, Rosemarie. *Staring: How We Look*. New York: Oxford UP. 2009. 72–3.
13 Berger, 27.
14 Berger, 5.
15 See Chapter 1 for a more in-depth discussion of these terms.

Bibliography

Berger, Ronald J. "Disability in Society." *Introducing Disability Studies*. New York: Lynne Rienner. 2013.
Garland-Thomson, Rosemarie. *Staring: How We Look*. New York: Oxford UP. 2009.
McRuer, Robert. *Crip Theory: Cultural Signs of Queerness and Disability*. New York: New York UP. 2006.
Mitchell, David T. and Sharon Snyder. *Narrative Prosthesis: Disability and the Dependencies of Discourse*. Michigan: University of Michigan UP. 2000.
Norden, Martin. *The Cinema of Isolation: A History of Physical Disability in the Movies*. New Brunswick: Rutgers University Press. 1994.

Rothwell, Kenneth S. *A History of Shakespeare on Screen: A Century of Film and Television*. 2nd ed. Cambridge: Cambridge UP. 2004.

Titus. Dir. Julie Taymor. Perf. Anthony Hopkins. Fox Searchlight Productions. 1999.

"*Titus Andronicus*." BBC Television Shakespeare. Dir. Jane Howell. Perf. Trevor Peacock. BBC. 1985.

Vertigo. Dir. Alfred Hitchcock. Perf. James Stewart, Kim Novak. Paramount Pictures. 1958.

Index

For Product Safety Concerns and Information please contact our EU
representative GPSR@taylorandfrancis.com
Taylor & Francis Verlag GmbH, Kaufingerstraße 24, 80331 München, Germany

www.ingramcontent.com/pod-product-compliance
Lightning Source LLC
Chambersburg PA
CBHW071115100726
47908CB00008B/2379